THE TEXAS TYCOON'S BABY

BY
CRYSTAL GREEN

AND

HIS TEXAS WILDFLOWER

BY
STELLA BAGWELL

D1355415

MILLS & BOON

Dear Reader,

Thank you so much for reading the BILLIONAIRE COWBOYS, INC, mini-series! This is the final book in the trilogy, and it's *finally* Chet's turn to find happiness.

He's the illegitimate son who's suffered through the Barron family scandal and, boy, does he need a good woman by his side during this personal crisis. Enter Mina Ferguson, his administrative assistant—and the lady who's been in love with this cowboy ever since she first saw him.

Love at first sight… This is one of my favorite kinds of romances, but not everyone believes it's possible. But what do you think? Does it exist? Has it ever happened to *you*?

I hope this story shows you that love is a blessing—however you find it!

I'd love for you to visit my website at www.crystal-green.com. You can enter contests and see what else I'm up to…

All the best,

Crystal Green

Crystal Green lives near Las Vegas, where she writes for the Blaze® and Cherish™ lines. She loves to read, overanalyze movies and TV programs, practice yoga and travel when she can. You can read more about her at www.crystal-green.com, where she has a blog and contests. Also, you can follow her on Facebook at www.facebook.com/people/Chris-Marie-Green/1051327765 and Twitter at www.twitter.com/ChrisMarieGreen.

To Alicia, Maria, and Cindy. Year after year, decade after decade, we're so lucky that we will always be able to rely on each other!

Prologue

"I'm not who they said I was."

Chet Barron stood in Mina Ferguson's doorway like the walking wounded, his cowboy hat in hand, his short, dark blond hair mussed and out of place. He might've even looked like a bronc buster who'd just been thrown off a wild horse if it wasn't for the gray business suit he had on.

But that was the worse for wear, too; his silk tie was undone, his jacket open to show the wrinkles marring his fine white shirt.

"Chet?" Mina asked.

Shell-shocked, her boss took one step toward her threshold with those Justin Boots—the last vestiges of the cowboy he used to be only eight months ago, before he'd become one of the most powerful tycoons in Texas, if not the entire country.

She took his hand and pulled him the rest of the way

into her home, toward the couch, forgetting about the T-shirt and cutoffs she was wearing—a far cry from the polished skirt suits he usually saw her in.

At the feel of his skin, her pulse jittered, and she knew what would come next—a surge of the blood in her veins. A flip of the belly.

But she knew how to hide how she felt around her boss.

"What's wrong?" she asked as they sat down.

"They lied to me. All these years…"

The cryptic words seemed to freeze in the air.

"What do you mean by that?"

"I mean," he said, his tone still dead, "I'm not his son."

It seemed like a full minute lumbered past.

"I don't understand," Mina said. "Are you talking about Abe? He's…not your father?"

Chet nodded, and when he started to say something else, he choked on the words, burying his face in his hands in a struggle to contain himself.

She exhaled, resting her hand on his arm. Even through his jacket, she felt a burn on her skin, just as she always did when she happened to brush against him while leaning down to set papers on his desk. Or if there happened to be an accidental whisk against each other as they passed in the halls of the offices of the Barron Group.

"It turns out that this was the real reason my dad brought me down here from Montana all those months ago," Chet said, tight sorrow taking hold of his words. "It wasn't just because he had cancer. It wasn't just because he was dying and he wanted me to sell my cattle spread and take his place as CFO of the Group."

Mina kept her hand on his arm, as if she could absorb his hurt. He gripped his hat in both hands as he stared at the floor, his gaze intense.

"Abe told me the whole truth tonight."

When he glanced at Mina, she crumbled inside, because she would do anything to take the obvious agony away from the man she'd loved ever since she'd first met him.

"He wanted me to come to him," Chet said, "so I could take my 'rightful place.' And as the words came out of his mouth, my uncle Eli just stood there next to him with this *look* on his face…."

Chet's words got twisted again, his eyes filled with anger, betrayal.

Out of instinct, Mina put her hand at the back of his head, cradling, soothing, almost thinking *she* could hold a strong man like Chet together.

"Abe told me," he said, "that I was set to inherit a third of the Barron Group, just like my cousins Tyler and Jeremiah. I didn't understand why he and Uncle Eli were going to give me such a big portion when Abe was the minority owner. Then they told me. Eli's my real father. *Eli.*"

His shoulders seemed to lose the steel that had been defining them and he crumbled, his voice gritty with anger and hurt. "My mom had an affair with that bastard years and years ago, and my dad is just telling me now… as he's *dying…*"

Garbled words. Decimated. But he was able to start up again.

"They said that I can claim my damned 'rightful place' now. And I left them standing there because I couldn't hear any more of it."

If a heart could explode, that's what Mina's did. As he fisted his hands, his neck straining with everything he was holding back, she pulled him against her, resting his head on her shoulder, wrapping her arms around him. He encompassed her, too, as if she was some kind of pillar, just as solid as she'd always been for him in the office.

His go-to woman.

But it'd never been like *this* between them, and even though she'd imagined holding him a million times, it wasn't the same now.

She didn't know how long they stayed like that, with him twisting her shirt, pulling at it as he fought emotion, but she heard cars passing by the front window of the tiny house she'd saved up for so diligently, heard the hum of her refrigerator in her kitchen, heard a siren off in the distance.

She didn't pay attention to much of it as his embrace grew tighter and his breath evened out, as she lay her head against his, feeling his thick hair against her face.

He inhaled, a ragged, uneven sound, then shifted, his mouth pressing against her shoulder, where her T-shirt left a patch of skin uncovered, sensitive to every one of his warm breaths.

She couldn't hear anything but her crazed heartbeat, each pump filling her with adrenaline and a growing awareness.

He needed something more.

He needed…

"It'll be okay, Chet," she whispered. "It'll be just fine."

Thuds marked the seconds, beating in her head, and

only a shell of the man she'd fallen for all those months ago, when he'd first appeared at the Group's offices.

How would a man who was having such issues with his illegitimate birth react to the news that he was having an out-of-wedlock baby?

A car's beeping horn tugged at her attention, and she went to her long window, where a view of the pure blue Utah sky and the ridges of the claylike mountains reached toward the heavens.

Her pulse started jogging double-time now, but it wasn't exactly the breathtaking scenery that did it.

In the near distance, Chet emerged from the back of a town car, shutting the door without waiting for the driver to do it for him. He sauntered over the stone-lined path leading to the offices, his cowboy hat pulled low over his brow, his shoulders wide, his chest broad under a long-sleeved Western shirt. He walked like a man in charge of everything around him, but from the way his gaze was shadowed, Mina knew better. Even from here she could imagine the darkness that turned his blue irises to a midnight hue, that made him resemble a mysterious—and dangerous—man huddled in the corner of an Old West bar, one hand near his holster, the other resting near a half-empty drinking glass.

Just a glimpse of him made Mina go weak, light and floaty in a nerve-racked way that also caused her to feel more alive than ever before in her life. A little sob wrestled itself down in her—she was so glad to see him. So scared.

Now that they'd be spending some quality time together, she would have to choose the right moment to tell him her news.

If there was a right moment...

He disappeared from her view, entering the administrative building, and her heartbeat got louder, as if the ground was vibrating and sending thunder through her veins.

All she could think about was that night... Or, more to the point, the moments after they'd made love, when the world had come crashing down around her.

But now wasn't the time to think of that, especially when she heard him at her doorway.

She exhaled once more, turning around and telling herself not to look as if she had a secret that might send him running.

"Long time, no real see," he said, leaning against the door frame, grinning, as if he was happy to confirm that she'd made it here from San Antonio safely a few days ago when he'd sent her ahead to inspect the property before he arrived.

Mina's insides did something like a thousand individual back bends, tying her up.

Was it because there was something in his gaze? A *pow* that turned the dark blue of his eyes into a second of firework brightness?

Was he remembering how perfect they'd been for each other just when he'd needed someone to hold him and ease him?

Mina had seen the same *pow* in him a couple of times since then, during car rides to or from the airport where she would debrief him on the run, or during their frequent long-distance teleconferences. But she could never be sure.

They'd never mentioned that night again. And she'd never told him that the condom he'd worn hadn't worked.

"How was the flight?" she asked.

"Just fine. I can't stand being cooped up though, even if I'm taking the corporate jet. There's something about being in an enclosed place, especially thousands of feet in the air where I don't have the choice of getting out."

"Sounds like a man who misses the open range."

He smiled, doffing his hat and holding it by his side, as if remembering the old days, before Abe had called him down to Texas from the comfort of a Montana cattle operation. Chet had sold his holdings to go to work for the Barron Group—a move that he'd made after finding out about Abe's cancer.

That was even before Abe had told Chet about his true parentage though, before his world had broken open. Mina couldn't imagine what that kind of news would do to anyone—making them doubt all the truths a person had ever known, shattering their trust in the people they depended on for honesty.

Abe had died a few months ago, further adding to Chet's sorrows, taking away the man he'd thought to be his father for a second time in under a year.

As he tossed his hat on a nearby wingback chair, Mina wondered if there'd ever be a right time to put another life-changing piece of news in front of him.

She slid her iPad onto her desktop, then made her way over, standing before him, not sure whether to hug him in greeting or not. Memory halted her as she recalled the heartbreaking aftermath of that night: how the lamplight had bathed them as they lay on that couch, her clothes on the floor, her skin singing with the afterburns of his touch, her body aching pleasantly after being filled with him.

Mina, he'd said, and she'd caught trouble in his tone. She'd held her breath as her giddiness—her bliss at how they'd finally come together—dissipated.

I took advantage of you…

As she'd reeled under that, he started talking about how he knew she wanted to be a serious businesswoman, and he'd never meant to cast a shadow on her reputation. He didn't want everyone to think that she owed her career to her sex life with him.

Even then, she'd known that he was talking around the real issues—how he couldn't handle a relationship in all the turmoil that'd come to him that night, how he'd let his anger and grief get the better of him. And every bit of it had rung through her like a punch that had deadened her chest, then the rest of her body.

He had no idea that she would've given up everything—a career, her solid reputation—for his love.

But with the way he'd looked into her eyes, as if he hated himself and was confused about everything around him, she had forgiven him. It was beyond her to despise him when she'd freely offered comfort. And even though it had torn her apart to say it, she'd told him that everything was okay between them—no harm, no foul. From there, he'd gone his way and she'd gone hers, always his stalwart. Always his girl, even if he didn't know it.

She'd thought about quitting her job, just so she wouldn't have to torture herself any longer, but the thought of being away from him was even worse. And they *had* been able to work with each other in the aftermath, thank goodness. Yes, she'd mostly stayed at their San Antonio headquarters while he'd traveled around the country on various projects, but there'd been one exception to that—when they'd spent a day at his brother Tyler's wedding. She'd only been at the festivities because she'd worked with the oldest Barron brother for years and she'd been invited. Chet hadn't asked her to accompany him.

Besides, that had been before the doctor had given her the official word about her pregnancy.

Now, as she stood in front of him, so unsure about how to act, Chet looked just as out of sorts as ever, his gaze searching hers.

Then he laid a hand on her arm, as if that was a good enough greeting.

Her skin tingled, even under the cotton of her blouse. She could feel the weight of his hand even after he removed it and wandered farther into her office, heading toward the window to take in that mountain view.

Just let him get his head together a little longer, Mina thought as dismay needled her. *Wait until he's in a better place to hear that he's going to be a dad, because if you tell him at the wrong time or in the wrong way you'll lose him completely.*

She went to the window to stand by him. Even though he had moments where she believed he was so damaged by what had gone on with his family, there were times when she thought he could come around, especially here, in the desert, away from the drama. This ranch spa was his dream, and a distraction, too. He was putting his heart and soul into renovating it, and it was almost as though, if he could build this place back up, he could do the same with himself.

Even with the positive thoughts, though, something niggled at Mina. What if she *had* only been there to cushion his fall that night, and she really didn't mean any more to him than that? Chet was the type who would marry a woman he'd gotten pregnant purely out of honor. But honor wouldn't be enough in a marriage.

And Mina didn't want that from him. She wanted his love. Her child deserved that, too. Mina knew exactly what it was like to be a surprise baby—she'd been an "accidental child," as well, except her own mom and dad had been very married.

She'd just been a "happy" accident for them during a hard financial time that they'd eventually recovered from. At least, that's what she'd overheard from a drunk uncle talking about it during a barbecue years and years ago.

Even now the thought stung as she and Chet stood at that window. Both of them, accidents. She related more to him than he knew.

She wished she could just reach out and touch him. She was dying to.

But she didn't.

While he surveyed the property, she could just about feel the pride radiating off of him. So many things in his life were messed up, but this resort wouldn't be one of them.

"It's going to be amazing," she said, a catch in her voice, because she wasn't just talking about the property.

"I aim to make it that way." He glanced at her, and her pulse skipped. "I hear we're scheduled to have the chef show off her menu tonight."

"In your cabin. I arranged a tasting for you."

"Just me?"

She hesitated. What did he mean?

"Please," he said lightly, "tell me you won't make

me test that menu alone. I'm counting on your opinion about how everything is shaping up here."

"I was going to get around to a tasting."

"Get it over with tonight. We'll catch up over dinner. We haven't been able to have a real sit-down in a long time."

There was a gleam in his eyes that she couldn't quite translate. Was he finally ready to be with her one-on-one again? Not even necessarily in a romantic manner, but just as friends?

"I guess I could use a good meal and a break," she said, determined to take charge of this relationship, to show him that she could always be there, along with a family who would love him through thick and thin.

"Good." He smiled, almost to himself, as he hitched his thumbs in his jeans pockets. "I was also thinking that you might want to take a horseback tour of the property with me right now."

When she'd been to the OB-GYN, she'd asked about exercising, as she did it regularly. Jogging, a calm horse ride, some light Pilates... But her doc wasn't a fan of riding during pregnancy, and she wasn't about to do anything to endanger her child.

"How about a walking tour instead?" she asked.

"Okay then." He backed away from the window, and really, his blue gaze was clearer than she'd seen it in a while. Was it because he was out here...or because *she* was here?

She could only wish.

He moved toward the doorway, scooping his hat back up and putting it on—a rough and rugged man who would surprise anyone if they were to see him in a business suit, looking slightly out of place, yet dashing just the same.

Mina even jellied a bit in the knees at the thought of him dressed up.

"You ready?" he asked.

God, if he only knew just how ready she was. She wished he had even an inkling of how much she wanted him to stroll off into the sunset with her.

She thought she saw that spark in his gaze again as he glanced at her, and optimism wove its way under her skin. Was it possible that he would see how much she adored him before she told him about their child?

Would it make a difference if she could show him that she wanted more than just a night with him?

Only time would tell, she thought as she went to the door.

He ushered her out of the office as her heart stuck in her throat.

They sauntered side by side on a trail that headed toward the hills, cutting through the stillness of the late afternoon.

It was actually nice to get away from the office, even though staying busy was good, Chet thought.

Very good.

While passing the scrub and barrel cactus at the foot of some red-tinged hills, he did his best to keep his mind off of everything—including his assistant. Thank God they'd settled back into an amiable pattern, especially after that night when he'd overstepped his bounds with her.

What had he been thinking, coming on to Mina? He'd never been so unprofessional in his life. In fact, he imagined that taking advantage of an employee was something a womanizer like his biological father, Eli Barron, might've done in the past.

But that wasn't Chet. Hell, no. He respected women, Mina more than most of them. And when he thought about what might happen if word about them ever got out around the Barron Group, he wanted to throttle himself.

She was ambitious, wanted to build a career. But was everyone going to think that she'd slept her way to the top?

Luckily, she'd been gracious and accepting of his errors, not holding Chet to any promises that his body might've made to her. Maybe he should've given her up, hired another personal assistant, but he wasn't about to punish her for his lack of judgment that night.

And she was too damned good at her job for him to give her up, too.

Besides, they'd worked things out. Certainly, it involved him traveling a lot, but he was getting a lot done for the Group, buying up land and property then renovating and building on it to add the Group's coffers. So it was a decent trade-off. He'd cleared his head quite a bit, and enough time had passed that they could go back to being...

What? What *had* they been to each other?

The wind carried a hint of Mina's perfume past him, and it made him light-headed, reminding him of what it felt like when he'd held her against him.

When he'd first seen her as more than an assistant.

That night he'd filled himself up with the scent of her, a combination of green tea and...calm. It was at odds with her sunset hair, which seemed so very lively against the quiet of the desert as the breeze cajoled a stray lock out of her upswept hairdo.

In spite of all his efforts, Chet stole an even better peek at her now. Wearing a skirt that came to her knees, she had the posture and the elegance of a lady, with high cheekbones sprinkled with freckles and clover-hued eyes that usually bore a sparkle.

But there wasn't much of a sparkle today. In fact, there was some kind of distance.

Did seeing him again for more than a debriefing make her think about what had happened between them?

Disappointment clawed at him, surprising him with its sharpness. From the way they'd fallen back into their boss-assistant relationship, he could've sworn that she'd let go of that night. Hell, he would've even said that she'd been relieved when he'd told her that he should've never put her in a position to assuage his anguish.

Even now, he still wanted to kick himself for how he'd acted with her after he'd held her, kissed her, been inside of her.

I'm sorry...I took advantage of you...

He just hadn't known what to make of what had happened. His emotions had been abraded, bleeding, and she'd been there. That's all.

And it had been wrong to pull her into his vortex of trouble.

How was it that he'd ruined so many things in his life without trying? Mina, and even his family. He hadn't meant to be born the way he was, but the truth of his birth had thrown everyone into chaos, anyway, and as ridiculous as it seemed, he felt responsible.

Rocks crunched under their boots. The silence between them was like a saw, and he had to turn it off.

"Where are we off to first?" he asked.

"How about the spa?" She motioned to the east where, just over the hills, the white dome of the building peeked up. Around it, there would be pools with waterfalls and serene sculptures.

Mina added, "You should see the inside. There's a meditation room with floor-to-ceiling windows, and a quiet lounge with fountains where the guests will go while waiting for their treatments. You should see the Paradise Room, too, with its waterfall and pool."

She seemed fine with the small talk, just as she was fine with everything.

When her phone rang, the sound split the air. She took it out of her pocket and glanced at her ID screen, then put it away.

"It's my mom. She's probably calling to chat." She laughed. "Or, should I say, to check up on me."

He knew from comments Mina had made here and there that her family was really tight. They had frequent get-togethers at her parents' home in the San Antonio suburbs, with her two local sisters and their brood usually in attendance.

Odd that he knew so little about her private life when she seemed to know so much about his because of the scandal.

"How's the family doing?" he asked.

"Great. Same as always—caring, nosy, all that."

Was there some dryness in the way she'd said it?

"You're not too keen on the nosy part," he said.

"Not really, but what family isn't that way? It just means they care about what happens to me."

Her words struck Chet hard. He'd been doing everything possible to avoid anything even near to "nosy" or "involved" with his own family. Then again, they weren't much like the Fergusons at all. First, there was Eli, who'd been hitting the bottle hard ever since he and Abe had announced that Chet was Eli's son. Then there were his brothers, who were doing their best to deal with the situation in their own ways.

The term "family" didn't really even apply to the lot of them. Actually, Chet wasn't sure what a family was since his own had obviously been a lie. His mother had passed on a few years ago in a car accident with Aunt Florence, who supposedly hadn't known about her sister-in-law's affair with Eli.

And Mom wasn't the woman he'd thought she was.

That left Abe.

Something in Chet's core took a fall at the thought of him. The man he'd called "Dad." The man he'd abandoned for a life in Montana just as soon as he was old enough to get out of the house and strike out on his own.

And Chet had *wanted* to leave because, intuitively, he'd always suspected there was something off whenever Abe and his mom had exchanged those heavy, sad glances when they thought "their son" hadn't been looking.

But there were other reasons Chet didn't want to be with his new family right now. Abe's recent death had made it hard. And how much *did* Chet have to do with Abe's passing? Had the truth weighed on his "father" so roughly that it'd helped to kill Abe?

Remorse bit at Chet once again. He only wished Abe were still alive. So many things to make up for. So many things that had been thrust upon Chet now that the truth had come out…

The desert breeze sidled up to him again, along with the scent of Mina. Chet kept his gaze on the path as a bird of prey cried overhead, and his mind went fuzzy, making him forget everything, just for a moment.

But then he sensed Mina watching him and his heart kicked as his gaze connected to hers.

She looked away, but not before he thought he glimpsed a wounded look in her eyes.

Was she more affected by that night than she let on?

Chet felt every cell in his body screaming. Yet what could he say to her?

That night, I did need you, and you were there for me. You were the best thing that could've ever happened...

A vibration shook his shirt pocket and, at first, Chet mistook it for another memory—of the way she'd grabbed hold of his heart, his entire being, and shocked both of them to life.

But when the vibration came again, he knew it was merely *his* phone now.

Mina grinned. "Not a moment of rest for us, even out in the boonies."

Her smile was like a warming beacon, and he only answered the phone because it was Tyler's number, and his cousin's—or, rather, brother's—calls were rarely unimportant.

Putting the phone to his ear, he said, "Hey, Tyler."

Mina walked on a few steps ahead of him, giving him privacy.

Tyler was already talking. "You have an ETA for when you'll be back in Texas?"

"I just got to St. George. Why?"

Tyler paused for one of those quiet moments that he'd used so well as the big boss of the Barron Group before he'd retired to start up a horse rescue with his new wife, Zoe. Back when Chet had first started working at the Group, he'd welcomed Tyler's competitive guidance. The same for Jeremiah, his slightly older brother.

But out here, Chet felt very much alone, especially with Mina strolling ahead, her back to him, her hips swaying under that skirt.

He forced himself to look away. "Is it Eli again?"

"Sure enough. He went on a real bender last night. Tore up the lounge at the Broadway, and our lawyers had to step in to run interference."

Chet wanted to throw the phone, but he kept himself contained. "The last time we were all together, he told us that he was going to change." They'd been planning an intervention, but when Eli had vowed he was turning a corner, they'd trusted him.

"He was wrong." Tyler paused. "Jeremiah and I confronted him, then helped him check in to the Whitehall Center for rehab."

Chet felt his shoulders stiffen.

"But," Tyler added, "I won't rush you to get back here because of that, Chet. He can't have visitors right now. It'd just be good if you could come back when he's improved enough to see us. Maybe it'll even happen around the time of Jeremiah's wedding."

"You know I'll be there for that."

But as for visiting Eli?

Damn it, Chet knew he should be anticipating the day it would be possible. Still, he held back the rest of what he wanted to say to Tyler—that if it was Abe instead of Eli who was in trouble, Chet wouldn't have gone out of town at all; he would have been around to help Tyler and Jeremiah deal with him. And if Eli hadn't been so selfish when he'd had the affair with Chet's mother—and if he wasn't being so self-centered now—it would've been so much easier to accept him.

Plus, Chet mentally added, it would've been easier to accept himself, too, because he was Eli's son now, and he wondered how much he'd inherited from the man he didn't really know.

"I'll check in tomorrow about my ETA," Chet finally said.

They both signed off. When Chet hung up, he stared at the mountains for a moment, feeling aimless.

Then he realized that Mina was waiting for him and for a moment—just a heartwarming flash—he allowed her to comfort him again.

Knowing he would have to rely on more than this to get him through the next months, he forced the dark look that he knew he must've been wearing off of his face and walked over to her.

As she faced him with those compassionate green eyes, he sank into another memory of that night, memories that always came unbidden whenever he saw her.

Holding her, because he didn't know what else to grab on to. Running his hands over her soft, smooth skin, her waist and hips, just before he entered the warmth of her...

His belly seized up, hot and sharp, but he pushed back the sensation. Again.

"Everything okay?" she asked, searching his gaze. There was something more intense about her than usual, though he couldn't put his finger on it.

Not wanting to lay anything more on her than he

already had, he nodded. "Ty was just putting things in order with the family."

A strange look crossed her expression. Was it because he was shutting her out of a more complete answer?

As she moved on, Chet frowned, wondering if they'd left that night behind after all.

Chapter Two

After showering, Chet felt a hell of a lot better. Good enough to kick back with a beer in his cabin near the main lodge before the chef would arrive with dinner.

And before Mina would get here, too.

Once more, an inexplicable warmth surrounded Chet's heart. All he'd done was just think of her.

What was going on with him?

Desperate to clear his head, he wandered to the outside deck, where a few hardy chairs and a stone fire pit offered welcome. Later that week, a designer would start putting the grace notes on the guest cabins, as well as the main lodge itself. He and Mina were scheduled to leave the resort in a matter of days—too many other projects to oversee, such as a renovated art-deco office building in New York, a condo project near the Vegas Strip, a grand hotel on the Florida coast. But they'd be back before the grand opening of this one.

As he leaned on the rail, his beer bottle dangling from his fingers, the A-frame of the cabin loomed, all rising glass windows and reaching upper deck—a rustic retreat for the rich clientele who would visit this resort for spa and adventure getaways.

A sense of pride welled within him as he took another drink. It felt good to be building something up rather than tearing it down.

Soon, the chef and her staff came, armed with covered trays, along with enough matched wines to keep a person going for weeks. He stayed outside while they prepared his table.

When he saw Mina coming down the path to his cabin, his blood rushed through his veins again.

There was no fighting it.

She'd pulled her auburn hair, with its sleekly styled layers, away from her flushed face so that the rest of it fell to her shoulders. The hairdo revealed a graceful neck and jawline, plus those cheekbones. Closer up, he knew that her thick lashes would be so long that a princess would kill for them. And the princess imagery didn't stop there—she was wearing a white peasant's camisole and yellow skirt that swished just over feet dressed in simple yet elegant sandals. With that stately posture of hers, she seemed like some kind of royal miss who was running off from the castle for an evening to be with him—the pauper, not the prince.

Or, at least, that was what he felt like, even though the Barrons had made him a rich, successful billionaire just like his brothers. Still, Chet didn't know how he fit in to their lives...his *own* new one, too. He felt as if...

Well, as if he was still on the outside, no matter

how hard Tyler and Jeremiah tried to make him feel differently.

Why couldn't he have been Abe's son through and through? Why had Eli been so irresponsible, creating him—a bastard who didn't really belong, no matter what his parentage was?

Mina's voice eased into his thoughts. "I got a special delivery a half hour ago."

She'd been holding something behind her back, and now she revealed the object: a small basketball hoop with a spongy ball, just like the one he had back in the San Antonio office.

He couldn't help but smile.

Mina's pale skin flushed, as if appreciating his response. "You're always saying that your office here—and even your cabin—lack a personal touch. I thought I'd take a step in remedying that."

"I guess it's obvious that I'm not so good at sitting still." Even when he was supposed to be kicking back with his boots on the desk and thinking. The motion of arcing a basketball—foam or not—through the air and getting all net gave him a measure of serenity. Not many other people knew that much about him.

She ascended the stairs to the deck and set the sports gear on a chair. His gut tied itself into knots as he thought of what it'd felt like to run his fingers over those bare arms, long, slender, pale, soft. He remembered what her skin had tasted like, too...

When her gaze caught his, it seemed to flare with the same desire he was feeling.

Her lips parted as if she wanted to say something.

But then the basketball backboard slid off the chair and hit the deck, making them both start.

They laughed awkwardly. She might've even been just as relieved as he was for the interruption.

Laughing. It was something he would have to do more. Sometimes he wondered what had happened to the old him—the guy who used to shoot the bull and laugh with his pals at the Watering Hole near his Montana ranch.

Where had that normal life gone?

And, worse yet, he wasn't even sure if the new him would ever be able to laugh, relax, trust people as he used to.

It was the trust part that worried him the most.

"Thanks for the special delivery," he said, raising his beer bottle to her, thinking that, if there was anyone to be trusted now, it was definitely Mina. "Care for a drink before dinner?"

"I'll have water when we get inside," she said.

"You usually like wine during dinner."

Her skin was really flushed now. "It's the desert. I feel...dehydrated."

"Then I'll be a proper host and get that water for you now." He motioned for her to take a seat in one of the chairs then went to scoop the backboard and ball from the ground. "Be right back."

She didn't protest when he went to get an ice-filled glass of water. He put down the sports items by the stone fireplace and came back out to see her face raised to the last of the turquoise sky, streaks of pale color etching it to dusk.

He handed her the beverage, and when she drank, he watched her lips—the lushness, the way her mouth tilted slightly up at the corners, as if it couldn't help smiling.

She leaned her head back. "I can smell the food from out here. It makes the place seem like home, doesn't it? Good food, I mean. All that's missing is a table weighed down with a week's worth of grub and my mom telling us that we need to take as many leftovers home as we can carry."

Chet let her description of home wash over him.

Then she sighed.

"What?" he asked.

"Nothing."

"That was a sigh for the ages, Mina. It didn't mean 'nothing.'"

She cocked her eyebrow at him. "Sometimes I think it's not a good thing that you can read me, boss."

Boss. It gave him some firmer footing with her.

He rested the beer bottle on the wooden railing. "People don't sigh unless there's something worth sighing about."

She waved her hand, as if dismissing something. "It's just… Well, that call from Mom today. Even though I'm twenty-eight, sometimes I feel like I'm still a teenager, and I can't go a few days without filing a report about my doings. She says that single girls like me need to have someone check in with them, just to see that they haven't fallen down and can't get up in their house or… whatever emergencies go through a mom's mind. She doesn't like that there's no one else around most of the time."

"You're the light of her life."

"I know… She loves me." Mina grinned. "And I know she's right about checking in with me. Still, sometimes I just want to untangle myself from my family a little. They have a tendency to overstep."

"And that chaps your hide."

She laughed at his colorful description. "Family's always going to be there through thick and thin when others might not be. That's the bottom line. I'll even withstand my mom's phone calls for that."

He thought of his own mom: how she'd betrayed his dad but still loved her son way up in Montana. She used to call him, too, fussing over him, making sure he realized he always had someone somewhere who loved him, even though it was far across the miles. And now he knew why she'd put out the extra effort—to make it up to him because, one day, he might know the truth about what she had done to him and Abe.

So *much* of it had been a lie.

Mina said, "I love having a mom—don't get me wrong. But she feels like she also…"

Trailing off, Mina took another drink, as if she regretted even bringing this up.

"She what?" Chet asked.

Mina got that look on her face that she usually adopted when she was balancing the consequences of something. Then she lowered her glass, holding it with both hands on her lap.

"My parents have this guilt trip when it comes to me, and my mom sometimes overcompensates." She got that expression again—the measuring, the hesitation. "I was never supposed to come along. I was a surprise for my parents."

As she watched him, Chet didn't move a muscle. Even after he'd learned about his own birthright, Mina had never told him this piece of news. And it'd probably been because of what'd gone on between them…because of how he'd let her down afterward and damaged their friendship, taking away their former closeness, which was just beginning to return now.

But he was ready to mend what he'd broken, and damned if he wasn't going to make great strides in it tonight.

She glanced away, yet he could see that her gaze was bruised. No one wanted to be an accidental baby.

"We have more in common than you ever expected, don't we?" she asked. "My circumstances are hardly the same as yours, but when I found out that I was just sort of thrust into this world without a plan, it pushed me to a place where I felt pretty alone for a while. My parents never even knew that I stumbled on the truth, but it sure shaped me, just as it's shaping you in a way."

"Shaping me," he said slowly.

"Yeah. I think it's what made *me* such a pleaser— you know the type." Her smile was wistful. "The Girl Fridays of the world, the ones who have to make sure everyone is happy with them. I spent years being the secretary of the school's governance team and every childhood club on my block, honing my skills at being the go-to person."

"So that's why you're so good at your job." And making herself relevant to others. When he'd found out that he'd come from the wrong side of the blanket, he'd felt as if he didn't have much of a place in the Texas Barron family, even though Eli had tried like hell to fit him into the company, making him a co-vice president right off the bat.

"Maybe you're right." She grew quiet, as if she had so much more to say but didn't know how to word it.

Chet even got the feeling that there was something

going on here that he would never understand, something deep in her that she wouldn't reveal easily.

And it scared him that he cared enough to know just what it was.

He tried to figure out a way to bring up the subject but was stopped short by Chef Arnett coming to the sliding glass door in her whites and announcing that dinner was ready to be served.

Going to Mina's deck chair, Chet offered her a hand, helping her up. Her flesh branded his and he backed off sooner than he meant to, recovering by ushering her ahead of him inside, where, in the living area, a fountain ran through the room. The water sculpture had been designed to recall a Japanese garden, with stone lanterns and raked rocks surrounding a pond that would hold koi fish when it came closer to the grand opening of the ranch.

They arrived at the dining space, a stone table with padded silk chairs. A lone candle burned in the midst of the settings. A bottle of wine rested in a silver bucket of ice, but when Chet went to pour it, Mina refused him again.

"I'm sticking with the water," she said, refilling her glass with the pitcher resting on the table.

As they sat, Chef Arnett folded her hands in front of her, smiling. Chet could tell that the young apple-cheeked woman was nervous about serving the big bosses.

"I've prepared sample dishes—tasting portions," she said, sliding two menus onto the table so they could see what was in store. "Five courses, and they're all made in the spirit of good health." Just like the resort would be promoting.

"Hellfire," Chet said, perusing the list. Like the menu of the San Francisco restaurant from which they'd recruited Chef Arnett, there were a lot of choices. Even after so many months of this life change—from rancher to business tycoon—he wasn't used to the luxuries.

They thanked her, and when she left them to enjoy the first course, they started with a choice of appetizers. Chet dug in to what the chef called a crab rémoulade salad paired with a Chenin Blanc wine, which Mina, of course, didn't want.

That's when Chet realized what might be going on. Was she actually afraid of dropping her defenses with him? Was she afraid that they might do something they regretted again, out here away from the office?

It was time to get everything in the clear.

"Are you angry with me, Mina?"

She put down her fork and lifted her linen napkin, dabbing at her mouth. It seemed to take forever as Chet waited.

"Angry?" she asked.

"For what happened after we were together."

She cleared her throat. "No. Of course I'm not angry."

"Good. Because you know there are reasons it had to end there."

"I know your reasons."

She lifted her gaze, and even though her green eyes were clear, there were depths that he couldn't fathom.

He added, "I told you that I'd hate for word to get around the Group that you were with the boss, so I've been standoffish. Maybe too much."

Blinking, Mina paused, as if she'd expected him to say something else, though he wasn't sure what.

But, hell, he *did* care about her ambitions, and if everyone knew that they'd been together, it would mark her, undermine her true talents.

Yet was that really the only reason he wanted to set their relationship back to rights?

Chet shut down the possibility of there being any more between them while waiting for his Girl Friday to respond.

Mina's head fizzed with confusion.

Was this the time to give him the news about the baby, now that they were getting matters out into the open?

A gnawing feeling told her that she should just stay quiet at this point.

One step at a time. They were doing well so far, getting back onto normal ground with each other.

She met Chet's blue gaze again, bracing herself for the impact that always hit her whenever he was close, and—*boom*. Stomach somersaulting, the acrobatics in her chest… They didn't disappoint, leaving her nearly breathless.

He looked serious, so she sat still, as if something was about to crack between them, like a piece of glass they'd been tiptoeing over.

He gazed at her a tension-filled moment longer, then shook his head. "Just look at us. Things are so thick in the air that I can practically carve it. And I'll be damned if our work suffers because of it."

Her heart sank so low that it might as well have crumbled to nothing. Maybe there really wouldn't be a future between them…

For the first time, panic hit her.

Was she going to be a single mom? Her—the woman who'd been so together?

She also had to admit that all the family talk from earlier had done a number on her, and she was extra sensitive right now. After chatting with her mom today, she'd started really thinking about how her nearest and dearest would react to Chet, the scandal-plagued man who'd been wreaking havoc on her. Her family would be real protective of Mina for certain, just as they'd been after her last significant other had broken her heart.

That's probably why she'd been so put out about her mom checking up on her today, when it normally didn't bother her as much. Facing Chet had just exacerbated her emotions.

"I'm only hoping I didn't damage our relationship permanently," Chet added.

"You haven't. We haven't." Mina reached for a piece of fresh bread from the basket.

"It's just…" He lost his words, then picked them back up. "Do you remember when talk used to come easier between us? We used to kid each other, like about how I never went on dates. And I'd do the same to you. These days, the very subject would take on new meaning."

"You think that we'd be keeping each other in check or something? That there'd still be strings attached to us just because of one night?"

"Don't you think so?"

One of the chef's assistants peeked out from around the corner, gauging their reaction to the first part of the meal. When Mina caught her eye, the young ponytailed woman drew back.

This wasn't exactly the perfect place for a life-altering kind of talk, Mina thought.

She gestured toward his salad. "What do you think so far?"

Chet's broad shoulders sank, as if he'd wanted to talk more. "Top-notch."

They continued eating. She suddenly noticed that Chef Arnett had even selected some music to go with the meal. Beethoven. The chaotic symphony did little to calm her racing thoughts.

"So," he said, as if he couldn't help himself. "After we get the resort manager in place, you'll have a breather from this project and the office altogether. I'll see to it. You've been running yourself ragged lately."

"I like working."

"I think you work too much sometimes."

"Look who's talking."

He grinned at that. "Look, indeed."

After a few more minutes, Chef Arnett appeared again, this time with more samples and paired wines: things like parmesan-crusted scallops, pan-seared salmon over risotto, grilled poussin with fingerling potatoes. At the delicious aroma, Mina wanted to dig in. Her appetite was growing by the week, but there was no way she would let Chet see that.

When the chef was gone, Chet continued, "All I'm saying is that I'm afraid business has taken over your life."

"Wrong."

At his quirked eyebrow, she realized what he was getting around to.

Was he attempting to see if she'd moved on from him? If she was "getting out of the office" with a social life, which might or might not include another man?

Well, wouldn't that be a nice break for Chet—her

falling for a different guy, one who was emotionally available. But it was disheartening, because he had to have felt *something* on that night—something that had stayed with him as much as it'd stayed with her. She knew it because of the way he'd touched her, whispered her name as if it was carrying him to a new, better place.

She'd never heard a man say her name like that before.

"I'll tell you what," she said, capturing a forkful of creamed spinach. "I'll hop right on to an internet social-networking site once we're done here and attempt to find some sort of real life if that'll make you feel any better."

All he did was smile again, appreciating her feistiness.

"What's so funny?" she asked.

"A man doesn't have to be told to back off of a conversation much more clearly than that, Mina."

Okay. Being defensive with him wasn't going to get them back on track, or to where she could measure how he was going to take the pregnancy news.

"It's just that it's—" she was still holding that spinach-topped fork "—been a while. For a relationship, I mean."

"Me, too."

"I know. You dated back in Montana but never got serious. And you've had a dry spell here because of all the drama. I have access to your social calendar, remember?"

"You have the advantage over me then. I don't know a thing about yours."

There was something in his tone that hinted he was truly interested, and Mina's heart bumped her chest.

"I haven't booked many dates for a while," she said, giving in, testing him further. "And it's probably for the best."

She ate the spinach.

"What was he like?" Chet asked. "Your last relationship?"

This was good, Mina thought. Chet showing a burst of curiosity about her personal life.

Did it mean he cared beyond just friendship?

She watched him carefully. "Michael was one of those free spirits. Reluctant to settle down, even though I kept thinking he was going to change his mind one day. Eventually, I realized that I wanted more from a man, and he didn't want more from a woman, so I did what was best for the both of us and broke it off." She put down her fork and wrapped her fingers around her cool glass of water. "Months of my life wasted. But I had time to recover, seeing as it ended about a year ago."

And then Chet had come along. From that moment on, she'd known that he was the one, and every other man she'd ever known had only been a lead-up to the real thing.

Her boss toasted her with his wine. "Good thing, then, that your family was there for you, for comfort and some shoulders to lean on."

As he drank, she realized that he was referring to their earlier discussion outside on the deck. And that there was a longing in his voice that he couldn't cover up.

Mina reached across the table, resting her hand on

his. When the contact sizzled, making both her and Chet start, she removed her touch.

Patience, she thought. *Don't rush things.*

"I'm glad to hear you say that about family." She fiddled with the napkin on her lap. If she kept her hands busy, maybe she wouldn't reach for him again.

"I'm sorting through my situation more and more." There was something in his voice—a break? Was it because she'd touched him? "There're just plenty of questions to deal with, like who my mom really was. And if I even *want* to be Eli Barron's son."

"I guess you do have a choice in that."

"Sure. I could still act like I'm Abe's and I could let Eli know that there's no chance that I'll ever be like a son to him. But that would be destructive when Eli's already in a black hole." He rested his hand on his wineglass. "That phone call earlier today, when I talked to Tyler? He told me that he and Jeremiah helped Eli into rehab."

Her heart almost broke at how much sadness cut into his apparent relief. "That's a good thing."

"Yeah. It is."

Just listen to him. He was worrying about Eli, even though the man should pay for the destruction he'd done to his own family.

Yes, Chet had a heart. He was a good man who would no doubt be a good father and, maybe someday, a good husband. But as they fell into more silence, Mina wondered just when he was going to realize that about himself, if ever.

Chef Arnett returned to bring a few more samples, which gave them the opportunity to heap praise on her. By the time they were ready for dessert, Chet was leaning back in his chair, looking more relaxed than he had in a long time.

Mina leaned back, too, her optimism revving up full force.

The time *would* come, she thought. She just needed to wait a bit longer.

They'd called it an early night, knowing that the next day would hold some major work, with contractors on-site to get the ranch going before its opening date as well as a few final candidates who would meet with Mina about the managerial position. Chet knew that she'd screened them beforehand, whittling them down to this elite group.

His day would consist of appointments with a few local ranches, where he intended to check out horse stock. But before he left the resort, he would have to check in with Mina about a locals preview night that they would be staging tomorrow: giving tours of the property, handing out samples of the cuisine and entertaining the crowd with music.

Thinking this would be a good time to take a more casual look at the resort's progress, he made his way to the main lodge, with its combination of Native American artwork and Asian-inspired comforts, such as the silk cushions that lined the furniture and the rock gardens that led to the reception dome.

There, he found Mina going over last-minute details for the glass-and-cedar decor that would distinguish this area.

The same shock-and-rock sensation he felt whenever he saw her rattled him. She had her hair in a French braid, and she was garbed in a smart, short-sleeved cool blue suit as she took charge with the contractor. When they were done, she checked her iPad while the man she'd been talking to started barking out orders to his workers, who'd been taking a break in the corner of the plank-scattered room.

Mina seemed content, and she smiled as she perused whatever she'd brought up on her computer screen.

Chet saw the old Mina—the constant who kept him steady—and a flicker of devilment snuck up on him as he eased on over.

"Mornin'," he said over her shoulder.

He saw some pastel blocks—the kind little kids played with in a nursery—decorating the edges of the site she'd brought up on her iPad. But she flinched and hid the screen from him before he could see much more.

Eyes wide, she got that same strange look on her face that he'd seen during their walk, as if she was guilty, or as if she'd been...

Caught?

Chet wasn't sure what was what as she touched something on her computer and acted just a bit too casual for him not to notice.

"Morning to you, too," she said, gesturing toward her computer. "I was just going over details for the day care center."

There it was then. She'd been gathering decorating tips for the guests who'd be toting their children.

She frowned. "I thought we were meeting in about an hour."

"We are. I'm just wandering around, getting a feel for the place. Where're you off to next?"

"The pavilion. The crew is going to finish it up today, and I want a look-see."

"Mind if I come along?"

She nodded, noncommittal, but her smile was welcoming as they walked out of the lodge and into the clear morning air. He liked how the sun played with Mina's hair, bringing out the deep red, flirting with the gold. He only wished she didn't have it in that confining braid.

But he had no business thinking like that. He'd danced pretty close to the fire last night, bringing up her social life, finding out about her ex-boyfriend. Maybe he'd just wanted to see if the sky would fall down around them, but it hadn't.

They were getting back to where they'd been before and he couldn't be happier about it.

Walking the rock-lined path, they passed what would be a gift shop with souvenir ranch items as well as sporting and spa essentials. Then they got to the barbecue area, which was coming together with picnic tables and a stage for entertainment. Nearby stood the restaurant, where Chef Arnett's healthy gourmet food would be served, then the sports center, which would offer a full gym as well as classes like yoga, dance and fencing.

They came to the pavilion, where hikers would meet early in the morning to hit the trails in guided groups. Wood was scattered around, but the rest of the spired structure hinted of the bands that would play there, the dance floor that would sit under the sparkle of fairy lights strung down from the ceiling and through the nearby Joshua trees.

"This'll look good by the end of the day," Mina said,

a grin on her face, as if she were imagining an innocent dance with someone.

With a blast of desire, Chet realized that he hoped it was him.

But…good Lord. He wasn't in a position to be hoping anything. He'd already taken too much from her, and to think that she would suffer the ups and downs of his life while he straightened it out was just too much. He wouldn't ask that of anyone.

Yet there he was, admiring how the sun slanted down and painted half her face golden. He adored how the light freckles dusting her nose and cheekbones gave her a playful air, even when she seemed so serious and professional.

Before he could even think about what he was doing, he touched her cheek, and it felt right, just like that night.

Just like he was made to be doing it.

And when Mina turned those green eyes on him, he didn't back away.

Even if every instinct shouted that he should.

Chapter Three

Tingles shimmied down Mina's body as she reveled in the feel of Chet's fingers skimming her cheek.

This was how it should be between them—no questions about what was right and wrong, or about office propriety.

He was a man, she was a woman, and right now it was achingly clear that nothing should hold them back from wanting and needing each other.

Or from having a family together.

She sucked in a breath, so ready for him. For a moment, she even thought he was just as ready, too. That he'd forgotten about everything except the here and now, the desire that kept bringing them together.

Her lips parted, a pulse away from a whisper in which she could say, *Just kiss me. Show me that we're not only about business. Show me what's really in your heart...*

But then something in Chet's eyes changed—that all-too-familiar darkness taking over and switching the hue of his gaze from passion to wariness.

The return of the world and all its problems.

As frustration gripped Mina, she could see that he was desperate to cover up whatever he was feeling. When he grinned, then tweaked her cheek, just as if she was some kind of little sister or pal, she didn't know how to react.

Not that she needed to respond, anyway, because Chet was already backing off from her, hooking a thumb into his belt loop and nudging his hat up an inch as he surveyed the pavilion again. Just as if that's what he'd been doing all along.

"Yeah," he said in that cowboy drawl—the one that would always mark him as a rancher who'd turned tycoon rather than the other way around. "This'll do real nicely."

Mina wanted to hurl questions at him, like, *What just happened here? When are you going to stop running from not only me, but from everything?*

But…baby steps, just like last night over dinner.

Had it all been an act though? Judging by how skittish he seemed right now, they weren't on any more solid ground than before.

"So," he said, "I'll see you in an hour?"

"Okay."

Chet was already on his way, obviously having decided that it wasn't the greatest idea to be taking this walk with her. It seemed as if he was on the other side of the earth with this gaping distance between them.

Back to business, she accessed her iPad, raising her voice to catch him before he was gone. "You didn't really test anything out in the spa yet. I'm going to do that later today. Should I schedule anything for you?"

"I think the spa's best left to you. I'm not a massage-and-facial kind of guy."

And there was that grin again—the one that might've fooled her if she didn't know him so well.

As he moved down the path, she restrained a sigh, trying not to watch him in those jeans. Trying not to notice the denim clinging to his rear, his muscular thighs or even the shirt that didn't do much to hide the corded muscles of his back through the linen.

Hopeless. She was incredibly, hopelessly in love and she didn't know how to pull herself out of it. Leave it to her to fall for the most inaccessible man on earth.

But Mina had no control over her heart and what it did—not even a perfect administrative assistant could line up her emotions like a well-ordered office.

Birds warbled around her in the morning air as she took a stroll around the rest of the property, marking "done" on the checklist that she carried on her personal computer whenever she noticed progress being made. She kept looking at the time, bound and determined to get back to her cabin in the next ten minutes, in time for the Skype conversation she'd scheduled with her older sister, Katie, on the computer. Mina's niece, Lizzie, had her first preschool open house tonight, and one of the activities that her niece was going to take part in was a dance number. Mina couldn't make it, but Lizzie had begged her mom to let her show off to Mina beforehand instead.

It would be a quick chat, leaving her just enough time to meet Chet in the offices before he went to his ranch appointments.

When Mina entered the cabin, the scent of cedar welcomed her. So did the trickle of water from the rock fountain in the midst of dimly lit granite nooks and ferns in the living area.

She sat on an overstuffed leather couch, opening the notebook computer that rested on the rough-hewn coffee table. Before she logged on for two-way visual communication through the Skype camera at the top of her computer screen, Mina checked her emails.

Most were from friends, not only those she'd kept in contact with from college, but a few from San Antonio, too. She hadn't told any of them about her pregnancy, although she'd been tempted to so many times.

Soon, it was time for her video chat, and her older sister Katie called her via the computer, which rang before Mina accessed it.

A video image appeared, featuring Katie, who looked just as tidy as always with her long strawberry-blond hair held back by a headband, her green eyes sparkling.

"Mina!" she said.

Then a tinier, younger voice came over the computer. "Auntie Mina!"

A head topped by a high red ponytail—one like Pebbles Flintstone had worn back in the day—blipped into view as three-year-old Lizzie jumped up.

"Hey!" Mina laughed at the antics of her only niece. So far, there'd been no nephews, either, so Mina was addicted to everything Lizzie did and said.

"Auntie Mina, Auntie Mina!" Lizzie was climbing onto her mother's lap. "Ready to see?"

"You bet."

Lizzie preened in front of the camera, this way and that, her freckled face delighted as she modeled the pink costume she would be wearing tonight. Her mom, a whiz with a needle and thread, had whipped together a fairy-inspired outfit for her.

Mina noticed a crucial element was missing. "Don't tell me you haven't earned your wings yet."

Lizzie giggled and veered closer to the lens. "No. Mommy said later."

Katie chimed in. "I still have a little more work to do on those wings, but she'll be wearing them for the show."

The little girl had already slid off Katie's lap and, seconds later, was back with the wings, which looked like gossamer daydreams that any little girl would adore.

"See?" she said, putting them so close to the camera that they merely looked like sparkly blurs.

"Gorgeous!" Mina said nonetheless. "I just wish I could be there."

Lizzie lowered the wings from the lens, and Katie wriggled her way out from under her daughter, standing up, then taking the wings from Lizzie. Alone now, the little girl's green-blue eyes were wide and sad.

"I wish you were here."

Something stirred in Mina's chest, then in her tummy. Yearning. A keening desire for a child just as sweet as Lizzie.

Once again, the news Mina carried begged to be revealed.

Soon, Lizzie would have a cousin. Four and a half months soon. But Mina wanted to see the joy on Lizzie's face *now,* wanted the rest of her family to celebrate this miracle with her, although she wasn't so sure about their response.

Good heavens—she could just imagine how Chet

might have to undergo a bunch of questions about his family scandal and why he and Mina weren't married yet. Could just picture her conservative family wondering if she'd hooked up with another commitment-shy Michael.

"*Can't* you come tonight?" Lizzie asked Mina.

"I'm afraid not. I'm far away right now, in another state called Utah."

Lizzie nodded, but Mina was pretty sure the girl didn't know what a state was. Or Utah. But Mina would show her next time she visited, telling Lizzie more about the places she got to travel on business. Her niece loved Auntie Mina's stories.

"But," Mina said, "I aim to see you dancing around in that fairy costume sometime soon, just after I get back to Texas. Will you put on a show for me then?"

This time, Lizzie's nod was even more emphatic. "And I can dance *now* for you."

And, with that, she hopped off the chair. Mina couldn't get a full view of her, since her niece was nearly out of the camera's view, but she got the impression that Lizzie was spinning around, her arms over her head like a pixie ballerina.

Katie came to the rescue and pointed the lens toward Lizzie, who still jumped and swept out her arms all around as she previewed her show.

When she was done, Mina applauded, wishing she could give her niece a great big hug, too.

Instead, she took solace in resting her hand on her belly after she was done with the bravos.

Her own girl or boy. She hadn't wanted to know the sex during her first ultrasound. Didn't want to know until she told Chet.

Or could it be that she'd put off the discovery because the news of the pregnancy hadn't seemed real during her visit to the doctor?

Now, though, it was getting more real by the day, and tears needled the back of Mina's eyes as she felt more alone than ever in this.

When a knock sounded on her front door, she prayed that her sorrow wasn't obvious.

Through the glass that decorated the thick door, she saw a hint of cowboy: jeans, boots, hat.

Chet?

"Come in!" she shouted. Then she turned to the computer. "Lizzie, you're going to be wonderful tonight. Big kisses. I love you!"

"Love you!" Lizzie blew kisses at the screen and flitted off.

Mina heard the door shut, then boot steps. She glanced over her shoulder to see her boss, his hat in one hand, leaving his dark blond hair ruffled.

It was as if the earth sloped, just like one of those walking ramps on a fun house that tried to throw you off balance. The irony was that Mina hadn't been having all that much fun lately.

Katie came back on, taking the camera over just in time to spy him, too. With a saucy, curious expression written all over her face, she said, "Doing business out of the office today, sis?"

Mina shot a don't-get-any-ideas glare at her sibling. It was obvious that Katie was trying to get an even better gander at Chet.

Great.

But whether things worked out with him or not, he was always going to be a part of Mina's life. Maybe they wouldn't end up married—God, Mina hoped *that* wasn't true—but he was her child's father, no buts about it.

Mina sighed. It was time to take baby steps with her family, too, introducing them to the father of her child, no matter how they might receive him.

"I'm meeting with my boss," Mina said, swiveling her computer so it would fully capture Chet on the screen. "Say hi," she said to him.

"Hi." He lifted a baffled brow at the sight of Katie on the computer.

Without any more ado, Mina turned the camera back on her. That's all Katie would get for now.

"Have fun at that open house tonight," Mina said, making it clear that Katie needed to keep any more comments to herself.

Her sister had the sort of perceptive look on her face that told Mina she suspected something was being kept from her. Mina was just too jumpy not to arouse suspicion. Heck, her own expression—lovestruck and dumb, no doubt—probably gave her away full force.

"We'll talk later?" her sister said.

Mina ignored her. "Love ya! Bye!"

And she signed off.

Before she could ask why Chet was here instead of the offices, he said, "I was antsy to get on with those ranch appointments, so here I am. Someone in administration said that they'd seen you go to your cabin. Hope you don't mind."

"Not at all." As efficient as always, she held out her hand for some papers that Chet was carrying.

But her heart was still beating from his entrance, as well as the gander Katie had gotten at the father of Mina's child.

"You know," she said, "you didn't have to print these memos out in hard copy. There're these newfangled things called computers that hold all this information."

He chuckled and took a seat in a chair next to the couch. "I don't like to stare at a screen all day."

"Right. You're an old-fashioned manly man." Her heart was beating so loudly that it overwhelmed the splash of the fountain.

She liked how old-fashioned Chet was—he was the type who would be all about slow walks through the country, slow summer nights as the crickets chirped, a slow hand...

He had found her iPad on the coffee table. "I'm not sure how my life would be much improved with all the doodads you carry around."

"Someone in your office has to be comfortable with the digital age."

"Better you than me."

Somehow, he managed to turn the "doodad" on. Mina didn't mind. He was already in her cabin, her personal space, and what she kept on her computer screens wasn't nearly as intimate.

But she changed her mind when he pressed a particular icon.

"Well, look here," he said, holding up the screen so she could see what he'd found.

It was her photo file, and it was showing a picture she'd taken about a year ago, soon after the breakup with Michael. She'd decided to take some vacation time—a rare occurrence—and go on a trip to clear her mind. She'd ended up in Savannah, Georgia, with her sister Amy, who wasn't just six years younger, she also looked more like their dark-haired dad than either Katie or Mina, the daughters who took after their redheaded mom.

This photo presented Amy, who'd been engaged to get married at the time, mugging on a park bench in one of the town squares.

"That's my baby sis on the Forrest Gump bench," Mina said. "They filmed some of the movie there in Savannah."

Chet lingered on the picture for only a moment, seeming just as unimpressed with the Hollywood trivia as he was with the doodad.

Mina tossed him a smart-aleck grin. "I don't have pictures of cattle drives or Montana wildlife on there, so I'm not sure there's much for you to get excited about."

Nonetheless, he was going from one picture to the next. And, wouldn't you know it—he stopped on a photo that Mina had meant to delete a while ago.

It was an image of him. A reflective moment she'd captured with her phone when he hadn't been aware of it. Before the scandal had hit and before all his family's skeletons had tumbled out of the closet.

He was leaning back in his office chair, one booted ankle propped on his knee as he gazed out his wide office window at the dusk-awakened lights of San Antonio. He'd almost seemed excited about his new life, the chances he might have to get to know the father who'd called him down from Montana so they might mend their fences.

Now, Chet turned off the computer screen as if he could turn off the memory of those days, too—the times when he'd been unprotected from a truth that had beaten him down not long afterward.

After the screen had gone dark, Mina swallowed hard, thinking that he might stay just as blank.

Just as tough to read and connect to as ever.

Hours later, Mina was still unsettled by her meeting with Chet. But, like most women who appreciated a good resort, she was hoping that some spa time might ease her mind.

Currently, she was wallowing in one of the thick, white terry cloth robes the facility provided as she navigated the circular indoor path that branched off into the private massage rooms. The hallway was dim, lit only by stone lanterns, with soothing music piped in through hidden speakers.

So far, she'd steered clear of the many massages on the menu—the tempting "desert rain shower" or hot stone or aromatherapy treatments. Mina had claimed to be too busy with tomorrow night's local event and had asked the rest of her staff to report their own experiences to her because, although she knew that pregnant women could get massages, she didn't want to tell a masseuse about her condition before Chet—or any of her friends and family—knew.

It just seemed wrong.

Instead, she'd decided to concentrate on the facials that the spa offered, today choosing one that used pearl powder to lend "luster to the skin," as the menu had said.

It'd done the trick, all right, and she was relaxed as she entered the Paradise Room, an area with a rock pool, a waterfall and a seductive, serene air so she could wind down before going back to work.

But, with a smile, she told herself that this *was* her work.

Best job in the world.

Water played against the pool's surface as it splashed from the rocks above. Mina took off the robe, tossing it over a nearby deck chair. She was wearing a one-piece suit that she'd plucked from the resort's gift shop stock— a modest light blue number that flattered and clung to her still basically normal curves.

Then she gave in to the lure of the room, breathing in the fresh, orange-blossom aroma.

Paradise.

But there was always a catch to it, and when she heard her phone go "ding," she knew she'd gotten a text message to interrupt her.

Since she was on the clock, she had to look.

But it was just from Mom. Then again, Mina had been expecting this after her chat with Katie.

A little birdy tells me you had a cowboy in your cabin. :)

Good heavens, it hadn't taken that long for the little birdy to spread the news. Thank goodness Mina had already decided it was permissible to let her family in on what was going on just as gradually as she was doing for Chet.

She texted back.

Don't get excited, Mom.

Her mother, who had fingers faster than any texting teen, came back with,

> Well, if it was someone to get excited about, you know that he'd always be welcome for dinner.

Mina shook her head, laughing a little.

> I'll keep that in mind.
> Love and kisses.

And she put the phone away, absently brushing her tummy at the same time. Even if they overstepped at times, her baby was going to have a family who loved him or her. Her mom and dad would help in any way they could, if worse came to worse and she lacked for anything as a single mom.

But she wouldn't. Mina had to have faith in Chet... and in herself if things didn't work out with him. She wasn't naive enough to con herself into thinking single parenthood would be easy, but she would be prepared, just in case.

She slipped into the cool pool, sighing, letting the murmur of water make its hushed way into the very core of her. Going under the surface, she came back up again, steeped, cleansed.

Climbing out, she sat on the ledge, kicking her feet and listening to the Native American flute playing on the hidden speakers.

She smiled. This spa was going to be a big success for Chet, and she was content to be a part of what would heal him. But was that all it would take to make him whole again—the triumph of a project that was dear to his heart and pride?

When she heard someone else in the room, she stood to get a towel or her robe. But too late.

There he was—Chet. And he'd stopped in his tracks at the sight of her.

Instinctively, she rested her arm over her belly, hoping she could still hide her secret.

Just for a little while longer.

Chet felt as if the breath had been slammed out of him.

Mina…

Legs that seemed to go on forever, slim hips, breasts that cried out to be palmed by his hands.

Was she curvier than he remembered?

No. Yes. He wasn't sure. He'd tried so hard to put her out of his mind that, right now, just by looking at her, his head was a mess, not settling on anything except for how much he craved her.

She snatched a robe off of a nearby chair, but it did nothing to douse the fire that was racing through him at lightning speed.

To feel her again. To be inside of her…

"I didn't think you were coming to the spa," she said breathlessly.

He had to clear his throat, because there was something lodged in it.

"I changed my mind. After being out in the sun all day, I thought a dip in a pool would be just the thing. You talked about this Paradise Room, so…" Damn it, his voice still sounded rough.

Out of gentlemanly instinct, he'd finally looked away,

knowing from the flush on her face that she was embarrassed to have been caught like this.

But they'd been intimate, and neither of them could pretend otherwise.

When he looked back up at her, she had that robe closed, the sash tied. Yet, even though she was dressed, she seemed so painfully vulnerable.

In the face of that, *his* walls went up. He hated what he'd done to her that night, hated that he'd caused this kind of tension between them.

Even so, he wondered what it might be like if his defenses ever stayed down. But what would he be left with if not for those walls?

She began to walk out of the room. "I've got a lot to do."

"Wait, Mina."

She halted, her posture stiff, as if she expected to be called out for something.

"Don't let me chase you away," he said. And he wanted her to stay, more than anything, because when she wasn't near him, he was wishing for it.

Then again, asking her to stay wasn't going to get them back to where they'd been before he'd touched her, made love to her. Even more importantly, being alone in a seductive room while she was half-naked under that robe wasn't going to go over too well in a conservative company like the Barron Group if a staff member came in and picked up on this sexual awareness between them.

Chet wasn't worried about his reputation so much as hers, because, if the rumors started up, even his most minor fears might come true and she might never be taken seriously again.

And Chet knew the power of words. The power of a lie.

But he also knew he was lying to himself right now, making up excuses about why they shouldn't be here, standing with a curtain of anticipation between them.

She was watching him again, with that weighted look he'd noticed last night, as if she was trying to figure what was running through his mind.

"You have no idea what to do with yourself, do you, Chet?"

Once again, she could see right through him.

"Things were so simple eight months ago," he said. "I'm trying to figure out why they can't be that way now."

"Things change."

Hearing her say it drove this new reality home. Things *had* changed, and he was sure doing a poor job of rolling with it.

That shamed him somewhat, because he'd always believed himself to be a stronger man than that. And what he was seeing in himself wasn't acceptable: this wasn't the person Abe had raised from boyhood up before they'd gone their own ways.

Was this *Eli* coming out in him?

Mina waited there in her robe, as if she was still wishing that he would say more.

But he couldn't and when she walked away, she took a little bit of his hopes with her, leaving him as aimless as ever.

Chapter Four

That evening after dinner, Chet's entire staff met at the pavilion, where they were having a "game night," just like the ones that would be offered to the guests once the resort opened. A few of the local contractors had shown up, too.

There was an excited buzz in the air, everyone getting to know each other outside of work as Danny, one of the young Barron Group staffers, stood next to Mina, his hands stuffed into his khaki pants pockets. Meanwhile, another staffer, Corrine, who'd put together tonight's activity, welcomed everyone.

Danny leaned over to Mina and whispered, "I'm gonna make sure I'm on your side." They were going to play a round of softball—a team-building exercise. "I figure backing up the boss might score me some points."

As Danny shot her a grin, she realized that he

wasn't talking about Chet—he was referring to *her* as the boss.

A glow of pride caught her right in the middle of the chest. This resort development had been the first big project that Chet had let her run with, but she'd never looked at herself as anything more than his assistant.

Yet, what would Danny and the others think if they knew that Chet had given Mina more responsibilities at this resort *after* they'd been together?

She tried not to believe that Chet had raised her status out of guilt or favoritism. Chet had gradually been giving her other projects with higher esteem for a while now, even before that night. Besides, he was a fair man in general, and when he said that he wanted to make sure that no one thought she had slept her way to the top, he'd meant it.

But maybe he was right about what might happen if the staff knew—they might not look at her the same way ever again. That's why it was imperative that, when she told Chet about the baby, it would be because she was more than just a one-night stand or the mother of his child.

It would be because he loved her.

Nobody would have any doubts about what she meant to him.

As Corrine led the group toward a field lined by rough bleachers, a chain-link backstop and lights that buttered the ground with illumination, Mina was determined to have some fun, to not think about anything else for a couple of hours.

But it was hard when all she was doing was glancing around for Chet, who hadn't shown up yet.

She sought a position in left field since she'd never

been a softball kind of girl. Danny, who'd indeed ended up on her team, stood next to her.

As he loitered with his arms crossed over the logo of his long-sleeved T-shirt—an ad for surfboards—Mina could tell that he was probably more into watching sports on TV than actually playing.

Their pitcher was lobbing high, slow balls at Corrine, the first up at the plate.

"Hey, batter batter," Danny said, almost as if he was poking fun at this entire exercise. Then, already bored, he turned to Mina. "If I didn't know any better, I'd say you almost look like one of *us* tonight."

"Us?" Mina peered down at her game-night garb. Roomy jeans, sneakers, an untucked blouse.

"I'm talking about someone who's just starting to climb the corporate ladder," Danny said. "*My* kind of person."

"I am your kind of person. I'm just a little further up the ladder." Mina smiled. "I've done my share of climbing over the years."

"You're lucky that you got assigned to Chet Barron. He's been a real good mentor for you."

Was Danny getting around to what she was afraid he was getting around to? Was it obvious that she and Chet had…hit it off?

"In business," she said, "you make your own luck, Danny. The rest is work."

"I know, and you've got a reputation as a hard worker. People around here like you, Mina. They're happy to see your fortunes rising."

Just when she was getting ready for him to deliver the zinger, Danny sent her a crooked grin.

And she realized what was really going on.

He was making small talk. Flirting?

Good heavens. Danny wasn't even out of his early twenties. Was he making his own luck, as he'd put it, searching for his own mentor?

There was a popping sound from the batter's box, and they both set their attention on the fly ball traveling toward first base.

As one of the contractors fielded it, Mina glanced around again, this time spying Chet near the bleachers, where he was leaning, arms casually crossed over his chest, his cowboy hat low over his brow.

A shock jolted her, in her chest and then lower, tightening.

Something wicked in Mina wondered if he'd seen Danny cozying up to her, if she should play this out just to get a reaction out of Chet—to determine if he cared. Or if he was jealous.

But she just didn't have the heart to test him that way, especially when Chet glanced away from her as if he knew Mina had seen him looking.

The shortstop called out to Danny, pointing toward the empty center field.

"I think that guy is serious about his game," Mina said. "Better get on over there."

Danny laughed. "Yes, boss."

And he wandered off toward center field. But he didn't stop there. He ended up in right field, where Chef Arnett's cute sous chef was positioned.

Mina peered back to where Chet had been lingering, only to find that he'd already left.

Did he care?

Her veins filled with rushing hope as she promised herself that she was going to find out soon, once and for all.

Chet had no right to be jealous.

None at all.

And he kept telling himself this after he settled back into his makeshift office, the halls empty, the lights shaded as the cleaning crew made their rounds.

It would've been nice to relax with the staff, letting off some steam out there, but the sight of Mina in left field with that young pup Danny Hogan, a known flirt, had stopped Chet cold.

He wasn't used to seeing Mina with anyone else but him. Wasn't used to seeing her in casual clothes, talking with other men, especially ones who were still young and untouched enough by the trials of life to have charming, carefree smiles.

Sure, Mina needed some levity in her life, but Chet was sure someone like Danny Hogan was too flighty for her needs, especially after what she'd told him about that ex-boyfriend of hers.

If Chet saw Danny making a play for Mina again, he'd...

What—shoo the kid off?

Or...

Damn, there was something else going on here— something Chet could barely admit. He was acting as if Mina had been getting ready to betray him, just as his own mom had betrayed Abe.

Chet leaned back in his leather chair, raking a hand through his hair. What did he expect—for Mina to become a nun after their one night together, after he'd made it perfectly clear that they didn't have a romantic future?

As he'd done before when life seemed to be piling up on him, he turned his attention to work. He worked until night covered the sky, until he knew that the softball game had to be over and Mina was back in her cabin.

Trying not to think about how much he hoped she was alone, Chet went back to his own cabin but had a hell of a time getting to sleep.

Fortunately, in the morning he was busy while the staff charged around, getting ready for the locals preview day that they were holding so that they could start establishing a reputation in the community. Hopefully, the resort could whip up some early enthusiasm and end up establishing regular customers besides their visiting clientele.

When Chet emerged from his cabin after an on-the-fly breakfast from his cabin kitchen, he found the property bustling with the staff setting up their tents and tables and a local band bringing their equipment to the pavilion. The resort's restaurant crew was preparing an area that would feature their food while, nearby, the spa and activities staff would be offering mini-massages, product samples and short hikes on the fringes of the common area, now that the weather was cooling off near the end of the day.

Somehow, he and Mina didn't see each other the whole time, although Chet heard her voice over the walkie-talkies that the staff carried. And every time he did, his blood caught on fire, heating him to distraction.

When he finally saw Mina, it was early evening in the food area, where a bunch of linen-covered tables boasted samples from the restaurant. There was already a casually dressed crowd, sipping wine, enjoying themselves.

Mina was schmoozing with some local politicians and businessmen, and she looked so fresh and beautiful in her prairie skirt, boots and white peasant top that she took Chet's breath away, leaving him standing there like a dolt.

When was he going to get over this?

Knowing he would have to start the process, he went over to join her group.

She saw him before he even arrived, and he recognized the same posture he'd spied in her last night, when she'd been in left field and he'd been standing by the bleachers.

Widened eyes. The obvious flare of attraction in her gaze.

She had to feel the same way he did, and it scared him to death, because he didn't know what the hell to do about it.

"Chet," Mina said when he arrived on the fringes of her social circle. She'd recovered nicely from their moment, going on to introduce everyone.

He shook hands all around, knowing that he would be wining and dining these people before he left to check on other Group projects later tomorrow; in fact, he would be having a lunch with several locals before going to the airport.

"Thanks for coming," he said to them. "Is there anything I can get for anyone?"

The mayor, a man with a handlebar mustache and a certain Wild West air, held up his glass of red wine. "I think you've provided nicely, Mr. Barron."

"Chet. It's Chet."

He and Mina traded a smile, and it had the power to let him know that things were going to be okay, that this resort was going to flourish.

But the crackling awareness between them didn't go anywhere.

He made it through the rest of the night, remembering her smile, remembering the way Mina's skirt fell over her hips, the way her hair rested on her shoulders and caught the last of the sun as it set.

In the end, when the visitors had left and the area was cleaned up, he found her on a bench in front of the administration building, exhausted, her skirt spread around her, her eyes closed.

A beat of concern seized his heart, but when she seemed to sense him, then opened her eyes and grinned, he knew that she was undergoing a good kind of exhaustion. The kind he'd grown used to over the years, after a decent day's work that bolstered the spirit.

"We did it," she said.

Chet pushed back the brim of his hat. "*You* did it. I just looked over your plans and gave my okay, that's all."

"You put your everything into this place. Give yourself some credit."

She was rubbing her arms, and for the first time tonight, he noticed a coolness in the air. Fall was definitely descending in the desert, and fast.

"Tonight might be a good time for a fire," he said. "What do you say I light up that pit on my cabin deck while we debrief?"

"I vote yes."

He held out his hand to her and she grabbed on to it,

just as she had the other night when they'd tested Chef Arnett's cooking.

The same jarring electricity traveled through him as he brought her to her feet. When he let go, they started to walk on the graveled path to his cabin, and he could've sworn that she was just as puzzled about what to say now as he was.

On the way, Chet saw Danny Hogan and that sous chef he'd been chatting up at the softball game in the near distance, walking over a hill.

"The spirit path," Mina said. "I'll bet he's taking her there."

"For some kind of deep religious experience?"

Mina gave him a little punch to the arm. "Nice."

"What?" It was easy to be in a good mood, knowing that Danny Hogan had decided to pursue a girl who wasn't named Mina. "The kid's known around the office for loving his entertainment."

"Kid? Listen to you, like you're such an ancient creature."

Who knew that thirty would *feel* so old? It was as if Chet had lived a lot of lifetime from birth to the present. But with the moon and stars shining down like they were, and with Mina walking right next to him, things seemed new right now.

He wished it would stay that way—that they could be locked in this moment under the stars, where he didn't ever have to go back to what he'd been running from.

"Are you looking forward to Jeremiah's wedding?" she asked, changing the subject.

He took a breath, let it out. "Yeah, for my brother's sake. Jeremiah's crazy about Ally, and I'm happy for him. It's just that Eli might be there, if he's earned any time out of rehab."

"Maybe you can avoid him."

Chet recalled how shamed he'd felt just yesterday, when he'd realized that it was high time that he faced his demons.

"No," he said. "There's no more avoiding what I need to confront."

Saying it felt right, as if he'd relieved himself of a burden he hadn't known how to release.

Mina paused, the moonlight brushing over her. She looked at him, the corners of her mouth turned up, her eyes shining.

"I'm glad to hear that, Chet."

"I'm glad I finally feel that way." Then he shrugged. "In any case, I've got two brothers waiting for me in Texas. And they've been waiting for a while. After Eli screwed up for the last time, we knew we'd have to figure out how to handle him beyond rehab."

"Just let me know what I can do. Promise you'll do that and not take all of this on yourself. You're not alone, Chet."

"I know."

He would never be alone—not with Mina around.

How could he have forgotten that she was the first one he'd turned to in his crisis? That she had never let him down, even when he'd done it to her?

He was talking before he knew it. "Did you get the wedding invitation for Jeremiah and Ally?"

"Yes."

She didn't add more. She didn't have to because, even though she'd attended Tyler's wedding as a business acquaintance, it'd been awkward. Maybe she'd been thinking about staying away from *this* Barron event, intent on avoiding more emotional clumsiness with Chet.

He talked before he even realized something had come out of his mouth. "Maybe we can go together."

"To...the wedding?"

Had he just asked her out?

He tried to recover. "It was just an idea. I figure we'll both be traveling at the same time, from San Antonio to the ranch, and it made sense for us to just do it together."

"Oh." Her voice was so soft, so vulnerable, that it nearly killed him.

Now look what he'd done—caused another weird situation.

He tried again. "Besides traveling together, I'd actually like to be around you there."

"You...would?"

"Yes." And he meant it.

With that one word—*yes*—he'd jumped off a mountain without anything to catch him below. Nothing but Mina.

They'd both slowed to a stand on the path.

"Weddings," she said. "They can be so boring unless you've got someone to talk to the whole time."

"Or to watch all the rituals with—like the bride and groom eating the first slice of cake."

"Or seeing everyone dancing to all the bad music."

Was she waiting for him to claim a spot on her dance card now?

Hell, he would love a dance with her—a slow one, where he could just hold her and sway to the music.

A worm of reality wiggled into his thoughts. Was

she what he really needed, or was he going to end up sucking her all the way into his problems, taking her down with him?

Goose bumps paraded over her arms, and he wasn't sure if they were from the cooling night or from this conversation that was fast swerving out of control.

"Damn it, you're probably freezing out here," he said, seizing the chance to save himself with another change of topic.

"I'm fine."

As he started down the path to his cabin again, she reached out, gripping his arm.

"I'm *fine,* Chet."

Did she mean more than just that though? Was she telling him that, if he stepped out of this self-imposed shell, if he were to seize the day and take up where their one beautiful night together had left off, she could handle it? That if he were to scoop her into his arms and sweep her the rest of the short way down this path and into his cabin, she might even welcome it?

Trouble was, he wasn't sure what would come after all that.

Or if *he* could handle it.

It was times like these, when Chet was being so darned wooden in the head, that Mina thought that she might have to start looking for a new job.

If she did, she might never have to let him know about their child. She could go off to a place where no one knew her, where they wouldn't care about who the father of her baby was, then start anew. That way, Chet could concentrate on his decimated life and not worry about anything else.

But, far below the surface, questions jabbed at Mina. Was there a chance that a child could mend Chet's fractured soul?

Couldn't *she* do that for him, too?

Believing in the possibility with every fiber of her being, she took the biggest risk ever.

Heart ramming against her chest, she lifted up to her tiptoes, pushing back Chet's cowboy hat, closing her eyes, tentatively touching her lips to his.

Paradise. As sensual as the sound of water falling. As perfect as any haven she could imagine.

It was as if something broke open in him, and he slipped his arms around her, holding her close as heaven swirled through her, as they sipped at each other, warm and lingering.

Chet.

Their second kiss, but this one was so much more wonderful than the first one, when he'd needed more than just her.

She breathed, pulled back a little, whispering against him. "You bet I'll go to that wedding with you."

I'll go anywhere, if you'd just ask.

But *he* had to be the one to bring up that he wanted more. He had to be obvious about wanting her, showing her without any outside influence that he had come to terms with his life and that there was room enough for her, plus one.

She'd obviously hit a button in him, and he guided them off the path, toward a large pine that spread its branches and blocked out the sky.

Privacy, she thought. He didn't want anyone to see.

Gently, he leaned her against the pine, cupping the

back of her head with a hand, tilting her face up to him just before he covered her mouth with his again.

And, just like that, she was in another place. A glass ball where nothing else mattered, just them, just this moment, an endless stretch of warmth and vibration that shimmered down her body.

Over her skin.

Under it.

Every inch of her was going liquid, hot and wanting.

She slid her palms up his back, feeling every muscle that had survived his time behind a desk, muscles that had been created by hard work on his ranch—riding, roping, straining under the sun as sweat dappled his skin.

Wanting to feel him all the way against her, she deepened the kiss, pulling him down, opening her mouth, nearly devouring him in her wild need. She was going tight all over—her breasts, the center of her—and she was going to need a release.

Him—her ultimate release.

She panted, "I've been wishing this would happen for so long. You don't know what it's been like, waiting for you, hoping…"

"I know," he said raggedly, his fingers threaded through her hair.

He knew.

He'd thought about kissing her again, too, holding her, pressing her against his body so that she could feel just how *much* he'd been wishing for her.

She pulled his hat off his head, clutching it as he came down for another kiss, just as hungry for her as she was for him.

This time he wasn't kissing her with the desperation of a grieving man, a man who was searching for a truth. Now, he took it slow, sliding his tongue past her lips, exploring as she melted beneath him, so overwhelmed that he had to hold her up when her knees gave out.

Her breasts were aching for a touch, more sensitive than she'd ever known because of the pregnancy but especially now, as he brushed a hand over one, tenderly....

Almost lovingly.

But Mina wouldn't believe that. Not until she *heard* him say it.

"Chet," she said on a near moan.

Encouraged, he circled her nipple with a thumb. With the lace of her bra and her blouse between her and his skin, all she wanted to do was strip off her clothing, be with him entirely.

She reached up, undoing one button, then another. If this went where she hoped it would go, she would be careful with him, be careful of the baby...

Nearby an owl hooted, reminding her that they weren't alone.

"Not here," he said, his breath warm against her ear, sending more sizzles through her.

"Your cabin?" she asked.

When he paused, she knew that this was a make-or-break moment.

Somewhere along the way, she'd dropped his hat, so she used both hands to cup his head, making him look right at her.

"You make me so happy," she said.

His gaze was unfocused, desire-ridden. "I do?"

"You always have."

And she brought him down for another kiss, no matter where they were, no matter who might come upon them out here in the open.

He held her, clearly unable to stop, and Mina wanted so badly to call it love.

Just thinking about it, she lost her balance again, and he caught her, then lifted her into his arms, taking her the rest of the way to his cabin.

Chapter Five

Chet crashed through his cabin door, holding Mina, kissing her.

You make me so happy, she'd said.

And she'd meant it in a way that went beyond anything he'd ever had with *anyone* before.

That should've scared the life out of him, but how could it when he knew that here, with her in his arms, she really was everything he needed and he'd just been too afraid to admit it?

Her face was nuzzled against his neck while she held tight to him, her breath like the tiny beat of butterfly wings against his throat. The fluttering sensation echoed inside of him, except a hundred times faster.

When he got to the staircase that led to his loft bedroom, he eased her down until she stood on the first step, bringing them nearly face-to-face.

She leaned toward him, feverish, running her fingers

through his hair. He remembered that his hat was somewhere outside, on the ground, but he didn't really care.

"Mina," he whispered, cradling her jaw with one hand, wanting to map every nuance of her face. First her cheekbones, curved and high, a work of art. Then her mouth.

She kissed the tip of his thumb. "This time, I want to wake up and see you in the morning, next to me."

The last time had been a maelstrom of feeling and urgency, and he wanted more between them, too. Wanted it to last all night long.

He answered her by coasting his fingers down her neck, her collarbone. She gasped, leaning back her head, exposing the white of her throat in the near darkness. He could barely see her, but he knew her through and through, just by touch, by his desire and affection for her.

Affection, he thought while dragging his fingers lower, down, between her breasts. He didn't know if he would ever be able to love anyone—trust was a part of love and he just didn't have that in him anymore—but he would come closest to it with Mina.

He would give her everything but that deep, dark place inside of him that he would have to protect from pain, because he didn't think he could take even an iota more of it.

She shivered as he traveled down the center of her upper stomach, but when he got to her belly, she grasped his wrist.

"Here," she whispered, leading him back up to her breast.

His hand opened over its fullness. Damn it, before

tonight, he'd forgotten how glorious it was to feel a woman. Feel Mina.

He braced one hand over her back, spread the other one over her breast, then used his fingertips to trace her nipple, which pebbled against her bra and blouse. Bending to her, he kissed her there, feeling the hard nub, rubbing his lips over it until she moaned.

A blast of heat made him realize that he was already hard, straining against his jeans. He used his tongue to lave her nipple, dampening her blouse, making her clutch at his shoulders.

Her breathing had turned to panting, his blood to a rush of molten lava, urging him on.

He pushed up her shirt, and he lowered himself, pressing his lips to her upper stomach. She inhaled harshly.

"Wait," she said.

Then she was undoing the rest of her buttons, practically ripping off her blouse. He helped her, pushing off the material, leaving her in a lace bra that he could see in the night-shrouded room.

She made quick work of that, too, dropping it to the ground.

Seeing the blush of her nipples against the pale of her skin was too much for him, and he cupped both of her breasts. They were beautiful, plump and round. Perfect.

He put his attention on the one that he hadn't kissed earlier, taking her nipple into his mouth, sucking, loving it while she whimpered.

Her little sounds drove him crazy, and he wrapped her in his arms, lifting her gently, bringing her to the top of the stairway to his bed—a span of pale quilt and mattress that welcomed them as he lay her down on it.

Moonlight spilled through the circular window above, casting silver light over the part of Mina that was caught by its illumination. Her smiling face, her hair, a spill of red on the white of the quilt. Her breasts, ripe and gorgeous. Her arms reaching out for him.

He wrestled off his shirt, his boots and socks, then crawled onto the bed, poised over her as she gripped his forearms.

"I tried to put you out of my mind," he said, his voice gritty. "But you stayed there."

"You stayed with me, too."

He slid an arm under her, then lowered himself until his chest came down on hers. Her breasts crushed against him, and he almost died, right there and then, stimulated beyond belief, flesh to flesh.

He kissed her again, deeply, thoroughly, slow, agonizing. His tongue explored her mouth with long, languorous strokes.

All night long.

The mere thought sent a deluge of warmth through him, down every limb, coating him, animating him for the first time in what seemed like forever.

He wanted to know more of her than he'd ever gotten to before, wanted to claim every inch of skin, every curve.

When he came up for air, he smoothed his hand over a breast again—damn, he couldn't get enough of them—then her waist. He felt her belt, the skirt beneath it.

Mina shifted underneath him, using her fingers to gradually hike up her skirt.

He took the hint and skimmed his fingers under the material and over her thigh, playing there, lightly tracing, making her squirm.

He smiled. It was so easy with her. So easy to be satisfied because he made her happy. He couldn't believe that he had the ability to draw such feeling from her.

When he coasted his fingertips between her legs, she gasped.

"Yes. There…" she whispered.

She parted her legs for him, and he tugged down her panties enough to slip his fingers inside the lace material.

She was ready for him.

Already ready.

And he was, too, pounding, throbbing for her. Nearly to the bursting point.

It wasn't time yet, though. Not nearly time.

As he slid a finger between her folds, she arched. And when he found the most sensitive part of her, she cried out.

He concentrated there, watching her moonlight-revealed face—every time she bit her lip, every time she opened her mouth to make another soft sound…

When he coaxed a finger all the way inside of her, she grabbed at his arm again, digging into his skin.

He barely felt it as her breathing escalated, heavier, faster.…

Moans.

Groans—

She cried out again, rocking her hips, saying his name.

He watched every moment, all twisted up inside, needing a release, too.

After she reached her peak, then relaxed on the bed, she didn't stay still for long, seeking the fly of his jeans.

"I've got it," he said, rising from the bed, standing and shucking off the denim. Then he removed her boots, her skirt, her panties, leaving her bare to him.

He could still only see from the waist up in that circle of moonlight and, when she spoke, he watched her mouth.

That gorgeous, full mouth.

"I want you so much."

It didn't take but a minute to go to his shaving kit for protection, then free the condom from its packet and put it on. He came to the bed again, lying down next to her, and she shifted so that she was facing him, side to side.

Without a word, just their breathing, just the night sounds outside the cabin, he rested his hand on her hip.

She didn't say anything, either. Then again, she didn't need to. He could see every thought written over her face.

Her affection for him.

And maybe even *more* than that?

His pulse jogged even faster as she pulled him close, wrapping one of her legs over him until his hardness nudged her.

"I'm so happy," she whispered again.

He was, too, but the words stuck in his throat. He was happier than he'd ever been.

Unable to stand it any longer, he eased into her, moving with a nice, slow rhythm so he could enjoy every pulsating instant.

She was with him all the way, pressing close, her lips against his throat.

"Chet," she said, and he loved to hear it, because

when it came from her, he had no doubt about who he was. She knew how to define him even when he couldn't do so.

The cadence of their lovemaking got faster, more demanding. Each moment nailed his heart, and it nearly beat out of his chest, taking over the rest of his body as it thudded hard.

Harder.

It was as if something was pounding at him, pulling him this way, that way, turning him upside down, in and out—

Finally, he did burst, and it felt as if he'd blasted right open, revealing everything about himself to her.

Afterward, as he held her close, he wondered if it was because he was overcome by emotion or if it was because he didn't want her to see the look on his face.

The complete and utter decimation of a man who would have to piece himself back together again come tomorrow, when he would have to go back to real life.

After they'd snuggled a bit, Chet left the bed, giving Mina a chance to slip under the covers.

She was glad that she wasn't obviously pregnant to the casual eye, otherwise she would've been cautious about having him touch or see her belly. The biggest change she'd undergone so far was her breasts, which had become so sensitized that even a brush of his fingertips had sent a blast crashing through her.

As she thought about how he'd responded to *her,* all fire and passion, she hugged a pillow to her chest. He'd lived up to every fantasy.

But what came next was all reality.

Was now a good time to tell him?

The most defensive part of her screamed "No!" It was still too early. Even though she'd hoped this would change everything between them, making love again hadn't done that. It hadn't meant his issues had disappeared and everything would be hunky-dory now.

And it didn't erase her concerns, either.

Her heart was blipping. Nerves.

Now, more than ever, Mina *needed* to hear him say, "I love you." She had to have a commitment. Maybe she could blame it on her last relationship, when she hadn't gotten anything close to promises or vows.

This time, she wanted to know that the man she'd chosen was with her because he couldn't imagine life any other way. And that's why she didn't say a word about the baby, even though she knew there would come a time when she would *have* to tell Chet, love or not.

But, after what had just happened between them, she was sure Chet was going to tell her he loved her. Maybe not tonight, but someday soon.

As he came back to the bed, she sighed. Looking at him always did that to her.

He had some height as well as heft, all muscle, as solid as they came. Feeling him against her had made her think that no other man would ever come close to doing what Chet did to her.

There would *never* be another like him, and that's the way it should be, too. The father of her child should be the end-all and be-all.

He lifted the covers, going under them, as well. A puff of air whisked over Mina, releasing goose bumps all over her body—especially when she caught scent of his skin.

Musky, manly, with a hint of sweet clover and hay.

"Hey, cowboy," she said softly.

He paused, as if thinking something over. Then he pulled her to him, bringing her back to his chest as he cradled her.

Heart banging with this show of affection, Mina hugged his arms against her chest, closing her eyes, her throat clogged.

Yes, someday he was going to tell her he loved her.

"I was thinking," he said, "that we should've tried to see more of the sights around here before we had to go."

Joy zipped through her. He was hinting that he regretted not being with her more outside of this bedroom.

"There're a lot of things to see around St. George," she said, encouraging him.

"Yeah," he said. "Zion Park's pretty close by. Maybe next time we're here, we can drive up there."

Mina was normally a pretty active gal, and under different circumstances she would've loved the type of challenging hikes Mt. Zion could offer. But she couldn't push herself physically in her state.

"I'd like Zion," she said. "But only if we'd do a wimpy hike or just…I don't know, strolled around."

"Since when are you a wimp? Weren't you the one who tried skydiving when we went to San Diego in April to check out that hotel property?"

"Yes, that was me. And I've never recovered." Actually, being a daredevil for the first time in her life had been loads of fun, but it wasn't something she would ever do again. "My heart barely survived the first time."

"All right then. We could go wimpy but, understand, you'd kill my male ego."

She nuzzled the crook of his arm. "We can build it back up again pretty quick, you know."

"You'll have to give me a minute on that," he said.

Then he laughed, and the vibrations carried through from his chest into her back. It was just more proof of a connection between them, a wire that ran between him and her.

She smiled into his skin, loving the smell of him. She'd read once that scent had a lot to do with attraction, and Chet did it for her. He was an addiction.

"The other night," she said, "you were talking about how I should take a real vacation. But what about you?"

She wanted to know where he would like to go, what he would love to do.

Who he would do it with.

"Vacation," he said. "I'm not sure I'll ever get one."

"You're that much of a workaholic?" Like his brother Tyler once was before he'd found his new wife, Zoe.

"I'm sure as hell turning into an office hound."

"But you won't be that way forever."

He stayed silent, and *that* didn't bode well to Mina.

"You like working that much?" she asked.

"I like staying busy…at least, I do lately."

Because of the scandal, but she wasn't going to mention it. Wasn't going to pop their bubble.

It seemed as if he'd just needed time to chew on her initial question—the one about vacation—and he swerved back around to answer it.

"Someday," he said, "I'd like to buy back the spread I gave up in Montana, then spend a lot of time there."

"Why didn't you keep it?"

"Because I didn't think I'd ever be going there again.

I really thought I could help my dad recover from cancer and we'd have this wonderful life down south." It was obvious that "dad" meant Abe, and it probably always would. "I can afford the land a hundred times over now, but…"

He didn't have to finish, didn't have to say that things were never going to go back to the way they'd been.

"What was your ranch like?"

"The Double R?" Chet tightened his arms around her. "Three hundred acres, a cabin that was built over a half century ago by a rancher who sold it to me after he retired. He was one of those old-time coots—you know, the kind you'd expect to see on a bench outside of a general store, whiling the hours away with a bunch of other oldsters who sit there spitting tobacco and exchanging gossip."

"Just like old pioneer women."

"Yeah. But these gossips would have scraggly beards down to their belts."

When he went quiet again, Mina could just about feel how much he missed his old home.

She leaned against his arms, enjoying the sensation of muscle, stalwartness. "You never would've left if it wasn't for Abe."

"Never. But I like Texas. And I'm okay at my job."

"You're more than okay. You're a natural at putting together development deals."

"Thanks."

She swallowed, getting to the bigger questions. "So you're going to stay for a while? In Texas?"

Although she didn't see him nod, she could sense it.

"I owe it to my brothers," he said. "And to Eli, even

if he's the one who made all this trouble. He's falling apart and I think the only thing that's going to bring him around is acceptance from all of us Barron boys."

She was so proud to hear him say that—to take matters in hand and turn them around. Shock had forced him away just after the scandalous truth had come out, anger had kept him on the periphery of his new family, doing what he could to help them but never fully allowing Eli the forgiveness he needed. But he sounded as if he was ready to tackle everything now.

That was another good sign for their future, yet time would tell if this was only pillow talk.

He was stroking her skin now, light fingertip brushes over her arms. Her pulse skittered, her flesh tightening with heat.

Until morning, she thought. That's what he'd promised her, and she was going to make him own up to it.

She stretched beneath him, angling her face so that her lips would meet his.

"I'm glad you're staying," she said against his mouth.

It turned into a kiss before she could say any more.

It wasn't easy to get out of bed come morning, but Chet forced himself to do it, even after awakening to the sight of Mina next to him.

The sheets gathered at her waist and her arms were flung over her head. Her positioning made her breasts all the more tempting, and he woke her up by kissing their pink tips.

She groaned, but when they both saw the time on his digital clock—6:07 a.m.—they got going soon enough.

Since he was leaving for the airport later today, neither of them made promises to meet again, just as they had last night. Nevertheless, being with her was all Chet could think about as Mina pulled her clothes on then rushed out of his cabin with a quick kiss to his cheek.

"See you at lunch?" she asked.

He knew that she had a meeting with some contractors in about forty-five minutes, and he would be dining with representatives from the nearby Chamber of Commerce at noon. Mina was scheduled to be there, too.

"See you then," he said, smiling, and that's the closest they got to making future plans.

After showering and putting on a gray business suit, Chet left the cabin. He even found his hat on the side of the path they'd traveled last night, and he beat it against the trunk of a tree instead of his leg, just to get the dew off. It might've even been the same tree he'd pressed Mina against when he'd kissed her.

He looked at it, hormones swirling around in him like fireflies.

Last night. God knew how he was going to get it out of his mind.

And he couldn't, though he put up a valiant effort while walking to his office, checking in with the main Barron headquarters via phone and then seeing to all the other projects he had going.

When lunchtime came around, he went to the dining room, which was one of the first areas to be fully decorated, with its elegant dark-paneled walls, Southwest-inspired art, massive fireplace and roses on every linen-covered table.

He arrived before any of the businessmen did, beating even Mina by a few minutes.

She was dressed in full business attire, too, in a dark blue suit with a lowered waist and wingtip pumps. The red hair that he'd combed his fingers through last night was pulled back in a pearl clip.

He wished he could just walk up to her and say, "Can't you wear it down?" As the businessmen arrived just after Mina, needles of emerging panic started to poke at Chet.

It was only during the meal itself that he got ahold of himself.

Work tended to do that though, whether it was out on the Montana range under the big blue sky or in an office. Still, he was all too aware of Mina as she sat at the other end of the table entertaining two men who owned local movie theaters.

He tried not to think about how taken they looked by Mina, how much attention they were paying to her beaming smile and bubbly laugh.

Good God, she was still in an afterglow and they couldn't help but respond to it.

Again, he thought about his mother—how she'd fooled Abe with her betrayal—and Chet fought to maintain the trust that Mina had built up in him again.

Mina wasn't like his mom. So why couldn't he remember that?

Somehow, Chet got through lunch and the niceties of escorting their guests to the resort limos that would drive them off and away. All the while, though, he kept an eye on Mina and those men.

They were the last to leave. One of them was even ruddy with all the whiskey he'd drunk.

He was wearing a hat with a snakeskin band and a

black suit. *An urban cowboy,* Chet thought, as the man whispered something in Mina's ear.

Chet had noticed that she'd refrained from alcohol during lunch, but that was Mina—always in control of business.

Except maybe for last night…

When she distanced herself from the man while still managing to seem friendly, the guy's associate, Todd Buckley, pulled him away.

"Come on, Jason. Time to leave our kind hosts."

Jason put an arm around Mina and she widened her eyes at Chet, who was just about to blow a gasket.

But this was business. A responsible tycoon wouldn't slam his fist into the face of one of the people he was trying to woo, now would he?

So he balanced his temper, went to the limo and pointedly opened the door.

"Great to see you, Jason," Chet said through gritted teeth. He nodded at the guy's friend. "Todd."

Todd Buckley pulled Jason inside as his buddy blew a kiss to Mina.

"Charmed," he said. "Everything about this place is charmed—"

Cutting him off, Chet shut the door and pounded on the top of the vehicle, letting the driver know it was safe to go.

When the limo was out of sight, Chet muttered, "Charmed. One more second of that nonsense and he would've been seeing stars, all right."

He'd said it low enough so that Mina probably hadn't heard. Even so, when she stood next to him, she had an air about her that he hadn't felt before—a sense that he'd claimed her, even outside of the bedroom, and she was claiming him right back.

That panic assaulted him once more.

With a slap of truth, he knew that *everyone,* whether they were a father or mother, had the capacity to betray. He'd already learned that well. So what the hell was he doing setting himself up for another fall, even if it was with a woman who seemed as if she wasn't capable of lying to him?

As some of the staff, including Danny Hogan, walked toward the restaurant, Chet tried not to act like a man in crisis.

Even though the whole thing about protecting Mina from office gossip—her sleeping her way to the top—struck false with Chet now, he realized that he truly didn't want the staff to know what had happened between them.

"Well," Mina said to him under her breath, "lunch sure was fun."

He tried to keep his dander down. "You handled Jason the drunk well."

"So did you."

She smiled up at him, showing him how she'd noticed that he'd barely contained himself with good old Jason, just as Danny shouted out a hello.

They waved, and Mina took a step away from Chet, as if she also was wary of causing office gossip.

For some reason, that was a warped relief. She wasn't going to announce their liaison. She wasn't going to press him, either, he hoped.

She'd been carrying that iPad at her side, just as she always did, and now she turned it on, accessing one of those images on the screen. He couldn't help but notice that it was as if she'd sensed all his panic and she was pretending it didn't matter.

"I need to get my schedule straight," she said, back to business. "Jeremiah's wedding is in a week...."

Wedding.

Last night, he'd invited her.

God, how deep was he going to get himself before things blew apart, as they definitely would? It was inevitable.

But he couldn't rescind his offer. Besides, she'd gotten an invitation herself, and she would be there, anyway.

"The wedding weekend starts next Saturday," he said. "I can arrange our transportation to Florence Ranch. You'll be back at the San Antonio offices by then, right?"

"Yes."

She seemed to notice this cooling off. Hesitating a moment, she started plugging away at that computer again.

Then she stopped, although she still stared at it.

Chet had a bad feeling about this.

"The thing is..." she said, halting as she bit her lower lip.

"What?" he asked.

She looked up at him, resolute in some way that he couldn't explain.

"I promised my parents I'd stop by their place on Friday night since it's on the way to your family's ranch," she said. "My dad's got his birthday coming up, but he and my mom will be away on a cruise on his big day. I thought I'd give him his present and eat some cake, just to celebrate with him."

What the hell else could Chet do—say no to her?

Half of him felt numb, the other half warmed up. He hadn't been to a girl's house and met her parents since…

Damn. High school. That was the last time he'd cottoned up to someone so thoroughly that he'd been summoned to meet the family.

"Feel free to make a change in plans," Mina said. She'd obviously noted Chet's minor freak-out, even though he'd done his best to hide it.

He gauged her expression. Casual.

Was he making too much out of this?

"Okay," he said. "Why not?"

He'd said it casually as well, and as they began walking to the administration offices, he thought he saw a flash of an unidentifiable emotion fly over her gaze.

But it was gone before he could be certain.

Chapter Six

Nearly a week later, the limo that had picked Mina and Chet up from the Barron offices drove down a white-fenced country lane, finally stopping in front of the Ferguson family home.

It wasn't anything fancy—just a beige, one-level ranch house set back on a couple of green acres and lined by oak trees. But as Chet stared out the window while they pulled into the long driveway, Mina wondered if he was getting the sense of stability she'd always felt when coming back here.

"So this is where you grew up," he said.

Mina nodded. "Not too far from the city, but just far enough in the country. We even had space for a horse. Lolly passed on years ago, just after me and my sisters moved out, and my parents never did buy another."

"Maybe you'll get a home someday that has enough room for your own horse."

"No one can replace Lolly."

She smiled at Chet, so glad to see him again. It'd seemed like months instead of just about a week since they'd parted ways for business purposes.

Sure, they hadn't had any big, romantic "nice to see you again" moment today when he'd brought her down from the office and to the waiting limo, but she was certain that was because there'd been Barron employees all around them. And during the drive, he'd been friendly enough.

Still, she kept thinking there was a little… Well, *distance* wasn't really the word. *Cool* wasn't a good way to describe it, either. But he sure wasn't acting like he wanted to whisk her off to bed again.

Maybe he would come to her after they got tucked into Florence Ranch tonight…

But they had to get through this visit to her childhood home first. It was an important night, although he didn't know it. She'd asked him here because she wanted to see how he got along with the family, if he could fit in someday.

The limo came to a stop, and Mina flattened her skirt, still grateful that her tummy hadn't "popped" yet. If she had, her mom, with her eagle eyes, probably would've noticed something going on with Mina, even if she'd worn baggier clothes.

Just hold on, she thought to her little passenger. *Help me out a little longer.*

As the driver opened the door for them, Mina poked out her head, seeing that her niece, Lizzie, was already sprinting out the perennial flower-decorated front entrance, dressed in her fairy dress with the wings flapping behind her.

But…*Lizzie?*

What was her niece doing here when Mina hadn't said anything to her mom about inviting Katie to this short-but-sweet hello for her dad's birthday?

"Mina!" the little girl shouted, crashing into Mina as she got out of the limo and hugging her legs so tightly that it was impossible to walk.

Mina bent down and embraced Lizzie, kissing her red-haired head. "Hey, there, Tinkerbell! Are you going to recreate your show from last week for me?"

"Yes!"

Lizzie backed up to get a good look at Mina, and the expression on her freckled face was so open and full of innocent love that it was almost heartbreaking. But in a way that let Mina know that she'd done something right to earn her niece's affection.

She fought the urge to rest her hands over her tummy, just to feel the other member of the family who would be joining them.

Lizzie was already staring at the limo, and at Chet, who'd come to stand beside Mina while he held the chocolate sheet cake and the wrapped present Mina had brought for her father—a computerized ebook reader that he could use on the cruise after she showed him how to work it tonight.

At Lizzie's unwavering curiosity with Chet, Mina fortified herself.

And so it would begin.

"Lizzie, this is Mr. Chet," Mina said. "I work with him."

Lizzie just smiled a little shyly and said a tiny, "Hi." For a rambunctious toddler, she could sure get quiet fast in front of strangers.

"We're on our way to a wedding," Mina added, as if she felt the need to explain it to a youngster. Then again, maybe she was just practicing for all the queries that were going to come from her family, since it looked like Katie was here.

Darn her mom. She'd sounded the alarms for the troops to check out the man Mina had finally brought home. There would be *lots* of explaining to do tonight.

"What's a wedding?" Lizzie asked.

"It's where there's a bride dressed in a beautiful white dress," Mina said. "You went to Aunt Amy's wedding a few months ago, and you've seen pictures from your mommy and daddy's."

"Oh, yeah."

Chet had gotten to a knee to bring himself to Lizzie's height, and Mina's chest closed in on itself.

"Hi there, Lizzie," he said, extending his hand for a shake.

The little girl returned his greeting, but just as quickly rushed back to Mina, burying her face in her aunt's long skirt.

Mina grinned at Chet, who was rising to his feet.

"Don't worry," she said. "Lizzie's going to be your best friend in about ten minutes."

"I'll be ready for it."

He'd better be, along with fortifying himself against the rest of the brood.

"Lizzie," she said, "did I tell you that Chet has a new niece? A baby?"

The little girl peeked at him, her interest awakened.

Chet said, "Her name's Caroline."

Lizzie let go of Mina's skirt a bit. "She's a *baby?*"

He laughed. "She's my brother Jeremiah's pride and joy."

By then, Mina's parents had come out the front door. Her mother, whose red hair was just beginning to be paled by strands of gray, made a beeline for Mina. Meanwhile, her dad made his way down the brick front steps, limping slightly, his salt-and-pepper hair in a buzz cut. Sometimes his joints got stiff, and it looked like today was one of those days.

After her mom enfolded her in a hug, Mina went to her father, greeting him the same way.

"Happy early birthday, Dad," she said into his shoulder.

When the hug ended, he said, "Good that you got to stop by before your mom drags me off on that boat for parts unknown."

Mom rolled her eyes. "Yes, I'm torturing him with this vacation. It's such a hardship."

He shrugged good-naturedly, and both her parents rested their attention on Chet…and that limousine.

Now the fun would *really* start.

"This is my boss," Mina said. She'd only told her mom that they were able to stop by tonight because the house was on the way to Florence Ranch. However, she hadn't said anything about Chet being more than a carpool buddy for the wedding. She'd even told her mom not to read anything into the visit.

Didn't matter though, because her mother had obviously conjured her own interpretation of tonight, since this was the cowboy Katie had spied during her computer call with Mina. From the "Hallelujah, my daughter's actually brought a man home!'" look on her face, Mina knew that Mom was in heaven.

She and Dad welcomed Chet with open arms, and he took it in stride.

Had she set him up unfairly though, testing him to see how much he could take before she unleashed even bigger things on him? Was he thinking that, after their second night together, she had turned into some nut job who'd assumed that they were engaged now and was whisking him into a situation that he wasn't ready for?

As everyone headed for the house, Mina kept Chet behind for a second.

"They don't know anything intimate about my personal life," she whispered.

What she meant was that they didn't know *much* about him and her.

He paused, and she just had enough to time hold her breath before he said, "It's okay. It's good to meet them." As she exhaled, he added, "Now I see where you get that hair."

A joke. He was using his sense of humor to ease the moment. But that was another good sign, wasn't it? He wasn't running back to the limo or anything.

Slow and easy, she thought. *Just keep it going that way.*

She crossed her fingers in front of her as Chet ushered her inside the door, to a hall with antique pitchers on old pine nightstands, plus a hat and coatrack where Chet deposited his Stetson. As they moved through the prairie-influenced living room, with its cow skull wall and wagon wheel wall hangings, the aroma of barbecue floated in the air.

When Mina heard more voices around the corner,

in the direction of the kitchen, she shot her mom the stink eye from behind. Her mother had invited Katie *and* Amy.

Mina took up Chet's side as her sisters peered around the corner, then came at her with arms extended.

"There she is!" Katie said, her unbound strawberry-blond hair brushing Mina's cheek as they hugged.

Amy, who'd just graduated from college earlier in the year and had gotten married right after, took Katie's place. She'd cut her black hair short, in a bob, since the last time Mina had seen her.

"What's this?" Mina asked, ruffling her younger sister's locks.

Amy shrugged away from Mina. "Scott likes it."

"Where is Scott?" Mina glanced at Katie. "And Jonathan?"

"The hubbies stayed at home," Katie said with a twinkle in her eyes that told Mina that the "hubbies" weren't quite as interested as their wives were in checking out Mina's traveling companion.

You'd think Mina was an old maid with all the fuss being put out over Chet. Then again, it'd been about a year since Mina had even talked about a man to her family. And before Michael, she'd been just as inactive.

They were only excited for her.

More introductions were made, and it didn't escape Mina's attention that Katie and Amy were in full inspection mode, looking Chet up and down, then trading a subtle, meaningful glance while Chet was otherwise occupied.

She wanted to ask them to tone it down, but that would require some privacy, and she wasn't about to let Chet out of her line of sight right now.

Lizzie was holding up her hands for Mina to lift her, so she scooped up her niece, saying, "Oh, my, you're getting to be such a big girl. When did you grow up so fast?"

"I don't know," Lizzie said.

Her mom had already relieved Chet of the cake and birthday gift and gone for some martini glasses in the freezer. Taking the cue, Katie was using the shaker to do some mixing.

"Let's go to the patio for cocktails," Mom said. "We'll eat out there, too, and catch the last of this good weather."

"Dinner?" Mina asked. "Mom, we can't stay *that* long."

"Sure you can." Mom glanced at Chet.

He slid a look to Mina, the familiar sparkle that she hadn't seen so much of lately in his eyes. Just witnessing it again turned her heart up at the corners.

"Dinner would be great," he said. "I'll just phone my brothers and let them know."

Mom looked mightily satisfied at that.

Katie put down the shaker. "Who wants a 'tini?"

Everyone but Mina accepted the offer, and when her mom gave her an inquisitive glance, Mina gestured to Lizzie.

"We pixies are going to have Woodland Punch instead."

Her niece clapped her hands as Katie said, "Suit yourself," and poured.

Soon enough, Mom, Katie, Amy and Dad went outside to the patio, where he said he needed to check the grill. That left Mina and Chet behind with Lizzie, and as he watched Mina with her niece, she thought she saw a certain appreciation in his gaze.

"What?" Mina asked.

The moment passed, and he shook his head. "It's nothing."

But she couldn't ignore the look she'd seen.

Was she just imagining it?

A short time later, out on the patio, Chet stood near the barbecue with Mina's dad, Ewan, as he minded the carne asada. Nearby, the bulk of the Ferguson women sipped their martinis while Mina and Lizzie partook of their Woodland Punch, which was nothing more than fruit juice with a maraschino cherry.

Ewan grinned at Chet, holding up his barbecue tongs. "Bet the last thing you were expecting to eat in the Ferguson household was Mexican food."

"I hadn't thought about it, really."

"Well, we've got some haggis in the fridge if you're in the mood."

Before Chet even answered, Ewan said, "Just a joke. In spite of our Scots blood, we're not much for sheep guts and Highland grub around here."

"What did you say, Ewan?" Mina's mom, Lorna, called out.

"Nothing, dear." He winked at Chet.

No wonder Mina had grown up so well. Judging from her family, they were a spirited, loving bunch, and when Mina commented about how they were perhaps a little too invested in her private life, Chet understood why.

Some families were like that. They looked out for each other, even after the kids left the roost. Abe and Laura had done that for Chet up in Montana to some extent. Hell, Abe had even procured Chet the job of a lifetime before he died, making sure that he would be set up in this new family of his—the one with Eli as a father.

Sure, Abe's gesture was touching, but it still angered Chet to have been left in the dark for so long when it came to knowing his true parentage. And he was enraged for Abe's sake, too. He hurt for him, because no man should've had to endure the humiliation he'd gone through with a cheating wife and brother.

Ewan broke into Chet's musing. "You're off to a wedding then?"

"Yeah. Florence Ranch is about a half hour away."

"Near Duarte Hill. I've been to that town. Quaint, isn't it? Still looks like there could be gunfights in the streets there."

Katie's voice interrupted. "Is that where you grew up, Chet? Duarte Hill?"

"No. My parents raised me on a ranch on the other side of San Antonio. My...other family lives near Duarte Hill."

Chet had the feeling there'd be questions during this visit. Actually, he'd guessed that this dinner wasn't really so much a "meet the boss" moment so much as Mina bringing him to her family—her support system—so they could get a general view of him.

Yup, now that he really thought about it, he'd had that suspicion the moment she'd asked him, but he'd still come. Why? He just wasn't sure.

Or maybe he *wanted* to meet the family....

He took a drink. Damn it, he didn't know where his head was. But the one thing he was sure of was that it would be a long time before he would be able to really commit to anyone.

Maybe he was making too much out of this visit, anyway. It could be that Mina truly *had* merely wanted to say "Happy Birthday" to her dad before her parents left on their cruise this weekend, and these traveling plans had matched perfectly with her needs.

Yeah, he thought, getting less antsy the more he thought about it. This was nothing to get worried about.

Little Lizzie had finished her punch by now and she was trying to pull Mina out of her chair.

"Come play with me."

"But…" Mina pointed to her unfinished glass of Woodland Punch, yet Chet could tell she wouldn't ever say no to her niece.

"Pleeeease?"

When Mina stood, Lizzie jumped up and down, her red ponytail bobbing. Then she went around to her grandma and tugged her up, too.

Like most grandmas, this one was only too happy to oblige.

When Lizzie got to her mom and Aunt Amy, both women held up their martinis.

"Maybe another time," Amy said.

Katie stretched out her legs in front of her. "We'll watch from here."

Undeterred, Lizzie brought her grandma and Mina out to the grass, where she proceeded to perform some kind of cute fairy dance. Mina stood there, hands clasped over her chest, so obviously adoring of her niece that Chet found himself looking at her as he'd done earlier when she'd been holding Lizzie in her arms.

Someday, some guy and some family would be real lucky to have her. She was meant to have children, meant to love them.

Chet just wished he was the man who could give her all that, but it was just a fantasy for now. There was a chance it might always be, too, because after the initial bloom of happiness, he might only end up dragging her into his sorry affairs, and what family needed *that?*

But there was something else, too—something that kept eating at him until he couldn't ignore it.

Deep inside, he kept thinking about what his mom had done to his dad.

Amy spoke. "So you've been working with Mina for a while now, Chet?"

"Months."

At the grill, Ewan glanced at Amy over his shoulder, then went back to the meat, taking it off and transferring it to a plate. "How's our superstar doing for you?"

Superstar. It sounded as if they held Mina on a pedestal, but she'd told Chet about how she'd always strived to be her best for them. Maybe that was what her family expected of her, too.

Chet smiled. "I couldn't ask for a better coworker. I'm lucky she was assigned to me."

"Damn lucky," Katie said as she traced the rim of her martini glass.

When she jerked in her seat, Chet wondered if it was because Amy had kicked her older sister under the table.

Katie sent a sweet grin to him, then said, "We're just huge Mina fans."

"That's right," Amy said. "And she's the same with us.

We're all close. Just like this." She wound her forefinger and middle finger together.

A tweak of longing got to Chet. His family—back when he'd thought it *was* his family—had been knit looser than the Fergusons, like a sweater that you could still wear, even though it'd started falling apart.

Katie chimed in again. "You'd mentioned something about your 'other' family, Chet? The ones that live near Duarte Hill?"

He should've just shut his big mouth earlier. They'd probably heard about the scandal and were starting to dig for more information, looking out for their sister.

"Extended family," he said vaguely.

Ewan broke in at that point, bringing the meat to the table and covering it with some tinfoil. "Next I'll hear you asking him how much he makes per year and what color toothpaste he likes to use."

"Dad…" both girls said.

He turned to Chet. "I could use some help plating the side dishes and bringing them out."

Thank goodness. "Consider me employed."

Chet nodded to Katie and Amy, then followed Ewan into the house.

Mina watched as Chet went inside with her dad, leaving Katie and Amy to chat in low tones with each other.

"They grilled him," she said in a near whisper to her mom as Lizzie performed her open house dance for them about ten feet away. "I knew I shouldn't have left him alone."

"He's a big boy, Mina."

"Why'd you have to invite them over?"

"They heard you were coming and there was no stopping them. You know your sisters."

"Yes—they're married. And once a woman gets married, she starts to wage a campaign for everyone else to get hitched, too."

She sounded testy. Maybe all her frustration with Chet was coming out now.

Lizzie paused in her dancing, and Mina and her mom clapped, encouraging the little girl to continue.

A second later, Mom said, "Sweetheart, you wouldn't have brought him home if there wasn't a reason."

Mina wanted to tell all, but then again, she didn't. Telling would put all her hopes and dreams for Chet out there in the open. It would expose a truth that she hadn't even addressed with Chet yet.

Worse yet, she was concerned about what her mom—her family—might think about her being with this scandal-ridden man.

She decided to meet her mom halfway.

"Okay, maybe he's a little more than a boss to me."

"And…?" her mom goaded.

That was enough information for now. "Mom, I don't know where this is going to lead."

She didn't add that this wasn't *exactly* the truth. It would lead to a baby soon enough.

Lizzie spotted a squirrel down the lawn and ditched the dancing to get nearer to it.

"Lizzie," Grandma said, "don't get too close."

The girl came to a skidding halt but still watched the squirrel with fascination.

Then Mina's mom smoothly transitioned back to the former conversation. "The course of true love never did run smooth, Mina."

"Tell me about it. It's just that Chet has got a...complicated life. More than most."

"I'm aware of the Barron scandal. And I'm sure Amy and Katie were back there trying to get to the bottom of it."

All right. This talk wasn't going so badly. If her family had heard about the scandal and they hadn't given him the third degree before even letting him in the house, that was a positive sign.

Her mom saw how she was watching her sisters again. "Your dad was there, too, and he clearly took Chet out of the line of fire."

"You mean the lion's den."

Her mom put an arm around her. "They mean well."

"At least *you're* not giving him grief."

"Why should I? I saw right away how he looks at you."

A flash of tiny fireworks lit her up inside. "What do you mean?"

"Please, Mina. He can't take his eyes off of you."

The fireworks continued in her, turning into the kind that zoomed and circled their way into the sky.

Her mom patted her on the shoulder, then removed her arm from around her. "He might be going through some significant troubles, but you can't tell it. He carries himself well. I like that. He gives me a good mom-feeling."

"He carries himself that way in public. But when he's out of it..." She thought of the night he'd come to her, a broken man.

"He lets you see him when his shields come down?"

"Yes."

"Then it sounds as if you don't have too much work to do with him besides waiting for his mind to catch up with his heart. And, unlike Michael, I can tell Chet's heart is with you."

It was about the last thing she expected her mom to say.

Wasn't her mom going to warn her, point out all of Chet's shortcomings in order to save her the sorrow?

Mina stuffed her hands in her skirt pockets. "I expected this to be harder, introducing him to you."

"Why?"

She sent her mom a caustic glance.

Her mother seemed taken aback. "Are you *that* worried about our stamp of approval?"

"You haven't ever been shy about giving it."

"Mina." Her mom sounded surprised. "You've always been so independent, as if you didn't mind so much what we think."

That's because she'd trained herself to feel that way for a long time, ever since she'd overheard her inebriated uncle at that barbecue.

It'd have been a shame if that little girl hadn't been born, he'd said to a cousin who hadn't known anything about the family secret as they'd lingered over beers. He'd gone on to explain how Lorna and Ewan had gotten the news one day and they'd decided to keep Mina, as if she'd been some kind of package delivered to their door by mistake and they'd warmed up to the contents enough not to send it back.

How could Mina ever tell her mom how that had felt? Nobody even knew that Mina had overheard while climbing under the nearby tables, playing hide-and-seek with the other kids. And she'd carried the secret with her for years, trying to please her parents, half afraid that they would, somehow, send her back.

She'd gone on to please everyone else, too.

A mix of anger and sadness crept up her throat as she thought of her child. He or she would grow up knowing they were wanted through and through, no matter what happened with Chet. It'd taken this accidental pregnancy, her own baby, to dredge up all her old feelings, but maybe that was a good thing.

Maybe it would force her to solve some of her own issues before her child was even born.

Needing some alone time, Mina began to walk back to the patio. "I've always cared what you thought, Mom."

"Mina."

Her soft voice stopped Mina, and she glanced back to find her mother's eyes teary.

"Don't listen to what *we* have to say," she said. "Because no matter what you decide, we'll be there to support you, not to give you more grief. Surely you know that."

Mina wondered if that would be the case even if they knew that their superstar daughter had been silly enough to have gotten pregnant when the father might not even love her.

Chapter Seven

Dinner at the Fergusons' went by without another hitch for Chet, mainly because Ewan kept training a fatherly "watch what you say" gaze on Katie and Amy for the next couple of hours.

Instead, Chet enjoyed talking about the cruise that Mr. and Mrs. Ferguson were going on—a long jaunt to the Caribbean. He liked how there was a teasing sense of adoration between everyone in the family, and he got the feeling that they would go to war for each other if it came right down to it.

And that was what really struck him. They'd go to war *for* each other, not against each other.

After the meal—and after a crash course that Mina held for her father for his new e-book reader—Chet and Mina were on the road to Duarte Hill and Florence Ranch again, where Chet just wasn't sure there would be the same loving atmosphere.

Outside the limo windows, darkness made the white fences into ghostly tracks along the road. Mina sat across from him, watching the scenery go by, a thoughtful expression on her face—one that just about wrenched Chet's heart because it turned the tips of her mouth down instead of up.

"Your family's good people," he said. "I'm glad you brought me along tonight."

Leaning her head back on the seat, she turned her gaze to him. "I'm glad you came."

She didn't say anything else about it, but Chet got the feeling that there was a lot more going through her mind than her dad's birthday and the cruise her parents would be taking.

"You all right?" he asked.

"Sure." She paused as the limo hummed underneath them, tires over blacktop. Then she said, "It's just…I had a little talk with my mom, and it made me realize something that I didn't expect."

"What's that?"

She tucked an auburn strand of hair behind her ear, as if it was a good excuse to hesitate again. "She said that their opinions shouldn't matter so much to me. At first, I interpreted that to mean that I wasn't important enough to care about. It stunned me. But when I started to really think about it, I understood that she *didn't* mean it that way."

"And?"

Mina looked so forlorn on the other side of the limo. "It really drove home how I've always believed that I was something my parents had to get used to, some-thing they had to fit into their lives, like a square peg in a round hole, so I tend to overreact about how *they* react to things. I suppose I've even come to like how the family is so protective and interested in everything I do, because it shows that they actually want me."

Chet leaned forward. "Everyone in that family thinks the world of you, Mina. You have to talk yourself into recognizing that?"

"I guess. Especially since Katie and Amy never had any big realization like mine, as far as I know. My parents were financially ready for another child when it came time for Amy, years later."

"I doubt your parents ever even think of what happened with you."

"You're right." She looked out the window again. "It's amazing to realize that I've spent so much of my life trying so hard to please them so they'd never regret having me."

Her words were a slight hit to his gut. "A man and woman should never regret having a child."

It'd just come out, bald and truthful.

As she watched him, her gaze was forthright. "No, they shouldn't."

Was she thinking about him now, and not her own life? Thinking about how he might've felt the night when Abe and Eli had taken him into a private room and told him who he really was?

Mina seemed ready to say something else—something with major substance to it, because he could almost feel it in the air between them.

But then she went quiet again, and Chet respected her silence, leaning back, his mind stretched in a million different directions.

And every one of them seemed to lead to Florence Ranch.

* * *

The ranch was smack-dab in Texas Hill Country, reigning on the top of a rise, surrounded by pines, a creek, meadows and guest cottages. There was even a swimming hole nearby—a place Chet had visited a few times during his youth when Eli would invite Abe and his family over.

More innocent times, as far as Chet had known.

The limo climbed the driveway up to the Greek Revival mansion, known affectionately as the "big house," and Chet couldn't help but think about how different it was from the home of Mina's parents, which had been far more modest and...

Well, cozy.

Theirs was a house that was more on par with his old cabin up in Montana. No fuss. No fancy stuff. Just a place to wander around in at your leisure, a place to set your boots in without having to worry about how they might dirty up the floor.

After the limo came to a halt, Chet didn't wait for the driver to open the door. He exited first, extending his hand to help Mina out of the vehicle.

When she alighted, she ran her gaze over the mansion, then removed her hand from his.

"I can never get used to this place," she said.

"Same here." And that was the truth. Every time he arrived, he felt like a visitor, even after all these months of knowing that he should belong.

The driver went to get their bags, and Chet took them from the guy, thanking him and letting him go to his cabin down the hill for the night. He was a Barron employee, so he stayed on the property, just as the ranch hands and other staff did.

While Chet and Mina climbed the few stairs that led to the entry, the front door opened.

It was Tyler, Chet's oldest half brother.

"Here they are." Tall and solidly built in his jeans and Western shirt, Tyler's coloring resembled Aunt Florence's, with their dark brown hair and green eyes. He didn't have much of Eli in him at all—not like Chet and Jeremiah did.

After Chet hung his hat and coat on an intricate iron rack, Tyler took his bag from him, then enveloped him in a fraternal hug. Chet was getting used to this kind of thing, so he returned the gesture, lingering for a second longer than he usually did.

Tyler seemed to notice, and he grinned, turning to Mina.

"We're really glad you could come this weekend."

"Are you kidding?" she said. "I wouldn't miss a Barron wedding."

He embraced her, too, then guided them to the lounge.

"Why don't y'all get settled in there," Tyler said. "Millie will have your bags taken to your quarters in the meantime."

Millie was the household manager. Chet knew that she would send his things to the room that was on constant standby for him here in the mansion. Mina had been assigned a guest cottage.

Without thinking, he put his hand on the small of Mina's back, intending to escort her into the lounge just behind Tyler.

Did she haul in a breath?

Removing his hand out of pure instinct—pure preservation, really—he followed her into the lounge, with its dark-wooded grandeur and velvet furnishings. Over a roaring fire, a painting of the "former" Barron family hung over the mantel: Eli, Aunt Florence, Tyler and Jeremiah.

Every time Chet saw it, he felt like a ghost in the portrait, felt just as empty inside of himself, too.

But he didn't have much time to think about that tonight, because everyone in the room—Jeremiah, his fiancée, Ally, and Zoe—came over to greet them.

Eli wasn't anywhere around, though.

Would he be able to get out of rehab to attend the wedding?

Jeremiah, who was taller than Chet by a couple of inches, though they resembled each other in so many other ways, slapped him on the back just before going to the minibar and getting out two glasses. Since he'd come straight from the office, he was dressed in a designer suit.

"My best man made it," he said to Chet.

Tyler cleared his throat. "*Co*-best man."

"That's what I meant." Jeremiah addressed Chet and Mina. "So what's your poison tonight?"

Chet waited for Mina to answer before he did.

"Nothing for me right now," she said.

He wasn't much in the mood for drinking, either. The weekend would be bringing a lot of opportunities for that.

"I'm good," he said.

Ally was holding a whiskey, just like Jeremiah. The fancy cut crystal glass went along well with her Grace Kelly looks—the long, straight platinum hair, a high-class bearing.

"Caroline's already asleep," she said, referring to the

newborn she'd adopted recently, before she and Jeremiah had fallen in love and decided to get married. "I wish she could've stayed up to see her future uncle."

Uncle. Chet liked the sound of that. Liked that whenever he got the chance to see Caroline, which wasn't often since Jeremiah and Ally sometimes lived in California, the baby smiled at him, making him a little lighter, too.

"I'll see her first thing tomorrow." Then Chet said to Mina, "You should get a load of Caroline. She's the cutest thing in creation."

"Except for Lizzie," Mina said, grinning.

"Of course." Chet laughed.

Zoe, Tyler's wife, said, "Sounds to me like you're a regular sucker for children, Chet." Her gray-blue eyes sparkled against her olive skin and shoulder-length dark hair. She was giving Chet and Mina "that" look, as if she'd already assumed he had brought a date to this wedding, that he and Mina might even be serious enough to have mentioned the possibility of having children one day.

What the hell?

Mina had shifted position, as if she felt the scrutiny. And why not, when they *all* obviously thought there was something going on? He could tell by the way they treated Mina—Zoe and Ally giving her those sisterly smiles, although this was the first time Mina had met Ally. Tyler and Jeremiah were even exchanging "uh-huh" glances with each other. And, this, after Chet had already told his brothers over the phone that he and Mina were traveling together because it was convenient.

Not that he thought that they were going to buy that or anything. But he tried.

Chet shuffled his booted feet. All right, so the "convenience" explanation had been a flat-out lie. He wouldn't have asked Mina in the heat of the moment that one night if he didn't feel right about it. It was just... Well, he didn't know what to do with her *now,* whether he dared to ever touch her again when he knew damned well that it would lead to some tough questions for him, like what if he couldn't get his act together?

When the women led Mina to a leather couch near the flickering fire, Chet couldn't help but to follow her with his gaze.

Unfortunately, Tyler and Jeremiah noticed.

Chet cut them off at the pass by clearing his throat. His brothers got the message, keeping their opinions to themselves.

There were more important things to talk about, anyway.

"Where's Eli?" he asked.

Jeremiah shot another look to Tyler, who nodded, as if he was telling his brother to go ahead.

"He's not here tonight," Jeremiah said, "but he's got a pass from the rehab center for the rest of the weekend."

Tyler added, "He'll be here tomorrow evening for the rehearsal dinner in town."

"Chet?" Jeremiah asked. "Is that okay?"

"Yes. I'm not going to make this difficult for everyone, especially during your wedding, Jeremiah." He looked up. "I'm finally going to make things right between me and Eli. It's well past time."

Tyler put a hand on Chet's shoulder, and Jeremiah patted his other arm. Brothers. Chet wasn't even going to think of them as half siblings anymore. Not if he wanted them all to come together.

He really was ready to face that.

Jeremiah held up his whiskey, as did Tyler. A toast, sealing a silent promise—one that Chet regretted having put off for this long.

Near the fireplace, Ally and Zoe were chatting up Mina pretty well. Mina looked comfortable with the others, smiling and talking just as if she belonged.

He watched the fire play with the color of her hair, watched how she tilted back her head every time she laughed. She fit in, all right, and for some reason, it sent a flood of warmth through him.

Being here on Florence Ranch was only highlighting how Tyler and Jeremiah had something with Zoe and Ally that Chet had never experienced. One look at Mina sitting so naturally among them made Chet think that everyone could have what his brothers did, even during the crisis they'd been surviving for the past months.

Everyone—even Chet.

Jeremiah, the scamp, was unable to hold back any longer. "Careful, Chet—the women are warming up to your assistant pretty thoroughly."

At the blunt observation, a familiar panic attacked once again. "Mina is just here because she's..."

Chet tripped over his words, and before he could search for the right ones, Jeremiah supplied them.

"Because she's your date?"

Straight-to-the-point Tyler looked baffled. "*Isn't* that what she is, Chet?"

Yes. No.

Damn it.

Chet turned his back on the women and lowered his

voice. "I'm not sure how to define it, so let's not define it at all, okay?"

His brothers just drank their cocktails, though Jeremiah smirked behind his glass.

There wasn't much else to say, not right now, when Chet didn't have anything figured out. All he knew was that he wanted to glance behind him again, keep Mina in his sights, because whenever she was in them, he felt better about life in general.

And about himself, too.

Mina and Chet hadn't stayed too long in the lounge. They'd bunked down in their respective rooms, and Mina had taken to her guest cottage like a bee to honey.

Her bed had soft sheets and was surrounded by pastel, sunrise artwork. She had a little kitchen where she could see bright flowers peeking out of a window box just outside, framing a view of the big house. It was "rustic chic," with a farmhouse-type minikitchen, complete with an old-fashioned lantern hanging over the stove.

She had just about everything she needed but Chet, who'd only said a quiet good-night to her before Millie, the household manager, had walked her to the cottage, explaining where things were and how to work them before leaving.

But why had Mina expected Chet to be in her cottage tonight when he'd come "home," to where all his problems were?

Even though her pulse limped along at his absence, she got a decent night's sleep, awakening just after dawn to a cloud-strung sky outside. After she got ready for the day, she went outside to sit on the stoop, drinking a mug of herbal tea that steamed in the cool morning.

It wasn't but fifteen minutes later that she witnessed Chet sauntering by on a nearby path, garbed in cowboy gear and carrying a fishing pole and tackle box in either hand.

Boom went her heart, and it didn't calm down, even as he walked farther and farther away.

Well, this wouldn't do—her on one side of the ranch and him on the other. She would never get him to see that he needed her in his life.

She set down her mug and walked as fast as she could to catch up to him, her skirt swishing around her legs and boots. The nippiness of the morning tweaked her arms, which were bared by her big, short-sleeved T-shirt, but she didn't go back for a sweater.

"Morning," she called out.

He stopped in his tracks, looking over his shoulder. Was there a *boom* moment in him, too?

"I thought you'd be sleeping in," he finally said.

"A girl can only slumber for so many hours."

He stood there a second longer, then nodded to her.

"Okay, then," he said, and it sounded like a dismissal. "There're horses in the stables if you want a ride. Lots of room for walking until our car leaves for the rehearsal dinner at six sharp."

"I'm invited to the dinner?" She'd thought the wedding summons had been just that—for the ceremony and reception, not for the family events.

He looked bewildered. "Of course."

She held back a smile. Chet wasn't making a big deal out of it, but this made her his date. It really did.

He cleared his throat, then tipped his hat to her with the hand that carried the tackle box. "I'll see you then."

"I heard there's a cute fishing hole on the property." She didn't want him to go. "Is that where you're off to?"

"A *cute* fishing hole?" he asked.

This certainly didn't feel like a date, with him clearly just dying to get going.

But Mina was tired of this limbo. She'd come here to get to the bottom of him, and he wasn't going to slip away that easily.

She was gradually finding out that the more personal room she gave Chet Barron, the more skittish he got. Obviously, a woman couldn't grant him too much time to think.

"I'd like to see where you're off to, if you don't mind," she said, walking over to him. "I grew up in the suburbs, remember? Fishing holes are a curiosity to me."

"All I do is use the pole to put the hook in the water, Mina. It's not a big event or anything."

"I know, I know—and too much talk scares the fish away, so I'll keep chatter to a minimum."

He spread out an arm, inviting her to walk next to him.

There was a slight bounce in her step as they strolled down a path that cut through the grass as it turned from a manicured lawn to that of a meadow.

"Last night," she said, getting the "chatter" out of the way before they got to the fishing hole, "Ally asked if I'd like to hang around while she gets ready tomorrow. I thought that was nice of her."

Chet kind of grunted, and she didn't know what to make of that.

"I guess," she added, "that she just wants me to feel

included for some reason." She realized she was twisting the hem of her T-shirt and stopped.

"She asked you to join her because she likes you." He slowed their pace, came to a halt. "And because we arrived together."

"In the same car." Testing. Test, test.

"No, *together* together."

So he was admitting it—that this *was* a date.

She wanted to bust out and ask, *So what exactly does this mean?*

But her common sense said that she had him on a hook, and it was quite possible that he would find a way off of it if she pushed him. The truth was that Chet had actually come a decent way recently, and she just had to get him a little further in.

Just a little.

But, much to her surprise, he was the one who went forward.

"I haven't been honest with myself lately, but I'm trying, Mina. Bit by bit, with my real father, my situation in life…my relationship with you…I'm trying."

She nodded, letting him go on.

"I want to be with you," he said, his gaze wounded, confused. "But I'm not sure if I'm in any shape for it. That's why I've been hanging back."

"You haven't hung back all of the time." She meant about how they'd been intimate, how he'd given her his body, but not anything else, at the resort.

"You're right," he said. "I haven't."

He sounded like he was being hard on himself, just as he'd been when he'd apologized right after the first time they'd made love.

The last thing she wanted was to regress back to those

days, so she reached out, touched his arm, showing him how she appreciated his efforts.

"You *are* trying," she repeated. "That's all I can ask right now."

He didn't say anything, and she tightened her grip on him.

"You're going to make it through everything, Chet. I'll be damned if you don't."

As if he'd come to the end of what he had to say for now, he faintly smiled, then walked on.

Progress, she thought. They were getting there.

They took a path that led downhill, toward a bunch of cottonwoods. Soon they came to a secluded pond with large rocks jutting into the water. A particular flat one made for a perfect seat, so they headed toward it.

To get there, they had to negotiate some smaller rocks that peered just above the water.

"Careful," he said.

She waited until he went first, and he offered his hand to her for balance.

But when she went to take it, her foot slipped.

As she went down, all she could think was, *My baby...*

Chet grabbed for her, barely getting hold of her arm. She slid partway into the water anyway, dousing her bottom half.

She sat there in the shallow water, realizing that she wasn't hurt. Just...embarrassed.

"Are you all right?" he asked, helping her out of the water and to a stand.

Everything was steeped: her boots, her skirt, the bottom part of her T-shirt. Dripping wet.

She was only starting to comprehend how thoroughly

her clothing was leeched to her when Chet ran a gaze down her body.

Too late, she laid an arm over her tummy.

Her T-shirt-plastered tummy, which wasn't showing a pregnancy as much as…

Well, as much as it just *felt* pregnant with him standing here looking at her.

This was like the day in the Paradise Room, when she'd instinctively thought to hide her secret from him, no matter how her belly looked.

She started back to shore, treading through the shallow water, praying that he hadn't noticed anything strange about her reaction, hoping against hope.

"Great," she said, trying to divert his attention. "I really liked these boots, too."

"You sure you're okay?"

"Definitely," she answered, "but I'm not hanging around here looking like a drowned rat."

If he noticed her babbling, he didn't remark on it, and she left as quickly as she could, wondering just how much longer her secret was going to hold up.

Chapter Eight

During the rehearsal dinner at a lively Mexican restaurant in nearby Duarte Hill, Chet leaned against a planked wall, watching Mina talking with Ally and Zoe across the room.

Right now, she was wearing one of those full skirts she liked—this one white, with a pink shawl dipping down over her shoulders and to her hips.

But this morning…

This morning she'd been a little more exposed, when she'd slipped into the water and her T-shirt had stuck to her skin.

The way she'd acted, hugging an arm over her lower stomach… It'd been a repeat of her reaction that day he'd come upon her at the resort, in the Paradise Room, when she'd been wearing a bathing suit. He hadn't noted anything out of the ordinary that day, but now that she'd repeated the gesture so obviously, his mind started spinning a reason for it. It was almost as if she was deliberately covering something up.

As if she were…

Pregnant?

He'd seen pregnant women touch their stomachs just as Mina had, back in Montana, wives of friends, but in Mina's case the notion was absolutely ridiculous, and as soon as he'd even thought it, he'd pushed it away. Hell, if she was with child, it would've happened months ago, when they'd first been together, and he'd worn a condom, for heaven's sake.

But that wasn't the biggest reason he'd dismissed the temporary suspicion so quickly. Condoms could fail, but he'd come to believe that Mina, out of anyone in this world, would never *ever* pull the wool over his eyes, keeping that big of a secret from him. She wasn't like his mother, who'd once lied to his dad about the affair with Eli. She'd done the same to Chet, as well, until Abe had come clean with the truth.

No, if *anyone* could be trusted with anything, it was Mina, he told himself for what seemed like the millionth time.

Nonetheless, Chet's insides were scrambled. See what his problems did? They tainted more than just him. They carried over to the people who didn't deserve to be judged or under suspicion.

He looked across the room again, past the red, yellow, blue and green lanterns hanging from the ceiling, casting rainbow shadows over the distressed hardwood floor and rustic tables.

Mina.

He thought about what he would've done if she had gotten pregnant that night, or the second one, and…

The image of a little redheaded baby floated over his mind's eye, and Chet smiled.

It disappeared quickly enough, though. It was a good thing that she wasn't pregnant. As if they needed more complications...

While she solidified in his sight again, part of Chet wanted to apologize to her for all he'd put her through and for thinking even for a second that she would lie. The other part told him that there was no harm done, that he should just continue to stand in his corner and listen to the mariachi band as they sauntered around the room with their guitars, trumpets and violins, serenading the crowd now that the dinner had ended.

A voice brought him out of his musings. Jeremiah, who slung an arm around Chet.

"How's my co-best man?" he asked.

Chet put on a smile. "He's hoping he'll remember his cues tomorrow at the ceremony."

"You did just fine during the rehearsal." Jeremiah clinked nonalcoholic beer bottles with his brother. "This is my last night as a free man, so I want you to live it up right along with me. Ready to go yet?"

Chet sent him a look that said, *You're happy to get married, so cut the bull.*

Jeremiah laughed at the obvious truth, dropping his arm from around Chet's shoulders. "Just be ready to leave in about fifteen minutes."

"You got it."

Since all Jeremiah and Ally's most loved friends and relatives were in the area for the wedding, they were both having their bachelor and bacherlorette parties after this dinner. Ally's old housekeeper, Mrs. McCarter, had already taken baby Caroline back to Florence Ranch, clearing the way for plenty of fun, although Chet knew that neither Jeremiah nor Ally were going to get too wild.

Yup, Jeremiah's life sure had changed for the better after he'd met his bride.

Once again, Chet's gaze strayed to Mina, as if every cell in his body was drawn to her.

Was there a chance for him, too, if he could just believe that he wouldn't go ruining her life with scandals and a lack of trust that didn't seem to disappear, no matter how hard he tried to banish it?

As if those problems had materialized, the room went a little quieter. Chet guessed the reason before he even saw it.

He'd been waiting all night for Eli Barron to show up.

The older man stood at the fairy-light-lined room entrance, his hat in his hands. Briefly, Chet pictured Eli as the very picture of what he, himself, might resemble in a couple of decades if he kept going down the same road he'd been traveling recently: gray-haired, still stocky but with the slumped shoulders of a beaten man, wrinkle-lined skin, lips in a nervous line as his wary gaze scanned the room.

Always alone, no matter how many people were near him.

Tyler was the first one to go up to his dad, taking the man's hat, welcoming him and sitting him at a table. A waiter came by and Tyler spoke to the man, obviously ordering food for Eli.

Jeremiah said, "I wasn't sure if his ride from the rehab center would get him here on time."

Even so, that was the reason tonight's drinks had been

alcohol free—for Eli's sake. There'd be time enough for carousing after the dinner, at the parties that Eli's curfew kept him from attending.

"I'll bet he busted his ass to make it," Chet said.

"I just hope he lasts through the weekend."

"He's going back Monday, right?"

"Yeah. Tyler said he'd keep a good eye on him, help him to avoid the alcohol that'll be served at the reception. I offered to keep everything dry, but you know how Dad is—he got red in the face and was mortified at even being thought of as the 'head case' who'd put a damper on my big day. I told him it wasn't a problem, that I'd already made plans to have a dry rehearsal dinner here, but he got huffy about how wedding reception plans were much more involved than just some meal's. He said being around regular social scenes would be a good test for him, that he wouldn't be able to ask everyone in the world to stop drinking so he needed to start getting used to being around alcohol now. We've already gotten rid of every bit of it in the mansion though, after last night's cocktail hour."

"So, aside from that, we're all supposed to pretend he's fine? We just go on about our business as if he's not going through rehab?"

"If it makes him feel more empowered in his struggles." Jeremiah paused. "His counselors would like to sit us all down together, just to fill us in on how we should be handling Eli's challenges, too."

"I'll make sure it's a priority." Up until now, Chet had been reading all the literature he could find on how to handle alcoholism.

Jeremiah added, "They'd also like us to look into Al-Anon."

Chet nodded. It wasn't just up to Eli to face his challenges; they'd all have to fight them together.

And, for the first time since the scandal broke, it seemed like everything was falling into place.

Like Jeremiah, Chet put his beer bottle—non-alcoholic of course—on a nearby table.

Eli was still glancing around the room, and when his gaze lit on Chet, it was obvious that he'd been looking for his third son in particular.

A mix of emotions seemed to pass through his eyes: happiness at seeing Chet standing with Jeremiah, embarrassment at having to put his sons through everything they'd endured.

"Here it goes," Jeremiah said, speaking for Chet, too, because they both knew what they needed to do next.

It was just hard to cross the room, say hello, as if everything was wonderful.

Chet felt someone else looking at him from across the way and he knew it was Mina. He met her gaze, inhaled at the zing of it.

One thing was certain—he needed to take care of his relationship with his biological father before he could be good for anyone else.

And when she smiled at him, so comfortingly, so naturally, something lifted within Chet, buoying him, making him think everything *would* be okay because she believed that he could do this.

Chet and Jeremiah made their way through the tables, which had started to clear out after the dinner itself had ended. By the time they got to Eli's table, the waiter had brought a plate of enchiladas, plus rice, beans and tortillas.

Jeremiah took hold of his father's shoulder, squeezing it. "Dad."

It was obvious that they were still working through years of hard times between them, but when Eli reached up to grip Jeremiah's hand, it was enough. Chet could tell by the smile on his brother's face. Even Tyler looked touched as he stood behind Eli's chair.

Eli peered up at Chet, and he saw that his biological father's eyes weren't red with drink. They were clear tonight.

Thank God.

Chet sat in the chair next to Eli. "We were all hoping you'd make it here in time."

And he didn't just mean that it was good to see him at this dinner—it was nice to finally know that Eli had found himself in a better place altogether, in time for his son's wedding.

Finally in the place he needed to be.

"Chet," Eli said, his voice cracking.

Chet glanced at his brothers, and they understood that it was time to leave Eli and his new son alone. That it was time to start the next phase of forgiveness, if they could manage it.

When they were by themselves, Eli spoke first. "How're things at the Utah resort?"

Starting off slow. Okay. That was fine.

"Perfect," Chet said. "No need for you to even think about it."

"I'm retired from the Group now, anyway. But it's tough, after all those years of knowing every detail about every project. I'm sure Tyler feels the same way, now that he's cut himself loose from the Group, too. But it looks like the business is in good hands with you and Jeremiah at the helm."

"It is. You can depend on it."

Eli went quiet, obviously fresh out of the beating-around-the-bush talk.

"Dad," Chet said, hesitantly. "I really am glad you're here."

At the word *Dad,* Eli's head had snapped up. One corner of his mouth twitched, his eyes going hazy.

Chet had never seen Abe, his "other father," cry. He'd been raised to think that men didn't do that.

Just thinking of Abe's lessons made Chet promise that he would remember what his first dad had taught him over the years, even as Chet moved on.

But an emotional snag remained. By forgiving Eli, would he be trading one father for another? Was he spitting on the memory of the man who'd raised him?

Brushing that aside for now, he put his hand on Eli's forearm, and the older man's eyes welled up as Chet's own gaze went bleary.

Mina left the restaurant with Ally, Zoe and Ally's aunt Jessica, but she didn't say goodbye to Chet. He was still with his biological father, and it was clear that they shouldn't be interrupted.

And that was the best news Mina could've imagined.

She couldn't stop smiling, even though there was a scratching in her throat that brought a little happiness/sadness to the sensation.

"Mina," Ally said in her refined, gentle voice as they got to the limo parked in front of their restaurant. "Are you all right?"

"Yeah. It's just the whole business with Eli…"

Aunt Jessica, a spitfire forty-year-old who looked more like a carefree thirty-year-old, put a hand over Mina's mouth. "Not tonight, okay? Y'all can talk about maudlin matters after we've drank and danced and made a bride-to-be fool out of Ally, and not a minute before."

Zoe laughed as they climbed into the limo. "Sensitive as always, Jess."

Jessica tossed back a lock of her sun-kissed brunette hair. "Honey, I'm the party mistress, and I take my task quite seriously."

"Yes, ma'am." Ally saluted.

But she wasn't so obedient when Jess pulled out a bag from under a limo seat, giving her niece a sparkly princess crown, a sash that read, "Kiss me!" and a glowing green wand.

Ally's crown was crooked as she sat back in the seat and the limo pulled forward. "This is degrading, Jess."

Zoe and Mina couldn't hold back a spate of giggles. So wrong to laugh, but Mina couldn't stop herself. She was absolutely giddy—for Ally, for Jeremiah, for Chet and his dad.

And for the baby who would soon be announced to his or her father, now that it seemed things were on track.

Jess broke out some champagne. "Drink up, my darlings."

Of course, Mina declined any.

Ally sat there holding her silly wand. "Where're you taking us, Jess?"

"Yeah," Zoe said. "It's not like Duarte Hill is the party spot of the millennium."

"Well, girls," Jess said, "you know I like to wing it, but this time I did my homework. If you'd done yours, you'd know that there's a social dance about two miles down a country lane off the main road in a community hall. I'm betting there'll be a buffet of cowboys there."

"Cowboys?" Ally asked. "I'm already getting married to one. Tomorrow, if you'll recall."

"Who said the cowboys are for you?" Jess asked.

Soon they pulled up to a building that resembled an old wood warehouse, with weathered gray walls and light peeking out from the slats of wood. Country music from a live band blared out.

"Yee-haw," Jess said, the first one out of the limo.

Zoe adjusted Ally's crown, then made her take off the "Kiss me!" sash, much to Ally's relief.

"Good call," Mina said. "I could just see that thing causing a lot of trouble." It would be bad enough that Ally was gorgeous and would attract every cowboy's stare within gaping distance.

Inside, streamers hung from the rafters; the smell of old hay, along with that of hops, was woven through the body-warmed air. All around them there were indeed cowboys, but there were a good many cowgirls, too, wearing tight jeans and curious looks as the bachelorette party strolled inside with Princess Ally and her glowing horny-green wand.

Mina and Zoe flanked the bride-to-be.

"Don't worry," Zoe yelled over the music. "We'll protect you."

But then Jess came over to pull Ally away, toward

a corner where a keg stood, surrounded by young, strapping ranch hands.

Zoe shrugged and said in Mina's ear, "Jess is harmless. She won't let anybody get near Ally." She nodded toward the keg. "I need some of that beer."

"Party away."

Zoe left, and within ten minutes, all of them were on the dance floor, whooping it up, fending off the cowboys, who joined in the whole bachelorette party fervor with friendly abandon.

They danced and danced—swinging, line dancing—and all the while, Mina imagined that every partner was really Chet. After a while though, the fantasy chipped away at her, because she realized that there would never be another man who would live up to him.

She *had* to tell him everything this weekend. Holding it in was breaking her down, day by day. And it just didn't seem fair to him, either, because what if the news actually brought him further along in his healing?

Then again, what if it didn't...?

As a swing dance ended and everyone applauded, the cowboy Mina had been dancing with bowed to her and went off to grab a drink, clearly sensing that he wasn't going to get anywhere with Mina tonight.

That was when a loud "Whoo-hoo!" broke the atmosphere.

Mina whipped her gaze to the building's entrance, where Jeremiah Barron was waving his hat.

Then he headed straight over to Ally, who jumped into his arms just before he swung her around.

Zoe rushed to Tyler, too, and he dipped her back in a long kiss that made a few of the nearby cowboys and girls hoot.

Then came the one man Mina had been hoping to see.

Chet sauntered over to her, tipping back his cowboy hat, revealing a tuft of his dark blond hair. Judging from the wide smile on him, things had gone well with Eli.

Her pulse gave a big bang.

The band hadn't started a new song yet, so she had no problems hearing him when he said, "Jess told Jeremiah where you girls were heading."

"Thank goodness. I was looking for a dance partner who could keep up with me."

Boy—for a woman who'd been playing her cards close to her chest ever since she and Chet had left the resort, her statement seemed pretty bold.

The band launched into a song that begged for a two-step.

Chet looked like he'd just come off of the range in his jeans and cowboy gear, but when he took Mina into his arms, it was as if the gentlemanly side of him—the part that was perfectly comfortable in a designer business suit—had come out to take over.

He eased her into the flowing dance, his mouth near her ear. Mina shivered as her temple brushed the five o'clock shadow on his cheek. His clover-and-hay smell sent her reeling.

She whispered, "So everything's okay?"

He knew that she was asking about him and his dad. "Eli and I are going to settle in for a longer talk tomorrow, before the wedding. His driver had to get him back to the mansion early. A curfew is a condition of this weekend pass from rehab."

Content, she rested her head on his shoulder.

He gripped her hand in his, tightening his hold on her hip, too. Her breathing spiked as heat banded every inch of her.

They weren't doing the two-step anymore—they were lost in their own world instead. Through her lashes, she could see the cowboys and girls on the edges of the dance floor, watching them. It was mainly the women who had such poignant looks on their faces—the type Mina knew she used to wear whenever she would think about Chet, longing for him, wondering if her love for him would ever be noticed or come to fruition.

Then she saw Ally and Jeremiah on the dance floor, holding each other, too. As the bride-to-be met Mina's gaze, she smiled, one woman in love to another.

A couple. Everyone seemed to be thinking that Mina and Chet were together, and she wanted to believe that with all of her soul.

She never wanted this dance to end, even as the notes swayed toward their inevitable finale, the music swelling, then fading off as everyone clapped.

As the band switched to a fast song, Mina glanced up at Chet, drawing away from him ever so slightly. They were still holding each other, as if he was just as unwilling to let go.

But their connection was broken when Tyler passed by, nudging Chet.

It only took an instant for Mina to see the reason.

Jeremiah was at the keg, and so was Eli.

Mina did a double take.

Eli?

Tyler joined his brother and dad, just as Chet cursed over the music, then headed over there, too, Mina's heart going with him.

* * *

Jeremiah's voice belted over the music as he burned a stare through Eli but addressed his brothers instead.

"Dad tells me that he wasn't intending to get himself any beer. He was just standing here, watching the party."

"It's true," Eli said, his aged skin going ruddy. "I wasn't going to pour myself a drink."

Tyler asked, "Then why were you standing by a keg, Dad?"

"I was just walking by. You have to believe me."

Whether or not he was lying, Chet had heard this all before. So had Tyler and Jeremiah. And they knew that when Eli got called out and felt backed into a corner, it never turned out well.

And he'd thought tonight was a turning point.

Chet said, "You're supposed to be in bed by now. That's what you told me back at the restaurant."

That stubborn bull-about-to-charge intensity heated up Eli's gaze. "I just wanted to come here and be with my family for a short time. Is that too much to ask?"

Tyler grit his teeth. "Is it too much to ask for you to stick to your guns, Dad? You were doing so well at rehab."

"And I'm still doing well, Ty." He took off his hat, jutted out his chin. "Want to smell my breath to see if there's any alcohol on it? Go ahead."

They all glanced at the beer keg, where a ranch hand was watching them from beneath the brim of his hat while pouring himself a cup.

Chet couldn't stand this farce anymore, and he took his dad by the shirtsleeve, thinking it'd be a good idea to get him away from temptation.

Eli resisted. "Hey—"

His face was so red that Chet let go of his shirt. He noticed that Mina had followed him over here, and she looked more devastated than he felt.

But why, when *he* was the one whose world was crashing, just when he thought it'd gone upright again?

Eli was breathing in and out, and Chet wondered if that's what they'd taught him at rehab—exercises to calm himself.

Finally, he said, "I'm not a child who needs babysitting."

Tyler shot another emphatic glance at the keg, expressing his doubt. Jeremiah just stared at the floor, shaking his head.

Eli looked to Chet, as if his third son was the only one who might believe him, even though he'd been the toughest one to win over.

"I'm telling the truth. You believe me, don't you?"

Truth. Chet wanted to ask him the definition of it, because it sure seemed to be a different matter to the man who called himself his father.

Eli apparently lost all the fight he had left in him, his shoulders slumping again as he straightened his jacket, then his bolo, mustering his dignity.

It was those little gestures that made Chet think that maybe there *was* hope for Eli yet. That all he'd wanted to do was be near the son who was getting married tomorrow, to take part in a bit of the happiness the rest of the family was experiencing.

The music cut off just before Eli said, "Forgive me for ruining your night. Forgive me for everything."

With that, he headed toward the exit. None of the brothers stopped him.

Chet looked to Mina, who'd always been the calm in his every storm.

But when he saw the sympathy and sorrow in her gaze, his heart sank to the bottom of his chest, where it always seemed to land.

Chapter Nine

The party had lost its air after Eli had gone home, and the brothers had decided to return to Florence Ranch, too.

Mina had left with the women in the limo. The only one of them who'd had any remaining will to celebrate was Jess, and she'd agreed to put an end to the evening when she'd heard about Eli's appearance.

Mina had gone back to her guest cottage, not expecting to see any more of Chet tonight, even after that dance they'd shared. That magical moment that hadn't lasted nearly as long as she would've liked.

It was morning when she saw him again.

She was strolling out in the gardens in back of the mansion with Caroline, Ally's baby daughter. Since the bride had a mile-long list of things to do today, along with her maids of honor Mrs. McCarter and Jess, Mina had volunteered to switch off with Zoe in watching over the child.

They were walking down one of the gravel maze paths amidst the roses, but Mina didn't see many of them. Caroline's little pink face, which was peeking out from under her knit cap and her swaddling blanket, outshone all the flowers.

Is my baby going to be a sweet little girl like you? Mina thought, brushing a finger down Caroline's soft cheek. *Or am I going to have a boy who turns out to be as big and strong as his daddy?*

Caroline smiled up at her, and Mina bit her lip. She wished she'd asked the doctor about her baby's sex.

She became aware that she wasn't alone when she heard the crunch of boots over the gravel. Looking up, she saw Chet, his hat in his hands, a mysterious slant to his gaze that seemed full of questions.

But there was a gentleness there, too.

He put his hat back on his head, as if that would cover what she'd seen in him, but she remembered anyway. Her heart had stamped his gaze all over the inside of her chest.

"I thought I should come out here and fetch you for breakfast," he said. "It'll be ready in about fifteen minutes in the smaller dining room."

"The smaller dining room as opposed to the big one, huh? Imagine living in a house with a choice of either."

"I don't really live here." He knit his brow, then gestured toward the house. "It's buffet style, so no hurry. No fuss."

Mina smiled. "Somehow, I don't associate the term *no fuss* with Florence Ranch."

"I never did, either—not until I got to know Tyler and Jeremiah better. They're different than when they were young, when I would come here to visit. They used to be boarding school rich kids." His own smile held a touch of wistfulness. "Abe didn't believe in sending me away for my education. He and Mom kept me at home."

"Seems to have worked out just fine for you."

A loaded pause balanced between them.

He broke it, looking at the baby, then coming toward her and Caroline, who locked her gaze onto him, enthralled.

"Look at that," Mina said. "She likes you."

"Maybe because I resemble Jeremiah a bit." He touched the baby's bunched hand. "I'm not used to being around children, but since I'm going to be an uncle, I supposed I'd better get used to it."

You're going to be more than an uncle, she thought. But then she recalled how coiled he'd seemed last night, after he and his brothers had confronted Eli at that dance.

More time. He just needed a little more time to come around, and then...

"Here you go," she said, handing Caroline to him, a lump in her throat.

Without hesitation, Chet took the baby into his arms. A natural, just as he'd been when he'd taken his place at the Barron Group.

It occurred to Mina that he was the type of man who might be good at just about everything, although he didn't make a show of it.

Would he be just as natural a father?

He was still pretty quiet, and she suspected he was waiting to say something, probably about the awkwardness of last night with Eli. It would be just like Chet to apologize for the situation, which had been out of his control.

Finally, he spoke. "You should see Jeremiah. He's fit to jump out of his skin right about now."

Not what she'd been expecting him to say. Maybe he was working his way around to it, as always.

"The former playboy's getting cold feet?" Mina asked.

"I think he just wants to get all the ceremonial stuff over with and be with his family in peace." Chet was grinning down at Caroline, and the baby was still enamored of him.

"Ally's as cool as ever," Mina said. "I was with her first thing this morning, checking to see if she needed anything."

"I have no doubt you were of great help."

He transferred that adoring smile to Mina, and she just about melted, even though he was talking about one of her sore points—her propensity to be such a people pleaser.

Then it hit her: had she been doing her best to please Chet, too, just like anyone else?

The more she thought about it, the more it seemed like a real possibility. She'd been dancing around him with the paternity situation, putting all the pressure on herself without seriously giving him the benefit of the doubt when it came to taking the news well.

Had she taken her neuroses too far? Was this more about *her* than *him*?

While she was mulling over that, Chet had taken to rocking the baby ever so slightly, and Caroline's eyes were beginning to close, little flutters of sleepiness.

The movement echoed in Mina's chest, and she struggled to maintain herself.

She started up the conversation again. "Ally's going to be such a beautiful bride."

Now she sounded downright yearning, and Chet looked up from the baby, noticing it, as well.

"Don't they say that every bride is beautiful?" he asked.

"Some more than others, I suspect."

"Well, I'll tell you what—you'll be outshining everyone in that ballroom today, Mina."

The sincerity of his tone bowled her over, weakening her in the knees and threatening to take her down.

The atmosphere had changed between them, going from tense to absolutely laden, weighed with things they couldn't, *wouldn't,* talk about.

"Mina," he said, "I owe you a long talk. As much as I'm ashamed to say it, I've been putting it off, just like I put off making my peace with Eli for so long."

She got the bad feeling that she was someone to "make peace with," too, and that didn't sit well.

Was he going to tell her that a romantic relationship just wasn't going to work out, even before she told him what *he* needed to know?

All of a sudden, it was as if she was hearing her drunken uncle at that barbecue all those years ago, and he was spouting another truth, this time directly to her.

No one wants you, Mina. You're an accident to everyone.

Her world spun, nightmarishly fast—images of her raising the baby alone or, worse yet, her having to trade off with Chet for visitation…

Before she could ask Chet to come out with what was in his heart, footsteps sounded on the path.

Mina turned to find Zoe rounding a tall hedge. Her dark shoulder-length hair was cut straight, and it swung with every step.

"Hi, there," she said, giving Mina and Chet the same glance from last night, when they'd been slow dancing like a real couple.

After Mina and Chet quietly greeted her, Zoe held out her arms for the sleeping Caroline.

"I grabbed some breakfast early," she said, "so I'm free to steal the baby while you take care of yourself, Mina."

Chet gave the precious cargo to Zoe, who shot a sympathetic glance to him.

"Chet," she said, "Eli's on the patio. He's been asking where you are."

"Thanks, Zoe."

She left Chet and Mina standing there, his hands in his jeans pockets, her arms crossed over her chest.

"You should go to him," Mina said, almost relieved that she and Chet wouldn't be able to talk until after the wedding. She was so afraid of what he might say… and about how this conversation with his father might ultimately affect everything.

"I'll see you at the wedding," Chet said, but he seemed hesitant to leave.

So she deserted him first, just as she might have to do anyway.

Chet kept thinking that there was something that he should go back and say to Mina before he went to his father, but he wasn't sure what it was.

I'm sorry for always having to leave you hanging?

I'm sorry my life is such a mess that it doesn't leave all that much time for you?

As he rounded the tall hedges and spotted his father standing on the patio in front of the French doors, a glass of what looked to be orange juice on the table near him, Chet fisted his hands by his sides.

He was sick of apologizing to Mina—just as sick as she must've been in hearing him. He was sick of how his life had spun out of control and he'd been too stubborn and angry to get a grip on it.

Most of all, he was sick of how Eli tested them, over and over again.

When the old man heard him coming, he forced a smile that seemed to wobble in its uncertainty. He also noticed how Chet gave a pointed glance to that orange juice glass.

"Nothing toxic mixed in," Eli said, picking up the drink and offering it to Chet so he could sample it.

Chet held up his hand. "No, thanks."

"I just thought that maybe, after last night…"

"You already told us that you weren't near that keg to nip a drink."

"Yes, I did. But what matters is that I think you still don't believe me."

Chet wanted to. Lord, did he ever.

Eli sank to a stone bench, which sat near an empty fountain, sapped of water.

"To tell you the truth," he said, "I'm not sure what the hell I was doing. One minute I was walking into that dance, the next I was by that keg." His face was ruddy again, but not from anger. "Maybe you boys saved me just in time. I don't know. It might've only taken a few more seconds before that beer was really calling to me."

His candidness struck Chet.

Eli continued talking. "I'm going to go back to rehab tonight, and I'm going to make every one of you proud. Before I leave though…" He put down his juice. "Chet, I'm not asking for you to really think of me as your father… But I'd like you to know that I love you just as much as I can love any son."

Chet mulled that over for a second, a sense of wrongness creeping up on him until he understood just what it meant.

He sat down on the bench, too, but there was still a space between him and Eli. "One reason that I've had such a hard time coming to terms with you is that I feel like accepting you is a betrayal of Abe."

"He wouldn't feel that way, Chet."

"That could very well be. But Abe was the victim in all this, and the last thing I'd ever do is stop backing him up, even if he's gone now. Abe and I had our tough times when I went off to Montana, but I *never* fully turned my back on him. To do it now is…unthinkable."

Eli apparently knew better than to offer his own opinion. But, then again, he knew Chet pretty well, because when he'd first moved down to Texas, Eli had been the first to welcome him home, the first to seemingly understand him. He'd been every nephew's dream of an uncle until he'd turned out to be something else altogether.

"I think," Chet said, his tone lowered, pained, "that when I left my parents all those years ago, I might've done it for more reasons than just wanting to experience some freedom. There was always something unspoken between my parents, and now that I know what it was,

I wonder if *that* was why I wanted to go. So I wouldn't have to endure those looks between them anymore." He shook his head. "Even then, I knew there were lies going on, and it's the lies that have bothered me the most about any of this."

And he couldn't stand any more of them. They'd nearly ruined so many people around him.

"I did the most lying, Chet," his dad said. "You need to put the blame squarely on me."

"Don't forget my mom."

"She was saving her marriage. I kept my silence so I could maintain my marriage, too, but..." Eli wilted a little. "I was also doing it so I could save face. Your mom didn't care about that as much as she cared about you and Abe."

When Chet looked into his father's eyes, he knew that Eli meant everything he was saying.

And, the thing was, they were the same eyes that Abe had: blue, forthright, clear as a Texas sky now that Eli was sober.

"I'm not going to put anything on you," Chet said. "Not anymore. You need to know that, and I should've been able to say it sooner. Resentment hasn't gotten me anywhere."

"Stop it, Chet. You have nothing to apologize for, especially after going through the scandal, then..."

Eli choked to a halt, and Chet knew why. He had the same rock in his throat that the other man probably did.

Abe's death.

Would the grief ever stop? It'd gotten buried these past months, a dusting of ground over the agony, a shallow grave where Chet had stored his sadness.

But what kept him from fully turning away from that grave was that he'd never gotten to know Abe as well as he could've as an adult. *He'd* been the one who'd blown that chance when he'd left his family behind, going off to Montana, telling his father he didn't want to be cooped up in an office.

Utterly leaving him until the cancer had come.

How could he get over that? When?

What scared Chet was there was even a chance that, if he didn't help Eli to bury his *own* sorrows, he would suffer from even more regret someday. He would've denied yet another father.

So cowboy up then, he thought. *Onward.*

But the last word made him think of Mina.

Was he ready to go onward, forward, clear to move ahead with everything he'd been denying himself with her?

He glanced at his dad. No more regrets.

Onward. With *everyone*.

Feeling as if he had shed about a hundred pounds, Chet took up where he and Eli had left off yesterday at the rehearsal dinner, before they'd had that setback at the party.

He rested his hand on his father's shoulder, neither of them needing to say much more as, in the distance, from the ballroom, the notes from the band rehearsing the wedding music floated through the air, celebrating today's unions and reunions.

The minute Mina saw Chet walk into the wedding, she knew everything had changed for the better.

As he came down the red-carpeted aisle behind Tyler and Jeremiah, he was all shined up, his normally tousled dark blond hair combed back to go along with the black suit he wore as one of the best men. When he caught her eye from his place by his brother near the altar, he gave her such a dazzling smile that her head whirled.

Whatever had gone on between him and Eli this morning, it'd been life altering.

Her pulse started bopping, and she hugged her hands over her belly.

The small orchestra, composed of three violins, a cello and a harp, played Bach while everyone got settled under the golden chandeliers. Outside the large French doors, the gardens bloomed under an overcast sky.

Eli came down the aisle next, dressed in a tuxedo with a bolo, and he and all the Barron boys exchanged a long glance before the older man took his seat in the front row.

Maybe it was pregnancy hormones, but Mina got the sudden urge to cry. She held it back magnificently until she realized that there were no more parents coming down the aisle because the bride's mom and dad had died, so there was no one to give Ally away.

It made Mina think of her baby and what it would be like to miss her own son or daughter's wedding because of a tragedy.

But she was being dramatic, maudlin.

Definitely pregnancy hormones.

Zoe, dressed in a blue sheath dress, slid into the seat next to Mina's. She was holding Caroline, who was making little sucking noises while swathed in her blanket.

"Just in the nick of time," she whispered as the symphony struck the first chords of the "Bridal March."

The small crowd, mainly consisting of Ally and Jeremiah's friends, plus a few work associates, stood, facing the back of the ballroom.

Ally entered, breathtaking in her Jackie O.–inspired gown, her platinum hair twisted into a classic upsweep. Her old housekeeper, Mrs. McCarter, was dolled up, too, wearing a sage satin dress with a matching cashmere sweater while using her cane to walk with Ally down the aisle. Mina realized that the elderly woman was the one who was giving Ally away to the groom, and that brought on the tears again. Ally had told Mina last night how Mrs. McCarter had just about raised her as the household manager for her parents. Even after they'd died, she'd been there through thick and thin, the closest thing Ally had to a family now.

Behind them, Ally's aunt Jess wore the same dress as Mrs. McCarter, but without the sweater. They were all gorgeous, and Mina couldn't help wishing that she and Chet…

No. She wouldn't get ahead of herself. Not before she could have that heart-to-heart with him.

When Mina saw how Jeremiah's love shone in his gaze as he watched Ally come to the altar, tears leaked out of Mina's eyes.

But then she looked at Chet, who was watching *her*.

And he seemed just as smitten with Mina as she'd always been with him.

She drew in a breath just as the preacher asked everyone to be seated.

Don't sob, she thought. *No matter how happy you are, don't do it….*

She managed to hold it back to mere tears as the ceremony went by in a stream of color and longing.

Afterward, the wedding party had to duck out for pictures, trying Mina's patience.

As she sat at the bridal party's table in a Victorian-wallpapered formal dining room that was even larger than the regular one, Zoe took a chair next to her. The other woman had gone up to Ally's room to put a tuckered Caroline to sleep, and a babysitter would be watching over the baby until the reception ended and Zoe could take over again, leaving Ally and Jeremiah to their honeymoon night.

Zoe sipped from a glass of sparkling water garnished with lime, inspecting Mina, who tried to seem as if she wasn't wishing for a certain cowboy to walk through the door.

Then she put down her glass. "He's probably just as anxious about getting those photos over with as you are."

Mina tried to play innocent, cocking her eyebrow. *Whoever are you talking about?*

Zoe just laughed. "Yeah. I haven't noticed how you and Chet are mooning over each other at all. And it can't be easy on your part, with all the Greek tragedy going on in this family."

Nailed.

Zoe continued. "Take a word of advice from someone who knows what it's like to fall for a Barron—just be patient. Things will calm down and life will go on. Tyler was just as angry and confused as Chet when the scandal first broke, and I swear, he was like a…" She smiled, as if deep in memory. "Well, like a horse that had to be gentled."

"I've been trying to hang in there." Mina smiled. "I'd do anything for him."

She might've been embarrassed to tell that to anyone else—to lay out her heart so thoroughly. But Zoe had gone through this, too. She'd been the PR rep who'd controlled the Barron scandal, but then she'd become so much more to Tyler.

The other woman said, "Even Ty knew what's been going on between you two a long time ago."

Mina stopped reaching for her water glass. Had Chet told his brother that he'd ended up in Mina's bed the night he'd heard about his parentage?

But Zoe put her fears to rest when she said, "It was in the way Chet acted around you at our wedding. The way Chet would light up whenever you called him on the phone. Not too hard to miss, even if you're an alpha male who refuses to even watch a romantic comedy with his wife."

Mina allowed herself to relax. Maybe no one knew just how far things had gone with her and Chet.

It wasn't long before the bridal party entered the room to much applause and toasts. But nothing else seemed to exist as Chet headed straight for the bridal party's table.

To Mina.

Her heart stuttered as she caught scent of him—the clover, the hay, the way no one else smelled and appealed to her.

When he took her hand under the table and squeezed it, she nearly flew with absolute joy.

A smile curved his mouth, and she didn't have to ask about how this latest talk had gone with Eli.

And when he leaned toward her to whisper in her ear, she closed her eyes, thinking that she'd never felt so dizzy, so in love.

"Let's scram as soon as we can."

She nodded, unable to speak.

She would be doing enough talking soon, when they were alone and she dropped her wonderful bombshell on him.

Chapter Ten

It seemed as if time trudged by during the reception, but Chet was going to make the most of it, dancing the hours away with Mina until they could escape.

Until they could finally be alone, now that he'd cleared some of the webs from his life.

But by the time the bride and groom were ready to cut their wedding cake, Chet was done waiting.

Most of the guests were on the temporary dance floor that was surrounded by the dining tables; everyone was standing in front of the tall, white layered cake, complete with a bride and cowboy groom at the top of it.

Chet leaned down to Mina, brushing back her hair from her ear, whispering into it.

"Are you ready to scoot?"

She smiled, and when she looked into his eyes, it seemed that she reached right into him and pulled out everything he had, heart and soul.

His pulse sped up, and, in the back of his mind, he experienced everything around him going faster, faster than ever before.

The ink isn't even dry on your new lease on life with Eli, yet here you are rushing headlong into a relationship with Mina?

But from the way he ached as she slid her hand into his, he knew that it was way past time.

Everyone cheered while Jeremiah and Ally fed each other the cake slices. Meanwhile, Mina whispered into Chet's ear.

"Why don't you grab a couple of plates and meet me at my cottage?"

Again, there was that out-of-control merry-go-round sensation of speed, of going too damned fast.

But he ignored it. "Will do."

As the band began to play, the crowd started dancing again, this time to some awful yet peppy chicken song.

Mina slipped out of the throng, toward the exit, virtually unnoticed. Chet watched her, wearing his heart on his jacket sleeve.

The way she looked in that bronze-colored dress, which rivaled her hair in color and shine...the way the silk draped over her hips as she swayed out the door...

She really was the most stunning woman in the room, just as he had told her she would be. He doubted he would ever find another person as beautiful, inside and out.

Feeling more light-headed than ever, Chet casually grabbed two slices of cake from the tray of a passing waiter, who was depositing the desserts at each place setting. Then he stealthily made his way out of the room, the weird chicken music left behind him.

Perfect time to get going.

He made his way through the big house, out a side door, then took a path toward the nearby guest cottage with soft light burning through the windows.

He managed to knock, even with two fistfuls of plate.

When Mina opened the door, the dim illumination shone from behind her, creating an aura that kissed every strand of gold in her red hair. She'd already kicked off her shoes, revealing scarlet-tipped toenails, and already taken off the wrap that had draped over her shoulders and arms. But she still wore that dress, and it fell nearly to her feet like a shower of bronze.

"I thought you'd never get here with my sugar fix," she said, taking the plates from him. "I've been craving cake all day."

As he came inside, he thought that she might've had a slight tremor in her voice, even though she was smiling.

Nerves?

He wasn't sure why she would be anxious around him, unless it was just the anticipation of what this night might bring.

But what was *that* exactly?

What was he expecting—for them to make love again? Or did he want much, much more this soon?

Again, his pulse raced.

If she didn't have nerves, he definitely did.

He shut the door behind him while she headed for the small kitchen, with its square wooden table smack in the middle of the tiled flooring. Coffee was brewing in a machine on the counter, and she'd lit a couple of candles. That plus a lantern hanging over the stove provided the only light in the area.

She set the plates on the table, then laughed.

"What?" he asked.

"I just realized...I think I've recreated that scene from *Sixteen Candles*. You know—the ending, where Molly Ringwald is celebrating her birthday with her dream guy?"

Dream guy.

There was a lot of pressure in that description, if Mina was indeed comparing him to the hero of the movie.

Adrenaline spun through him, but he told himself that they'd been heading to this point the entire time they'd known each other.

And it *wasn't* too soon.

"Sorry," he said. "That kind of movie really isn't my thing. I haven't seen it."

"It's a great one." Was she talking faster than usual? "Everyone around Molly has forgotten her sixteenth birthday. They're rushing all over the place, paying attention to other matters, like her sister's wedding. But she finally gets what she wants in the end."

Okay. He understood why the movie might've been significant to Mina, with how she'd felt about being an accidental baby, forgotten herself sometimes.

But she'd chosen *him* to make her feel special, just like the heroine in that movie had been with her dream man.

Mina had already put forks and napkins by the plates, and now she was pouring water into tall glasses. Putting down the pitcher, she blew out a breath, smoothed out her dress.

Everything was feeling real innocent right about now, as if it was the first time he'd been alone with her, boy with girl.

Man with woman.

Coming up behind her, he rested his hands on her arms. He felt her shiver.

But the same was happening to him—washes of desire traveling his skin, cool and warm at the same time.

He leaned down, his face against her hair. The scent of her—cucumber, green tea… Heady and clean.

"I can't tell you how it feels to finally be away from everyone else," he said. "Every*thing* else."

"Why don't you try to tell me, anyway?"

He ran his hands down her bare arms, and she crossed them over her chest until he was embracing her from the back.

"Freedom," he said. "It was like I was locked up and then let out. That's how it felt with all those lies—like they were pushing me back and keeping me from going anywhere. But they've all been cleared up now with Eli."

"Everything's in the clear?" she asked.

"Yeah." He tightened his hold on her, releasing a little when he realized he might be overdoing it. "I swear, if I'd had to deal with one more lie…"

She stiffened beneath him.

He thought he could feel the beat of her pulse under his own skin, a skittering rhythm. Or maybe it was just her breathing, faster now.

Was she afraid that he would never fully pull himself

out of his family drama? That the fallout from the scandal was going to linger and affect *them?*

"There won't be anything else coming between us," he said. "Don't worry about that."

"At least you've learned how to handle it when someone hasn't been entirely truthful with you," she said, her words seeming…careful. Very careful. "Did you get any perspective on why other people might've had to pull back on telling you the truth? I know what your mom and Eli did wasn't right, but…" She turned her head just a tad, still not looking at him. "Can you understand, even a shred, why they might've kept you in the dark?"

"I've tried. But it all keeps boiling down to this—Eli and my mom could've avoided hurting a lot of people if they'd come clean a lot earlier." He shook his head. "There's never a good enough reason to hide the truth."

"Never?"

She still sounded odd, but he couldn't read her face since she'd turned away from him again.

He eased her around so he could see her. "None of that matters now. Eli and I are starting up a new relationship." Even as he said it, there was something dragging at him—the truth of how he still felt. "Okay, maybe there's always going to be a part of me that remembers how he held back the truth for so many years. Same with my mom. But, with her, I'll never have the opportunity to tell her how much damage she did."

"I wish she was here, and not just so you could straighten matters out with her, too," Mina said.

He hugged her to him. Mina, his saving grace, the woman who always seemed to keep him balanced.

"I'm still angry at her," he said. "And if you hadn't come into my life, I even wonder if I might've ended up with a woman who would lie to me like my mom did to Abe at first. How's that for some neuroses?"

"You can't generalize like that, Chet."

Then she fell silent.

He kissed her head, wanting her to know that everything would improve from this night on.

"You're right—I shouldn't generalize," he said. "You're the most trustworthy person I know."

She was gripping his hand now, finally looking at him, but with a hint of anxiety in her gaze.

He strove to reassure her. "I was so afraid of bringing you into my life. My God, what woman in her right mind would ask to be a part of it?"

"I've told you before—I was always determined to be there for you throughout everything, thick and thin. All I've ever wanted was to see you heal up…"

Touched, he pulled out a kitchen chair, sat down on it, bringing her onto his lap. She snuggled against him, her face near his neck, her hair brushing his skin and driving him crazy. When she spoke, her breath tickled him.

"Everything I've ever done," she said softly, "it's been because I was thinking about what might be best for you."

"I know." He kissed her temple. "Because you're my girl."

It was as if that particular sentiment had twisted something within her, and she pressed her face against him harder.

He felt wet skin. Tears?

Leaning back, he cupped a hand under her jaw. "Why are you crying?"

She seemed on the edge of saying something, but then shook her head.

Why was she so sad when this should be the happiest moment of their lives?

All he wanted to do was bring her to where he was— happy. Finally happy.

He pressed his mouth to hers, tenderly, with all the affection he'd been fighting before now.

"I love you, Mina," he said.

They were the words she'd been hoping for, but she barely registered them through all the confused feelings that were tearing her up: wanting to love him right back, needing to tell him that maybe he wouldn't feel so kindly toward her after she revealed that she, too, was a liar.

But there'd been such good reasons for not telling him about their own big, life-altering news.

Would it be too late to explain that to him? Or was he going to put her in the same category as his mother, whom he obviously hadn't come to terms with yet?

Damn the woman for never telling Chet the truth. Yet Mina couldn't be angry at a ghost, not when there was a man, flesh and blood, looking down at her with such openness and hope in his blue gaze.

Her instincts told her to just show him that she would *always* be his, no matter what she'd done to him.

"I love you, too," she said, sadness making the words raw in her throat. "I love you so much, Chet."

His smile was so beautiful—relaying what no other words could've possibly accomplished—that it was beyond Mina to tell him to wait and hear her out.

Before she could say anything else, he kissed her, and it was everything to her—full of the true affection he'd never admitted before now, full of the unconditional love she'd been searching for all her life.

She wasn't a mistake to him, not this time.

Not until the truth would destroy everything she'd labored so hard to build with him. And she couldn't stand to injure him again, not after he'd finally found a measure of peace tonight.

She kissed him back with everything she had in her—months of watching him from afar, of having to keep a yearning distance between them at work. Surely she could hold on to this complete and utter happiness just a little longer....

Groaning low in his throat, he slowed the kiss down, gently nipping at her, weaving his fingers through her hair in a lazy exploration that sent waves of heat through her. Her blood pounded, marching toward the low center of her body, where it gathered, demanding.

"Mina," he said against her lips, and she couldn't let go of how that made her feel—as if she was wanted more than any woman could've ever felt wanted.

As he held her on his lap, brushing her hair back from her face, she saw in those eyes how much he did love her, had maybe always loved her.

He leaned over and blew out the candles on the table, one, then the other.

She longed for him to kiss her again, but he took her by the hand instead, leading her to the lantern over the stove. He doused that, too, then brought her to her bedroom, where moonlight rolled through the open curtains at her window.

Around them, the sunrise paintings breathed soft,

dim hues, the splash of them echoing inside of her, coloring her with a desire so strong that she could barely stand it.

His whisper dominated the semidarkness. "I'm never going to let you down again, Mina. I'm going to make up for all the times I disappointed you, starting now."

But *she* was going to disappoint *him,* and it seemed inevitable, even now, when she was trying so hard to show him that she hadn't meant to lie—had only had his best interests at heart...

An ache split her, and it had nothing to do with her desire for him. It started in her chest, as if prying her apart in two directions.

Was he going to call her a liar when she revealed the baby to him? Was he going to put everything in generalities again and tell her that, even though she'd only been looking out for him, there was no reason to ever keep such important news from someone you loved?

He ran his hands down her arms, up again, as if memorizing every inch of her. Then, with deliberation, he reached to the back of her dress, looking for a zipper.

Not finding it there, he skimmed a hand to her side, discovering it, laughing low—an intimate laugh that made her turn fluid.

He unzipped that dress, and the sound resembled what he was doing to her, too: dividing her, taking her apart.

As he peeled the material away from her torso, she churned with need, not only because of the air hitting her bared skin, but because she was getting more and more revealed, even if her body didn't scream "pregnant!" just yet.

Still, she didn't know what to do—stop him?

No. She wanted to keep going. Oh, she wanted it so badly.

Couldn't she just tell him everything after they made love?

Definitely. She would definitely do it then, in the afterglow, when the news couldn't be anything but beautiful and right.

Leaving her dress bunched at her hips, he coaxed off her bra. She didn't have the willpower to put a halt to it.

And when his hungry gaze devoured her exposed breasts, she felt such a rush of emotion for him that she couldn't do anything more than give in all the way.

Then he turned her around, her bare back to his chest. Cupping her breasts, he rubbed her with his thumbs, bringing her to even harder peaks.

She wanted to cry out, but all she could do was make little sounds of utter enjoyment.

"I love every curve of you," he said. "Every inch."

He kissed her neck and she shivered.

After he backed away from her for a moment, she heard the rustle of clothing, the crinkle of packaging.

It didn't take but a minute for him to return, and this time he was naked, except for a condom that he must've gotten from his wallet. She could feel him against her, hard and ready.

And she was as lost as lost could be.

He pushed her hair aside, kissed the bump on the back of her neck, then trailed down her spine, planting another kiss. Another.

"I love," he said, his hands braced on her material-shrouded hips, "the dimples you have just above your derriere."

Gasping, she thought just how much she wanted to worship him, too.

To show him how she would always be devoted to him, no matter what.

She turned around, pulling him up to a stand, then pushed him toward the bed. He fell back onto it, all muscled male beauty on the light field of her covers.

"I love so many things about you, too," she said, bending down, hovering over him on her hands and knees, her dress still around her hips, the material dragging over him. The sensation of silk over his bare thighs must've gotten to him, because he went even harder.

She sat on his thighs, her dress covering him. Then she rested her palms on his biceps. "I love your arms, because they look like they could carry anything."

"They can carry you."

Yes, she wanted them to carry her everywhere, to places she'd never been before. Places only he could take her.

She skimmed her fingertips to his chest, where there was a fine dusting of dark blond hair. "I love how you look like a man, not a boy. How you take care of things like a man."

His chest was rising and falling with fast breaths, and he slipped his hands under her dress, hooked his thumbs into the sides of her panties, starting to lower them.

"As pleasant as this is," he said, grit in his tone, "I'm not going to last much longer."

"Just so you know how much I love every bit of you," she said. "Forever and always."

The last words had a tinge of foreboding to them, even though she hadn't meant it to be that way.

Hoping to erase it, she slid off of him, scooting back

to her pillows so she was still sitting up as he worked her undies from her body, tossing them to the floor.

Even as passion-steeped as she was, she remembered their baby, how to be safe, even while making love.

He rested his thumbs on her belly under her dress, his fingers splayed over her hips.

She wrapped her legs around him just as he entered her.

Mina made a primal sound of ultimate pleasure as he brought her to him, then away from him, their skin slick with sweat.

As they moved together, she saw circles in her mind—rings of fire that danced with flame, waving, touching her skin, charring it, kissing below the surface until she was branded deep down.

And the flames got bigger, higher, licking her faster and faster until she felt torched....

Higher, faster...pushed to her limits, fire in her, on her—

She flamed out in a series of tiny explosions that culminated in one big burst of heat, making her say his name.

But she didn't cool off yet. He wasn't done, and she stayed with him until he climaxed, too.

Then she held him close, refusing to let him go, hoping that he'd seen and felt a thousand truths in her love before she did what she had to do next....

They were still in bed, but even afterward, Chet sensed that Mina was more anxious than ever.

Did she think he was going to say, *Well, now that I got what I needed, I've changed my mind?*

Who could blame her if she did though? He'd put her through too much.

She came to rest on her side, facing him, that dress still on her, gathered at her waist, just above the sheets she'd pulled up, too. She had one hand under her pillow, the other under her chin, making her seem so vulnerable.

He touched the tip of her nose, her cheek, but didn't say anything.

Her eyes were wide when she started to talk. "Do you know when I first fell in love with you?"

He thought for a second, but he wasn't sure he knew the answer. Mina had always been Mina, never changing.

"Tell me," he said softly.

She smiled, but it was a tiny bit sad. He wasn't sure why. Wasn't sure what was going on with her at all.

"When you first walked through your office door," she said.

His heart jammed upward. "It was love at first sight?"

"You say it like you don't believe in it."

"I'm not sure I do. There's lust at first sight." And he'd never felt that for his assistant until the night he'd first gone to her for comfort, seeing something else in her entirely that had only grown to what it was now. Love.

"I know," she said. "It seems that love is too complex for it to happen in the first instant. That's what they say, anyway. But I'm not so sure about that. I think love's very simple." She wound her hand into his, wrapping her fingers, twining. "There you were, in a new business suit and your cowboy hat. It was your smile that got me, though. It flipped my heart right around, and I thought,

'This is the man. This is the one I've been waiting for.' I knew it without a doubt."

Chet wasn't certain if it was possible that a heart could crack, but his seemed to be doing it. In a nice way, too.

She went on, but there was still something in her voice that he couldn't identify.

"From just a look, I could tell so many things about you.... That you were pure-hearted. That you were a straight shooter." Her voice lowered. "That you expected people to be the same way with you."

"That's what I thought about you the first day, too."

"It was hard," she said, "working with you day in and day out, trying to hide my feelings."

"Is that why you never went out with anyone, because of me?"

"Pretty much. When you feel about someone the way I feel about you, it seems tawdry to be with another person, no matter how low the chances are of success with your true love."

What she was telling him was so sweet that he wanted to take hold of it. She was so unlike everything else in his life.

He began to pull her toward him, but she grabbed his wrist. He could feel her unsteadiness.

"I just wanted you to know that I've loved you more than anyone could ever love another person, Chet."

This was starting to sound...

Like a warning?

"What's wrong, Mina?" he asked.

She closed her eyes, as if she was gathering every bit of strength she had. As the seconds passed, it felt like daggers in his skin.

Finally, she opened her eyes again, pushing the dress down the rest of the way over her hips, discarding it.

Taking him by the hand and placing it on her belly.

"Chet," she said in a quivering voice, "we're going to have a baby."

Chapter Eleven

The announcement rang in Mina's ears for what seemed like a full minute as she watched Chet for a reaction.

Would he turn on her for keeping this a secret from him?

Had she told him too late…

…or still too *early?*

"A baby," he said, as if it hadn't quite sunk in yet.

She tightened her hold on his hand, which was still on her bare belly.

"A baby," she repeated, her heart throbbing in her ears.

Just as she thought she might not be able to take another breath, a smile broke out over Chet's face. And his eyes…

They were shining, welling with what she thought might be incredible, glinting joy.

Then he laughed, hugging her to him, putting his

hand right back on her tummy. At the same time, he was kissing her forehead, cradling her, and now it took *her* a few moments to process his response.

He wasn't mad at her....

She held to him, hardly believing that it could be this easy. He stroked her hair, and for a while it seemed as if this would go on for hours.

Then the moment she'd been dreading arrived.

As he still hugged her close, he rested his chin on her head. Her hand was over his heart, and she thought she could feel his pulse underneath her palm.

The slowing of its rhythm.

His silence cut into her, because the surprise had clearly passed for him. Reality had set in.

She didn't want to look up, into his eyes. But she did.

And what she saw shot her into pieces.

The moonlight revealed shadows—the ones that she thought had gone by the wayside already.

Sorrow flooded her. "Chet?"

"It had to have happened all those months ago," he said, almost as if to himself. "That night I came to your apartment."

"Yes."

He didn't go on, but she knew just what he had to be thinking.

"You're going to say that you wore a condom," she said. "But I'm pretty sure it broke. Afterward, both of us weren't paying as much attention to it as we should have—there was so much else going on." With her still trying to comfort him about the scandal and everything. "And I didn't find out for certain that I was pregnant until fairly recently. I wanted to tell you right away, but…"

He had come to touch her belly again, looking down at the place where their child was growing. "But you wanted to see how things would go with me and my family before you said anything. You thought I might take the news badly."

She didn't even know if she should say yes, so she didn't move, just waiting for him to go on instead.

He let go of her, and she scooted from him a few inches. They merely lay there for a while, next to each other, and soon he put his hand on her tummy again, as if he wanted the baby to know that he or she wasn't responsible for this tension.

The quiet was excruciating, because Mina knew that all Chet's demons had arrived, whispering in his ear.

An illegitimate baby, just like you, they had to be saying. *History repeating itself.*

But this wouldn't be a forbidden baby. Or an accident.

Didn't he realize that Mina had lived through the same sort of scenario and she would never allow a child to suffer because of the way he or she had been conceived?

That wasn't the worst part, though. Those demons would also be driving home to Chet that Mina hadn't let him in on the secret until now, after she had already known for a bit.

Keeping the truth from him would be just the same as a lie in his book.

What should've been the most wonderful moment of their lives was quickly going dark as the night collapsed around them. What made it worse was that she didn't even know what to say now, while he was so lost in his own mind and emotions.

At least his fingertips were *still* on her tummy, as if he'd already fallen in love with his child.

Was it only the mom he was angry at?

Her?

And she knew why he might be disappointed in her, too, even if she didn't know how to remedy it.

"I'm not like your mother," Mina said.

"I'd rather not talk about her right now."

Sure. He was going back into that shell of his, just as he'd done after the scandal had reared its ugly head.

But she wasn't about to let that happen.

"Just today," she said, "you told me that you knew you'd made a mistake in how you handled Eli. Now you're going to deal with me the same—"

"Please don't, Mina."

It would've hurt her less if it'd been an actual slap. As it was, she felt the mortifying sting of it.

She pulled the sheets up over her chest, and that forced his hand away from her and the baby.

Already, she felt abandoned.

"Okay," she said. "I'll leave it alone then. But we're going to have to talk about this sometime."

"I just want to..." He was staring at the ceiling. "Jeez, I don't want this to matter—the way the baby was conceived."

It went unsaid, but she knew he was mulling over how she'd presented the news to him—belatedly. Maybe even, according to him, cruelly.

"But it does matter," she said, so eager to get past this if he would let them.

She rose up to a kneeling position, still covering herself with the sheets. His hands seemed so empty as he rested them on his stomach.

"I want to hear everything you have to say," she said. "I want you to lay it all out there so we can take care of it now, not later, after it's had time to fester. Tell me what's going on with you."

He pressed his lips together.

"Please," she said.

Then he sent her a long glance that she couldn't quite understand, sat up, got out of the bed to put on his pants. She hadn't meant to drive him away—not tonight.

But she couldn't live with a partner who resented her, either.

"Is this about lying?" she asked.

"I…" He dug a hand into his hair. "Damn it, Mina, I just have to wonder how long you would have waited to tell me."

"Until I thought you could handle the news. And maybe I should've waited even longer, until after your wounds with Eli had mended a little more."

"You didn't trust me." What might've sounded petulant from another man only seemed rock-hard coming from him, as if his reaction had been written in stone a long time ago and it'd been fruitless to try to change it, even for her, the woman he supposedly loved.

She swallowed, clutching those sheets now.

All she could say was, "You can't compare this to what your mother did. I would never have done that to you. It's not even remotely the same."

But Mina could see that no matter how happy he'd seemed when he'd first heard the news, as the reality had set in, so had the hurt.

* * *

His mind was popping with so many different things, right or wrong, that he didn't know what to think.

There was genuine joy at the baby they were going to have, and that's what had come out when she'd announced the news.

But then there was the resentment that had followed—an emotion he didn't want to have, even though it wouldn't leave him.

He'd thought he'd gotten over his trials and tribulations, but here he was, still a prisoner of them.

But there was something *else* eating away at him that he hadn't expected, a dark mass that was just now taking shape.

He recalled when Mina had told him about her exboyfriend back at the Utah resort. How she'd said her family had despised the other guy after the break up.

In light of that, had she worried about bringing Chet, the father of her child, home? Had she ever wondered how her all-important family was going to react to the Barron bastard who couldn't be any good for her, either?

Had she been embarrassed about who he was and how that would affect her and their child?

They were over-the-top thoughts, but he couldn't help thinking them. He'd gone through too much rejection—just like the illegitimate child that Eli had never claimed until he'd been forced to do so. Just like the man who'd been lied to his entire life.

And Mina had lied to him, too.

She wrapped the sheets around her even more, covering all the skin she could, and that slammed him hard, as if she was retreating from him when, just shortly before, they'd been as together as two people could be.

With a child besides.

He thought of the moment he'd heard the news, and it folded him up inside, warm and bright.

They were going to have a baby.

He told himself to go back to her right now, to talk this out. But he'd been optimistic before and look where it'd gotten him.

Nowhere.

Maybe he just needed time.… Maybe it'd just be best to get out of here so he could breathe and think.…

"This was what I was afraid of," Mina said from the bed.

She was pushing him and he wasn't in any place to tolerate it.

"You didn't think I'd be angry?" he asked. "Especially after you let me make love to you again? Were you buttering me up?"

Manipulating him?

He'd been manipulated enough.

"No," she said so forcefully that he immediately regretted the questions.

Then, softer, she said, "I knew you would be angry with me, and I deserve that. There were so many times I almost told you about the baby, but each moment never seemed right."

He wondered if his mother and Eli had ever talked together, asking themselves when the time would be right to let Chet in on their secret.

He *wanted* to be angry with Mina—it would feel so much better if he could direct it somewhere besides the vague world around him—but if there was a rational

side of him, it was screaming that he would've been
wary of sending a bombshell like this his way, too.

And he hated himself all the more for it.

Good God, what the hell kind of father would he
be?

What had they gotten this baby into?

He was so livid that he wished there was a way to
tell their baby that, no matter what, he or she would be
protected. There'd never be ugliness because of his or
her parents.

And that was why he put on the rest of his clothing,
thinking that he really *should* cool off, weighing what
to say to Mina next before he said something he couldn't
take back.

"Where are you going?" she asked.

"To get myself together. It's not good for me to be
here right now."

"Oh."

She said it as if he'd proven something, and good
or bad, Chet actually felt as if she was accusing him
of being a terrible father already. That she'd known he
was going to blow it, and *that* was the reason she'd put
off telling him.

He should've thought twice about that, but his nerves
were shredded from all the scrapes they'd been getting
into these past months.

"What does 'oh' mean?" he asked, even while knowing that he should've just left it alone.

He wanted to hear her say it, just as she'd wanted him
to talk this out instead of just appreciating that they were
going to have a baby together.

He added, "Did you think I'd walk out that door and
never come back?"

When she flashed an injured gaze at him, he realized that Mina was dealing with her own issues here, too—the woman who'd never quite believed that people wouldn't reject *her*.

That dug into him even more.

"You actually did think that," he said, hardly believing it. "You thought I might be the kind of man who'd turn his back on his child, just like Eli did."

"No." But even though she tried to deny it, he could see it on her face.

Bam. Right in the gut.

The real truth.

His mind grasped at what was going on here because he just wasn't sure anymore.

Would she *always* be thinking that he would leave?

In spite of all the I-love-you's, did she actually trust him?

Crushed, he buttoned his shirt, put on his jacket. Now he *really* needed to cool off.

"Don't walk out that door," she said, her voice cracking.

"Don't worry, Mina." His heart felt as if it'd been sliced up and was stretching, trying like hell to bring itself back together. But it wasn't working. "You're afraid that I'd leave the baby behind, but in spite of what you might think of me, that's not the case. I'll always take care of my child."

She dropped back to lean against the wall, cocooned in that sheet, clearly decimated at what he'd said.

He would take care of the baby.

But what about her?

He left the question behind him, taking his battered

heart instead as he walked out of the cottage to do that cooling off he so sorely required.

Little did he know that when he returned she would be gone.

The morning after, Mina stared at the dawn-grayed ceiling of her house, the expanse of pale paint like a blank slate.

When Chet had left her in the cottage, she'd been so angry at him that she hadn't stayed, heading straight home in one of the Barrons' limos without Chet's knowledge. She'd felt too numb in the chest, just like another blank slate, this one marked with slashes of pain that only emphasized the otherwise empty expanse inside of her.

She had turned off her phone so Chet couldn't reach her and, once home, impulsively written a resignation letter to the Barron Group, hopping in her car and driving to the closed offices, where she'd slid the paper under his door, then left.

This morning, she'd still been angry at him, but she felt the same way with herself, too. It was just that she'd been hoping for a miracle, hoping that Chet wouldn't just say all the right things but that he would somehow banish how he really felt, as well.

Had she driven him away for good?

Now, as she kept looking at the ceiling, she formed another version of her resignation letter, one she could have sent.

Dear Sirs:
Much to my regret, I'm resigning my position at
The Barron Group forthwith.

Working there would mean pretending that my boss, the man I thought I'd marry and be with for the rest of my life, still loved me. I'm not sure I could bear seeing him day after day.

She wiped a hand over her eyes, blocking her view of the ceiling. The real letter had been much more formal and professional, just as she'd always been. And she was clinging to the orderly, people-pleasingly simple Mina now, because she wasn't sure she had much more than that left.

Sitting up, she glanced at the old-school yellow phone on her secondhand coffee table, just as if that would make the thing ring. As if that would bring his voice on the other end of the line and he would beg her not only to come back to the office, but to return to him.

Yet she doubted that would happen, especially after what she'd said to him. He obviously hadn't *wanted* her enough to stay and, this time, it had been no accident.

This time, she'd earned the rejection because she'd wanted too much, too soon.

In fact, she feared that the only time she might hear from Chet was through an attorney, informing her that he was filing for custody.

Maybe she was overreacting, but that didn't mean the mere thought hadn't kept her up last night.

Tearfully, she rubbed her belly, wishing it was bigger, that her baby would be coming sooner.

Wishing she didn't want to take back the last couple of weeks to see if things could've turned out differently.

"I'm such a whiz," said Mina's father that same afternoon as they sat in the living room of her parents' home, avoiding the overcast weather outside. Since she'd been up and about since the crack of dawn, she'd come here early, needing the company.

The change in temperature had triggered some kind of cold in her dad, and his nose was stuffy, the scent of VapoRub wafting from him.

"This almost makes me forget that I'm not on the high seas with your mother," he said while he toyed with the new smartphone that Amy and her husband had purchased for him as a birthday gift. It did seem to cheer him up, because even though he'd pretended that he wasn't looking forward to the cruise, his sickness had caused her parents to miss it. They weren't even going to have a big impromptu party for his birthday tomorrow because he needed to rest.

Mina smiled at his interest in the phone, but her gesture wasn't natural. She had so many "wired up" devices herself—her own smartphone, her computer, the iPad—and even though they were supposed to connect a person with the rest of the world, Mina didn't feel linked to much of anyone at all, except for the baby.

To make things even worse, her dad's enthusiasm reminded her of Chet's level of expertise with newfangled "doodads."

Then again, everything reminded her of Chet.

Surely he'd read her letter by now, but did he even care? There'd been no phone calls from him—only a few from her friends in the office who'd checked in about her absence and learned of her resignation. Danny and Corrine had even invited her out to dinner tonight to say goodbye.

The aroma of chicken soup floated through the room,

and Mina's mom came out of the kitchen, carrying a couple of bowls with steam waving out of them.

"Eat up," Mom said, slipping a serving in front of Mina on the pine coffee table just before she gave one to Dad, too.

"I'm not that hungry." Her stomach was a mess because she hadn't just come here to nurse her dad.

She had some things to get off of her chest if she wanted to move on without Chet. To do that, she knew that her support system would help to pull her through.

True, she knew she could survive without interference from her family, but it felt darn good to have it if she wanted it.

Mom was spooning some of the soup and lifting it to Mina's mouth.

"Seriously, Mom," Mina said. "Not hungry."

"All right, crankypants." Her mother frowned as she put the spoon back into the bowl.

Dad laughed under his breath.

"Chicken soup is proven to lift moods as well as fight sickness," Mom said to him. "I could eat a whole pot of it along with ten bars of chocolate some days." She patted her stomach. "I'd pay for it, though."

"Honey," Dad said, "if there's more of you to love, I won't be complaining."

"Thank you, Ewan." Mom rolled her eyes.

Dad seemed to know just when to leave a room…and a woman's mild temper. He got up from his chair and headed for the hallway.

"I might get better reception back here," he said, pointing to his phone.

"You sure will." Mom still wasn't over his food comment.

Mina grinned at him as he disappeared, his slippers leaving soft footfalls on the carpet.

"I swear," she said, sitting back on the couch. "Years of marriage, and it's like he still hasn't figured out that I'm touchy when it comes to weight. There are just some things you don't say to a woman."

Mina pressed her lips together. There were some things you didn't say to a man, either, but she'd said them to Chet.

"Sometimes," she whispered, "we say things we don't mean." *And sometimes there's a big cost.* "Dad was actually being sweet to you, Mom."

She smiled a bit. "So he was."

Her dad had turned on the TV back in his room, and the murmur of it imitated the muddled noise in Mina's heart. It wouldn't quiet itself.

"So what's wrong?" Mom asked.

It wouldn't do to avoid the question. She'd come over here for that tender love and care, so why not admit it?

But it was the lingering shame of displeasing her mom with her behavior that made it hard to speak right now. Her parents had raised her to be a good girl, and Mina had been wondering about how they would react to her sleeping with another man outside of a committed relationship. It'd been bad enough with Michael.

Yet hadn't her mom told her she was independent? Hadn't she sounded as if she respected that, too?

Mina realized that, like Chet, she needed to put her family matters in order once and for all if she was going to go forward.

She steadied herself, then said, "I'm pregnant, Mom."

The moment her mother put her hands over her mouth and her eyes lit up, Mina broke open with a tiny sob she'd been holding back ever since things had gone to hell with Chet.

"Oh, sweetie!"

Mom hugged her, rocking her back and forth as the tears really started to come.

Pregnancy hormones. But crying was also profound relief, a load off of Mina's shoulders.

"When are you due?" Mom asked, looking at Mina, wiping the tears from her daughter's eyes, even as she cried herself.

"In about four months."

"And…Chet? I assume he's…"

Mina could only nod while her mom stroked the hair back from her face. She was sobbing now, an obvious signal that things were not going well with the father.

"What happened?" her mom asked softly.

It felt good to have an ally, and Mina told her almost everything—about the night Chet had found out about his illegitimacy, about how they'd gotten together, then closer and closer, until she'd dropped the news on him.

She almost expected her mom to say something about how Mina needed to stop picking guys who didn't deserve her, but instead, she got something else altogether.

"So when are you two going to patch this up?"

The surety in her mom's tone made Mina look up and say, "You're not going to give me 'the talk'?"

"Like the one you got last time?"

Mina nodded.

Her mom tucked Mina's hair behind her ear. "Sweetie, Michael was an engaging guy, but he was one of those slackers. There are little details that reveal everything about a man, and when I saw how he loved to be waited on hand and foot and how he disengaged from the family to sit here and watch TV while we'd sit out on the porch with each other... Well, that spoke volumes." She shook her head. "Chet felt real, though. A mother knows these things."

Mina almost started crying again.

"Have you talked to him at all?" her mom asked, saving her.

"No. I've wanted to call him, but...I'm afraid."

"Of what?"

Mina held up her palms. "What if he's always going to be angry with me for not trusting him?" Sorrow pushed up through her chest, making her words tangled. "I wouldn't be able to stand it. It'd be concrete evidence that he never cared that much in the first place. He's already put me aside, even though he promised to always take care of the baby."

Mom held Mina's face in her hands. "Your child deserves every chance you can give him or her. You've got to talk to Chet."

"I know. It's the most important thing in the world to do, especially for the baby's sake." She bit her lip, as if it would hold back everything else she wanted to say, but it didn't work. "Among other matters, children should never feel as if their parents didn't want them."

Empathy changed her mother's expression. She was obviously thinking about the circumstances of Mina's birth.

"I've known about it for years, Mom," Mina said.

"Uncle Dennis was drunk once, and I heard him talk about it during one of our family get-togethers. I just never told you."

"Oh, Mina." She stroked her daughter's hair again.

"It's no big tragedy. I mean, I grew up fine."

"But it's something no child should hear." Her smile was soft, like a mother's should be. "Your father and I weren't sure that we could afford to have any other children at that time. But there you were, in spite of any precautions we took."

She'd already known the circumstances, but she touched her belly, anyway, as if her baby could hear. As if shielding him or her from all of this.

"We started celebrating you right away, Mina," her mom added. "And it kills me to think that we might not have had you at all but for an 'accident.'" She touched Mina's cheek. "*Accident.* What a word for it when, really, it was as if someone or something out there was telling us that you needed a home, and we were the lucky ones who were chosen to bring you in to one. And there hasn't been a moment when we haven't thanked our stars for you."

Did you hear that? Mina asked her child. *That's exactly how I feel about you.*

"I could just throttle Uncle Dennis," her mom said, narrowing her eyes. "He had no business talking about that when we told him in confidence."

"It's okay," Mina said.

Because it was.

It really was.

It'd been a long time in coming, but hearing her mother say this with tears in her eyes made all the difference.

And it caused Mina to realize that *she* was going to be a mother. Really and truly a mother. She genuinely felt just how devastating it would be to not have been blessed with someone who was going to bring such joy into her life.

She understood so much now.

But what about the father of her baby?

Would he still consider Mina an accident…

…or was he thinking about her as much as she was pining away for him?

Chapter Twelve

Hours later that same day, Chet sat in the stables at Florence Ranch, holding a copy of Mina's resignation letter in his hands while sitting on a bale of hay. He'd cut out early from the office for some peace and quiet, because his mind sure wasn't giving him any rest.

He still couldn't forget the look that had been on Mina's face when he'd left her. It was as if he'd pulled the floor out from under her, and gradually, realization—and betrayal—had taken over her expression. Then he'd stupidly left her alone, just to do that cooling off thing of his, only to come back and find everything gone—her luggage, her clothing...

Her.

Then, even more foolishly, he'd told himself that she just needed a little space, so he hadn't called her, believing that he would see her this morning when he reported for work on a rare late day at the office, where they could find some time alone together to smooth things over.

And that was when he'd found the letter under his door.

A remote, polite, businesslike resignation from his life.

That was when he realized that a mere phone call wasn't going to erase the words they'd said to each other.

Unless he proved otherwise, was she always going to think he was too troubled?

He needed some advice on this, so he had come back here to the ranch to…

Hell, he might as well admit it. For the first time, he needed his brothers, and he'd left word back at the mansion asking them to meet him here.

He folded the letter while next to him in a stall, an Arabian mare stomped her hoof and nickered. Chet stood, just about ready to put the paper into his business suit pocket when someone walked through the entrance to the stables.

Scratch that—it was two people. Tyler and Jeremiah, who hadn't left on his honeymoon with Ally to Lake Arrowhead in California yet.

"Saddling up?" Jeremiah asked Chet, eyeing his business suit.

"I didn't want to go in the mansion, so that's why I'm here instead."

Since Eli hadn't gone back to rehab yet, Chet had wanted to avoid the big house and any talk about Mina with his father. Besides, he'd already said goodbye to Eli this morning, before he'd headed out for the office.

It looked as if Jeremiah and Tyler were ready to ride

themselves, with their jeans and hats. They were watching him expectantly. Everyone on the ranch knew that Mina had left already—Chet had only told them she'd scheduled an early day at the Group—and his hangdog expression was probably causing his brothers to wonder just *what* was going on.

Might as well get this over with.

Chet held up the letter. "Mina quit the Group."

Jeremiah nodded. "When I checked in with my assistant an hour ago, she told me. Some of the staff is going to be meeting Mina tonight to see what's going on with her, why she's leaving. I suspect some might even want to make a play at changing her mind."

Tyler stepped in. "Why did she quit, Chet?"

"We had…a falling out last night. And I'm afraid it was mostly because of my damned issues."

Tyler exhaled loudly.

"What's that mean?" Chet asked, immediately realizing that he was about to get his first real brother-to-brother-to-brother talk about something that had nothing to do with Eli.

Tyler said, "I won't presume to play big brother to you unless you're willing to hear it."

Jeremiah lifted an eyebrow to Chet, seconding Tyler's comment.

Chet didn't know where it came from, but he got one of those warm glows in his chest that he mainly felt when it seemed that Mina was watching over him, doing anything for him.

He'd hoped that he might have two brothers who'd do the same for him, except…

Well, this was different. They were family, not a partner.

"What do you have to say, Ty?"

Just like the Group leader he'd been for years before he quit, the oldest Barron dove straight in. "The way I see it, we were all given a mighty dose of bad medicine to swallow these past several months. I was ready to tear Eli apart with my bare hands for what he'd done. As for Jeremiah…I guess you could say he got a little lost, himself."

"Hey," Jeremiah said, with a smile. "I got found."

"And that's my point," Tyler said. "We had certain someones come into our lives at exactly the right time, just like answers to prayers. I don't know how I would've managed without Zoe."

"Ditto here, but with Ally, of course," Jeremiah said. "And I think I know where Ty is going with this. There were times when we both almost ruined what Zoe and Ally brought to the table for us when we needed it the most."

"But they're strong women," Tyler said, "and they took our guff. Each one of them is capable of that, Chet."

"Including Mina." Jeremiah had that eyebrow cocked again as he measured his younger brother.

Chet kept holding that letter. Damn it, he still loved her. He always would.

Would they know how to dig him out of this hole?

Chet pushed up the brim of his hat. "If I knew how to fix what I've done to Mina, I'd have made things right with her already. But what we have is more than just a simple misunderstanding."

"What's the problem then?" Tyler asked.

"She's pregnant. That's not a problem, though."

Both men had skipped right over that last part, dwelling on the baby news.

"Congratulations," Tyler and Jeremiah said at the same time, lighting up, and it seemed as if they were about to come forward to shake Chet's hand.

But then Chet told them the rest: how Mina had apparently seriously considered the consequences of being with someone like him—just as undependable as the last man who'd broken her heart. How she thought he might feel about his own illegitimate child, what with being one himself.

"I don't even know where it all started going downhill," Chet finished. "Where we began to argue and say the wrong things to each other."

Jeremiah had come to stand with his hands planted on his hips. "Did you tell her you'd never have her raise a child alone?"

"Of course." Chet crumpled the letter a little in his hand. "I told her that I'd always take care of the baby, but I was so taken aback by what we said to each other that I didn't say I'd take care of *her*. And I want to do that. I can't imagine a future without her."

"Damn," Tyler said. "I never realized it before, but for a mellow man, you're really bullheaded, Chet."

"I don't want to be."

Jeremiah said, "Listen, I made my mistakes with Ally, too, and I would've ended up crawling back to her on my hands and knees if I'd needed to. Luckily, it didn't come to that."

"You've got to stop thinking about everything bad that might happen," Tyler said, getting back into leadership mode, "and think about what good might come out of it instead."

Chet just stared at his oldest brother. When the scandal had broken, Tyler would've been the last person on earth to be talking in optimistic terms.

Taking a chance with Zoe had changed him though, just as Ally had done for Jeremiah.

The only difference between Chet and them was that they'd been strong enough to take a risk, to put their hearts on the line.

And he wanted to be like his brothers, a Barron through and through. But, even more importantly, he wanted Mina.

Chet appealed to them. "You two won Zoe and Ally back...."

They seemed to understand that he was looking for ideas on how he could do it, too.

Jeremiah leaned against the stable wall as he said, "For starters, if you want to make an impression, we know where Mina's definitely going to be tonight."

Chet fisted her resignation paper in his hand, taking it from there.

When Mina walked into the steak house where she was to meet some of her ex-coworkers for dinner, she had the feeling something was up.

She moved past the moose heads over the main fireplace, stone walls and antler light fixtures, finding about ten friends seated at a long family-style table in a back room.

"Mina!" they shouted.

Danny patted her on the back as Corrine pulled out a chair at the head of the table for Mina to sit.

So many people here. Gratefulness bunched in her chest as she realized that they cared about her quitting the Group. But it pained her all the more, knowing that, evidently, Chet didn't give a fig. He hadn't called or anything.

And the longer *she* waited to do so, the harder it got.

"I'm sorry we didn't have the chance to work together longer," Danny said to her. "But I see big things in store for you in the future, Mina Ferguson."

"Thanks."

"Are you at least coming to the opening of the resort?"

"I'm afraid not."

Her stomach knotted. She'd nursed that project just as much as Chet had done, but she wouldn't be able to see it come to maturity. Yet she still had her real baby, though she wasn't sure if his or her dad would even be at *that* birth.

As she tried to still her falling heart, Danny took a seat nearby while the others—mainly assistants she'd come up through the ranks with—aimed questions her way about why she was leaving.

She gave all the right answers, about searching out bigger opportunities, etc., while big family-style sharing plates were set down on the table and the group dug in. They'd already ordered, and she smiled, thinking that everyone in the Barron Group was just as efficient as she was.

That they would be very much okay without her.

She peered out a nearby window at the early evening sky, plus the autumn-tinged trees…and the view of the tall, stately Barron Group offices in the near distance.

Far enough away so that she already felt as if she'd left them behind.

But had she?

She nibbled at a bread stick, looking around the table, realizing how much of her identity was tied up with the Group. It'd been a home to her, a challenging place to go where she could excel and feel proud of her accomplishments.

She'd been a people pleaser, but, damn it, she'd pleased herself an awful lot, too. And that had to be worth something.

When everyone at the table suddenly shifted their focus behind her, toward the entrance of the restaurant, then waved in surprised greeting, a shiver played down Mina's spine.

A wonderful shiver.

"Chet!" a few of them said.

She froze in her seat, hardly believing she was hearing his name.

His name, which flowed through her like warmed honey.

"Mina," said Chet's voice, and she didn't dare look back at him for fear of losing her composure in front of all these people she'd once worked with, once tried to fool by acting as if she wasn't head over heels in love with the boss.

No, she would explode into tears in front of everyone if she looked.

Now she could feel Chet standing behind her chair. There was heat on her neck, and it was slipping lower, sending her into a pool of longing.

Danny had stood, pulling out a chair. "Take a seat, sir."

"Thanks," Chet said. "But, all the same, I'd like to stay where I am for a minute."

Now everyone seemed to be watching Mina, probably wondering why she was blushing so furiously and why she wouldn't look at her former boss.

She slowly glanced up at him, and if she thought she'd been heated before, the crash of flame that hit her now just about knocked her out of her seat.

He was as handsome as ever, strong, stalwart while wearing his hat, plus a casual Western shirt and new jeans. He was carrying a tote bag that was weighed down by something, but he didn't show anyone what it was.

This was the Chet no one in the office really knew. This was *her* Chet, any way he dressed, because she knew him inside and out.

"Hi," she said softly, testing him, hoping to God he wouldn't just walk away from her again.

As he looked down at her, the background music was the only sound, save for the other diners and the clink of silverware against plates.

He doffed his hat, and she saw that his eyes were blue like an early Texas spring sky that was just on the edge of renewal.

When he spoke, he kept that gaze on her, even though he was talking to the rest of the group.

"Sorry for the interruption," he said, "but I wanted to take the opportunity to try and talk Mina into staying."

Everyone applauded at that, and each clap was like a chop to Mina.

Really, that was the reason he'd come here?

Because he'd lost his assistant and he wanted her back?

That couldn't be. Not after she'd seen what she'd seen in his eyes just now.

He held up his hand. "Everyone knows that I'm never going to find someone like Mina. Not anywhere."

His words carried a double meaning—business and personal—and suddenly his first words did, too.

I wanted to take the opportunity to try and talk Mina into staying.

With him?

He came to the side of her chair, so close that her hands began to quiver. She folded her arms over her tummy without really knowing she'd done it.

"I wish to God you would come back," he said to her, so low that his voice combed over her, owning her.

It was as if he'd forgotten what they'd said to each other last night, what had made them both angry in the first place.

And they couldn't ignore that.

She turned to him. "You think this is going to do it? Bring me back?"

"I'm hoping it's a start."

She realized that the whole table was getting uncomfortable. This had gone beyond a conversation about Chet wanting her to return to the Group, and they could obviously sense it.

But he didn't back off.

He wasn't running away this time or making up excuses to hide how they felt about each other.

"Imagine me," he said so everyone else could hear, "on my first day, walking into the Group's offices. I'd seen the place when I was a little boy, and it was hellishly imposing even then. But as a new co-vice president?" He shook his head. "It made me want to go back to Montana and never look back. But Mina took care of me. She ran my schedules, made sure I looked good every step of the way. I knew that she was going to go far in the Group, and she did. But, even as she was moving up that corporate ladder, there was a hitch."

The love he'd confessed for her last night was even clearer in his gaze now.

My Lord, she thought. He was about to come clean after stubbornly using and reusing that line about how much he didn't want to sully her reputation at the Group.

He was laying it *all* out there.

"I finally saw what was in front of me all along and fell in love with this woman," Chet said.

Everyone was silent, wide-eyed. Mina was the worst of them all as her breathing quickened, her gaze going hazy.

He loved her, even after everything.

Danny was the first one to rise from his chair, followed by Corrine.

"Er," he said. "I've got to…"

He pointed toward the restrooms. One by one, the rest of them followed, leaving their food for later.

Chet remained, though edgy, as if wary of how she was going to react.

"Why did you say all that in front of them?" she asked.

"They're going to know anyway that we were together, and I wanted to make it as clear as day that I won't tolerate any gossip about you…or us…or how you earned your way through the Group." He took her hand in his. "I wanted everyone to know how much I treasure you, Mina—not just as my assistant, but…"

He held her hand over his heart.

"But as the woman I want to be with forever and always."

Last night, Mina had told him that, too, and suddenly she didn't care that they were in a back room in a public place where anyone could walk in on them.

She was only a woman who wanted to go forward with the man she loved.

Mina's eyes had a glassy look that told Chet she was about to cry. And when he reached into the bag he was carrying, showing her what was in it, the tears came.

"Here," he said, giving her a thick pastel book that he'd purchased.

A how-to baby book.

She hugged it to her chest, lowering her head. Chet wanted to touch her, just a brush of his fingertips over her cheek. Just a skim over the beautiful auburn hair that gleamed in the lights.

But they weren't quite to that point yet.

"I want to be the best dad I can be," he said, his voice thick. "When I said I'll always be there for the baby, I meant it. It's just that I left out the most important part besides that."

"What?"

He took a chance, laid his hand on top of hers as she kept hugging that book.

"That I want to be there for you, too."

A tear wiggled down her cheek, and she reached up to whisk it away.

"I just wonder though," he said, "if you can bear with me while I learn to trust again. While I get the rest of my life together and leave all my baggage behind."

She nodded, but obviously couldn't say much more.
"Mina?"

"Sorry," she said with a croak. "I just get so emotional lately. I'm sure that's why I overreacted when I told you about the baby."

"You expected me to put my issues behind me. You weren't asking too much, even though it felt like it at the time."

He heard the words coming from him and marveled that he was able to say them.

But Mina had shown him how. Only Mina.

"I was wrong to expect that of you," she said. "I thought you were going to bolt right out the door, but I came to realize that I've got to trust you, too."

"You know I'm never going to hurt you again, right?"

She finally met his gaze, as if she knew that he was talking about her previous heartbreaks, not just the one they'd had together last night.

As if she already was willing to put all of her soul into trusting him.

The power of their visual connection would've sent him to his knees if he hadn't already intended to get down on one of them.

He lowered himself to the carpet, reaching into his back pocket, coming out with a velvet box. A ring he'd bought on the way over here, too.

Now Mina really started to cry.

"Be my wife?" he asked. "Keep on being the best partner I could've ever found?"

She knelt down, too. "Yes, yes, I will."

As a trill sang through him, he rested a hand on her tummy. She'd worn a baggy skirt, although she was still slender and the baby hadn't shown him or herself much at all.

But he still knew his son or daughter was in there.

"And you?" he asked their baby. "How do you feel about this?"

"He or she wants you to just put the ring on me," Mina said, laughing.

It felt so damned good to laugh with her as she slid the diamond-studded band onto her finger. It was a little loose, but it would do for now.

"We'll get it fitted," he said.

"It already fits just fine."

They embraced, kissed, as if finding each other again after too long of a separation.

Then, suddenly, Mina sucked in a breath, drawing way from him.

"Oh," she said, her hands flying to her belly.

"Are you okay?" His heart was palpitating like mad.

"Yes, it's…" She brought one of his hands to her tummy. "This is the first time I've felt anything. Can you feel the baby?"

He thought he did—a little thump that brought the idea of having a child with her to full life.

Overwhelmed, he kissed her again, and Mina leaned her forehead against his.

"We're going to have a little person," she said.

"Yeah."

"Did you know that, right now, this little person probably has hair on his or her head and might even be able to hear us?"

"Really?"

"*Really.*"

Chet guided Mina back to a stand while he remained kneeling. He cupped her hips, pressing his lips to her tummy.

"Your mommy just made me the happiest man alive," he murmured against her, hoping the baby really could hear. "And you've only made me happier."

Mina rested her hands on Chet's head, all of them finally connected, father, mother and child.

Epilogue

"**S**o when's it your turn, Ty?" Chet asked his brother as the family gathered in the grand living room in the Florence Ranch mansion months later.

Tyler looked down at Chet, who was sitting on a love seat next to Mina, holding his newborn son, Colin. Tufts of reddish hair were already peeking out from under his blue baby cap.

Tyler only grinned in answer to Chet's question while tickling Colin's cheek.

Mina laughed. "Evasive, Ty?"

She didn't look as if she'd been pregnant just a couple of weeks ago, but she did seem like a newlywed, three months married in a ceremony that the family had held here on the ranch, just like the rest of the Barrons.

Zoe wandered over from where Ally was holding court with Caroline. Mina's mom was holding the rosy-cheeked infant, and little Lizzie, who'd begged to come with her grandparents for the weekend to the ranch, was fussing with the red bow in the baby's hair. The Barrons had invited the Fergusons over, just like they did at least once a month these days.

While glancing up at Tyler, Zoe pulled on his shirt-sleeve. She had a playful look on her face.

By the time Ty got around to talking, Chet had already guessed the news.

"We *are* pregnant," his brother said.

From the other side of the room, Jeremiah gave one of his victory whoops, and everyone congratulated Tyler and Zoe at once.

But no one seemed more excited than Eli, who got out of his wingback chair and enveloped Tyler, then Zoe, in a hug.

Chet watched his father, smiling. Eli was about four months sober now. He attended his AA meetings while his sons attended their Al-Anon gatherings on a regular basis.

It was all working out for the Barrons now, but who would've guessed it all those months ago?

"How far are you along?" Mina asked Zoe.

"Three months. We want to wait until the birth to see what the sex will be, though. It'll be a nice surprise."

Chet slipped his hand into Mina's. That hadn't been the route they'd traveled. Soon after he'd proposed to her, they'd gone to their first doctor's appointment together, and they'd found out Colin's disposition. Chet had gone a little nuts afterward, shopping for baby boy stuff until Mina had told him that he was likely to fill a semitruck before he got through.

He'd even had a hand in putting the final touches on the day care center at the resort, and during its grand opening, Mina had been there, proud as could be as they'd looked upon what they'd created as partners.

And they were that in the truest sense of the word. She'd come back to the Group, opening the resort with Chet, staying on right up until she'd been ready to give birth. Now she was taking time off to be with Colin.

Actually, Chet had cut back on work, too, finding that there was no need for all the business trips he'd been engaged in. Not when he had so much to come home to every night.

Near a silver beverage service that had been brought in for their gathering, Eli used a ladle to transfer some of Lizzie's Woodland Punch to plastic party glasses. The little girl put herself in charge of giving everyone the drink for a toast to Ty and Zoe's pregnancy.

As Eli held his punch aloft, he led the salutation. "Here's to my sons," he said, his voice scratchy. "Miracles, every one of them. And here's to my new daughters, too."

"Here, here," said Mina's dad, clinking cups with his wife, then kissing her on a blushing cheek.

"And," Eli added, bending down to Lizzie, "here's to the traveling band we'll soon have if my sons and daughters keep going at the rate they are."

Lizzie probably didn't know what a traveling band was, but she joyfully clinked with Eli, anyway. It was obvious the old man adored her, especially in the ladybug-decorated early spring dress she'd chosen for today.

As everyone started throwing around possible names for a traveling band, Chet noticed that Colin had gotten heavy-lidded, so he rose from the love seat, pressing a kiss to Mina's forehead.

"I'm going to walk him around a little, get him to sleep."

"You do that, Daddy."

She smiled at him with such love that he could barely contain himself. But Colin was such a sound sleeper that Chet would be able to spend a lot of quality time tonight with his wife.

And many nights afterward.

Chet walked his son through the halls, past the ballroom and the windows with their flowery views of spring.

Finally, he came to the lounge.

To the new portrait that hung over the mantel.

The Barrons had commissioned an artist to recreate the original painting, with Eli, Aunt Florence, Tyler and Jeremiah posing so stoically in it.

But there'd been some additions.

Now the portrait held more Barrons, including Abe, Chet's mom…

…and Chet.

He didn't feel like a ghost anymore, and he knew that, in time, he was going to have a picture of his own family in a place of honor in his home. Colin would see himself in it, along with any future brothers and sisters, and he would know that he had always been accounted for.

Always wanted.

He heard footsteps behind him and turned to see Mina entering the room. She came to him, slid her arms around his waist, rested her chin against his arm so she could look down on the baby, who was slumbering away.

They could've made for a beautiful portrait right

now—a family who'd made it through bad times to get to the good.

A family united forever and always.

* * * * *

HIS TEXAS WILDFLOWER

BY
STELLA BAGWELL

First published in Great Britain 2012
by Mills & Boon, an imprint of Harlequin (UK) Limited,
Eton House, 18-24 Paradise Road, Richmond, Surrey TW9 1SR

© Stella Bagwell 2011

ISBN: 978 0 263 89402 8

23-0112

Harlequin (UK) policy is to use papers that are natural, renewable and
recyclable products and made from wood grown in sustainable forests. The
logging and manufacturing processes conform to the legal environmental
regulations of the country of origin.

Printed and bound in Spain
by Blackprint CPI, Barcelona

Dear Reader,

Have you ever believed that you knew someone and then they did something so out of character that you realize you never really knew that person at all? Well, that's the way my heroine feels when she discovers her family has been keeping secrets from her—secrets that shake the very foundation of who she is and where she wants to go in life.

The family connection is what makes writing novels such a fun task for me. Whether we like it or not, the people who surround us as we grow up ultimately influence the person we become. Some families are tightly woven with threads incapable of being broken, while others are only connected by fragile cobwebs that break at the slightest pressure.

In *His Texas Wildflower*, Jake Rollins comes from the latter and Rebecca Hardaway is only beginning to learn that her family was never what she thought it to be. Neither of them believes they have what it takes to make a family of their own. But true love has a way of bonding two people together in the strongest and sweetest way!

Please join me on a return trip to Lincoln County, New Mexico, where the men are as rugged as the mountains and love is cast in the desert sunsets.

Happy trails and God Bless!

Stella Bagwell

Stella Bagwell has written more than seventy novels. She credits her loyal readers and hopes her stories have brightened their lives in some small way.

A cowgirl through and through, she loves to watch old Westerns, and has recently learned how to rope a steer. Her days begin and end helping her husband care for a beloved herd of horses on their little ranch located on the south Texas coast. When she's not ropin' and ridin', you'll find her at her desk, creating her next tale of love.

The couple have a son, who is a high school maths teacher and athletic coach. Stella loves to hear from readers and invites them to contact her at stellabagwell@gmail.com.

> To my husband, Harrell, for all those times he's taken me to the mall, when he'd rather have been on his horse. I love you.

Chapter One

Rebecca Hardaway swayed slightly on her fragile high heels and for one horrifying moment she feared she was going to topple forward and straight across the silver-and-white casket suspended over the open grave.

Dear God, give me strength, she prayed as she struggled to brace her trembling legs and stop the whirling in her head. She had to be strong. If not for herself, then out of an odd respect for the person who was about to be lowered into the earth.

Up until five days ago, Rebecca hadn't even suspected she had an aunt much less known Gertrude O'Dell existed. If Gertrude herself hadn't left strict instructions with a lawyer to notify Rebecca of her demise, she doubted she'd ever have known.

When the law offices of Barnes, Bentley and Barnes had called Bordeaux's, the department store in Houston where Rebecca worked as a fashion buyer, she'd thought a coworker had been pulling a joke on her. Her mother didn't have a twin sister in New Mexico! Surely there'd been some sort of mix-up.

But shockingly, there had been no mix-up and now questions continued to tear at Rebecca. How could such a secret have been kept for so long? Why had her mother, Gwyn, done such a thing? Her father had died eighteen years ago. Had he known about Gertrude? Or had Gwyn kept her twin sister a secret from everyone?

You don't understand, Rebecca. Gertrude and I were never close. Even though we were sisters, we were very different people. She had her own life and I had mine. We chose to go our separate ways.

Her mother's lame response to Rebecca's grilling hadn't answered anything. In fact, Gwyn was still evading her daughter's questions. And each day that passed without answers filled Rebecca with more and more resentment and puzzlement. She'd thought herself alone in the world except for her mother and now she realized she'd been cheated out of the chance of knowing her aunt!

And now it was too late. Too late.

At the head of the casket, a minister finished reading the 23rd Psalm, then added a short, comforting prayer. As Rebecca whispered "Amen," she felt a strong hand cup her right elbow.

Lifting her head, she looked straight into a pair of gold-brown eyes framed by thick black lashes. The face was partially shaded by the brim of a gray cowboy hat, but she recognized the man as one of the eight people who'd seen fit to attend her aunt's simple graveside services.

"I thought you might need a little support," he said

softly. "The day is hot and grief has a way of draining a person."

Grief. Oh, yes, she was feeling all kinds of grief. She'd lost more than an aunt. She'd lost the whole foundation of her family. And her mother was still evading the truth. But this man had no way of knowing that.

"Thank you," she murmured.

A few steps away, the minister concluded the services, then offered Rebecca a few consoling words before he walked away. Beside her, the young cowboy continued to hold her elbow. He was dressed in a starched white shirt and blue jeans, the creases razor-sharp, the fabric carrying the faint scent of grass, sunshine and masculine muskiness. His hand was warm, the fingers wrapped against her skin, incredibly tough.

Who was this man, she wondered, and what connection did he have to Gertrude O'Dell?

"They'll be lowering the casket in a few moments," he said in a low husky voice. "Would you like one of the roses for a keepsake?"

Grateful for his thoughtfulness, she glanced at the lone spray of flowers lying upon the casket, then at him. "Yes. I would like that."

He dropped his hold on her arm and moved forward to pluck one of the long-stemmed roses from the ribbon binding. As he handed the flower to Rebecca, her throat thickened and tears rushed to her eyes.

Up until this moment, she'd not shed a tear or given way to the emotions washing over her like stormy waves. But something about this man's kindness had pricked the fragile barrier she'd tried to erect between her and the awful finality of her aunt's funeral.

"Thank you," she told him, then lifted her watery gaze from the rosebud to his face. His dark features were masculine and very striking, making the soft light in his eyes even more of a contrast. "I'm Rebecca Hardaway, Gertrude's niece. Did you know my aunt well, Mr.—" She paused as a slight blush heated her cheeks. "Uh, I'm sorry. I have to confess that I don't know any of her friends."

Once again his hand came around her elbow and with gentle urging, he moved her away from the casket and over to the limp shade of a lone mesquite tree. "My name is Jake Rollins," he told her. "And I'm sorry to say I didn't know your aunt personally. I only saw her from time to time as I drove by her place. I came to the funeral today—well, because I thought she might like having someone say goodbye to her."

"Oh."

The tears in her eyes spilled onto her cheeks and she wiped helplessly at them with the pads of her fingertips. He pulled a white handkerchief from his back pocket and offered it to her.

She thanked him, then used the soft cotton to dab at the tracks of moisture on her cheeks. While she tried to gather herself together, she was keenly aware of his broad frame, the way his brown eyes were studying her. There had to be a lot of compassion in this man, she thought, for him to attend the funeral of a person he'd not really known.

He began to speak. "My friends, the Cantrells—the people I'm here with—own a ranch just west of your aunt's place. It's called Apache Wells. Maybe Gertie mentioned it to you?"

She shook her head. She didn't know how to explain to this man that she'd never spoken to Gertrude O'Dell. Never met her. It was all so unbelievable, yet terribly true. "I'm afraid not. But I do thank you and your friends for coming today. I—well, if it weren't for you and your friends, there would have been only a handful of people here to see her laid to rest."

Faint cynicism quirked his lips. "People nowadays tell themselves they don't have time to go to funerals. If I were you, I wouldn't worry myself over the lack of mourners."

Interest suddenly sparked in her misty blue eyes. "You called my aunt Gertie," she asked. "Is that how people around here knew her?"

Jake tried not to appear stunned as he studied the beautiful woman standing before him. This couldn't be Crazy Gertie's niece, he thought. The old woman had been a recluse who'd always been dressed in old clothing and was known for firing a shotgun at anyone she didn't deem welcome on her land. Rebecca Hardaway was the complete opposite. She looked exactly like one of those women whose photographs filled a fashion magazine.

She was wearing a black dress that hugged her slender hips and draped demurely across her breasts. Her high heels were just that—high. With little straps that fastened around her shapely ankles. A black straw hat with a wide brim and a band swathed with white chiffon covered her pale blond hair and framed a set of pale, delicate features. Her lips were red and so were her short fingernails. And even with her blue eyes filled with tears, all Jake could think was that she was one classy chick.

"Well, I'm not exactly sure about that," he said. "We—Abe, old Mr. Cantrell that is—always called her Gertie. I imagine that's what her friends called her, too."

Everyone around here had assumed Gertie had no family. Down through the years no one had witnessed any outsiders visiting. In fact, Jake figured he'd fudged when he'd pluralized the word *friend*. The only person who'd had much contact with the woman at all was Bess, an older lady who worked in a small grocery store in Alto. A moment ago Jake had seen her climb into her car and drive away from the cemetery. If Rebecca wanted information about Gertie, then Bess would be her best source.

"I see," she murmured.

At that moment, she glanced over her shoulder just in time to see the coffin being lowered into the ground. Sensing the sight was cutting into her, Jake moved the two of them a few more steps away from the grave site and did his best to distract her. "Did you make the trip here by yourself?" he asked.

"Yes. I live in Houston and—there was no one available to make the trip with me."

No family, husband, boyfriend? Even though Jake had already glanced at her left hand in search of a wedding ring, he found himself looking again at the empty finger. It was hard to believe a beautiful woman like her wasn't attached. And if she was, what kind of man would have allowed her to travel all this way to attend such an emotional ceremony by herself?

"That's too bad," he said. "You shouldn't be alone at a time like this."

She drew back her shoulders as though to prove more to herself than him that she wasn't about to break down. "Sometimes a person has no other choice but to be alone, Mr. Rollins."

His lips twisted to a wry slant. Women had called him plenty of things down through the years, but never Mr. Rollins. "I'm just Jake to you, ma'am." He tilted his head in the direction of the Cantrell family, then suggested, "Let me introduce you to my friends."

"I'd like that," she murmured.

For May in Lincoln County, New Mexico, the sun was hot in the cloudless sky. Every now and then a faint breeze rustled the grass in the meadow next to the lonely little cemetery and carried the scent of Rebecca Hardaway straight to Jake's nostrils. She smelled like crushed wildflowers after a rainstorm. Sweet and fresh and tempting.

Forget it, Jake. She's not your kind of woman. So just rein in that roaming eye of yours.

By now Abe, Quint and Maura had gathered near the wrought-iron gate that framed the exit to the cemetery. As Jake and Rebecca Hardaway approached the group, Maura, a pretty young woman with dark red hair, was the first to greet them. Quint, a tall handsome guy who was the same age as Jake, followed close behind his wife. Next to him, Abe moved to join the group. The elderly man was somewhat shorter than his grandson and rail-thin. His thick hair was white as snow and matched the drooping walrus mustache that covered his top lip. Abe was a legendary cattle rancher of the area and Quint was quickly following in his footsteps. Both men were like family to Jake.

Quickly, he made introductions all around and had barely gotten the last one out of his mouth before Maura reached for Rebecca's hand.

"You must be awfully weary, Ms. Hardaway," she said gently. "We'd love for you to join us at Apache Wells for refreshments. That is, if you don't have other plans."

Gertie's niece glanced at Jake as though she wanted his opinion about the invitation. The idea took him by surprise. A fancy woman like her had never asked him for the time of day. But then he had to remember that Rebecca Hardaway was obviously under a heavy weight of grief and probably not herself.

"Well, I don't know," she said hesitantly. "I wouldn't want to be a bother."

"Nonsense, young lady," Abe spoke up. "We always have the coffeepot on. And everybody's welcome. We'd enjoy having you."

Rebecca smiled at the old man, which was hardly a surprise to Jake. Even though Abe was in his mid-eighties, Quint's grandfather hadn't lost his charm with the ladies. What did surprise him was how the tilt of the woman's lips warmed her, made her appear all too soft and touchable.

"Thank you, sir," she said to Abe. "It would be nice to have a little rest before I drive back to Ruidoso."

"Great," Maura chimed in. "Just leave your car here and ride with us. The roads might be too rough for your rental car. Someone will bring you back to pick it up."

"That's kind of you," Rebecca told her. "Especially since I—well, I'm not sure I'm up to driving at the moment."

Quint suggested it was time to get out of the hot sun and be on their way. Jake didn't waste time helping Rebecca over to the truck and into the front passenger seat.

She gave him demure thanks, but no smile and as Jake climbed into the back bench seat next to Abe, he wondered what the old man had that he didn't.

Hell, Jake. If you want a woman to smile at you all you have to do is drive down to Ruidoso and saunter into the Blue Mesa for a cup of coffee or the Starting Gate for a cold beer. There were plenty of women around those hangouts who would be more than happy to smile at you.

Yeah, Jake mentally retorted to the cynical voice in his head. He knew plenty of women who were willing to give him whatever he wanted, whenever he wanted. But none of them were like Rebecca Hardaway. And if any of them were like her, he'd steer clear. He was a simple man with simple taste, he told himself. If a man understood his limitations, he was more likely to avoid trouble.

And yet as Quint guided the club cab truck over the dusty road, Jake's gaze continued to drift to the back of Rebecca Hardaway's head. Once she'd gotten settled in the leather seat, she'd removed her hat and now as she turned her head slightly to the left to acknowledge something that Quint was saying, he could see a drape of fine blond hair near her eyebrow and wispy curls tousled upon her shoulder. The strands were subtly shaded and obviously natural.

There was nothing fake about Rebecca Hardaway, he thought. At least, not on the outside. As for the inside, he'd have to guess at that. Because there was no way in hell she'd ever give a working man like him a glimpse.

Abe's cattle ranch, Apache Wells, consisted of more than a hundred thousand acres and had been in existence long before either Jake or Quint had been born. The property was only one of many the old man owned and though he was rich, Abe lived in a modest log house nestled at the edge of a piney foothill.

Once inside the cool interior, Maura and Quint quickly excused themselves to the kitchen to prepare refreshments. While Rebecca took a seat on a long couch, Abe settled himself in a worn leather recliner and Jake stood to one side trying to decide if he should escape to the kitchen with his friends or take advantage of these few minutes with the Texas wildflower.

"Don't just stand there, Jake. Sit down," Abe practically barked at him. "You're makin' me tired just lookin' at you."

Stifling a sigh, Jake pulled off his hat and carried it over to the opposite end of the couch from where Rebecca was sitting.

As he sank onto the cushion, and placed his hat on the floor near his boots, he said, "Sorry, Abe. I was thinking I should go help Maura and Quint. But I guess they can manage without me."

"Sure they can," Abe replied. "Besides, I need you to help me entertain Ms. Hardaway."

Since when did Abe need help entertaining a woman? Jake thought wryly, but he kept the comment to himself.

"Oh, please. You don't have to make conversation for my sake," Rebecca spoke up. "Just sitting here in the cool is nice and restful."

She'd leaned her head against the back of the couch and crossed her legs. From the corner of his eye, Jake let his gaze wander down the length of shapely calf and on to the delicate ankle. Like the black leather strap of her high heel, he could easily imagine his thumb and forefinger wrapped around her smooth ankle and tugging her toward him.

Jake's thoughts were turning downright indecent when Abe spoke up and interrupted them.

"I'm right sorry about Gertie, Ms. Hardaway. She wasn't an easy person to know, you understand. She liked her privacy and I respected that. As neighbors we got along. 'Cause we didn't bother each other—just exchanged a few words from time to time." He wiped a thumb and forefinger down his long white mustache. "She was way too young to leave this world."

"Yes. She was only fifty-six. But she…suffered from some sort of heart condition." At least, that was what Gertrude's lawyer had explained to Rebecca about the cause of her death.

"That's too bad," Abe replied. "Could be that's why she didn't socialize. Guess she didn't feel like it."

Rebecca's gaze dropped to her lap. Was the old man trying to say in a nice way that Gertrude O'Dell had been a recluse? If so, he was probably also wondering why Rebecca or other relatives hadn't been around to visit or check on the woman. Oh, God, the whole situation was so awful. She didn't want to explain to these people that for some reason her family had been split down the middle. She didn't want them to know that her own mother had refused to attend her sister's funeral. It was embarrassing and demeaning.

"Well, I wouldn't exactly say that, Abe," Jake countered. "Gertie visited some with Bess."

Rebecca looked at the cowboy named Jake. Without his hat, she could see his hair was thick and lay in unruly waves about his head and against the back of his neck. It was the color of dark chocolate and even though the lighting in the room was dim, the strands gleamed like a polished gem. As her gaze encompassed his broad shoulders and long, sinewy legs, she decided he was a man of strength. No doubt he worked out of doors. With his hands and all those muscles.

She swallowed uncomfortably, then asked, "Who is Bess?"

"Gertie's friend," he answered. "She was the older woman at the funeral. She left the cemetery before we had a chance to introduce you. I guess she must have been in a hurry for some reason."

"Oh. Yes." Rebecca vaguely remembered an older, heavyset woman dressed in a simple print dress standing on the opposite side of Gertrude's coffin. "I would have liked to have met her. And thank her for coming to the services."

"I'm sure Jake can make that happen for you," Abe said. "He knows where everybody works and lives. He gets around."

Rebecca didn't find that hard to believe. Even though she didn't know him, Jake Rollins looked like a man who would never have a problem socializing. At least, with the female population.

He had that rangy, rascally look. The sort that tugged at a woman's dreams, that made her want to learn how it felt to be just a little naughty, a bit wild and reckless.

Had Gertrude ever had those womanly feelings? Rebecca wondered. Had her aunt ever looked at a man like Jake and wondered what it would be like to make love to him? To have him make love to her?

From all appearances, Gertrude had died a spinster. And at the rate Rebecca was going, the same was going to happen to her. Men were drawn to her, but they didn't stick around for long. Once a guy learned she enjoyed her demanding career, he chose to move on and find a woman who could devote her time solely to him.

Rebecca was doing her best to push those thoughts away when Quint and Maura entered the room with a tray of refreshments. And thankfully for the next half hour, the conversation moved away from Gertrude O'Dell's untimely departure, and on to the daily happenings of these people who had chosen to show her a bit of hospitality and kindness.

While Rebecca sipped iced tea and nibbled on a sugar cookie, she learned that Maura and Quint had been married for nearly two and a half years and had two young sons, the latter of which had been born only a few months ago. Abe was a widower and had been for nearly twenty years. As for Jake, she could only assume he was a single man. During the conversation he didn't mention family of any sort and there definitely wasn't a ring on his finger. At the cemetery when he'd handed her his handkerchief, she'd noticed that much about him. But it wasn't the lack of a wedding band, or the mention of family, that told Rebecca he was a bachelor. He had that independent look. Like a mustang who knew how to avoid the snares and traps made by human hands. Even though she was a city girl, she could see that about him.

But in spite of the prickly awareness she had of Jake Rollins, Rebecca decided she could've sat in Abe's house for hours, letting the easy conversation take her mind away from all the hurt and betrayal she'd been feeling since she'd learned of Gertrude's existence. But the day was getting late and she needed to do so many things before she returned to Houston.

After placing her empty glass on a tray situated on the coffee table, she rose to her feet. "Thank you so much for the refreshments and for inviting me to your home," she told Abe, then included the others in a hasty glance. "You've all been so kind, but I really need to stop by my aunt's place before dark. If someone could drive me to the cemetery to pick up my car, I'd be ever so grateful."

Quint looked questioningly at Maura and then Maura smiled suggestively at Jake. "Jake, I know you'd be more than happy to drive our guest to pick up her car. Wouldn't you?"

"That's a fool question," Abe shot at Maura. "Jake would give up his eyeteeth to drive Ms. Hardaway to wherever she wants to go. And if I were twenty years younger I wouldn't give him the chance." Winking at Rebecca, he pushed himself out of the chair and fished out a wad of keys from the front pocket of his jeans. Tossing them to Jake, he said, "Here, son. Take my truck. That way you won't have to hurry back with Quint's."

With a bit of dismay, Rebecca watched Jake rise to his feet. She'd expected Quint or Maura to be the one to drive her. Not the brown-eyed cowboy with the charming dimple in his cheek.

"Thanks," Jake told him. "And don't worry. I'll take care of your truck."

"Dammit, I'm not worried about you taking care of my truck. Just make sure you take good care of Ms. Hardaway."

Abe walked over and with a gnarled hand patted Rebecca's shoulder. For a moment the old man's gesture of affection stung her eyes with emotional tears. It had been years since she'd had her father in her life and with both sets of grandparents passing on before she'd been born, she'd never had a grandfather. Abe made her realize what she'd been missing and how much she needed a wise, steadying hand right now.

Jake cast Abe a wry grin. "Don't worry about that, either. I know how to be a gentleman."

Behind them, Quint chuckled and Rebecca didn't miss the dark look that Jake shot back at him. Obviously the two men were such good friends they communicated without words, she thought. And from what she could read from the conversation, Quint viewed her as a lamb about to be thrown to a wolf.

That was a silly thought, Rebecca told herself. She was twenty-eight years old and had been around all sorts of men. She hardly needed to worry about one New Mexican cowboy.

But moments later, as he wrapped a hand at the side of her waist and helped her into Abe's truck, her heart hammered as though she'd never been touched by a man.

"I noticed that Mr. Cantrell called you 'son.' And you and his grandson appear to be very close," she remarked as he climbed beneath the wheel and started the engine. "Is Mr. Cantrell your father? I mean, I know you have different surnames, but—well, sometimes that doesn't mean anything."

He thrust the truck into first gear and steered it onto the graveled drive. "No. Quint is just a good friend. Has been since the third grade. And Abe isn't my father. I don't have a father."

"Oh." His last words weren't exactly spoken in a testy nature, but there had been a faint hardness in his voice. She wondered what that could mean, but realized she was in no position to ask. Besides that, Jake Rollins shouldn't be interesting her. Not now anyway. She was here to say goodbye to her aunt and deal with the woman's estate. Certainly not to get involved with a local. "Neither do I," she told him. "Have a father, that is."

He shot her a questioning glance and she explained, "He died when I was ten. He worked for a major oil firm and was involved in an accident while he was in the Middle East. Something happened to cause an explosion on the job site."

"I'm sorry. That must have been tough."

She shrugged. "It's been nearly eighteen years and I still miss him."

He remained silent after that and it was clear to Rebecca that her revelation about her personal life hadn't given him the urge to expound on his. Biting back a sigh, she forced her attention to the passing landscape.

Once they'd moved away from Abe Cantrell's house, the forest of tall pines had opened up to desert hills dotted with smaller piñons and huge clumps of sage. To her extreme right, the sun was quickly setting, bathing the whole area in shades of pink and gold.

During Rebecca's many travels, she'd never been to New Mexico. And before her small commuter plane had landed in Ruidoso, she'd not expected the area to be so open and wild or for it to touch something deep within her.

Was that why Gertrude had come to live in this state? Because she'd thought it beautiful? Or had she simply wanted to put a great distance between herself and her sister. Oh, God, there were so many questions Rebecca wanted, *needed* answered.

"What is that cactus-looking stuff with the pretty blooms on it?" she asked Jake as she forced her thoughts back to the moment. "See? Over there to your left with the pink blossoms."

He nodded. "That's cholla cactus. It blooms in the early spring and summer. You don't have that in Texas?"

"Not in the city of Houston."

His gaze slanted her way. "Guess you don't get out in the country much."

He'd not spoken it as a question but more like a statement of fact. As though he already knew the sort of person she was. The idea that she appeared so one-dimensional to this man bothered her a great deal. Though why it should, she didn't understand at all.

"Not in a while," she replied. "But I've been in the desert before. In Nevada. It didn't look like this."

"No. That state is pretty stark in some areas. But Lincoln County, New Mexico, is just plain pretty," he said with obvious bias.

Even though the cab of the truck was roomy, Rebecca felt as though there were only scant inches between them. His presence seemed to take up a major part of the space and try as she might, she couldn't seem to make her eyes stay away from him for more than a few seconds at a time.

While she went about her daily life in Houston, she was accustomed to seeing businessmen dressed in boots and Stetsons. Yet she had to admit that none of those men looked like Jake Rollins. He was the real deal and she was embarrassed to admit to herself that his raw sexuality mesmerized her.

"Well, here we are at the cemetery already," he announced as he geared down the truck and pulled to a stop in front of her rented sedan.

She avoided looking across the wrought-iron fence to the mound of fresh dirt covering Gertrude's grave. Instead, she smiled at Jake. "Thanks for taxiing me back to my car. It was very kind of you."

His grin was crooked and caused her breath to hang for a moment in her throat.

"And I didn't have to give up my eyeteeth to do it," he teased.

In spite of everything, she chuckled. "Mr. Cantrell is quite a character. I think I could fall in love with him."

He let out a humorous snort. "Most women who meet him do. How he's stayed a widower all these years is a mystery to me."

He climbed out of the truck and Rebecca waited for him to skirt the vehicle and assist her from the cab. Once she was down on the ground and standing next to him, she quickly started to step away, but his hand continued to rest on the side of her waist, causing her to pause and glance up at his dark face. His brown eyes flickered with a light that was so soft and inviting, she couldn't tear her gaze away.

"I guess this is goodbye," he said.

The husky tone of his voice sent shivers over her skin and she could only think how his touch soothed her, thrilled her in a way she would have never expected.

Her heart was suddenly hammering, yearning for some elusive thing she couldn't understand. Unconsciously, she moistened her lips with the tip of her tongue. "I—uh—don't suppose you would like to stop by Gertrude's house with me? I mean, if you're not in any hurry. I need to shut things up before I head back to Ruidoso."

His brows arched faintly, telling Rebecca he was clearly surprised by her invitation. So was she. It wasn't like her to be so impulsive. Especially when it came to men. But during her aunt's graveside services, Jake Rollins had been so kind and caring. And though she couldn't explain it, his presence made her feel not so alone and heartbroken.

"I'd be pleased," he said.

"Fine." She drew in a long breath, then stepped away from him and quickly headed to her car.

Gertrude's house was only two short miles from Pine Valley cemetery. As she drove carefully over the country dirt road, Jake followed at a respectable distance behind her. When she finally parked in front of her aunt's small house, she climbed out of the car and waited for him to pull his vehicle to a stop next to hers.

When he joined her, she said, "I only arrived in Ruidoso last night, so I didn't get a chance to drive out here until this morning. I've still not looked over the whole property. Only the house and its surroundings." She glanced at the house and tried not to sigh with desperation. "I have to admit it wasn't what I expected."

As she walked toward a small gate that would lead them to the front entrance of the house, Jake followed a step behind.

He said, "I take it you've never been out here to your aunt's home before."

There was no censure or disbelief in his voice and that in itself drew out her next words before she had time to think about them.

"You're right, I haven't. And I'm very sorry about that."

"Well, you're here now. That has to stand for something," he said, then with an easy smile, he touched a hand to her back and ushered her up the small steps and onto a concrete porch.

By the time Rebecca reached to open the door, his comment had tugged on her raw emotions. Pausing, she bent her head and swallowed hard at the tears burning her throat. What was the matter with her? She hadn't known Gertrude O'Dell and until an hour or so ago, Jake Rollins had been a stranger. Neither of them should be affecting her like this.

"Rebecca? Is something wrong?"

Lifting her head, she looked at him and her eyes instantly flooded with tears.

"Oh—Jake."

The words came out on a broken sob and before she could stop herself her head fell against his chest, her hands snatched holds on his shoulders.

She felt his strong arms come around her and then his graveled voice was whispering next to her ear.

"Don't cry, Becca. Your aunt wouldn't want that. And neither do I."

Chapter Two

The comfort of his arms felt so good. Too good, she thought, as she sniffed back her tears and pushed herself away from him. She didn't know how long she'd allowed her cheek to rest against his broad chest, or his hand to stroke the back of her head. For a while she'd seemed to lose all sense of control over herself.

"I'm so sorry, Jake," she mumbled in an embarrassed rush. "I didn't mean to fall apart on you like that. I— The day has been long and everything just seemed to hit me all at once. And now I've gotten mascara on your nice, white shirt."

She darted a glance at his face and saw that his brown eyes were studying her with concern. Amusement, disgust, surprise. Anything would have been easier to deal with than his compassion. She struggled to keep her tears from returning.

"Forget that," he murmured. "Are you okay?"

While she'd been in his arms, while her cheek had rested against him, he'd called her Becca, she thought. No one had ever called her that and she wondered why it had sounded so endearing and natural coming from him.

Drawing in a deep breath, she nodded and turned to open the door. "Yes. I'm fine now. Please come in and I'll show you around," she invited.

They stepped into a small living room crammed full of old furniture, stacks of magazines and newspapers, and shelves of dusty trinkets. The windows were open, but outside awnings shaded the sunlight and left the cluttered interior dark and gloomy.

As Rebecca switched on a table lamp, Jake said, "I suppose I was eight years old the first time I ever visited Apache Wells with Quint. As best as I can remember your aunt was living here then. It's going to feel strange to drive by and know that she's not here anymore."

With one hand Rebecca gestured around the room. "It's clear that my aunt lived modestly. I suppose she wanted it that way."

"Maybe she couldn't afford anything else," he suggested.

"My aunt wasn't exactly a pauper," Rebecca revealed. "She had a nice nest egg in her savings account."

"Guess she was saving it for something more important."

More important? The money, the property, everything had been left to Rebecca. Nothing about her aunt's life or final wishes made sense. Had the woman lived miserly just to leave Rebecca a small fortune? She'd not even known her niece! Oh, God, Rebecca wished she could understand what it all meant.

"Come along this way to the kitchen," she told him.

"I'd offer you something, but I'm afraid there's nothing in the house to eat or drink."

"I'm fine," he assured her. "It hasn't been that long since we had refreshments at Abe's."

The kitchen was a tiny room with one row of cabinets and a single sink with a window above it. Through a pair of faded yellow curtains, a ridge of desert mountains loomed in the far distance. Between them and the house was an open range filled with green grass, clumps of purple sage and blooming yucca plants.

"Would you look at that refrigerator," Jake remarked. "I'll bet it's at least fifty years old."

Rebecca glanced at the appliance with its rounded corners and chromed handle. In spite of the paint being worn and rusted in places, the thing was still working. Although someone, she didn't know who, had removed nearly all of the food from the shelves. In order to keep it from spoiling, she supposed. Perhaps Gertrude's friend, Bess, had done the chore.

"Yes. I guess Aunt Gertrude didn't believe in getting rid of anything that was still working." Which was the complete opposite of her twin sister, Rebecca thought wryly. In Houston, Gwyn was constantly refurnishing her house with the newest and best. The contrast of how the two sisters lived was completely shocking and made Rebecca wonder even more how the split had happened.

Rebecca pointed to a short hallway that led off the kitchen. "The bedrooms and bathroom are down there. I'd show you, but they're all a mess. Would you like to see out back?"

"Sure."

He followed her out of the kitchen and onto a porch. This portico was made of planked wood and shaded with a roof. At one end, the thin branches of a desert willow moved in the breeze and scattered lavender blossoms on the dusty boards. The grass in the yard was long, scraggly and full of weeds and Rebecca couldn't help thinking about her mother's well-manicured lawn in Houston. There, thick St. Augustine grass was fed and groomed on a regular basis by a hired gardener. Expensive lawn furniture was arranged in an eye-pleasing manner beneath the deep shade of a live oak. From the looks of it, Gertrude O'Dell hadn't even owned an old porch swing, she thought dismally.

"Looks like things need a little cleaning and fixing up here, too," Jake remarked. "I didn't realize there was a barn behind the house. The trees hide it from the road. Are there animals or equipment in it?"

"No tractors or anything that could be deemed as equipment," she told him. "But there are three barn cats. And a horse was here this morning. I think it must come and go in the pasture. At least, it wasn't locked inside a pen when I saw it. There's a dog somewhere around here, too."

"Let's go have a look," he suggested, then glanced down at her high heels. "Or maybe you'd rather not."

"The ground is hard and dry. I'm not worried about my shoes, Jake."

He smiled and for a moment she was reliving those few moments she'd stood in the circle of his arms. His body had been warm. Incredibly warm. And his muscles thick and hard. His male scent had engulfed her and she'd wanted to bury her face in the V of his shirt, to cling to him until nothing else in the world mattered.

Her strong reaction to the cowboy was startling and continued to confuse her. Although Rebecca had always enjoyed male company, she'd never relied on a man to keep her happy. How could she, when all the ones she'd known had been as fickle and unpredictable as the wind? Down through the years, she'd learned, somewhat the hard way, that men perpetually put themselves first. To them, sacrificing meant giving up football tickets to take her to the opera. She could do without that. And do without them. At least, she believed she could.

Still there were times, like earlier at Apache Wells, when she'd watched the loving exchange between Maura and Quint Cantrell, when she'd listened to them speak of their young sons, that she wondered if she would ever find that sort of love, ever have children of her own.

"Good," he suggested, breaking into her thoughts. "Lead the way."

As they stepped off the porch, a reddish-brown dog with long hair scurried beneath the yard fence and came loping toward them. From the wag of his tail, he was happy to see Rebecca again and she paused to bend and stroke his head.

"I was surprised to find that my aunt had left pets behind," she told Jake. "I suppose before I leave I'll have to take them to a place where they can be adopted out to new homes. And I need to find a trustworthy Realtor to deal with the property."

After giving the animal a few strokes on the head, she straightened to her full height to see Jake was studying her closely.

"Gertie didn't have a will?" he asked thoughtfully.

Color rushed to Rebecca's cheeks, although she didn't understand why his question should unsettle her. It wasn't a crime to be an heiress, even to a run-down property like this.

"Uh—yes. Actually, Gertrude made me the sole beneficiary."

She began walking on toward the barn and he strolled beside her. A stand of aspen trees grew at the back of the yard and as they passed beneath the shade, the air was dry and pleasant. She suspected that by nightfall the temperature would be downright cool.

"So why don't you stay on and make use of the property?" he asked. "Or do you already own something in Houston?"

As they walked along, she stared at him. "No. I rent. In the city. I don't have any use for property."

Was the man crazy? Why would he even think she'd want or need Gertrude's old homestead? Even though she'd told him and his friends that she worked as a fashion buyer, he obviously didn't realize the importance of her job. At least, its importance to her. He didn't understand that her mother and friends would be shocked to see her spend one night on this ramshackle property, much less want to hold on to it for herself.

But she kept all those thoughts to herself. She didn't want to give him the impression that she was a snob. Because she wasn't. She was just accustomed to a different life than this. That was all.

"That's a shame," he said. "With a bit of loving care this place could be a nice little home. But I guess a fancy lady like you would never settle for anything this simple."

There was no sarcasm or accusation in his voice. He'd simply stated a fact the way he saw it. And she wasn't at all sure she liked the image he'd formed of her.

Pushing a hand through her tousled hair, she wondered if she looked as bad as she felt. But that hardly mattered. When Jake Rollins had called her a fancy lady, he'd not been referring to her looks, but her substance as a person. She couldn't remember the last time anyone had noticed anything more about her than her outward appearance, the latest fashion she happened to be wearing. It was a jarring realization.

"Actually, I won't be leaving tomorrow," she told him, while trying to decide why she felt it important to give him that bit of information. "It will take me a few days to deal with everything and get the property ready to sell."

"Well, I hope everything turns out the way you want," he said quietly.

"I do, too," she murmured, then quickened her pace on to the barn.

The structure was built of lapped boards with a low roof made of corrugated iron. The outside had once been painted white but had long since faded to a tired gray. At one end, two wide doors stood open, allowing a shaft of waning sunlight to slant across a floor of hard-packed dirt.

Inside, two female cats, one gray striped and the other a solid white, were lounging on a low stack of old hay bales. Nearby, a yellow tom was stretched out in the shade of a metal water trough full of rusty holes. Everywhere she looked, everything about the place seemed to have been long forgotten, as though her aunt had quit living years ago, instead of days ago. The idea saddened her even more.

While Rebecca tried to get near the wary felines, Jake walked around the structure, testing the supporting beams for structural soundness. Perhaps he knew someone who was looking to buy a place like this, she thought.

"This morning the horse was standing out in that wooden corral. But the gate to it is open and I suppose he or she wandered away," Rebecca suggested.

"Grass is probably the only feed it's been getting. Do you know how much acreage goes with the house?" he asked.

"Two hundred and ten acres."

"Well, I wouldn't worry about the horse. With that much grazing area, he has plenty to eat."

Rebecca moved away from the cats and walked to where he stood gazing out the wide-open door. "Do you cowboy for a living, Jake?" she asked.

His expression faintly amused, he looked at her. "That depends on what you mean by cowboying."

She shrugged, while wondering why he made her feel just a bit foolish. She was an educated woman with a college degree in business, along with being well-read on a variety of subjects. She kept up with current events, politics and the stock market. She was independent and had lived on her own for some years now. Yet when Jake looked at her with those brown eyes of his, she felt like a piece of mush, a woman who didn't know the first thing about dealing with a real man like him.

"Well, I'll put the question this way, do you do your job on horseback?"

He chuckled softly. "Most of the time. I own a ranch over by Fort Stanton, near Capitan. I raise cattle and horses."

She looked at him with interest. "Oh. Somehow I got the impression that you worked for the Cantrells."

"I used to work for Quint. On his ranch, the Golden Spur. But once he got the place built up to the way he wanted it, I decided he didn't need me anymore. And by then—" he paused, his lips twisting to a wry slant "—I had fish of my own to fry. From time to time I still help Quint. Whenever he has roundup going. And Abe occasionally asks me to do things for him, too. For instance, a few of his special horses he won't let anyone shoe, except me."

Her brows arched. "You do farrier work?"

He nodded. "I did a lot of farrier work when I was younger. And then for a long time I managed the training barns at Ruidoso Downs."

"So you know a lot about horses."

He chuckled again and the sexy sound drew her gaze straight to his. There was a gleam in his amber eyes that could only be described as provocative and she found herself drawing in a deep, cleansing breath and releasing it slowly.

"I like to think so," he drawled.

Finding it more comfortable to look at her feet rather than him, she noticed her high heels were now covered with dust and one of the pointed toes scuffed. But she didn't care. Bordeaux's supplied her with clothing, shoes, bags, jewelry and anything she wanted as a way to advertise their merchandise. There were plenty more high heels where these came from.

"I don't know much about the outdoors," she admitted, then glanced over her shoulder at the lazy cats. "Or animals. I've always loved being around them, but never had the opportunity to have any of my own."

As a young girl, she'd begged her mother for a dog or cat, but Gwyn had refused. Yet that hadn't deterred Rebecca's interest in animals. She'd visited the Humane Society every chance she'd gotten and fussed over her girlfriends' furry pets. By the time she entered high school, she'd had her heart set on becoming a veterinarian and had tried to gear her studies in that direction. In her mind, it would be the perfect job. Not only would she get to spend her days with a variety of animals, she'd be caring for them, making them well and happy.

But once her mother had learned of her daughter's plans, Gwyn had been outraged. She'd absolutely forbidden Rebecca to even consider such a career, insisting that her daughter was too fragile, too beautiful to be dealing with animals in a dirty barnyard.

Rebecca had argued the point. But by that time her father, Vance, who'd been a gentle, easygoing man, had already died, leaving Rebecca with no one to help support her wishes or desires. Gwyn had always been a forceful, strong-minded woman and Rebecca had never wanted to be a rebellious child. So she'd tried to consider the fact that her mother could possibly be right and that years down the road, after Rebecca had grown to womanhood, she'd eventually see that her wish to be a veterinarian was ridiculous.

In the end, she'd caved in to Gwyn's wishes and put aside her own dreams. But now, after all these years, Rebecca often wondered if her childhood pursuit would have suited her, would have given her more fulfillment than the materialistic job she had now.

"Well, looks like now is your chance to change that," Jake remarked. "There are plenty of animals here for the taking."

Lifting her head, she smiled wanly. He made everything sound so easy and uncomplicated. How would it feel to live that way? To not be hurrying and scurrying, constantly flying from one city to the next, continually worrying about maintaining her looks and asking herself if any of it really mattered, did *she* really matter in the scheme of things?

"Perhaps," she murmured, then said, "If you're ready, I need to be shutting the house and driving to Ruidoso. I'd like to get back to my hotel room before dark and from here the trip is at least thirty minutes."

"Sure. I'll help you."

It didn't take the two of them long to shut the windows and lock the doors. Once they made their way back out to their vehicles, Rebecca paused at the driver's door of the sedan and extended her hand to him. When his warm fingers wrapped around hers, she was once again flung back to those moments she'd been wrapped in his arms. Somehow she knew she would never forget how it had made her feel to be that close to him, to have his voice in her ear, his hand in her hair.

"Thank you, Jake, for taking time out of your day to attend my aunt's services. It means very much to me. More than you can imagine."

"I was glad to do it."

Instead of dropping her hand, he continued to hold it tightly, his thumb moving ever so slightly against its back. Rebecca suddenly had to remind herself to breathe.

"Well, perhaps we'll see each other again—before I leave to go back to Texas," she said, trying her best to keep her voice light and natural, even while she was feeling the quiver of her words as they left her tongue.

"I'd like that, Rebecca. Very much."

She waited for him to drop his hold on her hand. When he didn't, she forced herself to extricate her fingers from his and turn toward the car.

Before she could reach to open the door, he did it for her and without looking his way she quickly slid beneath the wheel and started the engine.

When he shut the door between them, she dared to glance at him through the open window.

"Goodbye, Jake."

He lifted a hand in farewell, then stepped back and out of the way. As she turned the car around and headed down the short drive, she looked in the rearview mirror to see him walking over to his truck. As he went, he lifted his hat from his head and raked a hand through his hair as though he was either puzzled or weary, or simply gathering himself after the stress of dealing with an emotional woman.

Dear God, what had made her fall into his arms like that and weep against his chest? She wasn't that sort of woman. What could he be thinking of her?

It doesn't matter, Rebecca. You'll probably never see the man again.

The idea left her very, very empty.

Rafter R Ranch, the place Jake called home, was located only a few miles from Fort Stanton, a military facility that had once played an important part in New Mexico's early growth as a state, but was now only a preserved part of its history, where tourists could view the past. If Jake needed to drive to town for any sort of supplies, he had to head northwest to Capitan. The trip took more than twenty minutes and the town was actually only a village of about fifteen hundred people or so, but Jake didn't mind the isolation. In fact, he felt lucky to have snagged the precious river land.

Several years ago, when the property had gone on the real estate market, Jake hadn't seriously considered trying to purchase it for himself. At the time he'd been doing farrier work around the county, making a decent enough living for himself, but nothing that could secure enough money to buy choice river acreage. Besides, why would a guy like him want a house and several hundred acres? His mother already had a place of her own, and as for himself, he didn't need much to make him happy.

A place to eat, sleep and hang his hat was enough to satisfy him.

But Quint, who'd always been more like a brother than a friend, had insisted that someday Jake would want to settle down and raise a family, that one day he'd want a ranch, a place to build a dream.

At first Jake had laughed at him. Jake didn't have dreams, he dealt in reality. And the reality had been that he couldn't raise enough money to buy an outhouse, much less a house with hundreds of acres surrounding it. But Quint had stepped up and offered to help Jake get a loan and as a result, he'd somehow managed to purchase the first and only place he could truly call his own.

At that time it hadn't mattered that the property needed lots of work. The house had seen plenty of neglect and outside the fences and barns were crumbling. But he'd looked past the drawbacks and on to the possibilities. He might have been short on cash, but he was an able-bodied man who could do plenty of things with two hands and a strong back.

Acquiring the ranch had put a dream into motion for Jake. And along the way, he'd gone from farrier work to running the stables at Ruidoso Downs, to helping Quint build the Golden Spur into a cattle empire. His financial security had slowly and surely changed. Especially three years ago when gold had been discovered on the Golden Spur and Jake had purchased shares in the richly producing mine. Now, the Rafter R was taking shape. He was gradually building the place the way he saw fit and answering to no one but himself. And that meant the ranch's success or failure rested squarely upon his shoulders.

For Jake, it was a heavy weight of responsibility and

one he'd never grown accustomed to carrying. But he was trying. And for the most part, Jake couldn't complain. He had a large herd of cattle and horses, a home, and a ranch yard full of sturdy barns and plenty of equipment. He even employed two hands to take care of the animals. He had most everything a cowboy could want. Except a family.

That lonesome thought entered his mind as he pulled his horse to a stop outside the barn, then swung himself down to the ground. But he tried not to dwell on it as he loosened the sweaty girth and pulled the saddle from the animal's back. He wasn't the family sort. Being a husband and father and doing it right meant loving one woman for the rest of his life. He couldn't imagine putting himself in such a confinement, much less succeeding at it.

Jake had just finished putting away his horse and tack, when he heard his mother's voice calling to him from the edge of the barn door. More than surprised that she'd ventured away from Ruidoso so late in the evening, he strode down the wide alleyway to greet her.

Clara Rollins was a thin woman with wispy brown hair and a face that could only be described as tired. Jake could remember a time, back before his father, Lee, had left the family, that his mother had been a beautiful, vibrant woman. But that had been nearly twenty years ago, before his parents' marriage had begun to crumble and before she'd been diagnosed with cancer.

She'd beaten the disease, but the fierce treatments had weakened her heart and for the past five years Jake had watched her movements grow slower, the light in her eyes fade away. Not because her heart condition had worsened, but because she'd lost all will and hope. He loved his mother and wanted to make her life better, but her mind-set was always on the negative. She refused to get better, because she believed she had no reason to get better.

"This is a nice surprise," he said, as he leaned down and planted a kiss on her forehead. "You've not driven over here to the ranch in ages."

"I haven't seen you in days," she said in a faintly accusing tone.

Jake bit back a sigh. In spite of his affection for his mother, she often tried his patience. Probably even more than Abe tried Quint's. But at least Abe was full of life. The old man would go to the end kicking, joking and enjoying his time on earth. Clara was content to simply wait for her life to slip by. He hated her attitude, but as yet hadn't found a way to change it.

"I've been very busy, Mom. I've been riding fence line this week." He gathered his arm around her shoulders and urged her away from the barn. "Let's go to the house. I'll see if I can scrounge us up something for supper."

"No need for that. I've brought you some pot roast. It's already in the kitchen, waiting to be heated."

He rewarded her with a look of approval. "You've been cooking? You must be feeling better."

"I just like to know my son is eating right," she said wanly.

Jake's house was located about fifty yards from the block of barns and sheds that made up the ranch yard. Even though he kept his pace slow to match his mother's, she was breathing hard by the time they reached the back door and stepped into the kitchen. A part of him wanted to shake her for not following the doctor's orders and keeping herself in shape by taking routine walks.

"Sit down, Mom. And I'll get everything together

and on the table," he told her as he washed his hands at the sink.

She did as he suggested and he went to work putting plates, utensils and iced glasses on the table.

"I talked to Quint's mother yesterday," Clara said as Jake heated the meat and vegetables in the microwave. "She said she was home watching the babies for Maura, while you went to a funeral for Abe's neighbor."

"That's right. Gertie O'Dell passed away and grave-side services were held for her yesterday. I doubt you knew her. She—well, I don't think the woman hardly ever got off her place. She was a recluse. Abe said she'd been his neighbor for nearly thirty years and he could count the times he'd talked to her on two hands."

"No. I don't recall that name," Clara said thoughtfully. "How old was the woman?"

"Fifty-six, I believe."

A worrisome frown collected between Clara's brows. "That's only a few years older than me."

"That's right. It's unfortunate, but people of all ages die."

He carried a dish of potatoes and carrots over to the table, then went back for the roast.

"What was wrong with her?"

Jake wasn't about to tell his mother that Gertie O'Dell had died from some sort of heart failure. Clara already considered herself an invalid. He didn't want to add the notion that, like Gertie, she was headed toward her deathbed.

"I'm not sure," he said evasively. "Some sort of illness she'd had for a long time."

With everything on the table, he took a seat kitty-cornered to his mother's chair and poured sweetened tea into their glasses.

Clara spread a napkin across her lap. "I'm surprised you attended the funeral. Guess you made the effort for Abe's sake."

He paused to look at her. "No. I made the effort for Gertie's sake, Mom. I don't do everything in my life just to make an impression or score points."

Clearly flustered by his retort, she clamped her lips together. "Well, you didn't know the woman personally," she pointed out.

"Maybe not. But she was a fellow human being, a fixture in Abe's neighborhood. Whenever she saw me pass, she would always give me a wave. And coming from Gertie that meant a hell of a lot. She hated most folks."

"Her family—"

"She had none," Jake interrupted. "Not any immediate family. Only one relative showed up for the funeral."

Clara's expression was suddenly regretful as she looked at her son. "How awful," she murmured.

Jake sighed. "Yeah. That's my thinking, too."

He didn't go on to tell his mother about Rebecca Hardaway. She'd press him with questions that he couldn't answer. Like why Gertie had left her estate to a niece who'd clearly never been a part of her life. At least, not while Gertie had been living in New Mexico. And from judging Rebecca's age, he'd guess that had been as long or longer than the pretty blonde had been living.

"Wonder what will happen to her estate?" Clara asked as she ladled food onto her plate. "I suppose with no husband or kids, some distant relative will put it up for sale."

The image of Rebecca drifted to the front of Jake's

mind, the way her blue eyes had glazed with tears, the sobs he'd felt racking her slender shoulders. He'd been a bit shocked when she'd fallen into his arms. Not that a crying woman was anything new to him. Down through the years, he'd seen plenty of waterworks sprout for all different reasons. And most of the time he had to admit that tears on a smooth pink cheek left him unaffected. There wasn't a woman on the face of the earth who couldn't be a good actress when she wanted to be and turning on the tears was just a part of her act.

But Rebecca hadn't been acting, he realized, and her emotional state continued to puzzle Jake. She'd said she'd never been to her aunt's house before, but seeing it had disturbed her. She didn't appear to have even known Gertrude or how she'd lived, so why had the woman's death hit her so hard? None of it made sense to him. But then, Gertie had lived what most people would call a bizarre life. Maybe learning all of that about her family member had been too much for the Texas wildflower, he considered.

Jake had to admit he'd been disappointed that Rebecca had so quickly decided that she didn't want Gertie's property. As though it was all meaningless to her. For some reason he'd wanted to think she was a deeper sort of person than that. But then maybe he wasn't being fair. Maybe she wasn't in a position to care for the place, the way it deserved to be cared for. She obviously had a life back in Houston. She might even have a special man waiting for her return, he thought grimly. The lack of a ring didn't necessarily mean anything nowadays. She might even have a husband.

The idea bothered him far more than it should have.

Trying his best to shake it away, he glanced up at

his mother. "You're probably right," he replied to his mother's comment. "And selling it won't be much of an effort. The land joins up with Apache Wells. Abe would be glad to fork over a very fair price to make sure it becomes a part of his ranch, instead of watching it go to some developer."

"Maybe someone should give this information to Gertie's relatives?" Clara suggested. "They'd probably be grateful to have someone drop a buyer into their lap."

When Rebecca Hardaway had spoken of finding a Realtor to deal with selling the place, he probably should have spoken up and told her that a Realtor wouldn't be necessary. Abe would buy the property without batting an eye.

But something had kept the words inside him. Selfishness? The hope that Rebecca Hardaway would be forced to stay in New Mexico longer than necessary? The hope that while she was here he'd get the chance to know her, spend time with her, maybe even get physically close to her?

Dream on, Jake. Rebecca might have leaned that sexy little body against you once, but there won't be a next time. If you do see her again, there won't be any tears in her eyes and she'll see you for just what you are—a cowboy who can offer her little more than a lusty roll in the hay.

Picking up a steak knife, he sliced ruthlessly into the meat on his plate.

"Maybe I'll do just that, Mom."

Chapter Three

At the same time, some twenty miles south in Ruidoso, Rebecca sat in a luxurious hotel suite. From her seat on the long moss-green couch, she could look out the plate-glass wall at the picturesque view of Sierra Blanca. Next to her right arm, a telephone sat on a polished end table and all she had to do was lift the receiver from the cradle and press a button to have a full course meal delivered to her room.

But at the moment she wasn't seeing the beauty of the tallest peak in the southern part of the state, or concerning herself over ordering dinner. She was thinking about Jake Rollins. Something she'd been doing ever since she'd driven away and left the man standing in front of her aunt's house.

So why don't you stay on and make use of the property?

With a bit of loving care this place could be a nice

little home. But I guess a fancy lady like you would never settle for anything this simple.

Today Rebecca had planned to get a list of things done. First of all, to ask around town and find a Realtor she could trust. Secondly, to contact the nearest animal shelter to find homes for the pets Gertrude had left behind. But Rebecca hadn't attempted to do either of those things. She'd walked a short distance around town, ate lunch, returned to the hotel and for the past two hours sat wondering why Jake Rollins's words continued to haunt her.

It wasn't like the man had anything to do with her life, she mentally argued. Up until yesterday, she'd never met him. Yet the things he'd said to her, the way he'd looked at her, had done something to her thinking.

With a heavy sigh, she rose to her feet and walked across the room to where a gilt-edged mirror hung over a small accent table. The image showed a young woman dressed casually but fashionably in a pair of summer white jeans and a sleeveless cashmere top. Her blond hair was twisted into a sexy pleat and her face touched with just enough color to look pretty but not overdone.

Her friends would tell her that she looked perfect, but that had come to mean very little to Rebecca. On the inside she felt far from perfect. And she didn't understand why.

Even before she'd learned about Gertrude and traveled here to New Mexico, she'd been feeling empty, as though spinning wheels were quickly carrying her to nowhere. Then yesterday, when she'd stood beside her aunt's grave with hardly a soul there to tell the woman goodbye, a heavy sense of reality had stung her. She wasn't sure why thoughts of missed opportunities and connections were upsetting her, but she couldn't get rid of them.

Across the room, her cell phone rang. The sound cut into her dark thoughts and with a heavy sigh, she walked over to collect the small instrument from where she'd left it on a low end table.

Her mother's name and number were illuminated on the front and she braced herself with a deep breath before she flipped the phone open and lifted it to her ear. Gwyn had been ringing the phone all day, but Rebecca had ignored her calls. She wasn't ready to talk to the woman, but years of being a devoted daughter couldn't be wiped away in a matter of days. And Gwyn deserved to know that she'd arrived in New Mexico safely.

"Hello, Mother."

Gwyn let out a sigh of relief. "Oh, thank God you finally answered! Is everything all right?"

Rebecca's jaw tightened. "Is that question supposed to be some sort of joke? How could everything be all right? I just watched my aunt—an aunt I didn't even know I had—be lowered into the ground!"

"Now, Rebecca, honey, please let's don't start in about all of that now. Gertrude is gone. There's no use talking about her anymore."

If it hadn't been for disturbing the other hotel guests, Rebecca would have actually screamed into the phone. Instead, she tried to calm the rage boiling inside her. "Sure. Just forget her," she said, in a voice heavy with sarcasm, "and get on with our neat little lives. The way you've seemed to do for the past thirty years."

There was a long stretch of silence and then Gwyn asked, "When are you coming home?"

Clearly Gwyn was still refusing to open up about Gertrude and her indifferent attitude about her own flesh and blood caused something to suddenly click inside Rebecca. Feeling strangely calm, she said, "I'm not. At least, not for a good while. I have things to do here. And I want to make sure they're done right."

Gwyn gasped. "What sort of things? What are you talking about?"

"Listen, Mother, my aunt left everything she had in this world to me. And even though she's gone now, she still deserves my attention. I owe her that much—" Emotions suddenly filled Rebecca's throat, choking her. "That and so much more."

"But, Rebecca—she—your job—you'll have to be getting back here to Houston soon!"

"You worry about my job, Mother. You seem to love it much more than I do, anyway."

"Rebecca! You—"

"I'm sorry, Mother. I'm very busy. I've got to get off."

Rebecca hung up the phone, then purposely walked over to the closet and pulled out the luggage she'd brought with her. An hour later, she'd packed all her things, checked out of the hotel, and after purchasing a few items at the grocery store, headed north to Gertie's place.

As she drove northwest, out of the mountains and onto the desert floor of the Tularosa Basin, she picked up her cell phone and pushed a button that would connect her with her boss in Houston.

"You're going to do what?" the woman exclaimed loudly in her ear.

Rebecca felt the ridiculous urge to smile, but forced herself not to. Even before her father had died, she'd been a responsible child, who'd grown into an even more responsible adult. She'd never done an impulsive thing in her life and she was shocked at how good it felt to be doing it now.

"I need to take a leave, Arlene."

"Yes, but you said indefinitely! Surely this break you're taking won't require that much time! What will I do without you? The Dallas show is coming up and then New York City. I have to have a buyer there! Otherwise—"

Outside her car window, the sun was casting a purple and gold hue across the desert floor. She'd never seen anything so wild and beautiful. "Send Elsa. She knows what she's doing and she'll be more than happy to step into my shoes."

Arlene snorted and mouthed a curse beneath her breath. The woman's reaction didn't surprise Rebecca. Arlene was in her late fifties and had spent more than thirty years working for Bordeaux's. Still single, she'd made the famous department store her life and believed that Rebecca and its other employees should, too.

"Elsa doesn't have your taste or finesse with people. I want you back here in two weeks. That's all I can afford to give you, Rebecca."

The demanding ultimatum brought an angry flare to Rebecca's nostrils. She'd given so much of herself, her life, to Bordeaux's and all she could expect in return for her commitment was two weeks?

"That's not enough, Arlene. Not by a long shot."

Her retort must have shocked the woman because the line went silent. It stayed that way for so long that Rebecca actually pulled the phone away from her ear to see if the instrument was still receiving a tower signal.

"What's come over you, Rebecca?" the woman finally retorted. "I realize you must be grieving, but from what I understand this death was a distant relative. Surely you can put it behind you and get yourself focused on business again."

She was nearing the turnoff to Gertrude's house and the road that eventually led to Apache Wells. Jake and the Cantrells had shown her more compassion in one afternoon than this woman had shown her in the six years she'd been working for Bordeaux's. What did that say for the people she'd surrounded herself with?

"Taking this time off is important to me, Arlene. If you feel you need to replace me permanently, I'll understand. Just mail my final paycheck to my apartment."

Another long silence followed Rebecca's statement and then Arlene said in a mollified tone, "Now wait a minute, Rebecca. Let's not get so hasty about things. You're a great asset to Bordeaux's and I don't want to lose you." She paused and released a long sigh of surrender. "All right. Take as long as you need. Your job will be waiting when you do get back to Houston."

Arlene's concession should have inspired Rebecca, filled her with joy to know that she was that good, that appreciated at her job. Yet she felt nothing but relief that her conversation with the woman was over.

"Thank you, Arlene. I'll be in touch soon."

Ten minutes later, she parked her vehicle behind a Ford pickup truck that sat beneath an expanse of sagging roof connected to the left side of the house.

Rebecca recalled a truck being listed in Gertrude's will and she assumed the old red F-150 had belonged to her aunt. In this isolated place a person had to have transportation of some sort. She wondered if the vehicle was still in running condition and made a mental note to check the thing out after she'd put away the perishable groceries. Keeping a rental car for an extended length of time would run into a huge expense. The truck would solve that problem.

At the back of the car, she opened the trunk and started to lift a sack of groceries when she suddenly heard a low whine and felt a nudge against the back of her leg.

Turning, she saw the dog had spotted her arrival and come to greet her. His mouth was open and he appeared to be grinning as though he couldn't be happier to see her.

For a moment, Rebecca forgot the grocery bag and squatted on her heels to wrap her arms around her furry brown friend.

"Well, here you are again, big guy," she said to him, then stroked a hand down his back. Beneath his long, thick hair she could feel his backbone and realized the animal had obviously not been getting enough to eat since Gertrude had died. "I'll bet you're hungry, aren't you? I'll bet you'd like a big bowl of juicy dog food."

As if on cue, the dog let out a long, loud whine. Rebecca smiled and patted his head. "All right. Come along and I'll see what I can do," she told him.

With plastic bags dangling from both hands, she urged the canine to follow her onto the porch. Once she opened the door, she pushed it wide and invited him in.

"Just for a while," she warned him as he shot past her, his tail wagging furiously.

During her visit yesterday morning before the funeral, she'd discovered several dozen cans of dog and cat food stacked in a small pantry. She emptied two of the cans into a plastic bowl and set it on the floor.

While the dog gobbled it hungrily, she stored what

perishable food she'd purchased in the refrigerator and found places for the rest of the things in the cabinet.

By the time she was finished with the chore, the dog had cleaned the bowl and was looking up at her, his head tilted curiously to one side. No doubt he couldn't understand why his mistress was gone.

The notion was a sad one. Especially when Rebecca tried to imagine her aunt and the dog together. It was difficult to form such a picture in her mind when she didn't have the tiniest idea of what Gertrude had looked like. There were no photos of the woman sitting around the house and even in death, she'd clearly been a private person by leaving orders with her lawyer to keep her casket closed.

If Gertrude and Gwyn had been identical twins, then the woman would have been petite and dark-haired with hazel-green eyes and a square face. But her mother hadn't seen fit to tell her even that much about her sister, so Rebecca could only guess and imagine Gertrude's appearance.

Trying not to dwell on the loss and become maudlin all over again, Rebecca spoke to the dog, "I have no idea what your name is, boy. Is it Furry? Smiley? Buddy? No. None of those fit. What about Beau? Back in elementary school I knew a boy named Beau. The tips of his ears sort of flopped over like yours. But he was nice. And I liked him."

The dog responded with another whine and pushed his head beneath Rebecca's hand. Smiling, she gave him a loving scratch between the ears. "Okay. Beau it will be. Now let's see if we can start cleaning up this place."

A week later Jake was at Marino's Feed and Ranch Supply, purchasing several sets of horseshoes, when he heard a woman's soft voice call his name.

Turning, he was completely shocked to see Rebecca Hardaway standing a few feet away from him. What was she doing in a place that was mostly frequented by farmers and ranchers? More important, what was she doing still here in New Mexico? He figured she'd probably already wrapped up her business and gone back to Texas.

His heart was suddenly beating fast as pleasure ricocheted through his body. "Hello, Rebecca."

He started toward her and she met him in the middle of the dusty aisle filled with pesticides and grass fertilizer.

Smiling, she extended her hand to him. "Hello, Jake."

He took her hand, while his gaze quickly encompassed every inch of her. She was dressed casually in blue jeans and a pink hooded T-shirt. Her blond hair was pulled into a ponytail and her face was completely bare of makeup. She looked fresh and beautiful and rested. And just looking at her made something inside of him go as soft as gooey candy.

"This is a surprise to see you," he admitted. "I figured you'd already left the area."

She shook her head. "No. I've decided to stay on for a while. I'm living out at my aunt's place now."

It was all Jake could do to keep his mouth from falling open. That day he'd visited Gertie's place with her, she'd seemed almost indifferent to the place. What had changed her mind so much that she'd actually been motivated to move out there?

"Oh. How's that been going?"

She laughed softly and Jake warmed to the sound, warmed even more to this different, more approachable Rebecca.

"Well, let's say I've never done so much cleaning in my life, but the house is coming around. I've decided I'll have to hire a man to help with the outside. There's so much heavy junk that needs to be hauled away. But I did get the truck going and turned in my rental car."

He peered toward the front of the building where plate-glass windows looked out over the graveled parking lot. Was she driving Gertie's old truck? He couldn't imagine such a thing. But perhaps there had always been another side of this woman and he'd not yet had a chance to see it.

His mind racing, he said, "Uh—that's good. Is it running okay?"

She nodded proudly. "Great. I took it by a mechanic's shop and had it checked out. The only thing it needed was new tires so I had those put on."

"Sounds like you've been busy."

She smiled again and as he looked at her, he realized the expression on her face was genuine. The fact made him happy. Very happy.

"I've made a start."

He glanced at the red plastic shopping basket dangling from her hand. "You needed something from the feed store?"

"A few things for the cats and dog. Flea collars, wormers, things like that. They're probably not going to be too happy about it all, but I want them to be cared for properly."

"So you didn't give them up to a pet adoption agency?"

Her cheeks turned pink and her gaze drifted away from him as though she was embarrassed she'd ever mentioned doing such a thing. Jake was truly baffled by this turn of events.

"No. I changed my mind about all that." She directed

her gaze back to his. "That day of the funeral was—well, I was very upset and said some things before I had a chance to think them through."

And done some things before she'd thought them through, Jake decided. Like bury her face against his chest and grip his shoulders like she never wanted to let him go. Now she was probably embarrassed about that, too.

But she didn't appear to be uncomfortable with him holding her hand. In fact, she wasn't making any sort of effort to draw it away from him. The idea encouraged him.

"We all do that from time to time," he told her.

She let out a faint sigh and then a tentative smile curved the corners of her lips. Jake couldn't tear his eyes away from her face or even consider dropping her soft little fingers.

"I'm glad I ran into you like this," she said. "I've been wondering if you might do me a favor. That is—if you have the time and happen to be going by my place."

My place. So she was calling it *her* place now. He couldn't believe how such a little thing like that could make him feel so good. And he wondered if he was coming down with some sort of sickness that was throwing his thinking off-kilter. He'd always been drawn to women. Down through the years he'd probably had more girlfriends than Quint had cattle, but he'd never had one that made him feel like happy sunshine was pouring through him and painting a goofy grin on his face.

"I'd be glad to help if I can," he told her.

She said, "The horse has been coming up and hanging around the barn. I found some feed for it stacked away in a storage room, but I wasn't sure how much to give it. The cats and dog I can deal with, but I know nothing about horses. And I remembered that you do. If you would be kind enough to look it over and make sure everything is okay. Maybe show me the correct amount to feed it? I'd be very grateful."

God was definitely smiling down on him today, Jake thought. For the past week, he'd struggled to get this woman off his mind. He'd tried to think of any reasonable excuse to drive over to Gertie's place and see if she was there. But he'd figured if she was still in New Mexico, she'd be staying in a hotel in Ruidoso and hardly likely to be around the old homestead. And then, too, he'd tried to convince himself that she was off-limits, a woman who could never fit into his simple life, even for a short while.

Now here she was inviting him to her place as though it was as natural as eating apple pie. He couldn't believe his good fortune and it was all he could do to keep from shouting with glee.

"Sure," he said as casually as he could manage. "I was thinking about driving out to Apache Wells this evening, anyway. Would that be soon enough?"

She smiled. "That would be great," she said, then glanced around his shoulder. "You were looking at horseshoes when I first spotted you. I don't want to keep you from your business."

She extricated her hand from his and Jake felt ridiculously bereft. "It's nothing that pressing." He glanced at his watch. "I have to be over at the track—Ruidoso Downs—in an hour or so to shoe some racehorses for a trainer that I'm friends with."

"Oh. Is that something you do often?" she asked curiously.

"Occasionally. There are some folks I just can't say no to."

Like you, he thought.

"Well, I should let you go, then."

Before she could turn to leave, he reached out and caught her by the hand. She looked at him, her brows arched in question.

Jake was amazed to feel warm color creep up his throat and onto his face. Hell's bells, women didn't make him blush. Nothing did. So why was he doing it now?

"I was wondering if you'd like to go have a cup of coffee?" he invited. "That is, if you have the time."

"Do you?"

He grinned. "It doesn't take me ten minutes to get to the track. I have plenty of time."

"In that case, I'd love to," she replied. "Just let me pay for my purchases and I'll be ready."

They both took care of their business in the feed store, then walked out to the parking lot together. Jake was about to suggest that she ride with him to the Blue Mesa, but before he could get the words out of his mouth, he noticed Gertie's dog was sitting in the cab of the old Ford.

Surprised, he asked the obvious. "You brought the dog to town with you?"

"Yes. I discovered that Beau loves to ride in the truck. And I enjoy his company. He'll be fine while we have coffee," she added. "I'll leave the windows rolled down and there's a nice breeze. He'll probably curl up on the seat and go to sleep."

Wonder of wonders, Jake thought. Was this the same fashionista who'd walked across the barnyard in a pair of high heels? No matter. She was here with him now and he was going to enjoy every second of her company.

"Okay," he told her. "Then follow me. The café is only a few blocks down the street."

Since it was midmorning, the crowd had mostly dispersed from the little café and they both found parking slots directly in front of the entrance.

Jake suggested they sit at an outside table. That way she could keep an eye on Beau. As they climbed onto the wooden deck filled with small round tables, she looked around with obvious pleasure.

"How nice of you to bring me here, Jake. This is so quaint and lovely," she exclaimed. "Can we take any table we like?"

"Sure. As long as it isn't already occupied."

Since there was only one other couple making use of the outside seating, Rebecca chose a table at the far corner, where a few feet below them a small brook trickled through tall pines and blue spruce trees.

A waitress appeared almost instantly after they were seated and Jake didn't waste time ordering coffee and a piece of chocolate pie.

"You're having pie, too?" Rebecca asked with a shocked tone that implied eating such a thing in the middle of the morning was absolutely sinful.

Jake chuckled. "I have a lot of work ahead of me today. Besides, the Blue Mesa makes the best pie in town. Try some. It won't put any pounds on you," he added with a wink, then glanced up at the redheaded waitress. "Will it, Loretta?"

The waitress laughed and Rebecca could tell by the light in the young woman's eyes that she knew Jake well and found him more than attractive. Probably one of many, she thought, then wondered why the idea annoyed her.

"Not at all," the waitress answered. "I eat it all the time and I don't get any complaints."

Rebecca deliberately avoided giving the waitress's

curvy figure an inspective glance. "Okay," she said to Jake, "you've talked me into it. I'll have a piece of peach." Glancing up at Loretta, she added, "If you have peach."

The woman's smile was faintly suggestive. "We have every flavor a person would want. Just ask Jake. He's tried them all."

Rebecca assured the waitress that she'd be satisfied with the peach and the redhead quickly swished away to fill their orders.

"Don't mind Loretta," Jake said. "She's a big flirt, but she doesn't mean any harm."

He probably didn't mean any harm either, Rebecca thought. But she figured he'd broken plenty of hearts with that dimpled grin and amber-brown eyes. Was she trying to be the next woman on his roster?

No. She simply liked him. Liked being around him. That didn't mean she wanted anything serious to develop between them. In fact, where women were concerned, she doubted the word *serious* had ever been in Jake Rollins's vocabulary.

"So how has it been staying out at Gertie's—uh, your place?" he asked after a moment.

She leaned back in her chair and wished she didn't feel so self-conscious about her bare face and messy hair. But for the past few days she'd felt like a child again, free to be herself. When she'd driven into town this morning, the last person she'd expected to see was Jake.

"It's been different to say the least. I'm still not used to the lack of an air conditioner. Or the idea that I can't drive a couple of blocks to a convenience store whenever I need something. But I like the quietness. Last night while I was sitting on the porch I heard a pack of coyotes howling in the distance. It was an eerie sound."

"Guess a city girl like you never heard anything like that."

"No. Actually—" The sound of approaching footsteps interrupted the rest of Rebecca's words and she turned her head to see Loretta arriving with their orders.

Once the waitress had served them and ambled away, Jake prompted Rebecca to finish what she'd been about to say.

"It was nothing important," she told him as she spread a napkin across her lap. "I was only going to say that since I've come out here to New Mexico I've been learning about a lot of things. Mainly about myself."

His expression was gentle on her face as he stirred a spoonful of sugar into his coffee. "Are you liking what you're learning?"

She grimaced. "No. But I'm trying to change what I don't like."

He didn't ask what she meant by that remark and Rebecca was relieved. She didn't want to admit to this man that it had taken the death of her aunt to open her eyes about her own life.

As she cut into the peach pastry, he leaned back in his chair and studied her with open curiosity. "This probably isn't any of my business, Rebecca, but are you planning on staying here in Lincoln County for an extended length of time?"

A faint frown creased her forehead. For the past week, his question was the same one that had gone round and round in her head. Was she going to stay for long? At the moment everything about being in this new place felt right and wonderful. But was that only because she was away from her demanding job? Away from the rift between her and her mother? Or was the contentment she'd been feeling these past few days trying to tell her that she'd finally discovered where she was truly meant to be?

"Maybe," she answered slowly. "It depends. On a lot of things."

He sipped his coffee, then thoughtfully reached for his fork. "Well, I suppose there's a man back in Houston who won't take kindly to you staying out here for very long."

She looked at him with faint surprise. "Not hardly. I don't have a boyfriend. And even if I did, I wouldn't allow him to tell me what to do. Unless I was madly in love with him."

He arched a brow at her. "That would make the difference?"

"Of course. Love always makes the difference. Doesn't it?"

One corner of his mouth curved upward as he reached across the table and closed his hand around hers. "You're asking that question to the wrong man, Rebecca."

He was telling her that love was not an important commodity on his list of needs. The reality should have put her off, should have made the warmth of his hand insignificant, the race of her heart slow to a disappointed crawl. But it didn't.

Like the rich pastry in front of her, she understood Jake Rollins wasn't necessarily good for her. But he was too tempting to resist.

Chapter Four

"You're going where?"

Amusement slanted Jake's lips. Even over the cell phone, he could hear the dismay in Quint's voice.

"To Gertie's place. Or I guess I should be calling it Rebecca's place. Since it belongs to her now."

As Jake motored his truck down the narrow, two-lane highway he could have counted at least twenty-five fence posts before Quint eventually replied and even then Jake figured the other man was rolling his eyes.

"I always did think you'd make a good detective, Jake. Maura's brother, Brady, could probably find you a good job in the sheriff's department if you wanted it. You're better at pulling information from people than a dentist pulls teeth."

Jake chuckled. "I can't help it. It just falls in my lap."

Quint's groan could be heard over the telephone

connection. "Oh, sure. You've probably been harassing the lady all week. How many times have you called her? No. Better than that, how did you get her phone number?"

"Quint, I've not called her once. I don't even have her number."

"Really? How did you miss that piece of information? You seemed to know other, more personal things about the woman."

"Look, I just happened to run into her at the feed store. She asked for my help and I couldn't refuse her. Could I?"

"You? Refusing a woman? That might have actually killed you."

Jake frowned. Normally Quint's sarcasm would have made him laugh, but for some reason this evening he wasn't finding it amusing. More like downright annoying.

"You're being a real jerk about this, Quint. Especially when I was planning on driving on to Apache Wells to check on Abe—after I finish meeting with Rebecca."

Quint sighed. "I'm trying not to be. But you took me by surprise, that's all."

"Why? What's so surprising about me seeing Rebecca Hardaway? She's gorgeous and nice and I happened to like a woman's company."

"No bull," Quint said with a wry snort, then added, "If you want the truth, I figured Gertie's niece would have already left here by now. Along with that, she's not your type."

Jake's jaw unconsciously tightened. "You mean she's not a barfly?"

"I didn't say that," Quint countered. "You did."

"You meant it," Jake shot back at him.

"All right," Quint conceded with a dose of frustration. "You'd be the first to admit that you don't go around seducing schoolmarms."

"Rebecca is hardly a schoolmarm."

"No. But she seems like a nice, decent woman. And after five minutes of conversation, I'm not sure you'll know how to treat her."

Even though Quint was his childhood friend and the two of them always spoke frankly to each other, Jake was struck by his comment. It was true that Jake had always directed his likes toward "experienced" women. But he knew when and how to be a gentleman. He resented Quint implying otherwise.

"I'm not a heathen, Quint. Besides, she wants me to look over her horse. Not her."

"Poor thing. Someone should have told her you're an expert at both," Quint said.

"You're really on a roll this evening, Quint."

Quint paused, then said, "I don't mean to get on your case, Jake. I'm just thinking about you. From what I saw of Rebecca Hardaway, she's the type of woman who— well, who could hurt a man without even trying."

Jake let out a wry snort. "What are you talking about? She's a fragile little flower who couldn't hurt anything or anyone."

Quint didn't say anything to that. Instead he abruptly changed the subject. Jake figured his friend had decided he was wasting his time giving him advice about the opposite sex.

"So what did you decide about buying the alfalfa from the producer in Clovis?" Quint asked. "I thought it was a fair price. And they always have good, clean hay."

"I haven't decided yet," Jake told him.

"What are you waiting on? Cold weather? The price to go up?"

"I was hoping the price would fall a bit," Jake admitted. "If it doesn't, I might be better off sticking to creep feed. I want to do more figuring before I decide what feed program to plan for this coming winter."

"I can understand that. I just wouldn't wait too long, though. Otherwise, you might get caught with your pants down."

Jake realized that Quint's advice was well-meaning. He even appreciated his friend's guidance, but it did little to bolster Jake's self-confidence. 'Course, Quint didn't have any idea that his longtime friend lacked in that department. At one time, before Jake had purchased the Rafter R, Quint might have believed he needed a big dose of ambition, but never self-confidence. That was something that Jake had kept carefully hidden from his friend, his mother, anyone who was close to him. He didn't want them to know that he often lay awake at night wondering if he was on the right path, if the business decisions he made would be the right ones and hopefully keep the ranch out of the red.

"I'll make my mind up about the alfalfa in the next few days," he told Quint, then spotting the turnoff to Rebecca's place in the far distance, he added, "I'm almost here. I'll talk to you tomorrow."

He started to snap the phone shut when Quint's voice stopped him.

"Jake—all that stuff I said earlier about you and Ms. Hardaway, I didn't mean to sound insulting."

"I never thought you did."

Quint sighed. "I just worry about you getting involved with a woman here on a temporary basis. I don't want to think of my best buddy moving to Texas and away from me. And I sure don't want to think about you getting that hard heart of yours cracked open."

A surprised frown crinkled Jake's features. "Oh, hell, Quint, there's not a woman on this earth that would make me leave New Mexico. And there sure isn't a woman who can break my heart."

"I'm glad to hear it."

Jake grinned as he wheeled his truck into Rebecca's graveled drive and told his friend goodbye. But as he slipped the phone into his jeans pocket and climbed down from the truck, he wondered why Quint had made such a fuss about him seeing Rebecca in the first place. The other man had never voiced an opinion one way or the other over Jake's female conquests, he didn't see why he should start now.

Shoving that thought away, he started toward the house.

Rebecca had been down at the barn, locking the horse up in the dry lot, when she'd caught sight of Jake's white truck pulling into the drive. Now, as she hurried through the backyard, she called his name.

"Jake! I'm back here."

He spotted her immediately and quickly changed directions.

She stood where she was, taking in his tall, muscular stride until he reached her side. This evening he'd changed his denim shirt to a teal plaid accented with flapped pockets and a long row of pearl snaps down each cuff. He looked very Western and extremely sexy and as he smiled at her, she could feel her heart reacting like a runaway drum.

"I was going to the house," he told her. "I thought I'd find you there."

It was impossible for her to keep her lips from spreading into a wide smile. Though she didn't understand completely why, just seeing him made her happy.

"I've been down at the barn, shutting the horse in the corral so it wouldn't leave before you got here," she explained. "Would you like to go have a look at her now?"

"Sure. We're already halfway there anyway," he reasoned.

With Beau on one side and Jake on the other, she led the way to the barn. As they moved forward, she noticed he was taking in the heaps of neatly piled junk she'd gathered from all corners of the yard.

"I've been trying to clean up the clutter," she explained. "Gertrude must not have believed in getting rid of anything. Even after it was broken. I've never seen so many old tires and rusted buckets."

"I'm surprised at how much better the place is beginning to look. And while we're on the subject, I could haul this stuff away for you," he offered. "That is, if you don't already have someone to do it."

She gave him an appreciative smile. "It's nice of you to offer, Jake, but Abe has already offered to send some of his hands to come pick it up for me."

"You've talked to Abe?" he asked with surprise.

She nodded. "This afternoon after I got back from Ruidoso I drove down for a little visit. I wanted to let him know in person how much I appreciated his kindness the day of Gertrude's funeral. He's such an easy man to talk to. If I tried, I couldn't have picked a better neighbor."

He chuckled. "If Abe wasn't eighty-five I'd be jealous."

Jealous of her with another man? Even though the

idea was ridiculous, it thrilled her to imagine this man getting possessive ideas about her. But no one had to tell her he was teasing. This morning while they'd drunk coffee at the Blue Mesa, he'd confessed to her that he'd never been in love or intended to be. And she'd spent the rest of the day wondering why.

Trying to keep a blush from stinging her cheeks with pink color, she purposely turned the conversation in a different direction. "Did you get your work done at the racetrack?"

"Finished up about an hour ago. I'm still trying to get the kinks out of my back."

"Oh, I'm sorry. I shouldn't have bothered you with Starr. You should have told me to call a vet."

"Starr? Is that what Gertrude called the horse? Or did you find registered papers?"

"If Starr has papers, I've not found them. But then I haven't begun to sift through all the drawers and cabinets filled with Gertrude's papers and things." She glanced away from him as she realized there was nothing for her to do but answer honestly. "You see, up until the morning of her funeral, I had no idea my aunt had any sort of pets." Trying to smile, she directed her gaze back to him. "So I've given them all names of my own. They might not like what I've christened them, but it's better than calling them dog, cat or horse."

"Well, looking over Starr is hardly a problem for me," he assured her, then added with a wink. "And moving around helps the kinks in my back."

At the barn, they walked to the small fenced lot connected to the left side of the building. Inside the enclosure, the gray dappled mare that Rebecca had named Starr ambled over to them. Beau flopped down in a nearby shade, content to simply watch.

While Jake sized up the animal's overall appearance, Rebecca decided it best to keep her questions to herself until he had a chance to voice his opinion.

Finally, he said, "From this side of the fence, she looks like she's in reasonably good shape."

"Do you have any idea how old she is? Or what sort of horse she is?"

"With a closer look I might be able to give you a good guess about her age. Do you have a halter or bridle that I could put on her?" he asked.

"Yes. Just a moment and I'll get it," she told him.

When she returned with a rope halter, she found Jake already inside the corral and his hands on the horse. Rebecca scrambled over the fence to join him and he took the simple piece of tack from her and slipped it on the mare's head.

Dismayed at how easy he'd done the task, she groaned with frustration. "I tried putting that thing on her several different times yesterday. But each time she kept lifting her head higher and higher."

Chuckling, Jake glanced at her. "Don't let her beat you at that game. Before you try to slip it on her nose, put your arm behind the back of her head. That tells the mare to keep her head down to your level."

"Oh. Well, I did warn you that I know very little about horses."

He cast her an appreciative glance. "You knew enough to see that this one was a mare."

The color on her cheeks deepened. "Thank you for giving me that much credit."

His hand stroked down the mare's neck and then his fingers began to comb through Starr's long, black mane. For a man with big hands, Rebecca couldn't help but notice how gently he touched the mare.

"You're welcome," he said. "But I can't figure why you named her Starr. She doesn't have a star in her forehead."

She shot him a hopeless look. "Does everything have to be so literal with a cowboy? I wanted to name her Starr because she is one—to me. Isn't that a good enough reason?"

"Best reason of all," he answered, then with a soft laugh, motioned for her to come closer.

Since she was already standing only a couple of steps away, she could hardly get much closer without touching him, she thought. Confused by his gesture, she took a cautious step toward him and Starr, then paused.

"Come on over here," he coaxed, while pointing to the spot directly in front of him. "Neither one of us is going to bite you. I want to give you a lesson."

Rebecca wasn't sure she was ready for the kind of lesson he could give her, but she stepped forward anyway.

Immediately, he slipped the rope halter off the mare's head and pushed the dangling straps into her hands.

Gasping, she stared at him. "Jake, I can't do this! I've already told you—"

Before she could finish, he positioned her next to the horse, then situated himself close behind her. Rebecca drew in a sharp breath as the front of his hard body pressed against the back of hers. Heat flooded her senses, raced over her skin to leave every pore puckered with awareness.

She was trying to catch her breath and assure herself that she wasn't going to melt, when he suddenly aligned his arms with hers and slipped her hands into his.

"I'm going to guide you," he explained in a low voice. "Let's open the halter like this." With his hands moving hers, the strands of rope fell into the right position. "Now we're going to put this arm around Starr's neck and this one is going to loop the rope over her nose."

The subtle movement of his body against hers was sending currents of excitement shivering through her, making it difficult to breathe, much less think. Thank goodness he couldn't see her face or guess how overwhelmed she was by his nearness.

"She—she'll try to run away." Rebecca finally managed to speak.

"No. She won't," he murmured. "She likes human contact. Don't you?"

Rebecca shouldn't have to answer that question, she thought wildly. The mare wasn't trying to move away from them any more than Rebecca was trying to pull away from Jake.

Swallowing again, she admitted, "When the time and the place is right."

He didn't say anything to that. But then he didn't need to. The slow, sensual shift of his body was already telling her how much it liked being next to hers. How much he wanted to prolong the experience.

She tried to swallow and ended up gulping as his low voice vibrated close to her ear.

"This piece goes behind Starr's ears. And this one beneath her throat. Now latch the two together and pull it snug. But not tight." He easily thrust two fingers between the halter and the mare's jaw. "See. You should be able to get your fingers comfortably beneath the rope."

"Yes—I see."

Her voice sounded more like a strained squeak than anything and he glanced over his shoulder to look at her. "Are you okay?"

She tried to smile, but ended up merely nodding at him. "Sure."

"Want to try again?"

Again? She'd barely survived this one lesson. "Um... no. I think I can manage now. Thanks."

Before he could insist on another haltering session, Rebecca quickly stepped back until there was a safe distance of space between them.

Glancing over at her, he said, "You must be a fast learner."

Superfast, she thought, as she took in the faint grin on his face. In a matter of moments, she'd learned that standing next to Jake was like snuggling up to a piece of red-hot dynamite. "I am. I pick up on things—quickly."

"That's good. Especially around animals. You always need to be on guard around them." With his gaze still on Rebecca, he stroked a hand over Starr's rounded hip. "Just because Starr is standing still and behaving nicely now doesn't mean that something couldn't frighten her and make her rear or bolt. She wouldn't be trying to hurt you—she'd just be trying to save herself. But you could get hurt in spite of that. You understand what I'm trying to tell you?"

Yes, she understood far more than he could possibly know. That he and Starr could both be unpredictable. And that she needed to stay on guard when she was around either of them. Yet that wasn't the way to enjoy the horse, him or even life in general. Strange how she could think in those terms now that she'd traveled out here to New Mexico. Before, back in Houston, she'd carefully thought out every step she'd taken.

"Don't worry, Jake. I'll be very cautious when I'm around her."

"Good."

He gave her a lazy smile, then turned his attention back to the mare. For the next few minutes, he made a slow, thorough inspection of Starr's teeth, ears, feet and coat. Once he was finished, he led the horse over to the fence and loosely tied the lead rope to one of the cedar post.

"Well, I'd say Starr looks to be somewhere around ten years old. And she's a quarter horse most likely mixed with a bit of Thoroughbred. The kind we use on the ranch to work cattle."

"Is ten old? For a horse, that is?"

He ambled over to where Rebecca stood and lazily leaned a shoulder against the fence. "Not at all. She hasn't even reached her prime yet."

She smiled with relief. "Oh. I'm glad. I mean, well—I guess I've already gotten attached to her and I hated to think that she might be in her waning years. And—I might not have her for much longer."

He casually folded his arms against his chest. "Hmm. Does that mean you'll be taking her back to Houston with you?"

His question brought her up short. What had she been thinking? That she was automatically going to stay here from now on with her little family of animals? Had she been speaking her dreams out loud without bothering to think how ridiculous they must sound to this man?

She groaned inwardly. "I don't know about that, Jake. I've not thought that far ahead. I just like to think that she'll be with me for a while. You know what I mean?"

An easy smile came upon his face and she suddenly realized that he did understand what she was trying to say, that maybe he didn't find her dreams ridiculous after all. The way her mother had so many years ago.

"Sure I do."

A breath of relief escaped her. "So, is there anything else I should know about her? Any problems?"

"Nothing serious that I can see. She needs to be treated for parasites and her feet need attention. A set of shoes would help. Especially if you plan on riding her."

Rebecca's lips parted with eager surprise. "Oh! Could I ride her?"

The smile on his face deepened and her gaze zeroed in on the dimple at the side of his mouth. Oh, my, he was a charmer, she thought. And he didn't even have to utter a word. Just one long look from the man was enough to melt a woman's bones.

"I don't see why not. She appears to be gentle. If you'd like, I'll bring a saddle over and see how she handles first. Do you know how to ride?"

Rebecca shrugged. "I know how to get in the saddle and make them go and stop. That's the extent of it. My friend and I went to Padre Island one summer on vacation and we hired horses from a stable to ride on the beach. I'm sure they were what you'd call nags. But it was such fun."

He chuckled. "I don't know what Gertie was doing with Starr, but she's definitely not in the nag department."

Rebecca walked over to Starr and pressed her cheek against the mare's neck. Jake followed and as he came to a stop just behind her shoulder, she looked thoughtfully up at him.

"I wonder what my aunt *was* doing with Starr?"

His expression solemn, he shook his head. "I'm not sure if Abe or Quint ever spotted her on horseback. I certainly didn't. Maybe she wanted the mare for company," he suggested.

A tiny pain squeezed somewhere in the middle of Rebecca's chest. "Yes. She probably was lonely," she murmured, then embarrassed by a sudden sting of tears, she turned her gaze on Starr's gray coat.

Behind her, Jake cleared his throat, then closed his hand over her shoulder and gently squeezed.

Touched by his sensitivity, she turned toward him and tried her best to smile. He was so close that she could see the golden flecks in his brown eyes, smell the subtle scent of cologne clinging to his shirt. His lips were not exactly full, neither were they thin. The word *perfect* kept coming to her mind as her gaze inspected the way the lower one squared off at the corners, the way his strong jaws blended upward into a pair of lean, hollow cheeks.

Doing her best to curb the urge to moisten her own lips, she said, "There is something else about Starr that you can advise me on. A couple of days ago, I purchased feed for her. From Marino's—where I ran into you this morning. The man behind the counter suggested I give her a certain kind. But I'd like your opinion. I have it in the barn, if you'd care to look."

"I'd be happy to," he replied.

Drawing in a bracing breath, she stepped around him and started to the barn. When he didn't follow immediately, she glanced behind her to see him removing the halter from Starr and opening the gate so that she could come and go whenever she liked.

Rebecca paused to give him time to catch up with her, then led the way to the back of the barn where a small room with a door was located. When she opened it and Jake spotted the four sacks of feed, each weighing fifty pounds, stacked against one wall, he looked at her with surprise.

"How did you get that stuff in here?"

She shrugged as though it was no special feat. "I drove the truck as far as the fence would allow and then I used the wheelbarrow to get the sacks back here."

"But you had to lift them to get them inside this feed room."

"I'm not as fragile as I look. I work out at the gym and I have some muscles."

Whenever Jake looked at this woman, he didn't see muscle. He saw gently rounded curves and soft, soft skin. He saw things he wanted to taste and touch. This evening she was wearing a purple top with a scooped neck and tiny little straps over her shoulders. The garment exposed her creamy skin and for the past few minutes that he'd been here, he'd had to fight with himself, remind himself that he had no right to reach out and touch, to let the pads of his fingers savor all that smooth, heated skin.

"Then I guess I can quit worrying about you taking care of yourself."

Her brows arched faintly above her blue eyes, the corners of her lips curved upward. "Worried? Why? I've been taking care of myself for a long time now."

"Maybe so. But not out here in the country. Like this. With no one around."

"Abe isn't that far away. And if I needed help, he has dozens of cowboys."

Jake didn't want to think about dozens of cowboys coming to Rebecca's aid. He didn't want to imagine just one. Unless that one was himself. Dear Lord, could Quint be right? he wondered. Was this woman the type who could hurt him? Really hurt him? He didn't want to think about it.

"Yeah. I suppose he does," Jake murmured, then stepped inside the little feed room.

She stood outside the open door and waited while he bent to inspect the feed and read the nutrition list. When he finally rose to his full height she said, "I've been giving her two of those scoops full twice a day. Is that enough? Or too much?"

Jake looked at the plastic scoop lying inside a black rubber feed bucket.

"That's good for now. After a couple of weeks, you might increase it to three scoops in the morning and evening. By then she'll be getting used to digesting more food on a regular basis. From the looks of her she could stand to gain about fifty to seventy-five pounds."

He stepped out of the room and shut the door behind him. It looked as though his job was now finished and for the life of him Jake couldn't think of one excuse to stay longer.

"That's great to know. I'll mark it on the calendar to remind me when to give her more," Rebecca told him, then smiled brightly. "Thanks for giving me all the horse lessons and for being so patient with such a—greenhorn."

He laughed softly. "I'd be as lost as a goose if I had to tell anyone about the fashion business. All I know is that I want my jeans to bend, my shirts to snap and my boots to have enough heel to stay in the stirrup."

She laughed along with him. "Yes, I guess we all have our own fortes."

Fighting the urge to clasp his hands around her arms and draw her to him, Jake jammed his hands in the front pockets of his jeans. Saying the next words was going to be worse than downing a dose of bitter medicine, but Jake didn't want to overstay his welcome and have her thinking he was a man who'd take advantage of her privacy.

"Well, I guess if that's all you needed from me this evening, I'll be going."

The disappointment on her face was like a burst of sunshine to Jake.

"Oh, you don't have to go yet, do you?" she asked quickly. "I was hoping you could stay and have supper. I've made enchiladas and I can't begin to eat them all."

Jake was more than a little stunned. True, she'd asked him out here for his help, but he'd never expected it to go any further than a few minutes of pleasant conversation over the mare.

"Are you sure?" he asked. "I wouldn't want to intrude."

To his amazement, she reached over and looped her arm around his. "Intrude? I'm the one who's been asking for all the favors," she said. "And I hate eating alone. Don't you?"

If Jake truly wanted to be honest with this woman, he'd tell her that he hated doing everything alone. But he couldn't admit such a thing to her. He wanted her, wanted everybody to believe he was a man who was happy with his life and himself.

"I'm not particularly fond of it," he replied.

"Great. We'll be doing each other a favor. Then let's go on to the house. It won't take but a few minutes to get things together."

As they left the barn and headed toward the little stucco, she kept her arm firmly clasped to his and

Jake was amazed at how much the simple touch was affecting him.

It didn't make sense, he thought. Over the years, a heck of a lot of women had touched more than his arm. But none of those women or their touches had made him feel as though he was stepping two feet off the ground, as though he was someone important and wanted.

She's the type of woman who could hurt you without even trying.

Quint's words suddenly echoed through his mind and a nagging unease followed right behind them. He still had his ranch to improve, his mother to care for, and no experience of settling down with a woman—particularly one who wasn't used to hard work and the realities of "cowboying," as she'd said. His friend had been right, he thought. Rebecca could easily hurt him.

If he let her. And Jake wasn't about to do that. She might have a firm grip on his arm right now, but he'd never give her soft little fingers the chance to touch his heart.

Chapter Five

Moments later, at the house, Beau followed them onto the porch and before Rebecca could open it, the dog stuck his nose in the crack of the screen door.

With a wry smile, she looked up at Jake. "Do you mind if Beau joins us? He'll be a good boy and lie on the floor, out of the way."

"I don't mind at all."

Jake followed her into the kitchen and was instantly struck by the delicious smell of just-cooked food. Glancing around the small room, he could see she'd made major headway in cleaning the piled cabinets and dusty linoleum.

The evidence of her hard work surprised him somewhat. That first day he'd laid eyes on her at Gertie's funeral, she'd seemed like the last sort to pick up a mop or broom or manhandle heavy feed sacks. But then, he'd not known her any more that day than he really knew her now.

"Is cooking something you do regularly?" he asked.

She laughed softly. "Not in Houston. I don't have time for it. And I'm not really that good at it. I can do a few certain dishes. But now that I've moved out here, I'm trying to get the hang of making regular meals. It's not like I can walk down the road to a deli or restaurant."

"No," he agreed, while thinking what a drastic change in lifestyle this must be for her. About as drastic as him trying to survive in Houston.

Gesturing toward an open doorway on the opposite side of the room, she said, "I'm sure you'd like to wash Starr's hair from your hands. The bathroom is right down that hallway on the left. There should be soap and towels and whatever else you might need."

He nodded. "Thanks. I'll be right back."

Since the house was very small, it was no problem finding the bathroom. Along the way, Jake caught glimpses of the two bedrooms branching off the short hallway. In one, cardboard boxes and clothing were piled and strewn every which way. The other was neat and clean with a double bed made up with a white bedspread.

As he washed his hands, he tried not to think about her lying upon that white bed, the night breeze blowing gently across her body. No. Those were thoughts he shouldn't be dwelling on. Those were the kind of thoughts that could only get him into trouble. Yet he couldn't quite shove them aside or quit wondering what it would be like to kiss her, make love to her.

You can forget that, Jake. Rebecca might want you to share her supper table. But that's a far leap away from

*her bed. Remember, you told Quint she's not a barfly.
So don't expect her to behave like one. She's a lady. A
lady not likely to make love to rough-edged cowboys.*

Downright annoyed by the mocking voice in his head,
Jake switched off the bathroom light and hurried to
the kitchen. He'd told Quint that he knew how to be a
gentleman. So now was the time for him to prove it.

He found Rebecca setting the table with big red plates
that were chipped around the rims and tea glasses foggy
from years of handling. Even though Rebecca came
from an easier life, he thought, her aunt certainly hadn't
lived one.

"What can I do?" he offered.

"Nothing. It's all ready."

She plucked a bowl of tossed salad from the cabinet counter and placed it in the middle of the small
table alongside the casserole dish containing the enchiladas.

As she made a move to take one of the chairs, Jake
quickly pulled it out for her, then helped her onto the
seat. He couldn't remember the last time he'd done such
a thing for a woman, but somehow it felt right with
Rebecca.

She looked up at him and smiled. "Thank you,
Jake."

"My pleasure," he murmured, forcing himself to drop
the loose hold he had on her forearm and take a seat in
the chair kitty-cornered to hers.

"I have all the windows open," she said, "but the oven
has made it very hot in here. I hope the heat doesn't
make you uncomfortable."

The heat he was feeling had everything to do with
her. Not the oven. "Don't worry about it. I'm fine."

She picked up a spatula, then motioning for him to

hold out his plate, she ladled a hefty portion of the meat and tortillas concoction onto the surface, then did the same for herself.

A few feet behind them, Beau had curled up on the floor and now had one eye cocked curiously on their movements.

"For a girl who never was around animals, you sure seemed to take to them," Jake commented as he glanced at the contented dog.

Smiling faintly, she said, "I guess you could say I feel like a child let loose in a toy store. I'm so enjoying Beau and the cats and Starr."

"You never had pets when you were a kid?" he asked curiously.

Her gaze avoided his as she shook her head. "Not one. Mother wouldn't allow it. She said they were messy and costly and would require too much care."

"Sounds like she's not an animal lover."

Looking over at him, Rebecca grimaced. "Not hardly. She—uh—is not the outdoor sort."

"And you are?" he asked with an impish grin.

She shrugged. "I've always thought I could be." Her blue eyes caught hold of his. "You'll probably laugh when I tell you this, Jake, but when I was young, I desperately wanted to become a veterinarian."

His fork paused in midair as he looked at her. A sheen of sweat dampened her forehead and her cheeks were flushed from the heat. She looked beautiful and sad and sexy all at the same time, he realized.

"What happened? Why did you change your mind?"

Her lips pursed together. "I didn't change it. Mother changed it for me."

"Oh."

She helped herself to the salad bowl. "You see," she began, "when my father, Vance, was still alive my life was fairly rounded. He understood that I needed and wanted to do things other than what my mother had planned out for me. But after he died, I didn't have him to back me up on anything. And when it came to me wanting to become a vet, she thought doctoring sick animals was too primitive for her daughter. That it was just a childish whim on my part."

"Was it?"

She sighed and Jake sensed there was something lost in her, some missing piece that she was yet to find. But then he supposed most people were that way to some degree. For years now his father's leaving had left an empty spot in him and he'd often wondered how he would feel if he ever found the man and stood face-to-face with him. Yeah, he figured everyone was a little lost at some time in their life.

"I don't know," she said. "Being here with Beau and the rest of the animals makes me wonder if I should have stuck to my guns and gone after my own wishes."

"You're still very young," he pointed out. "You have plenty of time left to go after your wishes."

She looked at him with faint dismay. "You make it sound so simple. But it's not. I have a job that pays extremely well. I've worked hard to build my career to this point. In fact, it's taken years. Throwing all that away and going back to college would be a huge change in my life, not to mention a whole lot more work."

"Work isn't work if you like what you're doing."

She remained silent for a long moment and then she grinned at him. Jake felt his heart begin to kick like a trapped pony.

"And do you like what you're doing?" she countered.

He chuckled. "We were talking about you."

"Yes, but that's all we seem to do is talk about me. I want to hear about you."

"I'm not that interesting, Rebecca. I live a boring, everyday life."

"I don't believe that. Tell me about your ranch. What do you call it?"

"The Rafter R. That's my brand, too. A gable of rafters with an R beneath it."

"Abe says the property is a very pretty piece of land."

"Abe did, did he?"

"Yes. He says it's near an old fort that the cavalry used years ago."

"That's right. The Rafter R is out in the middle of nowhere. But the majority of the ranches around here have to be in the middle of nowhere. You need lots of acreage to run cattle in New Mexico. Forage is a scarce commodity. It's not like the area you live in where the Bermuda grows knee-deep."

"I see. So do you like being a rancher?"

Did he? There were many aspects of the job that he loved. Working outdoors, tending to the livestock, seeing the results of his handiwork. But working for Quint or managing the training stables at the Downs had been much easier. At those jobs, the responsibility of making major decisions had lain on someone else's shoulders, not his.

"For the most part. It's the sort of work I've done all my life. I went to college for a couple of years thinking I might eventually do something different in the agriculture field. I even got an associate degree, 'cause I believe everybody ought to learn. But doing a thing is sometimes better learning than what books can tell you. And it just isn't in me to be anything else besides a cowboy. Horses, cattle. They're what I know."

He didn't go on to tell her that he'd been born into ranching, that his father had taught him all he knew about raising cattle and horses. Even his ability to become one of the best farriers in Lincoln County had come from Lee Rollins.

You're like your daddy in every way, Jake. The good and the bad.

His mother had spoken those words to him more times than Jake could count. And he supposed Clara was right. He did take after Lee in plenty of ways. But Jake didn't want to believe he was exactly the same man as his father. He didn't want to think he was the sort of guy who could callously walk away from his own child, from the woman he'd sworn to love and cherish.

"And I'm sure you're very good at what you do."

Her reply broke into his roaming thoughts and he looked over just in time to see her cast him a furtive glance.

"I'd love to see the Rafter R sometime," she quietly suggested. "Whenever you're not too tied up with work."

Did she really want to see his ranch or was she simply trying to be sociable because he'd gone out of his way to help her with Starr?

Jake quickly decided to keep the questions to himself. He didn't want to take the chance of offending her. Especially if she really meant what she was saying.

"I'd be happy to drive you over to see it some evening," he said. "Just don't expect too much, though. I've only been working on the place for the past couple of years. It's coming along. But it's not quite where I want it to be yet."

"So it wasn't in tip-top condition when you purchased it?"

He grunted with amusement. "If it had been I could have never afforded it."

Her smile was gentle. "Well, I'm sure I'll be rightly impressed."

Impressed? With him? What was wrong with this woman? Couldn't she see he was just a regular Joe?

After that their conversation turned to less personal things. She asked him about the winters in Lincoln County and other local interests. As they talked and enjoyed the food, Jake tried to think of another time he'd had such an evening. But he couldn't recall even one.

He'd never really had many meaningful conversations with women he dated. Not that Rebecca could be considered a date. But she was definitely a woman and they were alone together. If this evening wasn't a date, it was pretty close to being one. Yet nothing about it felt like anything he'd experienced in the past. Most of those encounters had been spent throwing out sexual innuendos and nonsensical jokes, while subtly maneuvering his date to the bedroom. Getting to know his companion had never been important to Jake

So why did it seem important now?

"I'm so full I don't think I can eat another bite," Rebecca announced as she pushed back her plate. "Would you like something else? Dessert? I have chocolate cake that I purchased from a bakery in Ruidoso. I'll make coffee to go with it."

Jake wasn't sure he could eat another bite either, but the cake and coffee would prolong the evening. And he wasn't ready to leave. Not by a long shot.

"That sounds good," he told her. "While you make the coffee, I'll clear off the table."

Rising to her feet, she looked at him with surprise. "That's not necessary. I'll deal with the mess later."

Ignoring her, he got to his feet and reached for the dirty plates. "I insist," he said. "It's the least I can do."

As they moved around the kitchen, the close quarters caused their shoulders to inadvertently brush each other more than once. Each time it happened Jake warred with the idea of grabbing her and whirling her into his arms. If Rebecca had been any other woman, he would have already made his move and showed her just what her presence was doing to his libido.

But Rebecca wasn't any woman and even though his body was yelling at him to shift to a faster gear, his mind was telling him he had to take things slowly. If he didn't, he might scare her off and ruin the easy companionship that had developed between them.

When the coffee finally finished brewing, Rebecca filled two cups and placed a hefty serving of chocolate cake on a small plate.

"If you'd like, we could take our coffee and sit out on the back steps," she suggested. "It's much cooler than this kitchen."

And much safer, she thought, as she poured a dollop of cream into her cup. From the moment they'd entered the house and sat down to supper, she'd felt as though all the oxygen had been sucked from the room. She'd hardly been able to keep her eyes off him. And the more she'd looked at him, the more her mind had wandered to things she had no business thinking. Like how it would be to kiss him, to have him hold her the way a man holds a woman whenever he wants her.

"I'm good with that," he agreed.

Releasing an inaudible sigh, she called to Beau and the three of them passed through the door and onto the back porch.

"I apologize for not having a porch swing or lawn furniture," she told him. "I couldn't find any around the place and I've not taken the time to shop for much more than groceries and pet supplies."

"The steps are fine," he assured her. "I'm not used to doing a lot of chair sitting anyway. Most of my sitting is done in the saddle."

He waited until she'd eased down on the top step before he joined her and as he stretched his long lean legs out in front of him, Rebecca immediately wondered if she'd made a mistake by leaving the kitchen. At least in there their chairs had been a respectable distance apart. Now that they were sitting side by side on the wooden step, there wasn't a hand's width of space between them.

What are you whining about, Rebecca? You've been itching to get close to the man. Now that you are, you want to run like a scared cat.

She wasn't feeling scared, she mentally argued with the mocking voice in her head. She was only trying to be cautious. Jake was obviously a love 'em and leave 'em sort of guy. He'd never taken a wife, or as far as she knew a fiancée, but she'd be ready to bet he'd taken plenty of prisoners of the heart. Would she be willing to become one more?

Sipping her coffee, she tried not to sigh, to let him see that just sitting here close to him was shaking her like the winds of a hurricane. "I'm ashamed to admit that a lot of my work is done sitting behind a desk. I have so much reading to do, so many photos and catalogs to view, I don't get to exercise as much as I'd like."

"You look like you get plenty of exercise."

She'd not been fishing for a compliment and the fact that he'd noticed such a personal thing about her sent a flash of pink color to her face.

"At the gym," she explained. "I meant natural exercise."

Between bites of cake, he glanced at her, his mouth curved in a suggestive grin. "What sort of exercise do you consider *natural?*"

She cleared her throat and wondered again why he made her feel so naive and inexperienced. She'd had plenty of boyfriends, even a few lovers. This one shouldn't be causing a flash fire of heat to rush from the soles of her feet to the top of her head. This one shouldn't be making her heart pitter-patter like those first few drops of rain right before a storm.

Dating had never been simple or easy for Rebecca. Losing her father had taught her that loving someone with all her heart also carried risks. And for a long time after she'd first started dating, she'd kept everything simple and platonic as a way to keep her emotions protected. But then, as she'd grown older, she'd realized if she never allowed a relationship to grow between herself and a man, she'd always be living alone. Unfortunately, each time she'd let a man into her life, he'd found a reason to leave. Now Jake was knocking on the door of her heart and, crazy or not, she was desperately wanting to open it up and let him in.

"I meant like…riding a horse."

"Oh. So tell me, Rebecca, back in Houston what did you do for play?"

The question brought her up short and for long moments her mind was stuttering, searching wildly back through her regular routine. To her dismay, the days and nights of the past few years were mostly an uneventful blur of work and travel, exhaustion and sleep.

"Well—I go to the movies," she finally said. She didn't add that the outing was mostly a form of work, a chance to see what types of fashions were being worn on the big screen and how the more popular movies would influence the next round of designs to be introduced to the buying public.

"Is that it?"

She thought for another long moment. "I like going to the beach down at Galveston—whenever I get the chance. But that's not often."

His gaze slipped over her face and she could feel her lips tingling, burning beneath his lazy inspection.

"No dining, dancing?"

She looked away from him to focus her gaze on the open field sweeping away to the left of the property. Twilight had fallen and in the gloaming she could see a pair of nighthawks circling over the desert brush. As she watched the birds dip and dive for insects, she wondered how Jake's simple questions could make her see herself more plainly than looking at her image in the mirror.

"On occasions. I stay very busy with my work, you see."

"Yes. I am beginning to see," he replied.

He placed his plate and cup aside, then reached for her hand. Rebecca tried not to outwardly shiver as the pads of his fingers slid gently back and forth over the top.

"And I'm thinking it's a good thing that you decided to stay on here for a while. For me, 'cause I like your company. And for you, 'cause I get the feeling that you needed some time away."

Her throat was suddenly thick and she tried to swallow

the sensation away. "I hadn't planned on staying. Not at first. But I—well, I decided that my aunt deserved a little of my time. God knows she didn't have any of it while she was alive. And now—well, everything she had in her life, she left to me. It's—"

She was suddenly too choked to speak and she looked down at her feet as she tried to regain her composure. Finally, she spoke in a broken voice. "It's hard for me to bear, Jake. I don't deserve anything from her. None of it."

"Rebecca, why would you say such a thing?"

"Because I never visited her. Never spoke to her." She looked at him, her expression full of despair. "Jake, this is going to sound crazy, but I never even knew I had an aunt! I didn't find out about Gertrude until a few days before her funeral."

Clearly stunned by her admission, he stared at her. Then finally, he said, "I understood that you'd never been out here to visit. But I thought—well, sometimes people have good intentions that never come through and I figured you were busy with your own life."

Her head swung shamefully back and forth. "I wish it were that simple. But it's not. My family—everything feels like a lie—a sham!"

"Whoa now, Rebecca. That's a pretty harsh way of putting things. Maybe you ought to back up and explain from the beginning," he gently suggested.

Realizing half of what she'd just said probably hadn't made sense to him, she nodded. "You're right. I should start at the beginning. So I'll begin by saying that I've always been from a small family. I never knew my maternal grandparents. My mother had been born to them in their latter years. By the time she'd grown to adulthood they were both suffering from age-related health problems. They passed away before I was born."

"What about your paternal grandparents?" he asked.

"During the time I was a very young child they lived in Florida and came for short visits. But a few years before my father lost his life, they were killed in an automobile accident."

"That's hard," he said softly.

Her lips took on a wry slant. "That's life. At least, that's the way it is in mine." She drew in a deep breath and let it out in a heavy rush. "So neither of my parents had siblings. Or that's what I was led to believe. So I had no aunts or uncles or cousins. For most of my life it's just been my mother and me."

His forehead puckered in a frown, he squared around to face her. "How did you find out about Gertrude?"

"A lawyer from Ruidoso called me at the department store where I work. He explained that Gertrude had left strict instructions to notify me of her death, but not before. And that all of her belongings, including the land and mineral rights, go to me."

As she talked he rested their entwined hands upon his knee and Rebecca was amazed at how one minute his touch could be so exciting and the next comfort her like nothing had before.

"Dear God, that must have been a wham in the gut."

She sighed. "At first I thought someone was playing a tasteless joke. I even argued with the lawyer and told him that I ought to know my own family." The faint noise she made in her throat was something between a self-mocking groan and a sob. "Can you imagine how I felt when I learned that I didn't know my own family?

Initially I was in denial. Then when I realized he was serious, I was stunned and embarrassed."

He stared thoughtfully out to the stand of aspens and the barn partially hidden by their branches. "I can't imagine what any of it must have felt like. You learn you have an aunt at the same time you learn that she's already died." He focused his gaze back on her face. "How did all this happen, Rebecca?"

Shaking her head with defeat, she tried to keep her emotions in check. Yet her voice quivered when she finally answered, "I don't yet know, Jake. I've asked my mother to explain, but she's told me very little. She and Gertrude were twins. But at some point, after they became adults, they parted ways and lived totally separate lives."

"And she hasn't explained why?"

The dismay in his voice matched the disbelief she was still feeling. After years of believing her mother was a morally upright person, she now had to face the fact that Gwyn was deceptive. Not only deceptive, but unfeeling along with it.

"The only thing she says is that they were entirely different people and they simply chose to live different lives."

"Do you believe that's all there was to it?"

Rebecca let out an unladylike snort. "Of course I don't believe it! If it was all that simple, there would have been no need for my mother to keep Gertrude a secret from me."

"Hmm. Maybe she thought the woman would be a bad influence on you and didn't want you to be acquainted with her."

"Jake! Gertrude was the only other blood connection I could possibly have for most of my life. Even if she had been a bad person, that didn't give my mother the right to keep her existence from me! Every family has a misfit or two, but that doesn't make them any less a relative. Besides, I don't believe Gertrude was a bad person. Do you?"

He appeared surprised that she'd asked him such a thing.

"Why, no. I don't," he answered. "How could she have been bad? She kept to herself and as far as I know never caused anyone a problem. Did your mother try to paint her sister as a bad person?"

Rebecca grimaced. "Not really. She refused to say much at all. And that infuriates me. I can hardly bring myself to speak to my mother. Most days I don't bother answering her calls. It's always the same. Begging me to come home, but refusing to explain anything."

His hold tightened slightly on her hand. "The Cantrells noticed you were the only relative attending Gertie's funeral. They wondered why and frankly I did, too," he admitted. "Your mother didn't want to see her own sister laid to rest?"

Anger, frustration and an enormous sense of loss swept over Rebecca and for a moment she closed her eyes. "Mother refused to come out here. Said she wanted to remember Gertrude in her own way." Opening her eyes, she looked at him with all the pain and betrayal she was feeling. "I'm ashamed to tell you this, Jake, but I honestly believe the death of a stranger living down the street would have affected her more. She doesn't want to remember her sister in any way. Much less talk about her."

His head swung back and forth in contemplation. "You being her daughter, I'm sure you know more about that than anyone else. What I'm wondering is why Gertrude never tried to contact you. You say she told the lawyer not to contact you before her death, only afterward?"

Rebecca nodded, then stared at him as her thoughts took his direction. "That's right. And I've been so busy wondering about my mother's motives, that I've not stopped to think about Gertrude's. Why didn't she try to contact me? Why did she live here in New Mexico, when I know for certain that my mother was born and raised in Houston? So that means Gertrude once lived there, too." Wiping a hand over her face, she said in a strained voice, "Oh, Jake, maybe my aunt didn't want to know me. After all, she knew where I lived—where I worked. I can only believe that she wasn't that interested in spending time with her niece."

His expression full of empathy, he curled his arm around her shoulder and snuggled her close to his side. "Rebecca, you're agonizing over things that might not even be true. I didn't know Gertie, but I can't imagine her keeping you out of her life on purpose."

It felt wonderful to have his strong shoulder supporting her, to have the heat of his body seeping into hers, warming the empty chill inside her.

"You're just being kind, Jake."

"I'm being sensible."

She sighed. "I'm afraid I'll never get the answers I need to know about my aunt—my family."

He didn't say anything for a long time, so long in fact that Rebecca finally tipped her head back to glance up at him. She barely had time to catch the faint smile on his face when he tucked her head beneath his chin.

"Don't feel badly, Rebecca. I've wanted answers about my own family for years."

As he stroked fingers through her hair, Rebecca

realized she was probably allowing herself to get too close to the man. She also realized she couldn't resist him. At this moment, she didn't want to move. Didn't want to break the sweetness of his touch.

"What sort of answers?" she asked quietly.

"Do you remember me telling you that I don't have a father?"

Her mind whirled back to the day of the funeral. As he'd driven her back to her car, she'd asked him about his father and the answer he'd given her had been curt and evasive. At the time, she'd been too upset with her own problems to think much about it. Now she was wondering and wanting to discover more about this man who'd quickly stepped into her life.

"Yes. I remember."

She felt his body move slightly as he let out a heavy breath and the idea that this man could be troubled about anything took her by surprise. From the moment she'd first met him, he'd seemed like a happy, carefree guy.

"Well, the reason I don't have a father is not because he died in an accident, like yours."

He turned his gaze on the open meadow, but Rebecca knew he wasn't looking at the waning twilight or the busy nighthawks. His thoughts were somewhere far away.

"Oh. Are you trying to tell me that you've never had a father? That your mother raised you single-handedly?"

"No. I had a father up until I was thirteen years old. Then he packed up and left us," he said flatly.

Pulling her head from beneath his chin, she stared up at him. "Oh, Jake, why?"

His arm dropped from her shoulder and he rose restlessly to his feet. Unwittingly, Rebecca also stood as she waited for him to answer.

"He found another woman that he wanted to make a life with—more than he did my mother."

"So your mother and father divorced?"

"Yeah, they broke up," he said, his voice heavy with cynicism. "Just like thousands of marriages break up every year."

Puzzled, she watched him lean a hand against a porch post. "I don't understand, Jake. What sort of answers don't you have about your family? Your father cheated on your mother and they ended their marriage."

"It's not that cut-and-dried. Maybe for them. But not for me." He looked at her and for the first time since she'd met him, she saw cold hardness in his eyes. The emotion didn't match the man she'd come to know and the sight of it left her chilled.

"What do you mean?" she asked softly.

"Before Lee—that was my dad's name—left home we had a long talk. He told me that he loved me and that I had nothing to do with the reason he and my mother were getting a divorce. He promised that I would always remain his son and he would call and come back to visit as often as he could."

"So what happened?"

"That was eighteen years ago and I never heard from him since."

When he answered his voice was flat, yet in spite of that Rebecca could pick up on his pain, the sense of betrayal he'd been living with for so long now.

"So you see, you and I have something in common, Rebecca. Neither of us knows why our parents lied to us. Or why they made the choices that they did."

Moving forward, she placed a hand against his back.

"I'm sorry about your father, Jake. But I'll tell you like you told me a few minutes ago. I can't imagine the man keeping you out of his life on purpose."

He turned toward her and this time there was a rueful twist to his lips, a sad acceptance in his eyes. The idea that he'd been hurt as she'd been, that he'd lived with it for so many years, touched her deeply, drew her to him in a way she hadn't expected.

He said, "Well, I tell myself it doesn't matter anymore."

"But it does," she added softly.

"Yeah. Deep down, I guess it does. Just like this thing with your aunt matters to you."

Her eyes met his and it seemed like the natural thing to reach for his hands and move closer to him.

"Thank you, Jake."

His brows lifted ever so slightly. "For what?"

"Just for…being here."

She squeezed his hands and for long moments they simply looked at each other. And then Rebecca realized his head was bending down to hers and she was rising up on her tiptoes to meet him.

When their lips finally made contact, the jolt was electric. As his hard lips gently moved against hers, she lost her breath and a rushing noise sounded in her ears. She was wilting, she thought wildly, drowning in a wave of heat.

A tiny moan sounded in her throat and then she felt his hands moving to her back, anchoring a supportive hold just beneath her shoulder blades.

He thinks I'm going to faint! And maybe I will if he doesn't stop soon!

The thoughts sent her hands crawling up his chest and curling desperate holds on both shoulders. The movement pressed the fronts of their bodies even closer and, as it did, his mouth turned urgent, hungry.

She clung to him, her heart pounding fast, her lips a throbbing prisoner to his.

And then, just as her senses began to reel off into some heady place, he tore his mouth from hers and stepped backward.

"I—I'd better go, Rebecca. Now."

Before she could catch her breath to utter a word, he was already down the steps and rounding the back of the house.

Dazed, Rebecca stared after him. What had happened? Why was he leaving?

She didn't stop to think about the answers. Instead, she leaped off the porch and raced after him.

Chapter Six

"Jake! Wait!"

When Rebecca's voice sounded behind him, Jake was reaching for the door handle on his truck.

Pausing, he glanced over his shoulder to see her hurrying toward him. He'd not expected her to follow him out here and the fact that she had both stunned and frustrated him.

As he watched her come to a stop a few steps away from him, he braced himself as best he could and turned to face her head-on.

"Rebecca, you shouldn't have followed me," he said hoarsely. "I told you I had to leave."

Her head swung back and forth. "I don't understand, Jake. I thought we were having a lovely evening."

Something in the middle of his chest squeezed into a tight knot. It was a pain like he'd never felt before and the sensation scared him, almost as much as her kiss had scared him.

"We were. It has been…nice. Real nice. But—" He broke off, amazed that he was at a loss for words. He'd always been able to communicate with women. If words didn't work, then there were always physical ways to express his feelings. But he'd already expressed too much of himself to Rebecca in that way, he thought ruefully.

She stepped closer and for one ridiculous moment, he considered jumping into his truck. At least that way he wouldn't be tempted to jerk her into his arms and smother those luscious lips with more kisses. Instead, he stood his ground and tried not to think about the way she'd made him feel. The way he was still feeling.

Confusion filled her blue eyes. "But what, Jake? You didn't like kissing me?"

He couldn't stop a groan from slipping past his lips. "Of course I liked it!"

"Then why are you running from me?"

Why was he? he wondered. He'd never run from any woman. In fact, he was always happy to let himself be caught—for a little while. "Because what happened between us back there on the porch—I…never planned for that to happen."

No, but he sure as hell had thought about it, he thought grimly.

She said, "I didn't think you had."

He let out a heavy breath. "I don't want you to think—" He stopped, then started again. "Look, Rebecca, you're a lady and before I came out here tonight, I assured Quint that I knew how to be a gentleman."

A smile lifted the corners of her lips and Jake found himself staring at them, wondering why her kiss had felt so different. After all, they were just another pair of plump, pretty lips. They shouldn't have the power to rocket his senses to the moon. But they had.

"Ladies kiss, too, Jake. Especially when they're with a gentleman they like."

Shaking his head, he tried to laugh, but the sound was more like a helpless groan. "And you think I'm one of those? You're misguided, Rebecca. I'm just a regular Joe, who's good at pretending to be something he isn't. I'm not like the men you go out with. The men you want to kiss."

Her expression turned serious as she moved another step closer. "How do you know what sort of man I want to kiss?"

He tried to be cool and shrug his shoulder, but inside he was trembling. It was crazy. Laughable. What was the matter with him? Having a woman close to him was a pleasure. One that he often sought.

"I don't. I just know that it isn't a guy like me."

"Maybe I should have made myself clearer."

If she'd made herself any clearer, he thought, his self-control would have snapped like a fragile twig between her soft little fingers. It still amazed him that he'd found the wherewithal to pull away from her and end the kiss.

"It's clear enough, Rebecca. We're completely different people. Right now I suspect I'm a novelty to you. City girl meets rough-and-tumble cowboy. That's why the only thing you and I need to be to each other is... friends."

Sighing, she stepped forward and curled a hand over his forearm. He swiftly realized the touch of her fingers felt just as sweet, or perhaps even sweeter, now that he'd experienced the yielding softness of her lips.

"Jake, why are you doing this?"

He swallowed. "Doing what?"

"Making a big issue over one little kiss. I promise

I wasn't trying to tie a string to you while you weren't looking."

Any other time, Jake would have laughed at her remark. Especially when it was ludicrous for her to think he was worried about her trying to tie him up. After about thirty minutes she'd want to untie him, kick him in the rear, and send him on back to the rest of the herd. But nothing felt particularly funny to him at the moment.

"I wasn't thinking you were trying to do anything. And I'm not making a big issue."

"Really? Do you always just jump up and abruptly leave your female guests?"

"You're not my guest tonight. I'm yours."

Exasperation twisted her lips and then as she continued to study his face, her expression softened and her fingers gently squeezed his arm. "Jake, I don't want you to leave angry. I like you. And tonight has been very special for me."

The wall of resistance he'd been trying to throw between them suddenly crumbled like old adobe. "Rebecca, I'm not angry. Far from it. I'm just—" Trying to hang on to his sanity, he thought as he searched helplessly for the right words. When none came, he decided plain ole honesty would have to do. "Look, Rebecca, back there on the porch—if I hadn't pulled away from you I—well, if that kiss had went on much longer, I'm not sure I could have stopped."

"Would that have been so bad?"

Her question tied his gut into a hard knot. Which didn't make sense. She was intimating that his making love to her wouldn't have been out of bounds. Normally that was just the sort of green light he wanted to get from a woman. But he wasn't at all sure it was what he needed to hear from Rebecca.

"A moment ago you said that you liked me," he replied. "Well, I like you, too, Rebecca. And I don't want something happening to mess that up."

She searched his face for what felt like an eternity and then she nodded thoughtfully and dropped her hold on his arm. "I understand."

Did she really? he wondered. Because he sure as hell didn't. Liking a woman had never interfered with him having sex with her. Liking had nothing to do with a roll between the sheets. Until now.

Turning toward the door, he momentarily closed his eyes. "I'd better be going, Rebecca."

"Will you—will I see you soon?" she asked.

He dared not look at her, otherwise his pretense of being a gentleman might fall apart.

"Sure. I'll come by one evening and take you over to the Rafter R. If you still want to go."

"Of course I want to go," she replied. "And before you leave, there's something else I wanted to ask you."

This caught his attention and forced him to glance over his shoulder at her. "Oh. What's that?"

"The woman at my aunt's funeral—her friend, the one you called Bess. If you think she wouldn't mind I'd like to talk with her. Could you tell me how to find her?"

He angled his shoulders back toward her. "Sure. When you go through Alto there's a little grocery store called Frank's off to your right on 532. She works there in the mornings."

"Thank you. I'm hoping she can give me a few answers about my aunt."

"Maybe so," he said, then jerked open the truck door and climbed beneath the steering wheel, before letting himself look at her. "Goodbye, Rebecca."

She didn't speak as she lifted a hand in farewell.

With a shaking hand, Jake started the engine and drove away before he could change his mind.

The next morning after Rebecca had eaten a small breakfast and fed all the animals, she whistled for Beau and the two of them climbed into the old red Ford and set off for Alto.

Traveling down to the little community to see Bess this morning had been a last-minute decision. Mainly as a reason to get out of the house and away from her thoughts. She'd had a restless night and sunrise hadn't done a thing to improve her mood.

Over and over, she'd been asking herself what had happened last night between her and Jake. They'd talked. A lot. And then they'd kissed. Passionately. She wasn't exactly certain which one of them had initiated their embrace, or if that even mattered. What mattered was that she couldn't get it out of her mind. Nor could she understand his reaction to it.

Forget it, Rebecca. The man doesn't want to get tangled up with you. You're not his type. He practically spelled it out in big bold letters. What more do you want him to do? Say go away?

Rebecca huffed out a heavy breath and glanced over at Beau. The dog was hanging his head out the window, oblivious to her miserable state of mind.

"You're no help at all, Beau. Give you an open window and a little wind in your face and you think you're in heaven," she muttered.

At the sound of his name, the dog glanced around at her, then just as swiftly turned his attention back to the passing landscape.

Rebecca swiped her blowing hair away from her

forehead, while wishing she could just as easily swipe Jake from her mind. If he didn't want to get tangled up with her, then why would she want to get involved with him? She'd never had to plead or finagle for a man's attention. She had no intentions of starting now.

And yet, there was something about Jake that touched her, made her crave his company, made her dream about kissing him again.

The cell phone lying next to her on the bench seat rang and her foot eased on the accelerator as she glanced down at the illuminated number. Not surprisingly it was her mother ready to make another pitch for her daughter to return to Houston.

Rebecca didn't bother picking up the phone. She wasn't in the mood to have a go-around with Gwyn this morning. Besides that, she wanted her mind clear when she spoke to Gertie's friend, Bess.

In the small community of Alto, she turned right at the highway junction and immediately spotted Frank's, a small brick building with a plate-glass front and a wide dirt parking lot to one side. At the back of the parking area, two huge blue spruce trees shaded a handful of vehicles. She parked next to a dusty Jeep and, before she climbed out, rolled the windows down so that Beau would be cool.

"You stay here, boy, and be nice. I'll be back in a few minutes." Patting his head, she added, "And maybe I'll bring you a treat."

The dog grinned and pounded his tail with happy anticipation. As Rebecca left the truck and started toward the store, she thought about her mother and the many times she'd scoffed at Rebecca's wishes to have a pet of her own.

An animal of any kind would be a nasty nuisance,

Rebecca. You're going to have to get over such adolescent fancies. You have a telephone, stereo and television. Just how much more company do you need?

Even after she'd grown up and moved out, Gwyn had reminded her about how hard she worked, how much she traveled and how it wouldn't be fair to have an animal. Rebecca had been unable to make her mother understand that a pet would have been her own special confidant, something she could share her private joys and sorrows with. Gwyn hadn't understood because she was the sort of aloof person that didn't know how to share herself with anything or anyone. And sadly, that had included her twin sister.

Oh, God, don't let me think about my mother now, she prayed, as she stepped through the open door of the small grocery store. She didn't want to get all angry and stirred up. Not while she talked with the only friend that Gertrude appeared to have had.

After the bright sunlight outside, the interior of the store was dim. The scent of fried food immediately met her nostrils and as her gaze swung toward the one checkout counter to her left, she noticed it was connected to a small deli offering hot food.

Behind the counter, a plump woman wearing a pair of black slacks and a red blouse with the word *Frank's* embroidered on the left breast was counting change back to a young man purchasing bottled sodas. Her hair was a mixture of gray and chestnut and her skin was lined with wrinkles in spite of the fact that she'd probably not yet reached the age of sixty. Those minutes at the cemetery were sketchy for Rebecca, but she did recognize this woman's kind face.

Rebecca waited to one side until the customer had left the building, then stepped up to the counter.

"Can I help you, miss?"

"I think so. Your name is Bess, isn't it?"

The woman used her hip to shove the drawer on the cash register closed. "Why, yes. Do I know you?"

"I'm Rebecca Hardaway. Gertrude O'Dell's niece."

The woman stared at Rebecca as if she'd just announced she was from Mars.

"You're kiddin' me! You're the same young woman I saw at her funeral?"

Nodding, Rebecca unconsciously glanced down at her casual attire. For this trip, she'd made a point to wear her most faded jeans and a simple T-shirt. Her face was bare of makeup and her hair pulled back into a ponytail. No doubt she looked very different from the "Houston" Rebecca.

"That's right," she told the woman. "I'm sorry I didn't get a chance to talk with you that day. I wanted to thank you for taking the time to come to my aunt's funeral."

Bess studied her thoughtfully for a moment or two, then suddenly turned her head and yelled to someone at the back of the store.

"Sadie! Come here and watch the counter for me. It's time for my break."

"Hold on!" a voice shouted from somewhere in the back of the store. "I'll be there in a minute."

To Rebecca, Bess said, "There's a place we can sit outside and I got a few minutes if you'd like to talk."

Behind her, a very young woman with pink-and-black hair and a pierced lip trotted up. "Okay, Grannyma. I'm here. Take your time. It's not like we got a boatload of customers today." She glanced at Rebecca. "You been helped, sweetie?"

"She's here to see me," Bess said to the coworker, then grabbed Rebecca by the arm and quickly ushered her out the open door. "Sadie's a sweet girl, but she loves to gossip. If you know what I mean."

"Yes. I do," Rebecca agreed, while wondering if this woman intended to tell her something about her aunt that she didn't want other people to hear.

On the west side of the building, two aspen trees shaded a long wooden picnic table. Rebecca took a seat on one side, while on the opposite Bess plopped wearily onto the wooden bench.

"Oh, my," she said with a contented sigh. "That feels good to the ole feet. Been standing on them since five this morning."

Amazed, Rebecca glanced at her watch. It was nearly eleven. "You've been at work since five this morning?"

"If the truth be known it was a little before. 'Course the boss don't count that. I have to start the biscuits and breakfast tacos. The working men want something they can eat on the go. Guess they don't have wives to cook for 'em." She glanced at Rebecca and laughed. "I'm showing my age now, ain't I, honey? Wives don't cook nowadays."

A vague smile crossed Rebecca's face. "I wouldn't know about that. I've never been a wife," she admitted to Bess. And neither had her closest friends. Like her, they'd all been career women. As for her mother, Gwyn stayed as far away from the kitchen as possible.

"Well, you're not missing much. I know from experience. I had me a man once, but he was a no-account. Didn't like to work and didn't much like me when I tried to make him work. One day he lit out for richer pastures and never came back."

The woman appeared completely casual about the

whole incident and Rebecca could only presume it had all happened way back in Bess's younger years.

"Oh. Did the two of you have children?"

"Two. A boy and a girl. After that I raised them myself." She leveled a pointed look at Rebecca. "A woman has to do what she has to do, you know."

Yes, Rebecca did know. Even though it had been through no choice of his own, her father had left her. And without him her world had changed. After his death, she'd decided to never cling to any man or depend on him for her happiness. And so far that pledge had kept her from a broken heart. But it had also prevented her from obtaining a lasting relationship. A man wanted to be clung to. A man liked to be needed. But so far she'd never met a man that could make her shake her independence.

Jerking her thoughts back to the present, she said to Bess, "You must be a very strong woman."

Bess snorted. "Strong hell," she muttered. "Half the time I was scared to death. But that's another story and you didn't come here to talk about me."

"Actually, Jake Rollins told me where to find you. He said that you and my aunt were friends."

Bess's eyes squinted a curious glance at Rebecca. "Jake, eh? You know Jake?"

To Rebecca's amazement she could feel her cheeks fill with a heated blush. Just saying the man's name was more than enough to conjure the memory of his kiss, the taste of it, and the wild, reckless urgings it had elicited in her.

"We…we've gotten acquainted."

"You be careful of that one, honey. He's hell on wheels with the ladies."

Unwittingly, her fingertips fluttered to her lips as

unaccustomed heat burned somewhere deep within her. As far as she was concerned the man was a potent elixir and the dose she'd taken last night still hadn't worn off.

"I'd already assumed as much," Rebecca admitted, then attempted to steer Bess in a different direction. "Had you known my aunt very long?"

Bess took a few moments to mentally calculate. "Probably twenty years or more. That's when I first came to work here at Frank's. You see, she'd come in once a week and buy supplies. We never exchanged more than a few words until she happened to have a deck of cards in with her grocery items. I asked her what she was going to do with them. 'Cause it seemed out of character, her buying a deck of cards. She was a quiet, meek little thing always going around with her head down. She mostly dressed like a man. To keep from drawing attention to herself, I think. But then you probably already know all about that."

Rebecca's head swung regretfully from side to side. "No. I'm sorry to say I know nothing about my aunt. I didn't even know I had an aunt until I learned that she'd passed away."

"The hell you say!"

"It's true. And now I'd like to find out as much about her as I can. Did she ever speak of her family? Mention me?"

Bess's head swung grimly back and forth. "Gertie told me that she had family in Texas but she never talked about anyone in particular. I knew that her parents were dead and that she'd never been married. I asked her once why she never went back for a visit and she explained that she hated to travel and hated the city. Many a time, especially when Gertie wasn't feeling well, I wanted to ask her why none of her family ever showed up here in New Mexico. But I didn't. I could tell she didn't want to talk about that kind of stuff and I respected her feelings. There's a hell of a lot of things I don't want to spill my guts about, either."

Bending her head, Rebecca wiped a hand over her face. "Gertrude—Gertie was my mother's twin sister. I've only just learned this in the past three weeks. I don't know what happened between the two women, but my mother has kept these facts hidden from me. I was hoping that my aunt had confided in you and that you might be able to give me some answers about our family."

In contrast to her gruff appearance, Bess reached over and gently patted Rebecca's forearm. "I'm real sorry, honey. I wish I could tell you more. Gertie and me were good friends for many years. We played cards every week together—just me and her. She didn't like to get out much, so I'd drive to her place. She was a lonely woman and for a long time—back when she was a lot younger—I urged her to get herself a man." She paused and let out a mocking snort. "But I couldn't make much headway there. She could see what kind of shape Jim had left me in. So I wasn't exactly in the right position to argue the good points of the male race."

"Was there ever anyone special in her life?"

Once again Bess shook her head. "Not that I know of. But there were times, from some of the sad sort of things she said, that I got the feeling there was a man in her life at one time. 'Course that could just be comin' from my imagination."

"You never asked her outright?"

"Oh, yeah. Years ago, after she first came here I asked her if she'd ever had a husband or anything like that.

"She told me that men and her didn't mix. And all the time she lived out by Apache Wells, it's just been her and her critters. She might not have got along with men, but she surely loved animals. By the way, is anyone taking care of the ones she left behind? I figured whoever was taking care of her estate would find homes for them."

"I'm taking care of them," Rebecca told her. "At least for now, while I'm here."

"Guess you'll be selling out," Bess pondered out loud. "I can't picture a girl like you livin' way out there in the boondocks the way Gertie did."

Selling the property had been Rebecca's intentions all along. But it seemed like the longer she stayed here in New Mexico, the less she warmed to the idea. In a small way, she felt she was beginning to know her aunt and that made everything about the place more important and special to Rebecca.

"I'm living there for now. I'm not sure for how long, though," Rebecca told her, then added, "There is something you can tell me, if you would. What did my aunt look like? Was she petite and dark-haired?"

Bess frowned. "Why, no. Just the opposite. In fact, she looked a lot like you. Tall with blue eyes. Her hair was blond, too, only that darker kind—dishwater blond is what we used to call it. Why? That's not the way her twin sister looks?"

"No. My mother is a brunette and smaller in stature. That could only mean the two of them weren't identical twins."

Bess tapped a thoughtful finger against her chin. "Gertie having a twin," she mused aloud. "I still can't get over it." She leveled a meaningful look at Rebecca. "If your mother couldn't bother to see her own sister laid in the ground, then there must have been some pretty bad blood between them."

Rebecca couldn't argue with that. Not when she'd been thinking the very same thing. It had been bad enough to learn that her mother had kept Gertrude a secret, but when Gwyn had refused to attend her sister's funeral, Rebecca's eyes had popped wide open. From that moment forward, her mother had taken on an entirely different image and in Rebecca's eyes it wasn't a nice one.

"You're probably right. But I—well, my mother doesn't want to talk about Gertrude." With a helpless shrug, she gave Bess a grateful smile. "Thank you for telling me about her."

Bess gave Rebecca's arm another pat. "Glad to do it, honey. If you get to hankering to talk again I live about a mile from here. Anybody can tell you how to find me." She rose to her feet. "I'd better get back before Sadie gets restless and leaves the register to come looking for me."

Rebecca thanked the woman again then bade her goodbye. As Bess walked back inside the building and Rebecca returned to the truck, her mind was spinning with the bits of information Bess had given her.

What did it all mean? Maybe they hadn't been twins after all, she thought. Maybe the two women had not really been sisters and that was why it had been so easy for them to go their separate ways? One or both of them could have been adopted. But why had her mother told her that she and Gertrude were twins?

None of it made sense and short of confronting Gwyn and demanding answers, she didn't know how she could ever get to the truth.

* * *

Three days later, Jake spent the morning and part of the afternoon branding calves that he and his two ranch hands, Trace and Jet, had rounded up from the river bottom. Quint, being the friend that he was, had driven over to help and other than a few kicked shins and a burned thumb on Jet's right hand, the work had gone smoothly.

Once the calves had been returned to their mamas, Jake had insisted the two hands take the rest of the day off. Being young and single, and looking for any extra time for fun, neither man had argued and the two had hightailed it to town.

As for Quint, he'd lingered long enough to help Jake unsaddle the horses and put away their equipment. After sharing a cold beer, the other man had left for home, where Maura was making a special meal for her parents, Fiona and Doyle Donovan.

As soon as Quint was gone, silence fell around Jake and with the solitude along came Rebecca's memory. Not that it took a silent moment to think about her, he reflected, as he stared pensively out at the grazing horses from his front porch chair. For the past three days, he'd thought of little else.

That kiss. Never had one little mouth-to-mouth moment affected him in such a way. He couldn't forget it. Couldn't stop wanting to repeat it. Kissing her had probably been a mistake. The whole incident had certainly been messing with his mind. Yet he had to admit he'd never tasted a sweeter mistake.

With an inward groan, he reached for his cell phone and flipped the instrument open. The other night, while he'd been helping Rebecca clean her kitchen, she'd given him her cell phone number. The fact that he'd been carrying it around had been tormenting him, tempting him, while at the same time he'd been trying like hell to forget he had the precious combination of numbers. It had only been three days since he'd spent the evening with Rebecca and he didn't want her to get the idea that he was desperate for her company. He'd never been desperate for any woman. Not when there was always another woman willing and waiting to give him a bit of company.

Hell, who are you trying to kid, Jake? You're problem isn't what Rebecca might be thinking about you. The problem is what you're thinking about yourself. The urge to see the woman, hold her, kiss her again is clawing at your insides, tormenting your every waking moment. And just any other woman won't do.

Muttering a curse under his breath, Jake snapped the phone shut, closed his eyes and sucked in a harsh breath. What was coming over him? Was he turning into a sap?

With that thought he opened the phone and punched Rebecca's number before he could change his mind.

She answered on the third ring and from the faint swooshing noise in the background he could tell she was outside in the wind.

"Jake, how nice to hear from you," she greeted him.

Like a cool drink of water after a long thirst, pleasure poured through him and curved the corners of his lips. "Have I caught you at a bad time?"

"Not at all. I'm painting the yard fence so I welcome the interruption."

Painting the yard fence? That didn't sound like a woman with leaving on her mind. But then she could just be sprucing up the place and getting it ready to put on the market.

Hell, Jake, it doesn't matter one way or the other. Eventually she'll go back to Houston and you'll go back to your old roving ways.

Shoving that thought away, he said, "Well, I've wound up my work for the rest of the afternoon and wondered if you'd like to come over to the ranch?"

She paused, but only for a second. "I was thinking you'd probably forgotten about the invitation."

Forgotten? He could forget nothing about her or the words that had passed between them. If that was a romantic sap, then he'd fallen into that category.

"No. Just waiting for the right time. If you'd like to come I can be over to pick you up in about forty-five minutes."

"If you'd give me directions I can drive it, Jake. There's no need for you to make such a long trip to pick me up."

Rising from his chair, he started into the house. As he walked through the living room, he said, "I realize your old truck is fairly dependable, but I wouldn't like to think of you driving it through the mountains after dark."

"Oh. I'm going to be at your place for that long?"

Pausing near an armchair, he chuckled, then said in a husky tone, "It's a big ranch, Rebecca. And I want you to see everything. Everything that matters, that is. Still want to come?"

There was another short pause and at that moment, Jake wished he could see her face and read what she was thinking. Maybe she was biting her lip, trying to decide whether he was worth the effort at all.

"I'll be ready," she answered.

"Forty-five minutes," he reminded her, then after a quick goodbye, tossed the phone onto the cushion of the chair and hurried to the shower.

She'd be ready, but would he? Jake asked himself, as he peeled off his sweaty shirt and kicked off his dirty boots. For the first time in his life, he had a real home and a real lady to show it to. And the idea shook him.

He'd never cared much about other people's opinion of him or his way of life. He was an unpretentious man and as far as he was concerned, they all could take him or leave him.

But it was different with Rebecca. He wanted her admiration and respect. He wanted to hear her say he was doing things right and good.

Did that mean he was falling in love? No. He couldn't fall in love. He had too much of Lee Rollins's genes running through his veins. He wasn't a one-woman man. He was a man for every woman. And when he looked into Rebecca's pretty blue eyes again, he couldn't let himself forget that.

Chapter Seven

Rebecca had just finished changing into a cool sundress and dabbing perfume on her neck and wrist, when she heard Beau bark and a door slam.

Hurrying from the bedroom and through the house, she walked out onto the front porch just as Jake was climbing the steps. He was carrying a small potted cactus with a single yellow bloom adorning one of the branches.

Her gaze vacillated between the plant and the lazy smile on his face while her heart leaped into a higher gear. Three days had passed since she'd last seen him and although he'd never left her thoughts, the actual sight of him was like a delicious jolt of pleasure.

"Hello, Rebecca."

She smiled back at him. "Hello," she said, then inclined her head toward the plant he was carrying. "Is that for me?"

A dimple carved deep into his left cheek as one shoulder gave a casual shrug. "I thought you could set it on your kitchen windowsill. Or something like that. It'll brighten up the place."

Touched by his thoughtfulness, she reached to take the plant from him. "It's beautiful, Jake. Thank you."

"It's also very prickly," he warned. "Better let me carry it in for you. We wouldn't want to spend the evening picking spines from your fingers."

"All right." She opened the wooden screen door and followed him through the small living room and into the even tinier kitchen.

He placed the blooming cactus in the middle of the windowsill and glanced around for her approval.

"Very nice. The pot even matches the curtains," she said.

A few days ago, she'd replaced the faded fabric at the window with those woven of blue buffalo checks. The curtains had been one of many small improvements around the place and she was still asking herself why she was making them. For herself? Or for the aunt she'd never known?

"Sometimes a man gets lucky," he said, slanting her a wry grin.

Her heart, which was already thumping in a rhythm that was way too fast, somehow sped up even more. Clasping her hands together, she cleared her throat. "W-would you like something to drink before we go?"

Moving away from the window, he walked over to where she stood by the small dinette table. "No, thanks. We don't have a whole lot of daylight hours left and I don't want to waste them." His brown gaze slipped down the length of her tan-and-white-striped dress and the sandals strapped on her feet. "Are you ready?"

His inspection of her appearance made her hesitate. "Am I dressed appropriately for this tour? If you'd like I can change into jeans and boots."

His gaze settled back on her face and in spite of her weak-willed efforts, Rebecca focused directly on his mouth with its square, chiseled corners and the faint sheen to the curve of his lower lip. Since that kiss they'd shared on the porch, she'd thought of those lips, dreamed about them, hungered for them. And tried her best to forget them. All to no avail.

"I'm not going to put you to work in the branding pen," he said with an amused grunt, then added huskily, "I like you just as you are."

She drew in a deep breath and said, "I'll go get my purse and wrap and we can be on our way."

For a moment there was something in his eyes that made her think he was going to reach out and touch her, but if he was harboring those intentions, something must have waylaid them. Like common sense, Rebecca thought. Because she had the feeling if he touched her now, they'd never make it off the place.

"I'll wait on the porch," he told her, then quickly turned and left the room.

Minutes later, they were headed northward through mountainous countryside that Rebecca had never seen before. Traffic was light to nonexistent on the narrow highway and before long they were far away from any sort of settlement or civilization.

As Jake focused on his driving, Rebecca decided to speak the thoughts that had been racing through her mind. "I was surprised when you called me this afternoon."

Beneath the brim of his gray hat, she could see his brow arch faintly. "Oh. Why was that?" he asked.

She looked away from him and out toward the swiftly changing scenery. In the past couple of minutes the mountains were giving way to flat desert surrounded by low, balding hills.

"Because the other night when you left my place I couldn't help but think that—" She didn't know how to put her feelings into words and she groaned inwardly as she tried to fumble her way through it. "Well, that something about me had put you off. I figured you probably intended to avoid me. Because you considered me trouble."

He kept his eyes on the highway. "You are trouble, Rebecca."

Frowning, she stared at him. "So what am I doing here? With you?"

This time he chuckled and the sound released some of the tension inside of her.

With his eyes crinkled at the corners, he glanced at her. "Haven't you guessed by now that I'm a man who likes to flirt with danger?"

Oh, yes, he flirted without even realizing he was flirting. That was part of his charm, she thought. He didn't even know just how potent he was to a woman, how just a simple little expression on his face was enough to melt her heart.

She started to tell him that there was nothing dangerous about her, but instead she decided it would be best all around to let the matter drop and try to forget everything about that kiss.

"I talked to Bess the other day," she told him. "She wasn't exactly what I expected. But she appeared to have cared a great deal for Gertrude."

"Bess is a little rough around the edges, but that's understandable. Life hasn't been easy for the woman. Still, she's a good ole gal. The kind that would be the first to offer help if you needed it." He glanced curiously her way. "Was she able to give you any helpful information about your aunt?"

"Actually, she told me something that still has me puzzled. My aunt's physical appearance looked nothing like my mother's. She said that Gertrude was tall and blonde. Like me. Is that true? Did you ever see her up close?"

"Not what you'd call close. But she was a tall woman and her hair was light-colored. I used to see her out in the yard, watering the shrubs and flowers. At one time she had a lot of them that bloomed, but that was years ago, back when Quint and I were just young boys. Later on, well, she must have lost interest in the yard and the house. It all started looking run-down." He grimaced, then shook his head. "Sorry. I shouldn't have said that."

She looked at him with speculation. "Why? The place being run-down is an understatement. It needs plenty of home improvements."

"Well, yes. But that bit about her losing interest. That's just a guess on my part. Bad health is probably what made her let things go undone," he said flatly. "I've seen the very same things going on with my own mother."

Interest peaked her brows. "You've never spoken much about your mother. Does she live around here?"

"In Ruidoso. After her and my dad divorced she sold the ranch where I grew up and bought herself a place 'among the living' as she calls it."

The thread of sarcasm she heard in his voice was

probably wound around all sorts of family incidents, she decided, and none of them good. "And you didn't want her to sell?"

"Hell, no! She let the property go for less than half of what it was worth. The two of us could have made a good go of it, but she wasn't willing to try."

"I thought you said you were only thirteen when your father left?"

"I was. But I was a big strapping boy. I could do the manual work of a man. And Dad had already taught me all about caring for the livestock."

"Yes. But still it would have been only you and your mother to see after things. Keeping up a ranch of any size would have been a big job for the two of you."

"We would've had to hire day hands from time to time and a vet whenever one was needed. But—" He let out a long breath and shook his head once. "Sorry. Again. None of that matters anymore."

"But it still fires you up," she quietly deduced.

He smiled wanly. "You could tell?"

She chuckled. "Just a little." Squaring her knees around so that she was facing him, she asked, "Do you and your mother get along?"

He shrugged. "If you're asking me if I love her, then I do. Very much. God knows she worked hard to raise me—without any help from my dad. But there are times I get so frustrated with her. It's like she's given up on life. She only sees the negative side of everything."

"That's not good."

The corners of his mouth turned downward. "No. But then she has her reasons for being like she is. First she lost her husband to another woman. And then about ten years ago she had cancer and went through months of grueling treatment. That wiped the cancer out, but it weakened her heart."

"Poor woman," Rebecca murmured, while thinking what Jake must have gone through while his mother was ill. She didn't have to ask to know that he'd been at her side whenever she needed him, which had probably been a lot. "Is she disabled now?"

"No. And her heart problem wouldn't be that serious if she would only do what the doctors tell her to do. But she doesn't. I think—well, I think she's like your aunt Gertie was these past years. She's lost all interest."

Rebecca gazed thoughtfully out the windshield. "Do you think she's still pining for your father? That she can't get over losing him?"

He muttered a curse under his breath. "I've tried to tell her that the man isn't worth losing sleep over. And she agrees. She knew he was no good. Even before he left, she knew he had a string of women, but she loved him." He looked at her and shook his head with dismay. "Like love means more than anything—even living."

The tiny ache that settled in her chest confused her. It shouldn't matter to her that Jake had a cynical outlook about love. But it did and she couldn't quite understand why. Except that she was beginning to see him as a gallant knight in spurs and blue jeans and knights believed in love. Didn't they?

"I asked Bess if Gertrude had a man in her life," Rebecca told him. "She says she thinks there might have been someone a long time ago, but that's only speculation on her part."

"What do you think?"

That the right man could make a fool out of most any woman, Rebecca thought. Aloud she said, "Since I never met her I can't say. I'm thinking that I might be able to glean some things about her whenever I start going through her personal papers. The spare bedroom is piled with boxes of old correspondence. When I sort through them, I might find old letters to friends or someone that mattered to her."

"You've not dug into that stuff yet?"

Rebecca shook her head. "I've taken a quick glance at some of the things lying on top, but they all seemed to be bills and receipts. The past couple of weeks I've been focused on the animals, clearing the yard of junk and making the house livable." Bending her head, she absently plucked at a tiny wrinkle in her skirt. "To be honest, Jake, I'm a little reluctant to dig into the correspondence."

Surprised by her remark, he darted a glance her way. "Why?"

She shrugged. "Fear of the unknown, I suppose."

He looked even more confused. "I don't understand, Rebecca. I thought you wanted to learn more about your aunt."

"I do. When I first found out about Aunt Gertrude I wanted to find out anything and everything—all at once. But I—" She stopped and let out a long sigh. "Now, the more I dwell on it—well, sometimes I get the feeling that I might be better off not knowing. My mother has certainly made it clear that she wants to keep the past hidden. Maybe she's trying to protect me in some way."

"From what? Gertrude wasn't a criminal."

Sighing, Rebecca swiped a hand through her blond hair. "No. But, Jake, whenever you think about your father—maybe about searching for him—don't you get the feeling that you might not like what you find?"

"Hell yes. I think that most all the time," he admitted.

"I guess that's why I've never gone on a real search for the man. I'd like to know why he turned his back on me. But finding the answer might tell me more than I want to know."

"That's exactly what I'm thinking about Gertrude's correspondence." She cast him a helpless glance. "Are we being cowardly, Jake?"

He grimaced. "I like to think we're simply being human," he said.

Just being human. Jake's words continued to linger in her thoughts as the truck carried them toward a low rise of mountains. When she was near Jake she felt very human. And so much a woman. Whether that was good or bad, she didn't know. She only knew that Jake was the first man she'd ever allowed to see all sides of her, to view the woman she'd always kept curtained and private.

What did that mean? That he was simply a man that was easy to be with, talk to? Or was she falling in love with him?

Pondering that question, she looked over at his dark profile just as he pointed a finger toward the windshield.

"See that cedar post? You are now entering Rafter R land," he announced.

There was pride in his voice and the sound made her happy. "Abe tells me you've worked very hard on this place. That it's turning into a 'damned good ranch' I think were his exact words."

"You've been talking to Abe again?"

"Yesterday. He came over with two of his ranch hands to haul away the junk I'd gathered together in the yard."

"Well, I think I should warn you that you can't

believe everything that Abe tells you. The man likes to exaggerate."

She watched a dimple come and go in his cheek. "I got the feeling that he enjoys telling a tall tale now and then, but in your case, I think I can believe him."

He chuckled. "You're about to find out for yourself."

Five minutes later, Jake steered the truck off the highway and passed beneath an arched entrance made of iron pipe. Sheet metal, cut in the shape of the ranch's brand, hung from the center of the arch and swung slightly in the dusty breeze.

They traveled at least a half a mile on down the red dirt road when a sprawling log house with a green tin roof appeared beyond a stand of aspen and willow trees. As they grew closer she could see the structure was surrounded with a wooden fence painted brown, while massive blue spruce trees shaded a long, ground level portico.

"How lovely!" she exclaimed, then when he failed to pull into the short drive, her head whipped around in surprise. "Aren't we going to stop? Or is this someone else's home?"

A wry grin slanted his lips. "It's mine. I thought I'd show you some of the other parts of the ranch while we still had daylight. You can always see the house later," he reasoned. "Unless you need to make a restroom stop before we go on?"

"No. I'm fine," she assured him. "I was just confused. For a moment I thought that perhaps other people lived on your property. Do they?"

"No. My hired hands live on their own places near Ruidoso and my nearest neighbor is about six miles from here. The closest town, Capitan, is about twenty minutes away. "

"Do you go there often?" she asked.

"I go over there on occasions, to see a few friends. It's more of a village than a town. So if I need supplies for the ranch, I drive into Ruidoso."

"I see," she murmured, as he turned right, onto what appeared to be little more than a two-rutted track with short, stubby grass growing down the middle.

Straightening the steering wheel, Jake glanced at her from the corner of his eye. Did she actually see and understand just how isolated his home really was? he wondered. It was true that Rebecca's place wasn't exactly in the middle of a metropolis, but at least Ruidoso was a heck of a lot closer to her place than to his. And compared to Houston, even Ruidoso was a little tadpole of a city.

"There's not much out here except the wildlife and my cattle and horses," he told her.

"Yes. But it's very beautiful. I wasn't expecting to see this many trees." She gestured toward a band of trees lining the riverbanks. "I thought it was going to look like the desert area we passed through. And those mountains to our left! Does your property include part of them?"

"No. It runs right up to the foothills. Next to me on that side is protected national forestland. And on the right I butt up to Fort Stanton, which was turned into a museum several years ago. So I have a little strip of property running between federal lands. But the strip crosses the river. And best of all, it's mine," he added.

She smiled at him and Jake found it damned hard to keep his eyes on the bumpy track. In that simple little dress she looked every inch a woman and every inch of him wanted her.

"Where are the cows?" she asked, her gaze scanning the horizon.

"All over the place. But I'm sure we'll probably find some down by the river. The grazing is better there."

Five minutes later, a few yards away from the river, Jake parked the truck in a flat, shady spot and helped Rebecca to the ground. Then with his hand wrapped firmly around hers, he led her through a tangle of waist-high sage and drooping willow limbs until they were standing at the water's edge.

"Oh, my! There's a little waterfall. How perfectly beautiful!" She turned a grateful smile on him. "And how sweet of you to show it to me."

Sweet? Hell, he'd never been called sweet before. And though it should have made him feel like a sap, it somehow made him feel warm and wanted. Quint would definitely get a laugh out of that, he thought.

Hoping he didn't look as goofy as he felt, he grinned at her. "I thought you might like it. Want to get a closer look?"

"I'd love to."

They walked several yards upstream to where a ledge of boulders had created a tiny dam. The crystal-clear water rushed over the rocky rim and fell at least ten feet before joining the rest of the river.

"Is the water always this clear and deep?" she asked as they stopped just short of the bank's edge.

"No. Later on in the summer, the level will drop considerably. It's always clear then. But in the spring, the snow runoff sometimes makes it muddy."

She turned her head to look at him and as their eyes met he felt as though something had punched him in the stomach. She was so fresh and pretty. Like a bright bird flying through a blue, blue sky. He wanted to touch her. Desperately.

"Do you fish for trout?" she asked.

"Once in a while. But I go to the lake to do that."

"Is the lake far from here?"

He didn't know why he couldn't quit looking at her lips. Why he kept remembering the taste of her kiss. After all, she was just another woman, he tried to tell himself.

He said, "A few miles. Quint and I used to camp there together from time to time. But that was—before he got married."

"Does that bother you? That Quint got married? You two probably spent lots of time together before he became a family man."

"Yeah, we did," he admitted. "But Maura and the babies make him happy. That's what counts."

She sighed. "I don't have any married friends. Most of them are like me, I suppose. Too busy to have a family."

Jake's gaze lingered on her face as he tried to read what was behind her pensive expression. "That's too bad. I'd bet you'd make a good wife and mother."

Her short laugh was threaded with cynicism. "No one has ever told me that before."

She gave him a faint smile and Jake was surprised at the sadness he saw in her eyes. "That's hard to believe. Surely there've been men in your life that have mentioned marriage to you before."

Shaking her head, she looked away from him and across the river to where a herd of black cattle were idly grazing. "Not really. With me and men—well, things never get that far. It's hard to have a relationship when

I'm packing up every two or three weeks to travel to some far-off city."

For some reason, Jake wanted to wrap his hands over her shoulders and pull her back against his chest. He wanted to press his lips against the curve of her neck and tell her that she was a woman meant for loving, not packing. But that would be insinuating that he wanted to keep her at his side, wanted her to consider him more important than her job. And he was in no position to do that now. Maybe he never would be.

Worry is all a man ever does when he loves a beautiful woman. First he frets about catching her. And then when he does get his hands on her, he worries himself silly wondering if he'll be able to keep her.

Jake had told Quint those very words more than once. And he'd meant them. Having a taste of a smart, beautiful woman like Rebecca could only cause problems. But with her standing so close that he could see the fine pores of her soft skin, smell her flowery scent and gaze upon the moist curves of her lips, he could only think she'd almost be worth the risk.

"Well, your job is important to you. Isn't it?"

From the corner of her eye, she darted a dubious glance at him. "More important than what, Jake? Right now my job is all I have."

Why did he want to tell her that she—that the two of them—could have so much more if they were together? What was the matter with him, anyway? When it came to women he didn't think in terms of "together." And he damned sure never let the word *forever* enter his mind.

Clearing away an uncomfortable knot in his throat, he said, "I see what you mean."

She didn't reply and after a moment he reached for

her arm. "We're losing daylight," he told her. "We'd better be on our way."

For the next hour, he drove to random spots on the ranch where he'd made vast improvements in the fences and grazing land. Jake tried to keep the conversation light, yet something between them had changed while they were standing at the river. He didn't know exactly what or why, except that there was a strained sort of tension between them. As though both of them were trying hard to avoid making eye contact or say anything that could be construed as personal.

By the time they arrived back at the ranch yard and entered the huge barn, Jake was ready to give in and say to hell with being a gentleman and worrying about tomorrow.

"Did you have to do much repair work to the barn?" she asked as the two of them meandered slowly down the alleyway.

On the left side of the structure, ten tons of alfalfa hay were stacked to the rafters. On the right, horse stalls were standing empty. Jake stopped at one of the huge posts that supported the roof and gently thumped the heel of his palm against the creosoted wood.

"Shoring up the support and a new roof. I've spent more money on this barn than I have everything else put together."

She was standing next to him now and in the dim lighting, the angles of her face were softened, the curve of her lips even more inviting. The aching tension deep inside him coiled even tighter.

"You don't have any horses in the stalls. Why is that?"

"When the weather is nice and I don't need to use

them the next day, I turn them out. They like being free—to do whatever they want," he added lowly.

She slanted him a glance and he watched her lips suddenly begin to quiver. "And you do, too, don't you?" she asked softly.

Jake didn't bother trying to summon up any resistance. His hands reached for her so quickly they were a blur.

With her breasts crushed against his chest, he bent her head back over one arm. "Hell yes," he muttered, his lips poised over hers. "And right now I'm damned tired of not doing what I want to do. And I want to do this more than I want to breathe."

He heard her suck in a sharp little breath just as his lips were settling over hers and then his mind went blank as his arms tightened around her and he deepened the kiss.

She tasted just as good or better than Jake remembered and when her arms slipped around his neck and drew her body closer to his, he realized this was something she wanted as much as he. It was a heady notion, one that fueled his rampant hunger.

Long seconds ticked by as their mouths fed upon each other's, their hands began to roam and seek, clench and cling. Jake's senses began to slip to some foggy place he'd never been before where there were no sights or sounds, just warm, velvety heat.

If not for the fiery pain in his lungs, he would have kept kissing her forever. But the need for oxygen finally tore his lips from hers. Yet even then he couldn't quit touching her. Between ragged breaths, he kissed a trail down the side of her neck, then onto the fragile bones of her shoulder.

Her skin was like the petal of a flower. Satiny and

soft and so precious beneath his lips. And the more they explored and tasted, the more he wanted. At the back of his neck, he could feel her fingers digging into his flesh while at the same time her body was arching forward, pressing her breasts and the juncture of her thighs tightly against him. The silent invitation, one that he'd never dreamed he'd be getting from this woman, sent blood roaring to his head, making him almost forget where they were and why. She wanted to make love to him and there was no way he could disappoint her or himself.

"Jake," she whispered hoarsely. "I want you. Really want you."

Her words were enough to lift his head and as his heart continued to pound wildly, he looked into her eyes. Desire wrapped around his voice, strangling his question. "Are you sure?"

One hand lifted to trace the pads of her fingers across his cheek. The tender gesture was like nothing any woman had ever given him before and he felt an odd swelling in his chest, the urge to simply hold her and worship having her close.

"Very sure," she answered in a breathy rush.

"Then not here," he said brusquely and reached for her hand.

As he led her out of the barn and across the ranch yard toward the house, sundown arrived, sending slivers of pink across the lengthening shadows. The air was cool and quiet and he half expected the serenity of the evening to dash her ardor and make her think twice about becoming intimate with him.

But her fingers remained curled tightly around his and when they reached the porch and entered the house, she turned to him and smiled. And if Jake lived to be a hundred, he knew he would never forget the tenderness, the utter longing on her face.

If she'd looked at him with lust, Jake would have understood and felt at ease with her and himself. But this was something different, something deeper and sweeter. The realization shook him right down to the heels of his boots and for one wild second he considered telling her that he couldn't go through with it.

Jake Rollins couldn't make love to a woman! What a hell of a note that would be!

"Jake," she murmured softly. "Is something wrong?"

She stepped closer and as she placed her palm against his chest, his doubts slipped and the aching heat he'd been feeling in the barn returned twofold.

"Not one thing," he said with a growl of pleasure, then swinging her up into his arms, he carried her to the bedroom.

Chapter Eight

When Jake eased Rebecca onto a queen-size bed covered with a smooth blue spread, she wondered how things between them had escalated so quickly. One moment she'd been kissing him and the next she'd felt certain her whole body would go up in flames if he didn't make love to her.

Had she gone crazy? Or just now come to her senses?

He didn't give her the opportunity to answer those questions as he followed her down onto the mattress and gathered her into his arms. And when his mouth latched onto hers in a deep, mindless kiss, she realized the answers didn't matter. All that mattered was the moment and the pleasure of being close to him, of tasting his lips, feeling the hard band of his arms holding her tight against him.

Eventually, he ended the contact of their lips and nuzzled his cheek against hers. "Oh, Rebecca," he whispered rawly, "I never thought I'd have you here. Like this."

The wonder in his voice surprised her. Didn't he know his own sex appeal? Didn't he realize from the first time she'd met him, she'd thought of this very moment, of how it would be to make love to him?

"I never truly thought I'd be here like this. With you," she replied.

His shoulders were broad and the muscles surrounding them corded and hard. She ran her fingers along the strong slopes then down his arms until she reached the bulge of his biceps. There her fingers curled inward, until she was hanging on tightly.

He eased his head back just far enough to look at her. "Why?" he asked with a hint of wry acceptance. "Because you never dreamed you'd lie in a cowboy's bed?"

She smiled as her eyes dreamily scanned his dark features. "You say that like there's something wrong with cowboys."

"Only some of us."

"Meaning you have faults?"

He grunted with cynical amusement. "Faults? Look, Rebecca, I can't pretend. I like women."

She sighed with the sheer contentment of having his body next to hers. "That's good. Otherwise, you might not have ever looked at me."

He rolled his eyes. "That's only a part of my flaws, pretty lady. I like beer. And loafing. And I don't like being serious. And—"

"You talk way too much," she interrupted.

Bringing one hand to the back of his neck, she drew his mouth down to hers and that was all it took to end his litany. After that, she went to work showing him just how much she wanted to be in his arms and his bed.

Almost immediately the contact of their lips turned desperate and rough as they both tried to give and take more and more. As their tongues mated, Rebecca's hands wedged between them and began to fumble with the buttons on his shirt. By the time she'd reached the last one, her lungs were on fire, forcing her to drag her lips from his and draw in long, ragged breaths.

As she resupplied her oxygen, she shoved the fronts of his shirt aside and planted whisper-light kisses across his collarbone, down the middle of his chest and on to his flat stomach. His skin was hot and its masculine scent sparked the heat that was simmering low in her belly. Above her head, she could hear his breathing turn to quick, sharp intakes. Beneath the search of her hands, she could feel his heartbeat and the rapid rhythm matched the pounding in her own ears.

Ever since he'd first kissed her that night on the porch, she'd wanted him. Yet she'd not understood just how deep that wanting was until this moment. It was more than having the unbridled privilege to touch and taste him. It was being connected to him in any and every way.

When her tongue traced a wet circle around his navel, he gasped and thrust his hands in her hair and lifted her face up and away from him.

"Come here," he whispered.

She brought her face back to his and this time as their lips met his fingers left her hair to splay across her cheeks, his thumbs anchored beneath her jawline. He kissed her until she was moaning with need and then he went to work lowering the zipper at the back of her dress and pulling the fabric over her shoulders until it fell to a bunched heap around her waist.

Drunk with desire, her head fell limply back as she savored the sensation of his open mouth sliding slowly, deliciously down the front of her throat, then lower to where pink lace barely covered the tips of her breasts. With his tongue, he laved the open valley between them, then moved on to a peak, where he bit gently through the fabric and around one hard nipple.

Crying out, Rebecca arched toward the pleasure and tangled her legs through his. By now her breaths were coming in rapid pants and she almost screamed with relief when he finally lifted his head and began to remove the remainder of her clothing.

Once he'd tossed the garments out of the way, he quickly shrugged out of his shirt and kicked off his boots. Her gaze followed his every movement until he reached to unbutton his jeans and then their gazes met. And clung.

She could see a last-minute question in his eyes, as though he felt it was only right to give her one last chance to change her mind about this and him. The idea that he was thinking solely of her wants filled her heart with a wave of warm emotions.

Her lips parted to speak, to assure him she had no doubts or desire to end the path they were racing down. But her throat was too tight to utter a word. All she could do to convey her feelings was rise from the bed and wrap her arms around him.

As she buried her face against his chest, she heard him groan. But whether it was a sound of delight or reluctant surrender, she didn't know. Nor did it matter. At this moment he was hers and only hers.

His arms came around her and they stood like that

until the heat between them became unbearable and the need to be connected on a deeper level took over their actions. Jake removed his jeans in hurried jerks and pressed Rebecca back onto the bed.

When he left her long enough to fish a packet from the nightstand and start to tear it open, she finally found her voice. "You don't need that, Jake," she said softly. "I'm protected with oral birth control. Unless—there's something else we should be extrasafe about?"

Extrasafe? With her? He would make love to her even if there was the possibility of a pregnancy hanging over his head. That was how much he wanted her. Needed her. And he'd never taken that chance with another woman. Even as a randy teenager he'd always had the forethought to wear his own protection. Thankfully, she didn't realize how reckless she made him, he thought. Thankfully she hadn't figured out that the mere thought of making love to her was making him tremble in places where he wasn't supposed to be feeling anything.

He tossed the unopened condom back onto the nightstand and joined her on the bed. Then dragging her naked body close to his, he buried his face in the curve of her neck. The scent of wildflowers and woman met his nostrils and swirled around in his head like the drunken whirl of a carnival ride.

He gripped her waist to steady his senses. "Nothing about this—about you and me—is safe. But I can't help myself. I've wanted you from the first moment I saw you."

"And I want you," she whispered. "That's all that matters."

The urgency in her voice was his undoing. He'd passed the point of taking things slowly, of being a gentleman even with her naked and in his arms. Passion had taken over and now all he could do was love her.

Rolling her onto her back, he parted her legs, then entered her with one smooth thrust. The sensation of being inside her was so potent, so new, it snapped his head back and snatched the air from his lungs.

Struggling to hang on to his control, he sucked in several deep breaths and began to move against her. She was soft. Oh, so soft. And the moist heat of her was searing his body, his mind. He'd never wanted a woman like this before. Desire was blinding him, threatening to send him flying into the dark sky.

Beneath him, he could hear her soft whimpers, feel her long, smooth legs wrapping around his, her hands racing over his chest and belly. Sensations were rushing at him at such an incredible speed he couldn't take them in fast enough. And though he wanted to slow everything down, to make the pleasure last forever, the frantic ache inside him made it impossible.

And then suddenly she was crying out his name, her whole body arching desperately toward his and all he wanted to do was give to her. Anything and everything she wanted. Bending his head, he latched his lips over hers and the link of their mouths was the last sweet nudge that pushed them both to a high-flying cloud. Clutching her tightly, he thrust deeply, mindlessly into her.

"Becca. Becca."

Her name slipped from his throat just as he felt himself pouring into her and his body shuddered uncontrollably as he rode out wave after wave of incredible ecstasy.

By the time his body slumped to a depleted sprawl over hers, his heart was hammering out of control and sweat had slicked his skin. The roar in his ears made it impossible to hear his own labored breathing, much less hers.

He wasn't certain how long it took him to come back to earth, but eventually he became aware of her shifting beneath him and though she felt soft and warm and totally luscious, he forced himself to roll to one side to give her breathing space.

When he finally turned his head in her direction, he saw that her eyes were closed, her blond hair tousled in wild disarray around her head. The quick rise and fall of her breasts told him her breathing hadn't yet returned to normal. But then nothing about him had returned to normal, either. He wasn't sure if it ever would.

Leaning toward her, he reached out and gently lifted a heavy tendril of hair from her cheek. The movement caused her eyes to flutter open and when she saw him looking down at her, the corners of her lips slowly lifted in a weak smile.

"Jake."

The murmur of his name was all she said, but that one word was more than enough to thicken his throat with emotions he didn't quite understand, or even wished to acknowledge.

Giggles. Dirty pillow talk. Silly platitudes. Down through the years he'd heard plenty of responses from women after a round of sex with him. None of it had meant anything more than empty noises to fill an awkward moment. But that had been sex. This thing that had just happened with Rebecca was something else, something that had, quite honestly, blindsided him.

Lifting her hand to his lips, he kissed her fingers, while wondering how such small, fragile things could have such a potent effect on his body.

"Do you have any idea of how beautiful you are to me?"

For a moment he thought he saw a glaze of moisture fill her eyes. But the room had grown dusky dark and he couldn't be sure. Or maybe he didn't want to believe anything he did or said could touch her that much. It wasn't as though he was trying to ingrain himself in her heart. Oh, no. He didn't want her to love him. Like him, yes. But not love. She needed to save that for a worthy man. Yet to imagine her lying with another man, giving him the most intimate part of her was so repulsive to Jake that his mind refused to form the image.

Sighing, she shifted to her side so that she was facing him head-on. "I've never thought about it," she replied. "But I'm nothing special to look at. Especially like this."

"*Especially* like this, you are."

She closed her eyes and he leaned forward and placed his lips upon her forehead. It was damp and salty and her hair tickled his nose. With one hand, he pushed the long strands away from her face and onto the blue pillowcase. Her eyes fluttered open and this time they were dark and hesitant.

"Jake, I—"

She didn't go on and though he was almost afraid to hear the thoughts she had yet to put into words, he knew he had to hear them. Otherwise, he would always wonder.

"Go on, Rebecca," he said softly. "I'm listening."

A smile slanted her lips. "A few minutes ago you called me Becca. Did you know that?"

Barely, Jake thought. He'd been drunk on her and the shortened name had just slipped out, like a breath he could no longer hold on to.

"Yes. I remember. That's how I think of you," he admitted.

The smile fell from her face and her palm came to rest alongside his cheek. "Before I was only going to say that I'm so glad that I'm here with you. So glad that I came to New Mexico."

Suddenly there was an ache in his chest, as though two hands were reaching in and wringing his heart.

Closing his eyes against the unexpected pain, he murmured, "I'm glad you're here, too."

Two days later, Rebecca decided she could no longer put off going through Gertrude's correspondence. The task was slow and meticulous and with the phone ringing several times this afternoon her progress had been reduced to a snail's pace.

A few times throughout the day she'd been tempted to ignore the intrusive ring and let whoever was calling leave a message on her voice mail. But each time she'd snatched up the phone, hoping she would see Jake's number illuminated on the face of the instrument.

Instead the callers had been friends and coworkers from Houston and so far Rebecca had forced herself to talk with each of them. But she'd not given them any concrete reasons or hinted at a date when she might be returning to Texas. She didn't want to explain to any of them that she was presently living from day to day as she tried to come to terms, not only with Gertrude and her death, but also her newfound relationship with Jake.

Lincoln County was beginning to feel like home to her. And now that she and Jake had become intimate, she didn't want to think about leaving. If anything real and solid could develop between them, she wanted to give it a chance and the time to grow. Maybe that was foolish of her. After all, he'd told her that he was not the sort of man who wanted to get serious about her or any woman. And he'd not said a word to her to imply otherwise.

But he'd touched you like he loved you. He'd kissed you as though you were precious to him. More precious than anything.

Rebecca was trying to push that tormenting little voice out of her head when the phone rang again.

With a skeptical frown, she glanced over at the black instrument she'd left lying on the corner of a small wooden desk. "Beau, if that's Jake," she told the dog who was lying at her feet, "I'm going to shout hallelujah. If it's someone else I'm going to throw the thing out the window."

Only vaguely interested, Beau lifted his head and watched her walk over to retrieve the ringing phone, then decided to dismiss her threat and rest his chin back on his front paws.

Unfortunately, the number illuminated on the front wasn't Jake's. It belonged to her mother and for a moment Rebecca considered ignoring the call. There wasn't really anything she wanted to say to Gwyn. Unless the woman had finally decided to call and do some much-needed explaining.

It was that last hopeful thought that had Rebecca flipping open the phone and pressing it to her ear.

"Hello, Mother."

"Rebecca! Thank God you answered! Do you realize how many times I've tried to reach you? Why haven't you returned my calls?"

"Because I really don't have anything new to say. Two can play your game, Mother."

Gwyn let out an indignant huff. "That's not any way to talk to me, Rebecca. And I don't understand. You were always such a respectful daughter. Now you're like a stranger to me."

At one time, Rebecca would have agreed with her. She would have been ashamed to use any sort of sarcastic tone with her mother. But since she'd learned that Gwyn had been so deliberately deceptive, she'd lost all respect. Rebecca hated feeling that way. She desperately wished that Gwyn could give her a good explanation for her behavior. But so far she'd given her nothing but more frustration.

"It's funny that you should say that, Mother. Because you certainly seem like a stranger to me. I find myself questioning everything you say and wondering what else you're keeping from me."

There was a long silence and then Gwyn countered in a husky voice, "When are you coming home, Rebecca?"

Rebecca groaned inwardly. How many times was that question going to be thrown at her today? "We went over this the last time we talked. And I'll tell you the same thing as I told you then. I don't know." She stared across the cluttered room at Beau and then another thought struck her. "Have you been talking to my friends?"

"Why would you ask that question?"

She didn't sound indignant, Rebecca decided. More like cautious. "Because I've gotten several calls today and all of them were pressing me for a time when I'd be returning to Houston. You put them up to it, didn't you?"

"Has it ever occurred to you, Rebecca, that your friends are asking that question because they're concerned about you?"

Rebecca grimaced. "My friends normally don't pry into my private affairs. They show their concern by offering their ear, and that's it."

"All right." Gwyn suddenly spat out the admission. "I did talk to a few of your coworkers. Only because I love you."

"If you loved me—really loved me—you'd want to answer my questions about Aunt Gertrude. You'd want to explain and help me understand why you didn't want her in my life. Don't you understand this is all very hurtful and confusing to me?"

Awkward silence stretched between them.

"I didn't call to talk about Gertrude," Gwyn said brusquely. "I want to know if you're all right and what you've been doing. I want to hear your intentions about your job and—"

How could she begin to describe how she'd been spending her time here in New Mexico? Gwyn wouldn't understand any of it. Especially not Jake. She'd think he was far too rough around the edges for her daughter. Funny how it was those very rough edges that drew Rebecca to him even more, she thought. "I'm fine, Mother, just keeping busy with chores around the place and taking care of the animals. As for my intentions I've not made any plans yet."

"Rebecca! Arlene has been calling me every day to see if I've gotten any news from you. Sooner or later she's going to have to fill the void you've left behind. And from the frustration I'm getting from her it's going to be a lot sooner than you think."

Rebecca was amazed at how unaffected she was by this news. Her job at Bordeaux's had once meant everything to her. It had been her whole life. Now she couldn't imagine herself jumping back into that frantic pace, the stressful demands. Or most of all, leaving Jake.

"If Arlene feels she needs to replace me, then that's her prerogative."

To Rebecca's surprise her mother released several curse words. Gwyn had always striven to present herself to everyone as a first-class lady, especially to her daughter. She could only remember one other time she'd heard her mother cuss and that had been when Rebecca had announced she was traveling out here to New Mexico for Gertrude's funeral.

"Don't you even care?" Gwyn blasted at her. "All those years of college? All the long hours you've spent traveling, working to prove yourself? I'm not getting any of this, Rebecca. This thing with Gertrude is ruining you! And for what? You didn't even know the woman!"

"Thanks to you," Rebecca countered sharply, then forcing herself to breathe deeply and calm herself, she added, "This is not all about Gertrude, Mother. And right now I have to go."

"Rebecca, don't hang up! You're going to listen to me and get home—"

Rebecca dropped the phone from her ear and clicked the instrument together. Her hands were shaking as she placed the phone back on the desktop. She should have never confronted her mother, she thought with disgust. The only thing it achieved was making the both of them upset.

With a heavy sigh she walked back over to Beau and the box of correspondence she'd been sifting through. "Guess you could tell it wasn't Jake," she mumbled to the dog, then picked up a handful of papers and envelopes.

Thirty minutes later, Rebecca stopped the sorting long enough to make herself coffee. She carried the cup back to the spare bedroom and worked between sips. Eventually she finished one whole box and, after marking it, stacked it to one side. As she picked up a plastic container filled with more correspondence and placed it on the bed, a flash of midnight-blue velvet caught her eye.

On second glance, Rebecca noticed a jewelry box sitting on a cluttered nightstand. Expecting it to be full of costume pieces, she ignored the correspondence, and reached curiously for the rectangular box covered in blue velvet. The jewelry would certainly give her an insight into the fashion taste of her aunt, she thought.

At first she thought the tiny lock on the front was locked tight, but on second glance she could see the latch wasn't completely together. Easing onto the edge of the bed, she gathered the dusty box onto her lap and opened the lid.

Rebecca was instantly deflated. There were no pieces of jewelry, only more correspondence. The only other thing in the box was a newspaper clipping with Rebecca opening a fashion show at Bordeaux's—that must have been how Gertie knew where she worked.

Letters bundled with faded blue ribbon. She started to shut the lid, but then paused in midtask as she noticed the return address on the top envelope.

The letter was from Vance Hardaway, a post office box number, then Houston, Texas.

Her father had written to Gertrude? But why?

Her thoughts suddenly spinning, Rebecca untied the ribbon and quickly shuffled through the different shaped envelopes. Each one had come from Vance Hardaway and from the same post office box in Houston. Until she reached the last five. Those had been sent from Dubai City, the area where he'd been working before he'd lost his life.

Carefully sitting the box to one side, she picked out the envelope with the earliest posted date and opened it.

When she unfolded the two handwritten pages, a photo fluttered facedown onto her lap. Deciding to look at it before she began to read, she turned it upright, and gasped with shock.

The last thing she'd expected to see was an image of herself. Pulling the dog-eared pic closer, she scanned it closely and, as she did, faded memories rushed to life. Even though she'd only been seven or eight at the time, she remembered the day her father had taken the photo. They'd gone to the zoo. Just the two of them. When they'd stopped in front of the monkey enclosure he'd had her pose for the camera, saying he wanted a picture of his own little monkey. They'd had a fun-filled day; one of the most memorable occasions she'd had with her father.

But why had he mailed the photo to Gertrude?

Laying the faded image aside, she opened the letter and began to read:

Dearest Gerta,
I'm sorry so much time has passed since my last letter. But things have been hectic here. The company is expanding and they want to send me to a city on the Persian Gulf. I'm not keen on leaving the States, but the money would be good. And Rebecca's welfare is my main concern. I want to give her all the things I never had as a child and make sure doors open for her at the right time.

And I know you want those same things for her, too. You're living so modestly, Gerta, just so you can save and help me provide for her future. I don't want you to have to sacrifice that way. But if that makes you happy—makes you feel more like her mother—then I can hardly deny you.

As it stands, I'm scheduled to leave Houston in three weeks. My fondest hope is that you will allow me to see you before I leave for overseas. I could take two extra days and spend them with you. I understand that you don't want me to come out there, but I miss you, Gerta. And there's not a day goes by without my wishing that things could be different for you and me and our daughter.

Our daughter! Did her father's words mean what she thought they meant? Rebecca wondered wildly.

Her heart suddenly pounding with a strange mixture of fear and excitement, she scanned the last paragraph of the letter.

I'm sending these photos of Rebecca that I took at the zoo last week. Gwyn didn't go—said it was too nasty an outing for her. But as you can see Rebecca loves the animals. She's like you, dear Gerta, in so many ways. And as I watch her grow, I only love you more.

Dazed, Rebecca quickly read the last few lines of the letter and then as she lifted her head and stared unseeingly at the bedroom wall, the aged slips of paper fell to her lap.

Dear God, had Gertrude O'Dell been her mother? Everything about her father's words had said so! And there was no doubt in her mind that the letter was from Vance Hardaway. Rebecca had recognized his handwriting instantly. She still had letters that, as a child, she'd received from him.

What did it all mean? That a few weeks ago she'd watched her real mother being lowered into the earth? And never had the chance to know her? Love her?

Pain and confusion cut into her so suddenly and deeply that she clutched a hand to her stomach and choked out a sob.

Her life, as she knew it, had been one big deception! Lies on top of lies!

With tears sliding down her cheeks, she reached for the telephone and punched her mother's—no, she couldn't even use that title for the woman anymore, she thought bitterly. Now she was simply Gwyn Hardaway, a woman who owed her answers. Answers that had been twenty-eight years overdue.

Chapter Nine

Later that afternoon, Jake pulled his truck and horse trailer to a stop in front of his mother's modest house, which was located on the eastern edge of Ruidoso. He found Clara sitting on the front porch and as he climbed the steps, she rose to her feet to greet him.

Today she looked somewhat perkier and Jake was relieved that he'd not found her lying on the couch, bemoaning the state of her health.

"This is a nice surprise," she said, turning her cheek up for his kiss. "What brings you to town? On your way to Apache Wells?"

"Not exactly," he hedged. "I'm going to see…a woman. Gertie O'Dell's niece."

Clara peeped around his shoulder at the rig he'd parked in the driveway. "And you're taking a horse?"

She returned to the wicker seat she'd been sitting in and gestured for him to take the one nearest to her.

Jake eased his long frame into the chair and stretched his legs out in front of him.

"That's right. I thought Rebecca might enjoy taking a ride. She has a horse that I need to check out."

The skeptical look on Clara's face disappeared. "Oh. For shoes, you mean."

"No. I need to make sure the mare is broke to ride."

"I didn't know you were hiring out as a horse trainer anymore, Jake. You're so busy now you hardly have time to draw a good breath."

It was true that on a good day his time was limited, but the past few days had been worse than hectic. A sick bull had been discovered in a back pasture and it had taken him and his two hired hands several hours just to get him loaded and back to the ranch. Added to that, a broken pump had left the barns and feed lots without a drop of water for the livestock, then one of his best horses had cut his foot and required surgery at the vet's clinic in Ruidoso. And to make matters worse, he had no land telephone line at his house, so when he'd lost his cell phone signal it had been impossible to call Rebecca. He'd never planned for three days to go by without contacting her and now it felt like weeks since she'd been at his ranch.

"I know, Mom, but Rebecca is—well, I'm not hiring out as a horse trainer for her. I'm doing this as a favor."

Rolling her eyes, Clara groaned with misgivings. "Oh, son, don't tell me you've gone and gotten yourself involved with this girl from Texas. Don't you have enough women around here without adding her to your string?"

Jake didn't bother to stop the grimace on his face.

Linking Rebecca to the other women he'd known over the years seemed downright disrespectful. She wasn't like those women and neither was their relationship.

Who are you kidding, Jake? You've already taken her to your bed. And you can't wait to get her back in it. What makes this thing with Rebecca any different than the last woman you bedded?

Dammit, now was hardly the time for his conscience to start talking to him. His mother's voiced opinion was bad enough.

"I'm not—this is not what you're thinking, Mom."

She shot him a look of disgust. One that Jake had seen a hundred times before. "The woman doesn't even belong around here. Sooner or later, she'll be going back to wherever she came from. That tells me you're not serious about her. But then you're never serious about any of them, are you?" Shaking her head, she lifted her gaze to the roof of the porch and sighed. "You'll be like your father until the day you die."

Over the years Clara had said some demeaning things to Jake, all of them pointing back to Lee's failings as a father and a husband, and how Jake had inherited the man's shortcomings. But she'd never spoken to him in such a sarcastic tone before and Jake didn't know whether he was angry or hurt or simply weary of being linked to Lee's mistakes.

Leaning forward in his chair, he studied her sad face. "Why are you doing this to me? I'm not Lee Rollins. I've not left a wife and child behind."

She flinched, then turned her gaze away from him. "No," she said bitterly. "That's one thing I won't have to worry about. You'll make damned sure you don't have either one of those."

Disgusted now, Jake muttered a few choice words

under his breath. "I don't know what in hell you want or expect from me, Mom. You say I'm just like Lee and not fit to be a husband or father. And then in the next breath, you ridicule me for not having a family. I guess it would be too much of a strain for you to find anything worthwhile in your son, yourself or your life."

Her head whipped around and she gaped at him in shock. "That's a horrible thing to say to me!"

"Is it? I'm thinking I should have said it a long time ago."

"Jake—"

"Look, Mom, just because you want to be alone and miserable doesn't mean I want to be."

She looked at him in stunned disbelief and Jake suddenly realized that he was partly to blame for his mother's cynical attitude toward life. All these years of coddling had only fed into her self-pity.

"What are you talking about? You are alone, Jake," she shot back at him. "And that's the way the both of us are always gonna be. Your father ruined us."

His jaw tight, Jake rose to his feet. "Only because we've let him."

He started off the porch and Clara called after him. "Come back here, Jake. I'm not finished."

Stepping onto the ground, he glanced over his shoulder at her. "But I am finished, Mom. Finished with the whole rotten mess of Lee Rollins."

Minutes later, as Jake drove north of Ruidoso to Rebecca's place, he tried to forget the exchange he'd had with his mother. It wasn't like him to lose his temper with her. She was basically the only family he had and after his father had left, she'd worked hard and sacrificed to raise Jake. He respected her for that and he loved her.

But that didn't mean he had to abide her attitude toward him or herself.

You are alone, Jake.

Of all the things Clara had said to him that had cut the worst. Although, he didn't understand exactly why. A few weeks ago, he probably would have agreed with his mother's observation. He'd always been a man alone. Until Rebecca had come into his life. Now he felt different. Now he felt a connection.

Was it love?

Hell, how could he know the answer to that? He'd never been in love. And maybe this thing with Rebecca was just lust, he mentally argued. God only knew how much he'd wanted her the other night. He'd not been satisfied to make love to her once and then take her home. No, he'd had to make love to her a second time and then a third. And to make the matter even more worrisome, he'd wanted to keep her with him all night. He'd wanted to wrap his arms around her and hold her until morning filled the sky. Something he'd never done with any woman.

But somehow, in the wee hours of the morning, he'd found the strength, or maybe it had been fear that had finally pushed him, to drive her home and kiss her goodnight. Since that night his thoughts had been besieged with the woman and now he was beginning to wonder what tomorrow was going to bring to him. Once she returned to Texas, how would he go back to being the old Jake, the man who flitted from one woman to the next, the man who never thought about a wife, children or the future?

A half hour later, he rolled to a stop behind Rebecca's old truck. The sight of the vehicle assured him that she was home, so he climbed to the ground and went to work unloading his horse.

By the time he'd taken Banjo to the barn and turned him loose in a small catch pen, Rebecca still hadn't appeared, so he quickly returned to the house and knocked on the front door.

There was no sound coming from inside and he was beginning to think that maybe Abe or Maura might have picked her up and taken her to Apache Wells for a neighborly visit, when he finally heard footsteps rushing through the house.

After a moment, she appeared behind the screen door and he smiled with relief. "Rebecca, for a minute I thought you were gone."

She pushed the door wide and without a word fell sobbing into his arms.

"Rebecca! Honey, what's wrong? Are you hurt? Sick?"

Lifting her head from his chest, she tried to speak, but only more sobs passed her parted lips. Jake urgently wrapped an arm around her waist and ushered her into the house.

Once he had her sitting on the couch, he sank down beside her and pressed both her hands tightly between his. "Take a deep breath, Becca. Calm down and tell me what has you so upset."

Nodding jerkily, she drew in several bracing breaths. "I—I'm so sorry, Jake. I didn't mean to—to break down like this. But when I saw you—oh, Jake—I don't know where to begin."

Fresh tears rolled down her cheeks and he quickly pulled a bandanna from the back pocket of his jeans and wiped them away. Once he was finished, her trembling lips tried to form a grateful smile.

"Are you ill, Becca?"

She shook her head. "No. I guess you could call it… shock." She pulled her hands from his and swiped at the tumble of blond hair hanging near her eyes. "This afternoon I was going through Gertrude's correspondence and I found out—quite by accident that—she was…my mother."

Stunned, Jake stared at her. "Did I hear you right? Did you say mother?"

Rebecca nodded, then released a long, shuddering sigh. "That's right. I said that Gertrude was my mother."

"But how? Are you sure?"

Jumping to her feet, she began to pace around the tiny living room. "I found letters from my father written to Gertrude. He called her Gerta and talked about how much he regretted the fact that they couldn't be together." Her woeful gaze lifted from the floor and over to him. "Oh, Jake, the things he wrote—he clearly loved her. And—"

His heart aching for her, he watched her cover her face with both hands. "Are you sure about this, Rebecca? Just because he loved Gertrude, that doesn't make the woman your mother. And even if she was actually your mother, why didn't she raise you?"

Dropping her hands from her face, she stared helplessly at him. "I'm going crazy trying to figure that out, Jake. None of it makes sense."

"Does your mother—the mother who raised you—know that you've uncovered these letters?"

She nodded stiffly. "Right after I found the letters I called my—I called Gwyn and confronted her with the contents. She didn't try to deny any of it. She simply said she'd catch a plane to Ruidoso tomorrow and I'm to meet her there so that we can talk. Apparently she's decided she can't hide the truth any longer. But what that truth is—well, I can't imagine what I'll hear from her. All I know is that my real mother is dead. And I never had the chance to see her, touch her or hear her voice. It's killing me, Jake."

The agony in her voice pushed Jake to his feet and he quickly pulled her into his arms and cradled her head against his chest. "I don't know what to say. To say I'm sorry wouldn't be right. Because this might be a good thing, Becca. You've been confused and wanting answers about Gertrude. Now you have them."

Her hands gripped the front of his denim shirt as though he was her lifeline. The idea that she needed to be close to him, that she was even sharing this most private part of her life with him, left Jake overwhelmed with emotions.

"Yes. But I've lost so much," she said in a tear-ravaged voice. "And why?"

"Oh, Becca, I can't give you the answers. But please don't cry anymore." Gently, he stroked a hand down the back of her head. "No matter what the truth is, it's not going to change the wonderful person that you are. And trust me, this will all get better with time."

Tilting her head back, she focused her watery gaze upon his face. "Oh, Jake, I'm so glad you're here," she whispered hoarsely. "I need you. You can't imagine how much."

Need. Not want. Need. The notion that this woman needed him, in any capacity, amazed Jake, filled his heart with a kind of warmth he'd never experienced before. And as he watched the dark agony in her eyes turn to something soft and sweet, he couldn't stop his head from bending or his lips from finding hers.

A faint groan sounded deep in her throat. Or was it a whimper of surrender? Either way, the sound stirred him, made him forget that he was supposed to be consoling her. Heat flashed through him as he tightened his arms and crushed her closer against him.

The taste of her mouth was like sipping a favorite wine, one that he could never get enough of. As his lips plundered hers, his tongue slipped between her teeth and rubbed a bumpy track along the roof of her mouth. At the same time he could feel her hips arching toward his, her fingers crawling up his chest and linking at the back of his neck.

His body had forgotten none of the pleasures she'd given him the other night and the memories melded with the erotic sensations zipping hot and wild along his veins. The search of his lips turned rough and urgent and she matched each desperate movement with a frantic need that left his whole body aching to be inside her once again.

Eventually the need for air and the desire to take the embrace to a deeper level forced their mouths apart. His breathing heavy, he gripped her shoulders and looked ruefully down at her.

"I must be a bastard, Becca, for wanting you like this—now. You need—"

"I need you. Only you," she interrupted in a desperate whisper. "Make love to me, Jake. Make me forget everything. Everything but you."

He kissed her again. More gently this time and once their lips parted, she took him by the hand and led him down the short hallway to her bedroom.

The small space was equipped with only one window facing the backyard. It was bare of curtains and opened to the cool breeze. Now as she pulled Jake down on the bed beside her, the sage-scented air wafted across their heated skin and ruffled the blond tendrils of hair lying upon her shoulders.

For long moments as they lay with their faces mere inches apart, Jake could only wonder how much longer he would have her to himself like this. She was at a crossroads in her life. That much was obvious to Jake. And the road she eventually chose to take would more than likely be away from Lincoln County, away from him. The notion chilled him and he fought to push it away at the same time he reached to draw her close to his heart.

The next afternoon, Rebecca drove to the Ruidoso airport and waited for Gwyn Hardaway's small commuter jet to land. Their initial meeting in the lobby was worse than stiff and, though Rebecca allowed the woman to give her a brief hug, there was little warmth between them as they exited the building and walked to the parking lot.

When they reached Rebecca's old Ford, it was clear that Gwyn was disgusted by the mode of transportation and even more embarrassed to be seen in it, but Rebecca didn't make any apologies. The truck had belonged to her mother and that alone made it special.

Rebecca drove them to the hotel where Gwyn had booked a room for the night, then waited in the spacious lobby while the other woman checked in and dealt with her luggage. So far only a handful of words had passed between the two of them and the strained silence reminded Rebecca how drastically her life had changed since she'd come to New Mexico. She watched her real mother be laid to rest and the woman who'd raised her had become a distant stranger. And then there was Jake.

The man she'd fallen in love with. Would he want to be a part of her scattered life?

Her mind was replaying last night and how Jake had made love to her so tenderly and completely when Gwyn's voice abruptly sounded behind her.

"Would you like to go up to my room to talk?"

For some reason Rebecca had no desire to closet herself in a private room with Gwyn. She already felt as though the woman had isolated her. As far as Rebecca was concerned, it was time for everything to be out in the open.

"Let's find a restaurant," Rebecca suggested. "I need a cup of coffee."

Thankfully, there was an eating place connected to the hotel and after a short walk, they seated themselves in a booth looking out a wide plate-glass window. After the waitress left to fetch their drinks, Gwyn stared out the window.

"I wonder what Gertrude saw in this place," she mused aloud. "I admit it has a quaint charm, but it's so Western."

And Gwyn was so big-city, Rebecca thought. She loved the hustle and bustle, the shops, the arts and social life attached to them. On the other hand, from what Rebecca could gather from her home place, Gertrude had been just the opposite. A quiet loner who was content to live with her animals.

"Do you know why she chose to live here?" Rebecca asked.

Gwyn's gaze remained on the window. "No idea. In fact, after we parted ways, I never knew where she'd gone to. I didn't want to know," she added bitterly.

As the two of them had walked to the restaurant, Rebecca kept reminding herself to keep an open mind and not allow her temper to rise to the angry point. After all, she didn't yet know what had gone on between the twin sisters. So now she quietly studied Gwyn's stiff expression and wondered how the woman could've turned her back on her sister and deceived her own child.

"Why?"

Gwyn turned her gaze on Rebecca and this time she could see dark shadows of pure hatred in their depths. The sight shocked Rebecca and made her realize there were sides to this woman that she could have never imagined.

"Do we really have to get into all of this, Rebecca? Isn't it enough to know that she was your biological mother? The rest is…unimportant."

Unimportant? Rebecca wanted to scream. Before Jake had shown up at her door yesterday evening, she'd read all the letters that had been stashed in the jewelry box and they'd given her bittersweet glimpses to her parents' relationship. The words her father had written to Gertrude were full of anguish, love, sorrow and regret. His life had been torn between two women and a child. How could Gwyn have the gall to say none of it was important?

"I'm not a child, Mother. And don't insult my intelligence. I didn't come here to meet with you just so you could hem and haw. If you don't want to give me the truth, I'll be on my way."

Gwyn's nostrils flared with anger, but any retort she might have said at that moment was interrupted by the waitress returning to their table. After the woman had served them and gone on her way, Rebecca stirred cream into her coffee and waited with patience that was wearing thinner and thinner with each passing moment.

"If you walk away now, Rebecca," Gwyn finally said, "you'll never know the truth."

She made it sound almost like a threat, as though she wouldn't think twice about withholding the answers that Rebecca so desperately needed. The realization stunned her. Gwyn had always been a temperamental person and spoiled by having her own way, but Rebecca had never seen this sort of cruelty in the woman.

"That's where you're wrong. I have Daddy's letters. They explain a lot."

Gwyn had ordered iced tea. Now, after a long sip, she plopped the glass down with a loud thud and quickly reached for the sugar shaker. "Damn people! Don't have the slightest idea of how to serve sweet tea!" She dumped a small mountain of white granules into the drink and as she absently stirred the tea, she turned an unseeing gaze toward the window. "Oh, yes," she said bitterly. "Those letters you found. I wasn't expecting you to stumble across anything like...that."

"Why not? You knew I was staying in Gertrude's house. Surely you figured I would run across them at some point."

Gwyn's head jerked around and Rebecca could see her face was now mottled with red splotches. "I didn't— I never knew Vance had been corresponding with Gertrude. I didn't know my husband had been speaking to the woman in any form or fashion!"

Oh, God, this was worse than anything Rebecca had anticipated. She wanted answers, but unlike Gwyn, she wasn't a hurtful person. She didn't want to cause her mother more pain than she was already going through. But neither could she avoid the truth. "You never suspected that he was harboring feelings for Gertrude?"

Gwyn's gaze dropped shamefully to the tabletop.

"No," she said hoarsely. "I thought all of that was over—after—"

When she didn't go on, Rebecca pressed her. "After what? After I was conceived? For both of our sakes, I think you need to go back to the beginning, Mother."

With a long weary sigh, she lifted her head and looked straight at Rebecca. By now her face had gone very pale, making her red lipstick stand out garishly against her white skin.

"All right. From the beginning my sister and I were always very different people. Even our looks were nothing alike. Gertrude was tall and blonde while I was dark and petite."

"Was she pretty?"

Gwyn shrugged one shoulder, an expression she'd always reprimanded Rebecca for using. "I suppose you could've called her pretty. She was the outdoorsy, girl-next-door type. And so quiet and reserved that I often wanted to scream at her. Yet as children we—well, we loved each other and were actually quite close."

"I find that hard to believe."

"Well, we were. Even though we did have our differences at times. As teenagers I was always pushing her to be more outgoing. I wanted her to have dates and fun—I wanted her to be someone I could be proud of. Instead, she chose to be a bookworm and for the most part shunned any advances the boys made toward her. She said they made her uncomfortable and that she would have a relationship whenever it felt right and not before. At that time neither one of us had met Vance. That didn't come until much later when we were in our twenties and our parents—your grandparents—had already passed on."

"You told me that you met Daddy at a dinner party. Is that where Gertrude met him, too?"

Gwyn grimaced. "Yes. At the time I thought she hardly noticed him. But that could have been because I was too busy trying to catch his eye," she added thoughtfully. "Anyway, after that we began to date. When he asked me to marry him, I was over the moon. Your father was killer handsome and though he wasn't rich by any means, he was a man with prospects and all of that put together made him one of the most eligible bachelors in our social circle. After he proposed, I immediately began to plan a big wedding and with Mother already gone, I needed Gertrude to help me with the details."

"And did she?"

Gwyn's expression turned hard. "Oh, yes. She even seemed happy for me. Little did I know that she had her eyes set on my fiancé."

"When did you find out about the two of them?"

"Not until a couple of months after Vance and I were married. Gertrude came to me and told me that she was carrying Vance's child and that their…indiscretion had happened before the wedding. She'd planned to keep their tryst a secret, but that the pregnancy forced her to come out with the truth. I was completely devastated. I'd been betrayed by both my husband and my sister."

Rebecca clutched the coffee cup as she watched pain slip across Gwyn's face. "I understand this isn't easy for you to say. It's not particularly easy for me to hear. And I realize that you were wronged. Terribly so. But that hardly justified you living a lie."

Gwyn's mouth fell open. "A lie? Why, what do you mean? I'm not the one who cheated!"

"You cheated me out of knowing my own mother. As far as I'm concerned you cheated in the worst kind of way. What I can't understand is why Gertrude and my father allowed it."

Her eyes lit with vengeful fire, Gwyn leaned forward. "They allowed it because I held the cards, that's why! She was nothing but a backstabbing slut and I was ready to smear her reputation into the dirt. She'd always gone around acting so meek and mild and holier-than-thou when all along she was a nothing, a nobody! I was the social flower, not her! And I damned sure wasn't going to let our friends and acquaintances learn what she and Vance had done to me!"

Revenge. Nothing good could ever come from it. But apparently Gwyn had yet to realize that lesson.

"How were you going to smear her reputation without dragging Daddy into it?"

"I wasn't above making up a sordid story about her. That wouldn't have been nearly as bad as what she'd actually done to me. So when I threatened, she caved. And believe me, it didn't take much threatening. Gertrude was the type who always did have too much conscience. She felt as guilty as hell and wanted to make it up to me. And most of all, she wanted what was best for her baby. She didn't want you raised up under a cloud of nasty gossip and illegitimacy. So I immediately spread the news that I was pregnant and then a few weeks later, I made up a cock-and-bull story that Gertrude and I had a widowed aunt in California who had taken ill and we were going out to care for her until she could get back on her feet. The two of us did go to California, a little town on the southern coast where no acquaintances would likely run into us. Once you were born, I came back with you as a new mother. Gertrude went her own way and I never spoke to her after that."

"And Daddy? What did he have to say about all this?

About getting Gertrude pregnant? About this plan of yours?"

"He was contrite, of course. He assured me that he'd only made love to Gertrude one time and that it hadn't meant anything. He'd just had a last-minute panic about losing his bachelorhood and Gertrude had been handy and willing. He wanted to raise his child and once Gertrude agreed to turn the baby over to me, he had to stick by my side. He didn't have any other choice. And in the long run, I don't think he wanted anyone to think badly of Gertrude. He didn't want her hurt in that way. And he didn't want you to be raised up under a shroud of ugly gossip, either."

It was all Rebecca could do to keep from rolling her eyes toward the ceiling. The more Gwyn talked the more psychotic she sounded. "And why do you think that was, Mother? If it was just a physical thing between them, why would he care if Gertrude was hurt? Do you think it might have been because he loved her?"

The anger on Gwyn's face suddenly disappeared and in its place came a look of weary defeat. "For years I never believed Vance had ever cared for Gertrude. I believed his heart was truly mine. But I didn't know about the letters—that he'd stayed in contact with her until he died. Now I can only think that they probably continued to see each other—until Vance was killed."

Bitter nausea swam in the pit of Rebecca's stomach. So many people had lied and loved and lost. "I was an innocent baby and you used me as a pawn—to get what you wanted. You didn't care that you took me away from my mother or that I might have needed her. You didn't even care about me, did you?"

If possible, Gwyn's face turned even paler. She took a nervous gulp of tea and answered in a flat voice, "All right, you asked for honesty so I'm going to give it to you. In the beginning I didn't want you. Each time I looked at you it killed me. You were a constant reminder of my husband's infidelity, my sister's betrayal. But then—" Her eyes suddenly filled with tears as she reached an imploring hand toward Rebecca. "You were such a lovely baby and after a while I couldn't help but fall in love with you. And then it was easy for me to pretend that none of it had ever happened. That I had actually given birth to you."

Rebecca didn't allow Gwyn to clasp her hand. There was too much hurt and confusion going on inside Rebecca to summon up any tender emotions for this woman who'd turned a bad choice into a lifelong nightmare. "Why did you never speak to Gertrude again? Why couldn't you find it in your heart to attend her funeral?"

Gwyn was dumbfounded. "Rebecca! Do you actually have to ask those questions? The woman wronged me!"

"And what did you do to her? Extorted her child from her! Hid the identity of my real mother from me! That's not a little wrong, that's a massive one."

Refusing to acknowledge her own faults, Gwyn said through clenched teeth, "Sister or not, I could never forgive her. And I don't know how you could possibly pitch a defense for the woman!"

Sadness fell like a heavy cloak around Rebecca's shoulders and filled her heart with silent tears. "Yes, she made a bad mistake. But you retaliated and made even more. The way I see it, if a person doesn't have the capacity to forgive then they hardly have the ability to love."

As Gwyn stared at her, a flicker of hope lit her eyes. "Does that mean—you're willing to forgive me?"

Grabbing up her handbag, Rebecca rose to her feet. "It's way too early for me to answer that. And who knows, maybe being raised by you has influenced me more than you think."

Bewildered, Gwyn frowned. "What does that mean?"

"That I might just hold a grudge against you for the rest of my life."

Gwyn gasped. "Rebecca!"

"I've got to go," Rebecca said abruptly. "Goodbye."

The other woman rose to her feet as though she was prepared to grab on to Rebecca and prevent her from walking out of the restaurant. "But you can't leave now—like this! When are you coming home?"

Rebecca swallowed as a cold, hard lump threatened to choke her. *Home.* The one she'd grown up in had been built upon a foundation of lies. Where was her home now? She didn't know anymore. At this moment all she could think about was Jake, the comfort of his strong arms, the steadying sound of his rich voice. He was the only real thing left in her life. But even he was a temporary component.

"I don't know the answer to that. Maybe soon. Maybe never."

"Rebecca, I—"

Rebecca didn't wait to hear more. She'd already heard more than enough to break her heart.

Chapter Ten

Later that evening, when she arrived back at her little ranch, she was surprised to see Jake's truck parked in the driveway. When he'd left early this morning, he'd not mentioned when he'd be back and today while she'd been in Ruidoso, he'd not rung her cell. But then she was learning he didn't necessarily believe in notices or plans. He was a man who simply acted upon whatever he was feeling at the moment.

She found him sitting on the front porch waiting for her to arrive and as she climbed the steps he must have noticed the weary sag of her shoulders, because he stood immediately and held out his arms.

Wordlessly, she dropped her handbag onto the floor of the porch and rushed to him. As she nestled her cheek against his chest, she felt his chin rest atop her head.

"You saw your mother."

It wasn't a question, it was a statement spoken in a

flat voice, as though he already understood she was miserable. The fact that he could read her so well, that he was here at the moment she needed him most, filled her with bittersweet emotions. He might not think of himself as a permanent fixture in a woman's life, but he'd already found a permanent place in her heart.

But it wouldn't be right to tell him how she felt. He'd not asked for her love. He'd even warned her that he wasn't the loving kind. And she wasn't going to weigh his conscience down with declarations and demands. The last thing she wanted to be was like Gwyn, who'd demanded that Vance love her, or else.

"Yes," she said with a weary sigh. "And it was worse than I imagined."

He stroked a hand down her back. "I figured it might be. That's why I showed up. I thought you might need a little distraction this evening."

Tilting her head back, she looked at him with a mixture of curiosity and provocative surmise. "What sort of distraction?"

His grin was warm and sexy and just what she needed to make her feel as though she was actually going to survive.

"Since we—uh—got sidetracked last night and Banjo was already here, I thought we might try again. So I've saddled him and Starr. I thought we might ride across your land and check the fences. Do you feel up to it?"

Even though he was sounding like the quintessential rancher, she realized the invitation had nothing to do with fences or making sure livestock remained on the proper property. He was trying to take her mind off her problems and on to something simple and pleasant.

Touched by his thoughtfulness, she blinked at the moisture gathering at the back of her eyes. "I wouldn't miss the chance for anything. Just let me change into some jeans and boots," she told him.

A few minutes later, after assuring her that he'd already ridden Starr and found the mare to be extremely gentle, he helped her into the saddle and swung himself up on the gelding he called Banjo.

Even though it had been years since she'd been on a horse, it took her only a few minutes to get the hang of handling the reins and giving the horse the right cues to follow her directions. As the house and barn receded in the distance behind them, the sage-dotted land opened, making the trek easy for horse and rider.

"This is nice," she told him. "Being on Starr almost makes me forget about this afternoon."

His expression full of concern, he studied her closely. "I was hoping you found the answers you wanted."

She released a sharp, bitter laugh. "Oh, I got plenty of answers. They were just nothing like I'd expected them to be."

"Want to tell me about it?"

To her amazement, she did want to tell him about it. Of all the people she knew, he would be the one who would understand the most. And that idea told her more about herself and the life she'd been leading than anything yet.

"If you want to listen," she told him.

"I do."

Rebecca told him the whole unfortunate story, ending with Gwyn's attitude. "Her sister is dead, yet she's still harboring hatred toward the woman. You'd think after all these years she could forgive and forget."

Thoughtfully, Jake lifted his gray hat from his head and ran a hand over his thick waves. "You telling her about those letters probably threw her for a loop. She learned her husband really did love another woman and that she'd been hanging on to something she'd never really had in the first place. Including you. That would be a heck of a pill for most people to swallow."

Hanging on to something she'd never really had. Jake's observation struck her like a thunderbolt. Was that what Rebecca was trying to do? Hang on to regrets of a mother she never knew and resentment for a mother who had pushed her to always do more and be better? Maybe even hang on to a life here in New Mexico even though her home had always been in Houston? No! She didn't want to think about that now. If she did she might break apart completely.

"You're probably right," she murmured glumly.

Sage snapped against the horses' legs and filled the evening air with the pungent scent. Behind them the sun began to sink and the desert around them became washed in hues of gold and purple. For a long stretch, they rode in silence, but every now and then their mounts drifted together and Rebecca's leg would brush against Jake's. The connection comforted her. And each time she glanced over at his dark profile, her heart filled to the brim and ached with a longing she'd never felt before.

Her love for Jake was growing and so was this new life she'd found with him. But he wasn't going to hang around forever. He simply wasn't that type. And when he moved on to the next woman, where was that going to leave her? Without him would there be any reason for her to stay here?

For the next few minutes, she did her best to push those questions from her mind and soak in her surroundings. After all, this land belonged to her and, other than a few short walks in the pasture, this was the first chance she'd had to look it over.

Eventually the landscape began to change to low rolling hills and washed-out gullies. As they topped one particular rise, a windmill and water tank came into view.

Jake tilted his head in that direction. "You probably need a break," he said. "Let's ride over there and give the horses a drink."

"Sounds good," she agreed.

It took them another ten minutes to reach the windmill and by then Rebecca was feeling the effects of being in the saddle. When Jake helped her to the ground her legs were trembling with fatigue and for a moment, she clutched his arm.

"Sorry," she said with a self-deprecating laugh. "I guess when it comes to riding I'm a bit of a wimp."

He smiled down at her and as their eyes met, Rebecca had to fight back the urge to slip her arms around him, to tell him that she loved him, that she would always need and want him in her life. If he knew how she felt, would it change anything? Or would she simply be making a fool of herself? Oh, God, she didn't know what to do about him, herself or anything.

"I wouldn't say that. It's something you have to get conditioned to," he told her, then reached for the reins of both horses. "I'll lead them over to the tank for a drink while you find a place to sit down."

As Jake saw to the horses, the thought came to mind that this was the first time he'd ever taken a woman horseback riding. The pleasure was one of those things he'd never wanted to share with a female. For the most part they were too chatty to appreciate the bond a man had with his horse and too soft to deal with the heat and the flies and the grime that went with it. Besides all that, when a cowboy acquired a saddle pal he kept him for life. That was a code he didn't break.

So what was he doing here with Rebecca? he asked himself. He wasn't planning on keeping her for life. He couldn't. She wasn't the keeper type. Not for a man like him, a man who changed women more often than he changed the oil in his truck. And even if he was the family type with dreams and hopes for a wife and kids, he could see she wasn't ready to deal with such plans. This thing with Gertie and her parents had turned her world upside down and he figured it was going to take Rebecca a long time to get things figured out. Or she might never come to terms with it. He'd spent the past eighteen years trying to figure out why his father had deserted him and he still didn't have the answers.

Yet in spite of all this, he wanted to be with her. He wanted to take away the confusion and hurt in her heart. He didn't know what that meant or why he was feeling this way. But he was beginning to understand what Quint had been trying to tell him. It was going to hurt and hurt bad whenever he had to let her go.

After the horses had their fill of water, he tied them loosely to the wooden frame of the windmill. While he'd been dealing with their mounts, Rebecca had taken a seat on a grassy slope a few feet away. Now he walked over and sank down next to her.

"Feeling better?" he asked.

She looked away from him and he could see her throat work as she swallowed hard.

"A little."

He rubbed the back of his fingers against her upper arm, while wishing he could wipe away the pain inside her just as easily. "It's hell learning that your parents are something different than what you always believed them to be. I know."

She looked back at him and the misty glaze in her blue eyes very nearly tore a hole in his chest.

"Yes, you would understand, Jake." With a wan smile, she touched her fingers to his cheek. "I'm sorry I'm not very good company this evening."

"I didn't come here for company. I came because—" He stopped and cleared his throat. "I thought you might need me."

The glaze in her eyes swelled to full-blown tears and with a choked groan she flung her arms around his neck and pressed her cheek against his. "Oh, Jake, I do need you! I—" Pausing, she eased her head back far enough to look into his eyes. "I want you to make love to me. Now. Please."

Jake didn't know what he'd been expecting her to say, but that was all he needed to hear. Galvanized by her plea, he circled his arms around her and found her mouth with his.

The moment their lips met, Jake knew she was not in a gentle mood. Her tongue plunged between his teeth, while her fingers dug into his shoulders and pulled him tight against her. A groan rumbled deep in his throat as hot desire slammed into him and sent his head reeling from the force of it.

If she was using him to wipe her mind of her troubles, Jake didn't care. The taste, the very scent of her, wrapped around his senses and cloaked him from the whys or what-ifs of tomorrow. He was connected to her and her to him. That was more than he could ask for.

In a matter of moments, the wild demands of their kiss caused them to tumble sideways and onto the pad of cool grass. Something hard and sharp jabbed him in the side, but Jake ignored the pain, which was an easy thing to do given the fact that his whole body was already humming, throbbing with the need to be inside her.

When their mouths finally ripped apart, Jake rolled onto his back and pulled her atop him. In a thick, raspy voice, he explained, "The ground is too rough for you."

Propping her forearms against his chest, she lifted her head to look at him. "For you, too," she pointed out.

The sound he made was something between a chuckle and a groan. "The only thing I feel is you, little darlin'. Now, come here."

Tunneling his hand beneath her hair, he cupped it around the back of her neck and drew her face down to his. She didn't resist. In fact, her lips made such a slow delicious feast of his that his whole body began to burn and ache. And when she unsnapped his shirt and planted little wet kisses down the middle of his chest and onto his abdomen, he could do nothing but surrender to her sweet ministrations.

But eventually that pleasure was not nearly enough for either of them. Clothes and boots were quickly removed and tossed aside. Then she was pushing him onto his back and straddling his hips.

Jake was vaguely aware of the dusky sky above, while a few feet behind them the horses swished their tails and gently stomped away the pestering insects. Water trickled in the tank and the windmill slowly creaked in the cool evening breeze. Somehow his mind managed to register all those things.Until she positioned herself over him and thrust downward.

The moment he slid into her, sensations rushed wildly

through him and didn't stop until they'd whammed the top of his skull and sent his whole head reeling back against the ground.

Trying to catch his breath and hang on to what little self-control he had left, he anchored both hands at the sides of her waist and attempted to slow the pace of her thrust. But that was like stopping the wind. He couldn't brake a wild gale down to a gentle breeze. All he could do was ride it out and let the frantic motion of her body carry him to a mindless place he could only call ecstasy.

When Jake finally returned to his surroundings, Rebecca was draped over him with her cheek pressed against the middle of his chest and her hands curled over the top of his shoulders. Except for the rise and fall of her lungs, she was motionless, but her soft breath caressed his skin like a gentle finger. Her golden hair spilled over his ribs and in the process hid her face from his view.

Sliding his fingers into the silky strands, he lifted them away from her cheek. She stirred and tilted her head just enough to be able to meet his gaze. As Jake looked into her blue eyes he was stunned at how replete she made him feel. In the past week he'd lost count of how many times they'd made love and by now he would have expected the familiarity of her to bore him. Instead, it thrilled him. Each curve, each texture and scent of her body was a treasure to experience over and over. Each whispered word and touch, every kiss from her lips was the most precious thing he'd ever been given. Loving her was like coming home. And each time grew sweeter.

That was a scary realization for Jake; one that he didn't know how to deal with. A part of him wanted to tell her what he was feeling, but the other, bigger part of him wanted to hide those tender emotions, bury the thoughts of longing going on in his heart. He didn't want her to know just how vulnerable she made him feel. That would only make it more clumsy and uncomfortable when she did finally say goodbye.

"It's getting dark," he murmured huskily. "We'd better mount up and get back."

She gazed at him for long moments, then with a wistful sigh, she placed a kiss on his cheek. "Give me just a few minutes longer, Jake. Please."

How could he deny her, he asked himself, when all he wanted to do was hold her forever?

"All right," he murmured. "We'll go in a little while."

He held her quietly in his arms until dusk faded into darkness and a crescent moon appeared above the jagged line of mountains to the east. After that they dressed quickly, mounted their horses and headed them homeward.

The ride back to the house was done mainly in silence, while they carefully maneuvered the horses through sagebrush and clumps of cacti. Rebecca seemed lost in thought and Jake could hardly resent her quietness. Especially when his own mind was absorbed with questions and doubts. Something had changed her or the both of them on that grassy bed. And once they'd left it to dress and return to the real world, he'd felt certain he would never be the same man. As for Rebecca he could only guess what was going on inside her.

She'd clung to him as though she loved him. Yet he told himself that couldn't be the reason why she'd wanted to stay in his arms with her cheek pressed against the beat of his heart. That idea—that she could possibly love him—was too incredible for Jake to wrap his mind around.

When they reached the barn, Jake unsaddled both horses and while Rebecca poured a bucket of feed into Starr's trough, he loaded the tack and Banjo into his trailer for the trip back to the Rafter R.

Once the animals had been dealt with, Rebecca invited him into the house for a light supper of cold-cut sandwiches and iced tea. Throughout the simple meal, their conversation came and went in brief, awkward spurts. Until finally, Jake reached across the little table and brought her chin up with his forefinger.

"What's wrong, Rebecca? And don't tell me it's all this stuff about Gertrude and your parents. I already know you're upset about that. There's something else. Tell me."

She closed her eyes and swallowed. "I can't explain what's wrong, Jake. I guess today, after talking with my mother—" She broke off and with a shake of her head, let out a humorless laugh. "Dear God, I can't call Gwyn my mother anymore, can I? Because she isn't or wasn't. She's my aunt. Gertrude was my mother."

"Rebecca—"

"I'm sorry, Jake. I'm not going to say any more about her or what happened. I just—well, I guess the whole thing has confused me. And I realize that these past few weeks that I've been here in New Mexico I—I've been living in limbo."

An ominous chill crept down Jake's spine. "What does that mean?"

She gave him a long, searching look, one that made Jake feel cowardly and worthless. Two things he'd never felt in his life.

You'll be like your father until the day you die. Oh,

God, why were his mother's words haunting him now? Jake wondered. Because she was right about him? Because he lacked what it took to be a man who could faithfully love one woman?

She reached for his hand and clung to it tightly.

"It means that I've been going through the motions of living without really knowing who I am or where I belong. I wanted to think I belonged here. But I'm beginning to see I—well, that I'm deluding myself."

"I thought you liked it here."

Her gaze swung away from him as she pulled her hand back to her side of the table. "I was. I do," she said. "But I need to do more than just exist. And I—well, I have nothing to hold me here."

That cut him deep. So deep that he could feel the blood drain from his face. Did she think of him as nothing?

Whoa, Jake. Before you go getting all hurt and bothered, you'd better stop and take a good look at this situation—at yourself. You've had some incredible sex with this woman, but you never told her what it's meant to you. What she means to you. How can you expect her to see you as anything more than a passing affair?

The voice traipsing through Jake's thoughts brought him up short. For a minute there he'd almost forgotten that Rebecca was only a temporary pleasure in his life. That was all he'd set out to have and he couldn't expect to have more with her now.

"You have this place and the animals."

Avoiding his gaze, she rose from the table and carried her plate over to the sink. With her back to him, she said, "Yes. But I have to have a means to live. Gert—my mother left me a nice sum of money and I do have some of my own saved. But all of that will go quickly if I'm not working."

"And your job is in Houston." He knew his voice sounded flat, maybe even accusing. But dammit, he didn't want her to go. He wasn't ready to give her up. Not just yet.

"Well, I really doubt there's any need for a fashion buyer around these parts." With a wry smile, she turned to face him. "And I'm not trained to do anything else."

In spite of the warmth of the kitchen, he felt cold, his face stiff. "I'm sure it's a very good job and that you do it well."

She drew in a long breath and let it out as though she was exhausted. Jake stared at her and wondered how things had quickly moved from making love to this?

"I've put in years of college and long, hard hours of work to get to the coveted position I have. I'm putting it all in jeopardy by hanging on here."

With a shake of his head, he rose from the table and walked over to her. "You didn't seem all that concerned about your job before. I don't understand this sudden change in you, Rebecca. Earlier—out by the windmill— were you already thinking this?"

Her gaze dropped to her feet as a blush washed her cheeks with pink. "Not exactly, Jake. I— To be honest, there's nothing sudden about it. I've been thinking about this every day. And tonight, as we rode home, I realized I couldn't put it off any longer. I—I'm going back to Houston."

She might as well have slapped him, Jake thought. And then it dawned on him. For the first time in his life, he was getting exactly what he'd dished out to his lady friends over the years. A few romps between the sheets and then a quick goodbye. He'd just learned how it felt to be on the receiving end.

But in his defense, he'd never given any of those women rosy promises or pledges of love, he thought.

And Rebecca never gave them to you, either.

Wiping a hand over his face, he turned and walked to the middle of the room. Beau was lying just inside the screen door and the sight of the dog made it somehow even harder to deal with her decision. He'd thought she loved the dog. But then, he'd begun to think that she might love him. What a fool thought that had been.

"I see. So what about Beau and the rest of the animals?"

She didn't answer immediately and he glanced over his shoulder to see her wiping her eyes. And suddenly he was angry. Angrier than he'd ever felt in his life. Why hadn't she packed up and left a long time ago? he wondered. Why in hell had she stuck around and made him and the animals fall in love with her?

"I want Starr to have acreage to roam over instead of taking her back to Houston and confining her in a stable. And since I live in an apartment that doesn't allow pets, I'll have to find homes for the cats and Beau with someone around here."

"They already have a home," he said gruffly. "They'll be lost anywhere else."

Lifting her head, she looked at him with an anger that matched his own. "Don't make this any harder for me than it already is, Jake."

Turning, he walked back to her and gestured around the small kitchen. "What about this place? What are you going to do with it? Sell it?"

Her nostrils flared at his accusing tone. He made it

sound like she was a criminal for leaving. "This was my mother's home. I'll never sell it for any reason."

"You just won't live here."

She shot him a daring stare. "Why should I?"

"Why should you?" Earlier he'd laid his hat on top of the refrigerator. Now he pulled down the stained gray Stetson and levered it onto his head. "If you have to ask, Rebecca, then I sure can't tell you."

She took a halting step in his direction. "You have no right to be judgmental with me, Jake."

That was true enough, he thought ruefully. Where she was concerned, he had no right to feel anything, think anything. And the less he did, the better off he'd be.

Closing the space between them, he touched a hand to her cheek. "I'm sorry, Rebecca. I don't want our time together to be marred by these last words between us. That's why…I'm going to say goodbye. And if you do decide to come back, you know where to find me."

So they could have another casual affair? Rebecca was tempted to fling the loaded question at him. But he robbed her of the chance by quickly turning and walking out the door.

Seconds later she heard the engine of his truck fire to life and then the rattle of the trailer as he pulled away. In the far distance she heard Starr nicker loudly and the sound of the mare calling out for Banjo to come back to her brought a wall of tears to Rebecca's eyes.

She wanted Jake to come back, too. She ached for him to walk back into the kitchen, take her into his arms and tell her that he loved her. That the only place she belonged was with him.

But she'd given him all kinds of chances to speak the words, to ask her not to go. Instead, he'd said goodbye and now she had to deal with a breaking heart.

As she tried to fight back her tears, she felt something cold and wet nudge against her hand. Glancing down, she saw Beau's sad eyes staring up at her, as though he knew their time together was over.

It was more than Rebecca could bear and she dropped to her knees and hugged the dog close to her breast.

Chapter Eleven

Three weeks later, Jake was walking from the barn to his house when the sound of a vehicle had him looking over his shoulder to see Quint's truck coming up the driveway.

The sight of his friend at this late hour was a bit surprising. Once Quint had gotten a family, he didn't roam from the Golden Spur after working hours, unless he had to deal with some sort of business outside of the ranch.

Jake waited for his friend to park and climb to the ground before he walked over to join him at the side of the truck.

"Hey, bud, what are you doing over here at this hour? It's nearly dark."

"Maura sent me on a mission," Quint explained, then reached inside the back door and pulled out a long casserole dish covered with aluminum foil. "She thinks you're starving to death so she made something to tempt you."

With a wry shake of his head, Jake asked, "What makes her think I'm in need of food?"

Quint shoved the glass dish at him, forcing Jake to accept it before it fell to the ground. "When you came by the Golden Spur yesterday, she said you looked thin and terrible. Her words. Not mine."

"Well, I should have known my good looks would start to go sooner or later," Jake tried to joke, then inclined his head toward the house. "Let's go inside and have a beer."

"You finished with the evening chores?" Quint asked as they walked through a gate and across the front lawn.

Unlike Quint, who had a roster of hands to deal with the mundane chores of feeding, watering and spreading hay, Jake only had two men to help with the everyday tasks. Sometimes it was long after dark before they were finished and the men headed for home. "Yeah. Before you drove up I was down at the cow lot. I got a problem."

"What's wrong?"

"A hell of a lot!"

At the house, the two men entered a side door that led them directly in the kitchen. While Jake set the casserole on the cabinet counter, Quint straddled one of the tall stools at a breakfast bar.

"I'm waiting," Quint prodded. "What's happened?"

"Nothing. That's what's happened. This morning me and the guys pregnancy tested the herd on the east range. Ten of the cows are empty. And you know what that means—ten less calves this spring!" Jake went to the refrigerator and pulled out two long-necked beers.

After shoving one in Quint's direction, he twisted the top off the one he was holding and downed a third of the contents.

Quint eyed him closely. "So how many cows did you have in that herd? Two hundred? Two-fifty?"

Jake grimaced. "Two hundred and thirty."

"Well, ten out of that many is not a big enough percentage to raise a ruckus over. This kind of thing happens to every rancher."

"Yeah, I know. But that doesn't make it any easier to take," Jake muttered.

"Have you had the bull tested?"

Jake shook his head. "I don't see any need for that. The rest of the cows in his herd are all carrying calves. That's what makes it so bad. I'll have to sell and replace them. And with the cows being open, I'll hardly get a decent market price."

"I doubt it. But that's part of ranching, too. There will always be ups and downs in the business. This is just one of those downs and if I were you, I'd call it a very minor one."

Jake shot him a cynical glare. "You would. Ten cows wouldn't count much to you."

Quint plopped the beer bottle down on the bar with a heavy thud. "Dammit, Jake, don't talk to me that way! Every cow on my ranch is important to me. Right now I have twenty that are too old to calve anymore. They've not produced in two years and they never will again. But I don't have the heart to send them to slaughter. So I feed and care for them just like the others. It's not good business sense, but it makes Maura happy. And I guess, to be honest, it makes me happy, too."

Heaving a weary breath, Jake walked over to a pine farm table and sank into a chair at one end. He felt awful and spouting off to the man who'd been like a brother since they were very small boys, only made him feel worse.

"Sorry, Quint. I didn't mean that like it sounded. But you can absorb the loss much easier than I can."

Quint mouthed a curse word. "You're not exactly poor, Jake. Not anymore."

They both knew he was referring to the dividends he received from shares of the Golden Spur Mine. And Quint was basically right in saying Jake wasn't poor anymore. He owned more valuable assets now than he'd ever dreamed possible. Yet he still couldn't think of himself as solvent. Maybe that was because he'd never felt confident that he could hang on to all he'd acquired.

"I believe you ought to have the bull checked," Quint went on. "I don't see ten cows having a fertility problem. But that's just my opinion."

Jake stared at him. "If the bull is the problem that's even worse! Replacing him would take a hunk of money!"

Quint frowned. "Look, Jake, if you're so worried about taking losses, then you might as well pack up and sell this place, because every good rancher knows he's going to take some hammering at times!"

Jake's gaze slipped to the beer bottle he was gripping with both hands. "I'm thinking about doing just that!"

"What?"

The incredulous tone in Quint's voice had Jake looking up at his longtime buddy. "You heard me right," he muttered. "I'm thinking about...doing something else."

With slow, purposeful movements, Quint climbed down from the stool and walked over to the table. "What are you talking about?"

The censure in Quint's voice made Jake feel even worse. Like it was possible to feel worse, he thought grimly. His mind, his whole body felt as if he'd been whipped, beaten down by a hand that he couldn't see or defend himself against.

"I was at the track a couple of days ago and—"

"I should have known," Quint interrupted with disgust. "You just can't stay away from that place, can you?"

Angry now, Jake glared at him. "And why the hell should I? Shoeing racehorses, managing the stables, those jobs made me a living for many years, Quint. And I have good friends there. Friends that don't preach to me because I'm not perfect," he added hotly.

The caustic remark didn't send Quint packing out the door. Instead, he eased down in the seat across from Jake and gave his friend a long, troubled look. "All right, Jake," he said quietly. "I'm sorry. I was out of line and I shouldn't have said anything about you visiting the track. I understand that place will always be a part of you."

"Damn right it will. And they've offered me a huge salary to come back to work."

Quint stiffened. "Are you considering taking it?"

Jake couldn't look him square in the face. "Maybe."

Shaking his head, Quint mouthed a curse word under his breath. "So you're just going to throw all this away? All you've worked for?"

"Look, Quint, I'm not cut out for this. In the end, I'll probably lose it all, anyway. Better to sell out and get what I can while the getting is good."

"That's a hell of a thing to say!" Quint spat. "And I don't know where this thinking of yours is coming from. You were my ranch foreman for a few years—*you know everything* about ranching. Your dad—"

"My dad is gone!" Jake interrupted flatly. "So don't go trying to bring him into this!"

Unfazed by Jake's anger, Quint said, "The man taught you a lot about horses and cattle."

And women, Jake thought bitterly. Oh, yes, Lee Rollins had charmed them, loved them and left them. Just like Jake. Until one important woman had come along. Until Rebecca had taught him that giving up his heart was something entirely different.

When Jake didn't reply, Quint leaned back in his chair and folded his arms across his chest. "All right, Jake, my father is gone, too. So what do you think we ought to do? Sit here and cry in our beer? Convince ourselves that we're losers?"

Jake glared at him. "Sometimes you can be a real bastard, Quint, and if we were eight years old again, I'd knock your head off. Or at least try."

Quint shrugged a shoulder. "If that would make you feel any better, we can go outside and pretend we're eight years old again."

Realizing the absurdity of that notion, Jake scrubbed his face with both hands and let out a long, weary breath. "Things were simple back then, weren't they?" he asked softly. "We both had fathers and I had no idea that mine was going to leave me behind."

Quint leaned forward and laid a hand on Jake's shoulder. "I thought you weren't going to let that—him—hurt you anymore."

"I believed I'd put it all behind me," he admitted, "until Rebecca came."

"Ah."

The one knowing word from Quint put a rueful twist to Jake's lips. "Yeah. I guess she reminded me all over again what it's like to lose someone you care about."

Quint studied him for long moments. "The racetrack, this ranch, the land, you're not agonizing over any of those things, Jake. You're just learning that none of it means a damn thing without someone to love. And someone to love you back."

Pain smacked the middle of Jake's chest and he fixed his gaze on the tabletop in hopes that his friend wouldn't be able to spot the misery.

"Well, she doesn't. Love me back, that is," Jake muttered.

"How do you know?" Quint countered. "I doubt you asked her."

"I didn't have to. She left. That was the answer she gave me."

"Did you give her any reason to stay?"

Jake looked dismally up at him. "No. I don't guess I did."

A week later, Rebecca lifted the stainless steel lid covering the main course of her dinner and gave the piece of glazed salmon a disinterested glance. It might have whetted her appetite if she'd gone down to the hotel restaurant instead of ordering room service, she thought. At least she could have sat among the other diners and pretended she wanted to eat. Now the food was growing cold and she had little desire to fork any of it to her mouth.

Across the opulent hotel room, piled upon the bed, were a countless number of flowing ruffled dresses, lightweight spring jackets, handbags, shoes and chunky pieces of jewelry. All of which she'd collected at to-day's fashion bazaar. None of those things interested her, either.

With a heavy sigh, she walked over to the outer wall

of plate glass and stared out at the dark night. The twinkling lights of the Chicago skyline stretched endlessly in all directions and directly below on the well-lit street, people were entering and exiting cabs as they made their way to some of the nearby nightspots.

There were times when an assistant traveled with Rebecca, but this time she'd made the trip alone to the Midwest Fashion Fair. Yet even if a friend had accompanied her, she wouldn't have had any desire to go out for a night on the town.

Face it, Rebecca, you're confused, miserable and missing Jake Rollins something fierce.

The voice going off in her head was suddenly interrupted by the ring of her cell phone.

Turning away from the untouched meal, she walked over to the nightstand where she'd left the phone and immediately frowned. She'd expected the caller to be her boss, Arlene, but the number illuminated on the front of the instrument was totally unfamiliar.

And then it dawned on Rebecca that the area code she was seeing was from New Mexico! Dear God, could it be Jake?

Snatching up the instrument, she fumbled it open and finally managed to slap it next to her ear. "Hello," she answered in a rush.

"Rebecca? That you?"

Stunned to hear Abe Cantrell's voice, she sank weakly onto the edge of the bed. Had something happened to Jake and the older man had called to let her know? The mere idea left her hands trembling.

"Yes, this is Rebecca. How are you, Abe?"

"Fine and dandy. Been sittin' outside watchin' the sunset and it was mighty pretty. Made me think of you. So I gave you a call to see how you're doin'."

A hot, painful lump filled her throat. While she'd lived on her mother's place, she'd not spent a great deal of time with her elderly neighbor, but enough to get to know and love him. Before she'd left for Houston, she'd told Abe about Gertrude being her mother and how confused and hurt the whole thing had left her. Surprisingly, Abe had understood her distress more than any of her friends in Houston. Perhaps that was because he was much older and wiser. Or maybe she'd simply opened up to him more. Either way, his thoughtful support had bonded her to him in a way she'd not expected.

"Well, right now I'm sitting in a hotel room in Chicago," she told him.

"You on a vacation?"

Rebecca closed her eyes as images of everything she'd come to love in New Mexico swam to the forefront of her thoughts. "Nothing that pleasant. I'm on a business trip. My job requires a lot of traveling."

"Went right back to work, did you? Guess that means you haven't had time to miss much about this place back here."

"Actually, I—I've been missing everything out there."

He said, "Your mother's place looks deserted now. I don't like seeing it that way."

Before she'd left for Houston, Abe had taken her animals and given them a nice home on Apache Wells. Another reason she was very grateful to the man.

She said, "It would be better if I could find a nice little family to live there and keep the place maintained. Maybe you know of someone?"

"I'd rather see you there."

She swallowed hard as she struggled to blink back a wall of tears. "Well, you know how it is, Abe, a person has to work to keep their head afloat." She cleared her throat, then asked, "How is Beau?"

"After you left he moped around for a few days. But he's okay now. I never was one to have a dog for a buddy, but he can't seem to shake me and I can't seem to shake him, so we're stuck together. The cats are in mouse heaven down at the barn and Starr has made a few friends in the remuda. And I know you didn't ask me to, but I sent someone to mow your grass. Just in case you decide to come back."

Beyond the door to her suite, Rebecca could hear a group of people passing in the hallway. From the sound of their laughter, they sounded happy and young. Had she ever been that way? Yes, she'd been happy, but that had been eons ago. Long before she'd grown dissatisfied with her job, before she'd learned Gertrude was her mother, that Gwyn had been harboring secrets, and her father had been unfaithful. And definitely long before she'd met Jake and fallen in love with him.

Tugging her attention back to Abe, she said, "Unfortunately, that won't be anytime soon. But thank you for the lawn work. It makes me feel better to know the place doesn't look raggedy."

"You haven't asked about Jake," he said pointedly.

The old man was crafty, Rebecca would give him that much. She breathed deeply, then asked, "How is Jake?"

"He ain't good. That's about all I can say."

Rebecca instantly gripped the phone. "Why? What's wrong with him?"

"You'd have to ask him to get the answer. All I know is what Quint tells me. And he tells me that Jake is considering taking a job at the track and selling the Rafter R."

"Selling his ranch?" She was stunned. "But, Abe, that doesn't make sense! He's worked so hard on it! And he seemed so proud of the place."

"Well, Jake never was one to want a pile of material things. To a certain point, Quint's the same way. Guess that's why the two boys have always been such good friends. Frankly, I think he needs to get rid of every damn cow on the place and focus on raisin' his horses. That's what he loves to do and that's what he ought to do."

"Then you should tell him so, Abe! You're his friend and I know he respects your opinion."

Abe chuckled. "He wouldn't appreciate me tellin' him what to do. Now you, that's another matter—if you was to tell him that might carry some weight."

A tear slipped from Rebecca's eye and fell onto her cheek. At one point during her stay in New Mexico, she'd believed that Jake might actually grow to care for her, maybe even love her. But once she'd met Gwyn in Ruidoso and learned the truth about how she was conceived, something had happened to her. She'd felt sick and desperate and lost.

And when she and Jake had ridden out to the windmill and made love under the open sky it had been so beautiful, so bittersweet, that her heart had ached. She'd desperately longed to hear him say that he loved her. Or at the very least, he wanted her to remain in New Mexico. But while he'd held her for those long minutes, he'd not said anything and his silence had opened her eyes. Suddenly, she could see she was deluding herself in thinking he would ever love her and the longer she stayed, the more her heart was going to break.

Then later, at the house, Rebecca had once again attempted to draw out his feelings, to get any sort of sign from him that he wanted her in a permanent way. When she'd told him she no longer knew where she belonged, she'd done so while hoping and praying he would open his mouth and tell her that she belonged with him. For always. But he'd failed to say anything meaningful, except goodbye.

"I don't think so, Abe. I've not even heard from Jake and I don't expect to."

"There ain't no law written that says you can't call him, is there?"

Call Jake? What good would that do, except tear her heart wide open again? she wondered miserably. "Jake doesn't want to hear from me."

Abe snorted. "And grass don't grow in the spring."

Closing her eyes, Rebecca rubbed fingertips against her furrowed brow. "In order for grass to grow it has to be fed sun and rain," she reminded the old man.

There was a long pause and while she waited for Abe to reply, in the far background she could hear a horse neigh softly. Was it Starr still calling out for Banjo? The notion put a hard lump in Rebecca's throat.

"Jake is like a son to me," Abe finally said. "I don't want to see him mess up. Think about calling him, Rebecca. That's all I ask."

"I'll do that much," Rebecca conceded.

Abe thanked her and after a quick good-night ended the call.

Rebecca placed the phone back on the nightstand, then dropped her face in her hands and sobbed.

* * *

The next morning Jake was on his way to the Downs to shoe three racehorses when Clara rang his cell phone and asked that he stop by her place before going on about his business.

Jake had agreed to see his mother, although he'd been surprised by her request. Only last night he'd dropped by for a visit, the first one he'd had with her since the day he'd raked her over the coals about his father and how she'd allowed the man to dictate her life. Taking all that in account, Jake had expected to find Clara more than a little frosty, but she'd met him at the door with a welcoming hug. And when he'd told her about Rebecca going back to Texas, he'd braced himself to hear a bunch of I-told-you-sos. Instead, she'd appeared truly sorry for him. He'd been inwardly shocked by the pleasant change in her and though he'd wondered what had brought it about, he'd decided it best not to ask and simply be thankful for it.

Now this morning as he walked onto the porch of his mother's house, he could only wonder what was going on with her and hope that she'd not had another health setback.

Rapping his knuckles slightly on the storm door, he opened it and stepped inside. "Mom? I'm here."

Clara immediately hurried through a doorway leading to the back of the house. She smiled at him with a measure of relief.

"Jake, I'm so glad you took the time to come by. I know you're busy, but I have something important to give you. At least, I think it will be important."

Walking over to his mother, Jake dropped a kiss on the top of her head. "What is it? You sent plenty of baked things home with me last night. I don't need any more food."

She let out a short laugh that sounded strangely nervous to Jake. Which only confused him more. In the past Clara had often complained and whined and accused him of being like his father, but one thing she'd never been with him was nervous.

"It's nothing like that." She took him by the hand and led him over to a short couch. "I—uh—I didn't tell you last night, but I talked to Quint the other day."

"That's nothing new. You two have always been friends."

A sheepish expression stole over her face. "We talked about you."

Jake grimaced. "Oh. You shouldn't have done that, Mom."

"I didn't. He's the one who approached me. And frankly, I'm glad that he did. I didn't know—well, that day we argued—I didn't understand about Rebecca, not really. I thought she was just another one of your women. I think—well, I've been so wrapped up in feeling sorry for myself that I couldn't really see what was going on with you and the girl from Texas."

Jake stiffened. "What makes you think she's any different?"

"Oh, son, don't try to pretend with me," she said gently, then attempted to laugh and lighten the moment. "I mean, your mother has finally opened her eyes, don't try to hide from me now."

Dropping his head, Jake stared at the scuffed toes of his boots, but all he was really seeing was Rebecca's face, her sweet smile, the warm shine in her blue eyes. "I miss her," he mumbled. "So much."

He felt his mother's hand rest upon his back and then she said softly, "That's how it is when you love someone."

Lifting his head, he looked at her with remorse. "I'm sorry, Mom. I've been hard on you at times. I said things to you that I didn't know about or understand."

Smiling faintly, she shook her head. "You had every right to say what you did. I've been wallowing in self-pity for far too long. I lost Lee and let the hurt ruin a big chunk of my life. I don't want that to happen to you."

She pulled a small piece of paper from a pocket on her blouse and thrust it at him. "Here. I think you need to use this."

He glanced down to see a phone number scratched across a torn piece of notebook paper. "I don't need that. I already have Rebecca's number. Besides, I wouldn't know what to say to her."

With a smile of encouragement, Clara pressed the paper into Jake's hand and folded his fingers around it. "When the time is right you'll know what to say to her. But before you talk to Rebecca I think you should make this call."

Bewildered, he asked, "Why?"

"Because it's a link to your father."

Less than a week later, Rebecca was sitting at her desk, sifting through a stack of fashion sketches, when Arlene's voice came over the intercom.

"Rebecca, I need you on the second floor. We're having a disagreement that only you can settle."

"I'll be right there."

She walked out of her sumptuous office and took the elevator up to the second floor, a space used exclusively to display Bordeaux's formal evening wear. At the front entrance of the department, she found Arlene and her young assistant, a guy named Nigel, trying to put the finishing touches to a mannequin dressed in a designer frock fashioned from yards and yards of shiny faille. She considered the dress far too flamboyant for the store, but this was one time Arlene had dismissed Rebecca's opinion and purchased the garment in several sizes anyway.

Now as she approached the bickering coworkers, Arlene split away from the young man and grabbed Rebecca by the arm. "It's about time I had some help," she said with a flustered wave at her assistant. "Please tell Nigel that I'm right and he's wrong. This dress needs more than a single strand of pearls."

The young man cast an imploring look at Rebecca. "Arlene thinks the chunky gold and ruby thing would look better. I think it's too much for all that dress. But what do I know? I only work here."

Rebecca took the tiny pearls from his hand and draped them around the mannequin's neck. "He's right, Arlene. The pearls."

The other woman gasped, then spluttered, "But, Rebecca, pearls are so—so retro and ho-hum!"

"They're also classy," Rebecca pointed out. "And this dress definitely needs something to give it a little elegance."

Nigel smiled with smug triumph while Arlene jerked on Rebecca's arm until the two women were standing some distance away from the display.

"Rebecca, I realize you're still angry with me, but you don't have to carry it over to our work," Arlene said under her breath so the women browsing nearby couldn't overhear.

Arlene had always been a bit of a drama queen, but she'd never taken this sort of tone with Rebecca. "You wanted my opinion and I gave it. That's what I'm paid to do. Besides, I've never been angry with you. Impatient at times, but never angry."

Arlene's lips pressed to a thin line. "Well, you were all out of sorts with me when you decided to take that vacation in New Mexico. And from what I can see you're still not behaving like yourself."

It had been more than a vacation and they both knew it. The truth was that Arlene had never quite gotten over Rebecca's challenge for a leave of indefinite absence, but she wasn't in the mood to have an out-and-out confrontation with the woman. "I have a lot to deal with, Arlene."

The other woman let out a disgusted huff. "Don't we all."

Rebecca stared at her. "Are you finished?"

"No! I just want to say that you need to wake up and look around you. There are other employees here at Bordeaux's who've had a family member die, but they don't go around taking out their grief on others. They handle it with maturity."

In other words, they don't go against your wishes, Rebecca thought. She should have been angry with the other woman for behaving so childishly, but she couldn't summon up that much energy.

"I've lost more than a family member, Arlene."

The woman frowned. "What does that mean?"

"It means that everything that ever mattered to me is gone. That's what it means."

She walked away from Arlene and, after an encouraging word to Nigel, took the stairs down to the first floor where the street clothes were displayed, along with fragrance, jewelry, and makeup counters, the facial area and countless dressing rooms. This was the store's hot spot and since it was a Friday afternoon and shoppers were readying themselves for the weekend, every area was busy.

At one time Rebecca would have been excited to see the throngs of clientele. But that was back when she'd considered Bordeaux's her second home. Back when she'd been excited about her job and determined to be a success at it. For years now she'd made it her life and along the way, she'd convinced herself that she was happy. She'd even quit dreaming that a man and a family could be in her future. She'd told herself those things were for other women, not her.

Until she met Jake. Dear God, he'd shaken the very depths of her. And try as she might she couldn't go back to being the old Rebecca, the fashion buyer, the career woman. Arlene had been right on one count. Rebecca hadn't been behaving like herself. Because she was a different woman now and she needed more than a position at Bordeaux's. She needed Jake.

Gwyn and Gertrude had wasted their lives trying to hide the truth from each other, Vance, their friends and even Rebecca. She couldn't allow herself to go down that same path. She had to let Jake know how much she loved him, how much she wanted him in her life.

If he still wasn't interested, then at least she could tell herself she'd gone down trying rather than hiding.

The decision quickened her steps as she turned toward an exit that would take her back to her office. Once she reached the private spot, she was going to call Jake and tell him they still had things to talk about and she would be flying out to Lincoln County as soon as she could arrange it. And then from somewhere behind her she heard a salesclerk say, "There's Ms. Hardaway now. If you hurry you might catch her."

At the sound of her name, Rebecca paused and turned

to see who wanted a word with her. And then she saw the object of her thoughts. Jake was standing there as big as life in his boots and Stetson and staring straight at her.

In a daze, she wondered what *he* was doing here and then she noticed the women customers around him were apparently wondering the same thing. All eyes were on him as he began walking toward Rebecca and the closer he got to her, the faster her heart pounded.

By the time he came to a stop only a few inches separated them and as Rebecca looked into his familiar brown eyes, she feared her knees were going to buckle.

"Jake. What— Why are you here in Houston?" she asked in a voice faint with shock.

The half grin on his lips was a bit sheepish and completely endearing. "Isn't it obvious? You."

Rebecca didn't realize she'd been holding her breath until a long gush of air rushed past her parted lips. "I don't understand. You haven't called."

"Neither have you."

She swallowed as hope tried to bubble up inside her. Surely he was here because he cared, she thought. Why else would he travel all the way to Texas? "I decided today—a few moments ago, to be exact—to call you. But—"

He moved close enough for her to smell the sunshine on his cowboy shirt, see the faint lines at the corners of his eyes. Since they'd been apart, his skin had browned even more from the summer sun, giving him a swarthy appearance and as she looked at him everything inside her melted with longing.

"I was going to call you, too," he said. "But then

I decided that what I had to say needed to be said in person."

Suddenly the store, the customers and salesclerks all faded into oblivion. The only thing she could see was him.

"And what was that?"

Stepping forward, he wrapped his hands around her upper arms. "Before you left, you told me you didn't know where you belonged. Well, I'm here to tell you exactly where you belong. With me. Forever."

Stunned with joy, she tried to find her voice to respond. And then it didn't matter because he lifted her completely off her feet and planted a long, thorough kiss upon her lips.

Behind them she could hear several oohs and awws and then a spattering of applause. By the time their heads came apart, they'd garnered a gawking audience.

Laughing, Rebecca grabbed him by the hand and hurried him out of sight and down a large corridor to her office. When she shut the door behind them, she turned to see Jake inspecting the room.

"This is where you work?"

She came up behind him. "This is my office."

He whistled under his breath. "It's really something."

Now that they were completely alone Rebecca's first inclination was to throw herself into his arms and cling with all her might. She was hungry for the taste, the touch, the very scent of him. But she also needed explanations.

"Jake, I've got to know why—"

Before she could finish her broken question, he turned and put his arms around her.

"I came to my senses and realized that I love you?" he finished for her.

To hear him say the word *love* very nearly wilted her and she snatched holds on the front of his shirt to steady herself. "You love me?"

"With all my heart," he answered. "But I was afraid to admit it to myself and especially to you. I'm not exactly molded out of family-man material, Becca. And I always believed the greatest favor I could do for a woman was walk away from her before I caused her the same sort of pain my father caused my mother. But I can't walk away from you. So here I am asking you to give me a chance to be something I never thought I could be. A husband. A father."

Her heart brimming with love, she reached up and brushed her fingers against his dark cheek. "You're not Lee Rollins. You're your own man. The man I love."

His hands splayed against her back and tugged her close against him. "Since you left, I've spoken to my stepmother and learned that my father died a couple of years ago. And that I have a half brother and sister," he told her.

"Oh, my. And how did she react to you contacting her?"

"Surprisingly, she was very warm and understanding. She even insists that my half siblings want to meet me."

"That's wonderful. But what about your father—did she have any explanations as to why he left you totally behind?"

"His widow told me that Lee believed I'd be better off without him in my life. He realized he wasn't exactly the best of role models for a son to follow. Plus, there was so much anger and fighting between him and Mom that he figured the constant warfare would only hurt me more. His way of loving me was to stay away so I'd look to others to learn how a real man should conduct his life, rather than patterning myself after him."

She carefully studied his face. "And how did that make you feel?"

He let out a long breath. "Very sad. But strangely free. For years I'd thought about searching for him. I had this idea that it would give me some sort of satisfaction to tell him face-to-face just how much he'd hurt me and Mom and what a sorry human being he'd been. But, you know, when his widow told me that he'd passed away, none of that really mattered anymore. I realized there were so many more important things in my life. Mainly you."

With a sob of relief, she pressed her cheek against his chest. "Oh, Jake, I'm so glad. You and I might not have come from the best of homes, but we're going to make a good home together."

Tilting up her chin, Jake motioned to her luxurious office. "Can you give all of this up for me?"

Her eyes shining with love, she smiled at him. "Can you love me for the rest of our lives?"

"Easy," he whispered.

She slipped her arms around him. "You took the word right out of my mouth. Easy."

Epilogue

Fourteen months later, Jake stepped down from the chestnut colt he'd been breaking to the saddle and tethered him to a nearby fence post. The sun had shown its face only a half hour ago, but long before daylight the ranch hands had arrived to tend to the early-morning barn chores.

"That was real fine, Smarty Cat." He gave the horse an affectionate pat on the neck. "You're going to be ready to gallop on the track soon and by this time next year you might be ready for the Sunland Derby."

"That's a big prediction."

At the sound of Rebecca's voice, Jake turned to see his wife walking up with their three-month-old daughter cradled in her arms and Beau trotting happily at their heels. The morning was sunny, but there was still a definite chill to the early March day. Rebecca had the baby bundled in a thick yellow blanket and a pink sock cap.

Jake couldn't resist pulling the blanket away from his daughter's cheek and smacking a kiss on her cherub face. Having a child filled him with indescribable joy and the moment he'd first held her in his arms, he'd understood what Quint had meant when he'd talked about Jake having a real home.

"Hi, Jacklyn," he crooned to the baby. "Did you come to see Daddy work?"

"You call that work?" Rebecca teased. "I thought you were playing."

Chuckling, Jake leaned forward and planted a soft kiss on his wife's mouth. "I can't fool you, can I? Riding Smarty Cat is play for me."

Since he and Rebecca had married more than a year ago, many changes had taken place at the Rafter R. With Rebecca's encouragement, he'd taken Abe's advice and sold every cow on the place. Broodmares now filled the pastures and race prospects were stabled in a huge horse barn equipped with heated stalls and a foaling area. A galloping track had been built and horse walkers erected. Jake was doing what he loved and thriving at it.

"Do you really think Smarty Cat might become that good? To race in the Sunland Derby? That's only a step away from the Kentucky Derby," she reminded him.

Chuckling, Jake curled his arm around her shoulder and gathered her and the baby close to his side. "I know it's a big dream, Becca. And if I sound confident, you can take the blame for that. I'm not settling for just existing—just hoping to keep the ranch in the black. I want our horses to be champions."

"And they will be if you have anything to do with it," she assured him.

"So what are you and Jacklyn doing down here at the barns so early this morning?" he asked. "Getting your exercise?"

"Well, I could have called you on the cell, but I wanted to see you."

The half grin on his face was a sensual reminder of the lusty lovemaking he'd given her last night. "Just can't get enough of me, can you?"

She wrinkled her nose playfully at him. "I don't want to burst your bubble, but I'm down here for a different reason. I wanted to ask if you'd mind quitting work a little early this evening. I just talked to your mother about having her over for dinner tonight. She's coming and bringing a friend."

Jake arched a quizzical brow at her. "A friend? Are you talking about a man? A date?"

Rebecca laughed softly. "That's exactly what I mean. Believe me, I'm just as surprised as you."

"Hmm." He stroked his thumb and forefinger thoughtfully over his chin. "Did she tell you his name?"

"No. Does it matter?"

A slow grin spread across his face. "Not really. I'm just thrilled that Mom is starting to live again. Her health has improved by leaps and bounds. And she seems actually happy now. Thanks to you."

"Me? I can't take the credit for your mother's turn-around. I think when she made the choice to help you find Lee Rollins it freed the demons she'd been carrying for so long."

"You may be right. But I know for a fact that seeing how happy you've made me has inspired her."

"Her son makes me very happy, too," she said, then lifting her gaze to the distant mountains, added, "I only wish things with me and Gwyn could be fixed so easily. I've been thinking about inviting her out here for a little visit. Would you mind?"

"Now why would I mind? You were such a great hostess when my brother and sister came a few weeks ago."

"That was fun—they're both just as charming as you, my dear husband. But this thing with Gwyn could get awkward," she warned him.

"Maybe. But you've got to start somewhere, Becca. And the invitation would let her see that you're willing to forgive and begin working past the problems between you. But do you think she'll come?"

"Who knows? She doesn't like the big outdoors. But if she wants to understand me, she needs to see what I'm all about. She also needs to see where her sister lived and where she's now buried."

"Gwyn might not go for that idea."

Rebecca shrugged. "She might not. But I'm hoping she's had time to think about doing some forgiving and letting go. And I think she'll jump at any chance to be with Jacklyn. I believe if there's anything that can help heal the wounds of the past, it will be our daughter."

Glancing down at the dark-haired baby, Rebecca adjusted Jacklyn's warm cap, then handed her over to Jake. While he cooed and talked to the baby Rebecca stepped over to stroke Smarty Cat's blazed face. The horse immediately nudged her hand for a treat and she pulled a piece of apple from her jacket pocket and fed it to him.

From behind her, Jake teased, "Just what I thought. You didn't come down here to see me. You came to spoil the horses."

"I can't help it. I love them."

A smile bent the corners of her lips as she felt Jake's hand come to rest upon her shoulder.

"You miss working at Dr. Adams's, don't you?"

A few months after she and Jake had married, a vet with a clinic near the racetrack had offered her a job as an assistant in training. And up until Jacklyn was born, she'd worked full-time for him. The learning experience had taught her much more than how to deal with animals, she'd come to realize her long-ago dreams as a young girl hadn't been a foolish aspiration.

"I loved the job. But I also love being a mother. Besides, taking maternity leave has given me the opportunity to start some online classes toward that animal husbandry degree I always wanted."

"It's going to take you a long time to get that degree with just a handful of classes at a time," he pointed out.

Twisting her head around, she gave him a provocative smile. "I'll have plenty of time in between babies to get a degree."

Both of his brows shot up. "Babies? As in plural?"

She chuckled. "Why, yes. You wouldn't want to have just one horse in your racing stable, would you?"

"No. But you can rest assured—" His eyes full of promises, he bent his head and rested his cheek alongside hers. "I only want one woman in my bed and in my life."

"That's good to know," she said with a contented sigh, "because you're going to have me around for the rest of our lives."

* * * * *